P9-CQR-918

TWO TALES
· · · OF THE · · ·
MOON

Jennifer Sun

 iUniverse®

TWO TALES OF THE MOON

Copyright © 2015 Jennifer Sun.

All rights reserved. No part of this book may be used or reproduced by any means, graphic, electronic, or mechanical, including photocopying, recording, taping or by any information storage retrieval system without the written permission of the author except in the case of brief quotations embodied in critical articles and reviews.

iUniverse books may be ordered through booksellers or by contacting:

iUniverse
1663 Liberty Drive
Bloomington, IN 47403
www.iuniverse.com
1-800-Authors (1-800-288-4677)

Because of the dynamic nature of the Internet, any web addresses or links contained in this book may have changed since publication and may no longer be valid. The views expressed in this work are solely those of the author and do not necessarily reflect the views of the publisher, and the publisher hereby disclaims any responsibility for them.

Any people depicted in stock imagery provided by Thinkstock are models, and such images are being used for illustrative purposes only. Certain stock imagery © Thinkstock.

ISBN: 978-1-4917-7769-5 (sc)
ISBN: 978-1-4917-7770-1 (e)

Library of Congress Control Number: 2015953747

Print information available on the last page.

iUniverse rev. date: 10/7/2015

P R O L O G U E

• • • • •

SEPTEMBER 1966, WEST SIDE OF SHANGHAI, CHINA

IT WAS A COOL and crisp autumn night. The full moon was like a giant silver plate brimming with luminous liquid light. It was a night, for reasons unknown to mortal souls on earth, when the moon seemed to have decided to hang right outside the rusty metal-framed windows of a small apartment bedroom. The moon shed bountiful light on the room's interior, dusting multitudes of frost-white patches on the paint-stripped walls and bare floorboards.

A silk-canopied, wrought-iron bed rested in the middle of the room, shrouded in the moonlight like a dreamy white cocoon. A gentle breeze drifted in from an open window, stirring up the canopy and revealing a doe-eyed little girl and her silver-gray-haired grandma inside, sitting against the headboard and leaning on each other.

"Grandma, look, the moon is full. You promised that Papa would be home when the moon was full." Expectantly, the little girl gazed up at the moon and then at her grandmother.

"Yes, Lu, your papa will be home soon," Grandma said, her lips quivering and her voice tremulous.

"Are you crying, Grandma?"

"Don't be silly. Grandma is just tired."

"Is Mommy coming home soon too?"

"I hope so."

"When?" the little girl pressed.

"Maybe tonight, maybe tomorrow. But for now, it's late; you need to go to sleep."

"Do you have to go to the meetings again tomorrow? I don't like to be alone at home."

"Yes, Grandma has to get up early. That's why you need to go to sleep. Lie down, and Grandma will tell you a story you have never heard before."

"Okay." The little girl was happy and quickly slid herself under her cotton quilt. It was her favorite time of the day, drifting to sleep listening to her grandma's stories. Whether the stories had tragic, happy, or uplifting endings, she liked them all. She loved the story of Mulan, a brave young woman in ancient China who disguised herself as a man to fight battles for her aging general father and who later married the man she loved. For days after her grandma had told that story, Lu had imagined that she would grow up just like Mulan, strong and accomplished, living a life of loving and being loved. The butterfly-lovers story, on the other hand, had saddened her for days. She had been tremendously disappointed that the young man and young woman in love could not get married simply because one came from a rich family and the other from a poor one. Her heart had gone out to the young lovers in the story, both dying of broken hearts because they could not be together. The ending of the butterfly lovers story was an eerily beautiful scene that often haunted her dreams—the dead young lovers, reborn as two butterflies, fluttering out of their grave sites into the blue sky, where they were free to be together forever. The Mulan and butterfly-lovers stories were Lu's favorites. She did not remember how many times she had made her grandma tell them to her at bedtime. Now she could not wait for the new story.

"Remember Grandma told you that the moon gets round like a silver plate every month? But this month it is a special moon; we call it the midautumn moon. It is bigger, brighter, and fuller than any other full moons in the year."

"Why?"

"Well, that's the story Grandma is going to tell you today. Once upon a time, there was a beautiful fairy living a good life on the moon with all the other moon fairies. She had everything she needed, but she was bored and curious about what was happening on the earth. With the permission of the mother of the moon fairies, she was transformed as a baby girl and born into a peasant family in China on a moonlit autumn night. Her parents named her Qiu Yue (Autumn Moon). She grew up and became a beautiful young lady. She and her brothers and sisters helped their parents in the rice field every day and lived a simple and happy life. One day, while working in the field, Qiu Yue saw a handsome young man on horseback passing by. At the same time, the young man also spotted her, and they immediately fell in love with each other. The young man's name was Yi, and he was a brave soldier who was loved by the people and the emperor of China. With the blessing of the emperor, they got married and lived happily together for a while.

"Unfortunately, Yi began to change after the emperor gave him a lot of money and made him the general of all the soldiers in China. He became evil, ordering his soldiers to do bad things, robbing village people of all the money they had, beating them, and sometimes killing them if they didn't give him what he wanted. He would take pretty young girls away from their parents and make them slaves in the palace where he lived. He was so bad that everybody hated him. Qiu Yue was heartbroken and regretted ever marrying him. One night the mother of the moon fairies visited Qiu Yue in her dream. She told Qiu Yue that Yi had convinced the emperor to give him the elixir of immortality, a magic pill that would let Yi live forever and become the most powerful man, ruling China forever. 'What can I do, Mother?' Qiu Yue asked.

"'Well, you have two choices. One option is to do nothing. You will continue to live on earth, and Yi will live forever, making your life and other people's lives miserable forever. The other option is to steal the pill from him and swallow it. After that Yi will die soon, but you will return to the moon and live in a separate palace by yourself forever.'

"'Can I go back and live with all the other goddesses like before?' Qiu Yue asked, longing for what seemed to be happier days on the moon before she'd left for the earth.

"'No you can't. You have been a human, and according to rules on the moon, you can never live with your ethereal siblings ever again.'

"To celebrate his soon-to-be immortal status, Yi ordered his servants to make him a feast and announced to his wife that he was going to take the pill and live forever. Qiu Yue, heartbroken that the husband she had once loved had become an evil person, decided to take the pill herself, even though it meant she would live a lonely life forever. She asked Yi if she could take a closer look at the pill. Yi was in a good mood that evening and agreed to let her hold the box that contained the pill. Qiu Yue quickly took the pill and swallowed it. Suddenly her body was as light as a feather, and she floated out the window and toward the moon. She never had a chance to say good-bye to her parents and siblings, whom she loved."

"What happened to the evil husband? Is Qiu Yue still living on the moon by herself?" Eyes heavy, Lu was eager to find out the ending before she fell asleep.

"Well, he died of some bad disease shortly after Qiu Yue left. Qiu Yue still lives on the moon by herself, but she misses her parents, siblings, and all the people she loved on the earth, especially every year on the anniversary of her going back to the moon. And of course, everybody in China remembers her because she saved them from evils like Yi. So in Qiu Yue's memory, we celebrate the midautumn full moon because that was the time she left the earth. It has also become a tradition at this time for people to think about loved ones in faraway places, and that's why the midautumn moon is extremely bright and full."

"Grandma, Qiu Yue must be very lonely," Lu mumbled, her eyelids fluttering as she struggled to stay awake. But exhaustion overcame her, and she drifted away into darkness.

In her fitful and restless sleep, the little girl dreamed of her grandma sitting at the small desk next to her bed, writing something. Then her grandma was standing by the open window in her white nightgown, gazing at the silver moon. Strands of her grandma's silver-gray hair fluttered in the gentle breeze after escaping from the neatly coiled chignon pinned by a single mother-of-pearl clip.

Dawn came, and Lu awoke to loud human voices outside the window. "Grandma?" She looked at both sides of the bed, but Grandma was not there. The voices were louder, more frantic. "Call the police!" someone screamed.

Worried and scared, Lu slipped out of bed and hurried to the window, where she climbed on a stool so she was tall enough to look out. She strained on her toes and craned her neck out of the window, all the time worrying her grandma would come into the room at any minute to stop her. "Don't do that; you will fall out," her grandma used to scold her.

In the pale light of early dawn, on the ground directly under the fourth-floor window Lu peered from, people stood in a circle around a body in white that was sprawled like a snow angel in a pool of crimson red, head twisted to one side at an unnatural angle. Meshed in the loose strands of silver-gray hair obscuring the face, a single pearl shimmered.

• • •

SEPTEMBER 1966, LONG ISLAND, NEW YORK

JUST ABOUT EVERY DINER who'd been to Autumn Moon, a Chinese restaurant in Montauk, had been impressed by the *Moon Fairy Flying Back to the Moon* motif on the center wall of its dining area. Inlaid on a lacquered wood panel, a willowy mother-of-pearl lady nestled in the ripples and waves. Her sweeping gown in sea-foam green floated out toward the iridescent full moon on the distant horizon where the deep-blue sea and the midnight sky seemed to melt into one. Her face, slightly turned earthward, was pensive, almost sad, as if something she cherished had been left behind.

On a Saturday evening, standing still underneath the expansive motif was a tiny figure, a little girl about five years old. She gazed at the moon fairy in wonderment, mouth half-open. Her little pink straw sun hat had slipped off the back of her head, revealing a crown of blazing auburn ringlets. Her eyes, as if counterbalancing the riotous nature of her hair, were a mix of soft green and silver gray, crystal clear and serene like a koi pond.

"It's beautiful, isn't it?" a melodious voice said behind the little girl. The girl turned and saw a woman of her mom's age smiling down at her. She was as willowy as the moon fairy on the wall, in a knee-length, cap-sleeved blue-and-green silk dress. She had thick, shimmering black hair that cascaded all the way to her waist, lips colored with cherry-red lipstick, and an ivory complexion. The little girl thought the woman pretty but not as pretty as the dress she was wearing. It was like a painting (hand painted on silk, she would learn later), two blue birds sitting on a delicate tree, looking out at the pale-orange moon in the sky through red-leaf-adorned branches.

"Your dress is pretty," the little girl said to the woman.

"Thank you. You are so sweet." The woman gently wrapped one of her arms around the little girl's shoulder. "Now, you tell me where you are sitting, and I will tell you the story of the moon fairy on the wall."

The little girl nodded and pointed at a table a few feet away where her parents and her twin brother were sitting.

"Sage, don't bother Mrs. Wong; she's busy." The little girl's mom beckoned her daughter to return to the table.

"No problem, Mrs. Donavan. She is adorable. She has such beautiful, unusual eyes," said Mrs. Wong, the chef's wife, as she walked the little girl back to her mother.

Smiling, Mrs. Donavan said, "Thank you. When she was born, her father and I had different takes on the color of those eyes. He thought they were greenish; I saw silver gray. We finally agreed they were the color of sage spears, grayish green, and so we named her Sage."

"What a beautiful name, Sage," Mrs. Wong said to the little girl.

"Will you tell me the moon-fairy story, Mrs. Wong?" Sage asked, her grayish-green eyes flickering with anticipation. Mrs. Wong smiled and pulled a rosewood chair next to the little girl. Her voice soft and dreamy, she began as if she was telling a bedtime story.

"Once upon a time, a beautiful fairy lived in a palace on the moon. One day she became curious about what was going on outside the moon and decided to come down to the earth. She transformed into a beautiful young lady, living in the kingdom of China. At that time, there were ten suns in the sky, scorching the land and killing many crops. People were starving, so to try to save his kingdom, the emperor of China ordered his bravest soldiers to shoot nine suns down with bows and arrows. All of them failed, except one by the name of Yi. He shot down nine suns and instantly became a hero. The beautiful young lady from the moon fell in love with Yi, and with the emperor's blessing, they got married."

"Does this mean the fairy from the moon is now a princess?" Sage asked. In her mind, the girl from the moon was starting to sound like the princesses she knew from her storybooks.

"Yes, you could say that," Mrs. Wong said. "To reward Yi for saving the kingdom, the emperor awarded him a very rare magic pill. If Yi took the pill, he would live forever. Yi and the princess were very much in love. They wanted to live and die together, so Yi hid the pill in their house. He later left home to fight battles against China's enemies. While Yi was gone, an evil soldier came to their house one night, telling the princess that if she didn't hand over the magic pill immediately, he would kill her husband and then take it. To protect her husband while not letting an evil person live forever, the princess swallowed the magic pill. Instantly, her body became weightless, floating out of the window, up and toward the moon. That's what you can see on the wall: the princess is floating back to the moon, and she is very sad that she's left her husband behind." Mrs. Wong paused to look at the moon-fairy wall.

"What happened when her husband came back?" the little girl asked anxiously.

"Well, Yi was very sad to find the princess gone. He begged the emperor to give him another magic pill so he could also fly to the moon to be with the princess. But the emperor didn't have any left, and he also wanted Yi to stay on earth to defend the kingdom. Yi was brokenhearted and prayed to the moon every night, hoping he could go there to see the princess. Finally, the mother goddess of the moon was touched by Yi's love for the princess. On a midautumn night when the moon was bright and full, she flew Yi to the moon with her magic, reuniting him with the princess."

"And did they both live happily together forever?" Sage asked, hoping for a happier ending.

But Mrs. Wong was interrupted by the arrival of more guests as well as dinner for the Donavan family, a plump duck on a large white platter. Roasted to perfection, the duck was translucently golden, garnished with freshly chopped green scallions, sun-kissed orange wedges, and garnet-red radish slices. The platter was followed by small plates of stir-fried green vegetables, creamy plum sauce, and paper-thin white pancakes. Once the duck was shown to everyone at the table, a server, in a white shirt and a tall white chef's hat, sliced the duck with surgical precision. Within a few minutes, the plump duck was transformed into a pile of thinly sliced juicy meat, its fragrant steam spiraling up into the air. To demonstrate the traditional Chinese way of eating the duck, the server

7

laid a single pancake on a dinner plate, spread a dollop of plum sauce in the middle, added a few pieces of duck meat, and sprinkled some chopped spring scallions on top. Then he folded, tucked, and rolled the pancake until it looked like an oversize spring roll and placed it on Mr. Donavan's plate. "No forks and knives, Mr. Donavan; all you need is your hands. See how you like it," the server said cheerfully.

Mr. Donavan nodded, clumsily picked up the roll with both hands, and cast a hesitant look at the server, who gave an encouraging wave of his hand. Carefully, Mr. Donavan took the first bite.

"Mm, mm, mm ..." Mouth full and head bobbing, he pointed at the platter containing the sliced duck meat and then at his wife and his children, as if saying, "You've got to try this," but not wanting to open his mouth for fearing of interrupting the savory moment.

As Mr. Donavan continued to relish the rest of the duck roll, stopping only to sip his martini, the rest of the family got busy, positioning, arranging, rearranging, folding, tucking, and rolling. A few minutes later, everyone had managed to create something resembling a wrap or a burrito. "Good enough," Mrs. Donavan said. "Now eat."

Sage took her first bite. She did not know how exactly to describe the experience. The crispy skin and tender meat melted in her mouth, and she tasted the bursting flavor of the tangy and sweet plum sauce, savoring the lingering mild fragrance of spring scallions. Temporarily the moon fairy left her mind and flew back to the wall.

"Is everybody enjoying the duck?" Mrs. Wong came to check on everyone.

"Best duck we've ever had." Mr. Donavan was louder after two martinis and many duck rolls.

"It is delicious. The skin is so crispy and the meat so tender without being greasy," Mrs. Donavan said.

"So what happened to the princess?" Sage asked. After a few bites of the duck roll, her mind had gone back to the moon-fairy-princess story.

"Yi and the princess loved each other and lived on the moon together when Yi was not fighting the bad people on earth. But in the end Yi was killed by his enemies on the battlefield, and the princess lived on the moon forever, by herself. She thinks of Yi every day and will never forget him. That's why Chinese people have the Mid-Autumn Festival every year to celebrate love, being together as a family."

Sage was quiet for a while. She glanced at the moon fairy now and then, happy but perplexed too. She was happy that the princess and Yi loved each other and lived happily together, at least for a while. But where was the ever after? Weren't princes and princesses supposed to live happily together ever after?

After dinner, Mrs. Wong brought special dessert for the Donavan family, moon cakes with small scoops of vanilla ice cream on the side. The cakes looked like golden medallions with centers of sweet red-bean paste.

"The moon cake symbolizes a happy family, full and whole, just like the full moon," Mrs. Wong explained as Sage's parents and brother dug into their dessert enthusiastically. But Sage seemed pensive. Her lower lip slightly protruding, she pricked the ice cream ball with the tip of her fork. "What's the matter, Sage? You don't like the dessert?" Mrs. Wong asked.

"The prince and princess should be together forever; they loved each other," Sage declared. To her, Mrs. Wong's story was against all logic of the happily-ever-after stories she had been told.

To calm Sage down, Mrs. Wong said gently, "Well, the princess and Yi did love each other. When they were together, their love was like the moon cake, perfect. I bet you are your parents' little princess, and when you grow up, you will meet your own prince and have your own perfect family."

Mrs. Wong's words seemed to cheer Sage up. She scooped a spoonful of moon cake coated with half-melted ice cream from the plate and smiled a beaming smile before the cake touched her lips for the first time. Across the table, her parents watched her adoringly.

C H A P T E R 1

. . . . .

IT WAS A COLD, early-spring day in April 2009. At seven that morning, Lu Li stepped into her Lower Manhattan office in New York City. She put down her Starbucks coffee cup on her desk and turned on the desktop computer. As the machine awoke with beeps and flashes, she looped out of the strap of her black leather messenger bag and plopped the bag down on the floor next to the swivel desk chair. She shook herself out of her Burberry trench coat and draped it on the heavy wooden hanger on the back of her office door. By the time she sat down at her desk, the computer had fully fired up, waiting for her password. She logged in. Then she leaned back in her chair, savoring the first few sips of coffee as well as the early-morning quiet in the office.

For the almost ten years she had worked at Lehrer & Schuler Investment, her morning routine had always stayed the same. She woke up every morning a few minutes before five. After downing a glass of water, she went for a one-hour run, either at the gym or outside, depending on the season and weather. To her, running was a daily cleansing of mind and body that rid her of mental cobwebs and bodily toxins. Often she would start the run pondering a work-related problem and would see the solution or the approach to the problem by the time sweat tricked down her face and dripped down her back. If she began the run feeling blue, her mood was uplifted, and every fiber of her body glowed as her strides lengthened and her pace quickened. After the run and a quick shower, she left her apartment and descended into the subway station around the corner. Fifteen minutes later, she emerged from the subway station a block away from her office building. After a quick stop at the Starbucks, she was in her office around seven.

She considered the first half hour or so in the office a luxury, reading online financial news and current affairs while enjoying her one and only daily dose of caffeine. When the coffee was gone, the real workday began. As the head of the firm's equity-investment research team, her days were often jam-packed with numerous meetings. But the first couple of hours in the morning were usually reserved for checking e-mails and reviewing and double fact-checking stock research and recommendations prepared by the staff before they were issued to the investment public.

One e-mail flagged "priority" popped up. It was from her boss, Jack Earnest, with the subject "IPO, China" and two attachments. She clicked on the message: "Review attached. Prepare to discuss ASAP. J."

She opened the attachments and did a cursory review of the executive summaries. Two Chinese companies, Golden Seafood Ltd. and Great China Telecom Inc., were planning to go through initial public offerings (IPOs) and to raise capital in the US financial market. She had been noticing for a while that more and more Chinese companies were seeking capital on US stock exchanges, and the big investment firms on Wall Street had all jumped on the bandwagon to underwrite the Chinese IPOs. It was not surprising to her that Lehrer & Schuler, a second-tier investment firm on Wall Street, was itching to get on the wagon too. "I guess it's the in thing," she murmured to herself as she took off her tailored black jacket. After unbuttoning the collar of her gleaming white cotton shirt, she delved into the detailed information about the two companies.

At ten o'clock, Jack Earnest dragged himself into the office, his charcoal-gray suit jacket draped on his shoulder, an almost-empty Starbucks extra-large coffee cup in hand. At sixty-one years old, his six-foot frame still stood tall and erect, and his silver-gray hair was still full and wavy. He still ran a few miles every day but found it increasingly difficult to jump-start in the morning after a long night of client entertaining and deal making, even if he kept the alcohol intake as little as he could get away with.

Lately, he had been seriously contemplating retirement. The world of investment and high finance had been changing, too rapidly for him to keep up and too far away from the principles and philosophies the founders of Lehrer & Schuler had espoused: focus on the fundamentals and aim for the long term. These days everyone focused only on an investment horizon of the next couple of quarters. For quick profit, the whole investment world had been packaging, selling, and buying convoluted investment products nobody could understand. As a senior managing director of the firm, he had considered the firm lucky to have largely dodged the catastrophe of the dot-com bubble burst and the 2008 financial and mortgage market meltdown, mainly because of senior management's relatively conservative business strategies. But old birds like him had been retiring or dying, and the generation succeeding him seemed to be willing to take on greater risks for quick bucks. At strategy meetings now, his opinions and recommendations were subtly dismissed or fell on deaf ears.

"Lu, my deer, how is your morning going?" He stuck his head in Lu's office.

"It's been a fire drill if you mean the Golden and the Great planned IPOs." Lu smiled both at her own impromptu abbreviations and Jack's term of endearment for her. For as long as she had been with the firm, Jack was the only one who occasionally called her *deer*, the English translation of her Chinese name Lu. Jack knew the meaning because he was the only one who had asked her when she had been interviewing for a junior-research-analyst job.

At the end of the twentieth century, when the dot-com bubble had just burst, Lu had applied for the equity-research-analyst position at Lehrer & Schuler. Before meeting Jack, Lu had gone through several rounds of interviews with a number of managers and soon-to-be peers at the firm. The report on her technical knowledge, academic training, and interpersonal skills was glowing. The interview with Jack, one of the senior managers of the firm, was just a matter of formality. After a firm handshake and a warm hello, Jack maintained eye contact a few seconds longer than usual. He found something intriguing in this doe-eyed woman, as he later told Lu. Her black eyes radiated enthusiasm yet were guarded and, under the circumstance, a bit nervous.

"So Ms. Lu or Ms. Li? I know the Chinese put their last names first. I guess that's why China and the US are on opposite ends of the world." Just like that, Jack broke the ice and put Lu at ease.

"I guess I have adopted the American way, having been here for almost thirty years."

"So what does it mean?"

"It means 'deer,'" Lu answered shyly. "When I was a baby, my grandmother thought I looked doe-eyed, so she called me Xiao Lu, Little Deer ..." She stopped abruptly, fearing she was being too personal in a formal interview setting.

"Interesting. So you are your grandma's dear little deer." Jack smiled.

And Lu thought that was the moment Jack coined his term of endearment for her: Lu, my deer.

Scanning down her resume, Jack continued, "I saw you came here from Hong Kong many years ago. You have a BS in accounting and a master of business administration, both at the University of Maryland. What made you decide to come to the US?"

"I had a good friend in high school. When we graduated, her parents decided to immigrate to the US for fear that Hong Kong would sooner or later be under the control of the mainland Communist Party, which became a reality when Hong Kong went back to China a few years ago. I was alone and had no family in Hong Kong at that time, so they helped me get a student visa," Lu answered matter-of-factly.

"I saw you started working right after you received your accounting degree and never stopped. You must have completed your MAB part-time?"

Her doe eyes brightened with pride. "Yes, I worked full-time during the day and went to school in the evening. It took me three years to complete the program, but I felt extremely lucky. The company I was working for not only sponsored my permanent resident status here in the US but also paid all my tuition."

"You must be a good worker for them to do that." Jack was impressed but followed up with a pointed question he had planned for Lu. "Your résumé is impressive, and you advanced rapidly in your field. I see you were the chief financial officer at a couple of technology companies and have lived and worked in the Washington, DC, area ever since you came to this country. Why do you want to move away and to be a research analyst on Wall Street? Aren't you getting off your career track?"

Lu had anticipated the question. With great confidence, she answered the questions truthfully. "I know my training and background may not be conventional on Wall Street, but I believe I have something that is valuable and important to being a successful research analyst."

"What's that?"

"I believe I have knowledge of the nuts and bolts of running a company, especially from a financial perspective. I know accounting and finance is not just counting money spent and projecting money to be made; neither is that important."

"Why?" Jack asked, curious.

"Because accounting is for something already happened. There is nothing you can do about it if the result is not good, though some are willing to play with the numbers to delay the inevitable. We can see what that brought us in the dot-com world. And financial projection is something we hope will happen in the future, and things seldom happen exactly according to our hopes and wishes."

"So what is important to a professional like you?"

"What's important for me is what is happening in between, the time between last year's results and the projections for what will happen next year. That means we have to know what story the numbers are telling us on a weekly and monthly basis and have to figure out quickly what actions to take if the story is a bad one."

"And how does that make for a good research analyst?" Jack was smiling; he knew exactly what Lu's answer would be but asked anyway.

"It gives me the ability to make investment decisions by asking in-depth questions regarding a business's real-time financial and operation health and the ability to peel back the surface layer of a set of financial statements to determine a business model's long-term viability." With that answer, Lu had sealed the deal. She had received the formal job offer the next day. A week later, she had moved to New York and started what she considered a stressful yet rewarding career in the Big Apple. For Jack, hiring Lu was one of the best decisions he had ever made.

"So what do you think of those two Chinese companies?" Jack was anxious for Lu's reaction. "I got the leads last night having dinner with a few big boys of the Street. They invited us to be part of the underwriting team since these two companies are much larger and wanted far more capital than the ones already listed on the exchange here."

"They sound good and solid in the executive summaries, but if you drill down in the details, I have my concerns." Lu looked straight at Jack.

"Of course you do; that's why I think you are the perfect lead person for these projects." Jack laughed. "Why don't you come to my office, and we'll compare notes so we can be ready for the big boys this afternoon. They will be coming to our office to discuss. See you in a few." He took the last gulp of coffee, cast the cup into the trash can next to Lu's desk like shooting a basketball into a hoop, and dashed off.

• • •

A FEW MINUTES BEFORE TWO, Lu was standing in front of the floor-to-ceiling windows of the conference room a few floors up from her office. She was in her typical work attire. Her soft black crepe jacket subtly curved in at the waist and flared out slightly at the hemline a few inches below. Her black dress pants were fitted at the hip with relaxed lines all the way down to the three-inch heels of her black pumps, which elongated her slender runner's physique and made her five-foot-four frame look much taller. Her light-caramel skin tone, set off by her straight, shoulder-length black hair, gave her the perpetual just-came-back-from-a-beach-vacation look, a look that was at least a decade younger than her forty-seven years of age.

She looked straight ahead, taking in the narrow view of the Hudson River sandwiched in between two skyscrapers. From where she was standing, within a tall building surrounded by even taller buildings, she could not see the sky. But she could tell it was beautiful out by looking at the river—only the sun could make it look that way: a river of dancing diamonds.

She clasped her hands behind her head and leaned slightly backward. Then she took her seat at the beige-colored conference table and mentally went around one more time about her views on the to-be-discussed Chinese IPOs.

Fifteen minutes after the scheduled 2:00 p.m. meeting time, the boys from the big firm made their entrance. Leading the way was Fred Armstrong, managing director of the largest investment firm in the country. Over the years, he had established himself as the giant of Wall

Street by successfully engineering and launching numerous large and high-profile IPOs. And he had the right physique to go along with his professional reputation. He was in his midforties, and one might say his six-foot-four bulky form was still solid and in good shape, but the slight paunch under his unbuttoned suit hinted the start of middle age. "Hey, Jack, Lu, sorry we are a bit late," his equally big voice boomed as he vertically and horizontally filled the door frame.

"No problem, guys," Jack and Lu greeted simultaneously. They were used to Fred's habit of being late. They expected his long-time right-hand research assistant to emerge from behind him, but trailing behind him that day was a young man of no more than thirty years old, clad in an expensive, well-tailored dark-gray pin-striped suit. Neither Jack nor Lu had seen him before.

"Jack, Lu, I want you to meet Dick Witherspoon, our new head of the equity-research team."

"Hi, Jack, nice to meet you," Dick said as he quickly walked past Lu and shook hands with Jack.

"Dick, this is Lu, your counterpart at Lehrer & Schuler." Jack motioned him to face Lu for the introduction.

"My pleasure." Stiffly, Dick extended his hand halfway, his head leaned slightly backward so he appeared to be looking down at Lu.

"Nice to meet you." Lu shook his hand, amused by Dick's gesture of self-importance. He was a man of average height, but standing next to Fred seemed to diminish his stature. He had slender shoulders, like a coat hanger that was too small for his well-tailored, expensive suit; squinty eyes closely set on a painfully bony face; and a narrow, long nose with a pointed tip jutting out right above a pair of thin lips.

"Shall we get started?" Fred sank into a chair and motioned Dick to begin talking.

"Yes, sir." Dick quickly pulled several xeroxed pages out of his compact Montblanc briefcase. "This is the summary Golden Seafood has provided of its financial history and its projection for the next ten years." He distributed a page to everyone around the table and continued in a pitch designed for potential investors. "As you can see, the company has experienced tremendous growth domestically over the past decade as China's premier frozen-seafood company, mainly by consolidating smaller frozen-seafood processing and packaging companies all over the country. Now with growing demand for frozen seafood from Europe and here in the US, they have made significant investment in their facilities in China to increase production. But they feel they could achieve even faster growth by establishing distribution and warehouse facilities in Europe and the US. That means if a vendor in the US calls Golden to buy seafood, Golden would have the inventory already in its warehouse somewhere in the US instead of having to ship every order from China." Dick paused and looked around the table, obviously very happy with his grasp of the proposed business model.

"Why do they want to raise capital here instead of domestically?" Lu asked. "The Shanghai and Hong Kong exchanges have become quite robust over the years."

With a subtle eye roll, Dick said, "Believe it or not, there is appetite for equity investment in Chinese companies on the Street, and the Chinese think they face less red tape and bureaucracy here than in their own country. After all, the country has become the manufacturing backyard of the world and has had the highest GDP growth for how many years? Go to any store these days, and just about everything is made in China or from China. And we should be happy that the Chinese consider it prestigious to list their stock on Wall Street. It's a win-win situation; everyone will make some money."

With a faint grin on his face, Jack asked from across the table, "So how much money are they looking for?"

"A couple of hundred million," Dick said casually, as if the amount was insignificant to the importance of the company asking for it.

"Is all the seafood they distribute produced in China?" Lu asked.

"I think so, and most of it will be farm raised," Dick said confidently.

"Their proposed business model is okay, but I think we need to make sure that reasonable quality-control and safety measures have been established on those farms," Lu said. Her eyes swept around the table with vigilance.

Jack grinned knowingly, and Fred raised an eyebrow slightly. Dick asked, a bit unsure, "How is that our job? Shouldn't it be left for the FDA?"

"Well, I found several investigative reports on the way some of the Chinese seafood companies are operated. Whether the seafood is wild caught or farm raised, there is a chance that it's coming from heavily polluted water. The farm-raised fish often live in crowded facilities and are given high doses of growth hormones, antibiotics, and hazardous color additives to make the product more visually appealing."

"Don't we use that kind of stuff here too?" Dick interrupted.

"Yes, but their dosage can be much higher than the maximum allowed here. It has serious health implications. Domestically, the Chinese government has already cracked down on a few food-processing companies for questionable ingredients in their products. I am not saying no; we just have to be extra diligent regarding our due diligence. The FDA can't inspect each of the hundreds and thousands of containers arriving in this country every day." Lu delivered her concern calmly, with a smile.

"Okay, maybe we can send somebody for an on-site visit then," Dick murmured, mostly to himself.

Jack turned to Lu and said casually, "Good idea. Do you think you can swing it? A trip to China?"

There were a few seconds of awkward silence around the table as the three men waited for Lu to say something.

"My schedule is quite full for the next several weeks, but I'll see if I can shuffle a few things around. I'll let all of you know later, okay?" Lu shot a please-don't-put-me-on-the-spot look at Jack as Fred and Dick uttered their obligatory expressions of how much they would appreciate it if Lu could help, and the meeting moved on to the discussion of Great China Telecom.

It turned out Great China Telecom was a far more complicated case than Golden Seafood. Everyone, including Dick, agreed there were too many missing pieces in the proposed deal. They would schedule a follow-up meeting if Dick could convince the company to produce more detailed information.

They ended the meeting, and as Jack and Lu walked back to their offices, he asked, "Are you okay, Lu? I don't mean to put you on the spot, but if anybody at that table is going to China for due diligence, I think you would be the best person." He must have felt that Lu's reaction to his question at the meeting was more complicated than simple annoyance at the proposed China trip interrupting her business schedule. In all the years he had known her, they had talked about a lot of things, professional and sometimes personal, but when it came to her family in China, she was often evasive, and he had never pushed.

They were at Lu's office door. She paused and turned to face Jack. "I'm fine, Jack, just a lot on my plate. But I will see if I can swing it. I'll let you know soon."

"Good. When was the last time you were in China?" Jack asked but regretted right away.

"Believe it or not, I have never gone back after I left it more than thirty years ago." Lu forced a smile.

"That long? Then you should go visit. Aren't you afraid you won't remember everything that is China anymore?"

"Yeah, it's been a long time ... Anyway, I'll let you know my schedule soon and do my best to help with the project." She turned and walked into her office.

It was almost the end of the workday. The unexpected Chinese-IPO discussion had eaten a big part of her day. She needed to finish reviewing and approving several due diligence and research reports before she could go home. After a couple of deep breaths, she sat down in front of the computer and tried to start what looked like a long evening, but Jack's question kept gnawing at her: "Aren't you afraid you won't remember everything that is China anymore?"

"Lu, focus, focus, finish the work, and go home. It was just an innocent question; it didn't mean anything," she told herself. But it was no use. Her problem wasn't that she could not remember but that she had tried to forget but could not. The past had never stopped haunting her dreams. The questions she desperately wanted answers for yet was afraid to ask continued pestering her. She knew she had been hiding from herself, behind a promise she'd made to her father so long ago to never go back. She had kept that promise so far, hoping that by never going back the painful memories of the past would slowly fade. She had known that keeping the promise also meant never having a chance to seek the answers to so many questions she'd had since she was a little girl. She had convinced herself maybe it was all for the better.

But recently she'd been thinking it was a matter of time before her profession would require her to go back. China had been seducing the capitalist West with its cheap labor and prospects of economic growth and profit. It was actually surprising that she had been able to stay away from anything China for so long while working on Wall Street. If Jack formally asked her to go to China, she would not be able to refuse. It was business; she had made a living out of it, and she was good at it. Slowly, she moved the cursor to the calendar icon on the screen and clicked it open. As she suspected, for the next few weeks, numerous reports and researches needed to be completed and reviewed, but nothing would absolutely require her physical presence in her Manhattan office.

"Lu, you will have to go," she murmured to herself as she clicked Jack's e-mail address and entered on the subject line, "China Trip." As she began to type the message, her heart murmured, *You are breaking a promise. You are breaking a promise ...* She stopped typing and stared at the blinking cursor until it was replaced by the screen saver, a photo she'd taken years ago, the first time she'd vacationed at Montauk in New York. She remembered the moment she'd taken the picture on the beach. Everything around her had been black or white yet magnificent: a white full moon in the dark sky casting a shaft of silver light over the black water of the Atlantic Ocean—her only companions, solitude and tranquility. The moment had made the deadlines and demands of her job less than one hundred miles away seem insignificant. She'd come back to Manhattan refreshed and renewed.

She studied the photo as it faded in and out on different parts of the screen, but it did not evoke the Zen-like feeling it usually did. Her mind was pulled back to a different body of water and that fateful day thirty-three years ago on the Hong Kong–China border.

• • •

It was a night in August 1975. She and her father had been hiding for days on a mountain near the Shenzhen River, a border river that separated Mainland China and Hong Kong. For almost a year, she and her father had carried a secret that no one else knew, not even her mother. They had been planning to escape from China to Hong Kong, and they were going to swim across the Shenzhen River to leave the

Communist country behind, forever. At the tender age of thirteen, Lu understood it was going to be a night of either death or freedom.

When she was not quite five years old, Chairman Mao, the leader of the red Communist government, had started the Cultural Revolution. His goal was to reform and exterminate people who were presumably influenced by the capitalist West, people who had become rich on the backs of the working class of the country. The target group, the capitalist elite, was small considering the country had almost a billion people. It included university-educated professionals, some of them with degrees from colleges in the West, and former business/property owners whose assets had already been confiscated when Mao and the Communist government had taken over China in 1949. With clever propaganda, Mao convinced the working class, including farmers and factory workers, that they had been exploited by the capitalist elite of the country all along and that it was time they took back what was theirs. So it began, the Cultural Revolution, one of the bloodiest class warfares in human history.

A couple of months after the Cultural Revolution started, Lu's father was dragged away from home and thrown in a labor camp. For two years, he was beaten, tortured, and forced to complete hard labor, a reform process prescribed by Mao for his crime. He was a successful surgeon. He had been educated in the United States but had chosen to return to his country to practice medicine before the Communist Party had defeated the Nationalist Government and taken over China in 1949. He was classified as a capitalist who made money on poor people's illnesses, a counterrevolutionary, and a spy for the West. The punishment was either execution by bullet or a slow death in the labor camp. For two years, he thought he was never going to see his family again. Then one day, his profession, for which he was being punished, saved his life.

It happened that a high-ranking general of the People's Liberation Army had developed stomach cancer and the only way to save his life was surgery. By then, almost all reputable doctors had been banished to labor camps or tortured to death. The only doctors available in hospitals were barefoot doctors, most of them sons and daughters of factory workers and farmers who had undergone a maximum of a couple of weeks of first-aid training. The general was not stupid. He was not going to let those barefoot doctors operate on him. So he gave an order to seek out the most qualified surgeon for the job. Lu's father had been a renowned surgeon before the Cultural Revolution and was relatively young. Despite the brutal torture he had suffered, he was one of the few doctors left who could still hold a scalpel steadily.

Lu's father performed the surgery successfully. The Communist Party saw the value of keeping him alive. After all, they were all human, and they might need some real doctor to take care of them one day. So Lu's father was taken out of the labor death camp and sent to a duck farm on the outskirts of Shanghai. His job was to tend ducks and be on call to treat important party officials. For years he lived on the duck farm. He was allowed to go home to see his wife and daughter every other weekend but was forbidden to have any visitors except immediate family members. He was not able to attend his mother's funeral after she jumped out of their apartment window and killed herself, the only way for many people at that time to avoid endless torture and interrogation for their so-called crimes against the Communist government. He'd also never had the chance to say good-bye to many of his good friends and colleagues when they wasted away and died in labor camps or prisons. For a long time after the nightmare began, he still held some hope that all this lunacy could not last forever, thinking that anybody who had a tiny bit of humanity left would band together and stop the brutality being inflicted on their fellow human beings. Years went by, and the madness continued. He realized he could not just wait and slowly rot away in a country that not only did not return his love but also was willing to crucify him because he loved it enough to have given up a position in the British Royal Hospital in Hong Kong right after completing his medical degree and residency in the United States. His gravest concern was his daughter, Lu. She was only four years away from graduating high school. Because of her father's sin, she was for sure to be expelled to the most-remote farm communes to be reeducated by the local Communist farmers. Like many before her, she would most likely be raped and forced to do hard labor for many years to come. He could not let that happen; he would rather die. When a fellow duck caretaker had told him that many Mainland Chinese had tried to escape to Hong

Kong by swimming across the Shenzhen River, he'd decided to take the risk.

The night was hot, humid, and moonless, and thunder rumbled in the distant sky. Lu and her father came out from the shrubbery on the mountain where they had been hiding. At the foot of the mountain, a narrow dirt trail led to the dark water of the Shenzhen River. They ran tiptoed along the trail, and within seconds they were wading toward the deep of the river. "Remember, Lu," her father whispered, "conserve energy as much as you can. Don't swim until your feet cannot touch the bottom anymore, and don't forget to cover your head with the watermelon rind the whole time."

As Lu submerged deeper, she welcomed the sensation of the cool waves of the river gently lapping against her body, washing away the sweat and filth. When her toes could not feel the bottom anymore, she floated forward on her stomach on a piece of thin plank wood tied to her waist for minimum buoyancy. Under the half rind of a large watermelon, her head was barely above the water. Her father had trained her to swim like this in a small creek on the duck farm for almost four months, all to create the illusion that the person under the water was nothing but a watermelon rind thrown in the Shenzhen River from a local fishing boat.

In the darkness, she floated forward. She could not see her father, but she could feel his presence next to her. The gentle movement of his arms and legs made sounds in harmony with the sound of the gentle waves. Preparing for this moment, she had been nervous and sick to the stomach for days. Her father had not sugarcoated what the two of them were about to embark on. It was a life-and-death event; they could swim to freedom, or they could be shot by the Chinese border-patrol guards or captured and sent back to prisons to die slowly, which her father ruled out as an option. Before they'd left their hiding place on the mountain, he'd handed her a small package wrapped in layers of wax paper and said, "Tie this to your body, inside your shirt. Your grandma left you this. You can read it when we arrive in Hong Kong. Promise me that no matter what happens, never, ever go back to China." Lu had never heard her father speak with such seriousness. She'd made the promise, the first promise she had ever made in her young thirteen years of life.

Strangely the cool water eased the sick feeling in her stomach, and adrenaline kicked in. Her mind was laser focused on what her father had repeatedly told her: "Take it easy; conserve energy; swim straight forward."

It seemed that they had lucked out. The river was calm and the waves gentle that night. Half an hour after they were in the water, they were well on their way to reaching the other end. But fate was about to deal them a cruel hand just as they thought they were going to make it safely after all.

In the beginning, it was a faint, distant humming sound. The next moment, all was quiet again except for the gentle sound of waves. "Papa, did you hear that?" Lu asked in a hushed voice.

"It's probably somebody's fishing boat. Keep going; we are almost there," her father whispered back.

A few seconds later, the ominous humming sound started again, louder and closer. It did not sound like a small fishing boat. "It could be the border patrol. Don't panic. Stay under the melon rind, and float forward," her father said as a flood of bright yellow light from a large motorized boat sped downstream and straight toward them. As the boat roared closer, there was an explosive bang, followed by gasping sputters, and the boat skidded sideways, stopping several yards away from the two watermelon rinds.

"Dam it, I told you to take it easy. Now what do we do?" a man from the boat said.

"We weren't going that fast! With this piece of old shit, how the hell do they expect us to catch any escapees?" someone else said.

"Stop complaining, you idiot. Turn on all the lights, will you? Let's see where we are. Hope we're not stranded here all night."

Lu could hear several men arguing loudly on the boat. She kicked harder as the water around her turned daylight bright.

"I can see the riverbank on the other side … the border sign … Shit, we're almost on the Hong Kong side," one man grunted. All was quiet again.

Knowing she was close to the destination, Lu's legs worked harder and kicked up small splashes.

"What was that?" a gruff voice asked.

"What was what? I don't see anything out there," a younger, boyish voice asked.

"Look at those watermelon rinds!" the gruff voice said. "Something is strange. They should be floating with the stream, not sideways."

"So you think there's something down there?"

"Hey, didn't we catch a few people just last month using watermelons as camouflage?"

"Yeah, but not here. The river is almost three kilometers wide. Not too many could swim for that long. Now we'd better send signals back so they can come to get us."

"All right, but just in case," the gruff voice said.

Lu heard the click of some metal device. Instinctively, she knew what was going to happen in the next split second. She took a deep breath, deserted the watermelon rind, and dived down to the bottom of the river before rounds of bullets splashed the water above her.

Frantically, she rid herself of the plank wood so she could propel herself deeper into the dark water. Just when she could not hold her breath any longer, she felt her toes touched something hard. She thrust her hands down and realized she could touch the bottom; she was coming ashore. She struggled into a vertical position, steadied her feet on the river's muddy bottom, and carefully surfaced her head above the water.

When she was sure she was safely away from the Chinese patrol guards, she crawled out of the water. Her first thought was to find her father. "Papa, papa, are you here?" she whispered into the darkness around her. But all was quiet. She heard only the rumbling of thunder rolling in, louder and louder. She turned and stared into the dark water. It began to rain. In the distance, angry white lightning zigzagged across the sky, illuminating the Chinese border patrol boat floating out there like a ghost.

She huddled amid a patch of shrubs, telling herself again and again that her father would be walking out of the water soon.

But he never did.

The next morning, the Hong Kong border patrol guards found her father's dead body in the shallow water of the river. He'd died of fatal wounds from two bullets. And they found his daughter, unconscious, lying in some bushes a few hundred feet away.

• • •

IN LU'S DOWNTOWN MANHATTAN office, a cleaning crew member turned on a vacuum. The noise jolted Lu out of the dark water of the Shenzhen River. With a gentle shift of the mouse, she was back in her e-mail. For a few seconds, she stared at the subject line of "China Trip" and then discarded the message. This was one of those few times in her life that decision making was not going to come easily. The noise of the vacuum had invaded the hallway, right outside her office. She would not be able to finish reviewing those reports this evening. She turned off the computer and decided to go home.

C H A P T E R   2

· · · · ·

As Lu rode the subway back to her apartment in Midtown Manhattan, her good friend and former colleague Sage Donovan was walking down Pennsylvania Avenue toward the Farragut West Metro station in downtown Washington, DC. She'd had a tough, nerve-racking day. As the human resources director of the Nationwide Bank, she and the senior vice president of the Washington, DC, branch had terminated many employees of the branch's residential mortgage group. What was worse was more heads would roll tomorrow. All this was the ripple effect of the 2008 housing and financial market meltdown.

It was early spring and had been dreary, cold, and windy all day. Shortly after she'd stepped out of the office building on Pennsylvania Avenue, it had started to drizzle. She pulled up her trench coat collar and scurried toward the Metro a few blocks away. She could not wait to get back to her apartment, only a few stops away, to ease her frayed nerves, take a hot shower, maybe order a pizza or Chinese takeout, and fall asleep in front of the TV, an evening routine she seemed to have fallen into ever since this mass layoff had started months ago.

She was forty-seven years old and a working woman in a profession of dealing with human beings on a day-to-day basis. She had accepted long ago that having a bad day or two at work was as common as dealing with broken air conditioning in the middle of summer or frozen plumbing in the dead of winter. Bad days were not pleasant, but they were part of life and had to be dealt with at one time or another. One did not sink into a prolonged period of gloom and melancholy because of it. Sure there were times she would return home after a mentally trying and physically exhausting day, and the darkness of night would make everything seem depressing. Then morning would come. Her body may be weighed down and bloated from the previous evening's greasy and salty food, but her heart would be somewhat lightened by the beginning of a new day, the potential of something good around the corner, and the reality that had happened yesterday, no matter how bad, would stay forever in yesterday. In that spirit she would unfurl a yoga mat and begin to bend, fold, and stretch her five-foot-seven, svelte body in various positions impossible to average women of her age. An hour later, her body agile and her mind flexible, Sage Donovan would be ready to face the world again.

But on this particular day, she wondered how long it would take her to snap out the mental slump she had been in for the past several months.

At the Metro station, the descending escalator was not working. "Not again," she muttered with a frown as she realized she had forgotten to put on her walking shoes before leaving office. One hand holding firmly on the railing, she was about to walk down the broken escalator steps when her cell phone vibrated in her coat pocket. Fearing bad reception underground, she stepped back and pushed the answer button. "Sage Donavon."

"Hi, sis!" her brother's cheerful voice radiated through.

"Hi, Will. What's up?"

"What's the matter? You don't sound too good. Having a bad day?"

"It's bloody. We almost let go a whole department today. The office is starting to feel like a ghost town."

"I'm sorry to hear that." Will modulated his voice to a tone more befitting to his sister's mood and continued, "Hey, how about I buy you a drink after work today? It will cheer you up."

"Can we maybe do this another day? I'm beat." Sage was still looking forward to her hot shower and Chinese takeout.

"Okay, I confess," Will said, sounded more serious. "Something's just come up, and I need your professional help ASAP. Besides, a drink will help you relax, please ..." He mock pleaded.

If he's begging, something important indeed has come up, Sage thought. She once had joked with Will that when it came to his business, he would coax, cajole, pester, or beg shamelessly, if necessary, to get what

30

he needed for the benefit of his company. "All right, all right, I'll be there. The usual place?" Sage said.

"Great, see you in a bit." He clicked off.

Shaking her head, Sage put her phone away and, with measured steps, walked down the broken escalator. She hopped on the Blue Line heading toward Old Town Alexandria, Virginia, a harbor town on the bank of the Potomac River outside of Washington, DC, where Will's office was located. She was grateful that the train was not too crowded, and she slid into a window seat close to the door. She leaned her head against the window and closed her eyes. As the train whooshed into a dark tunnel, the fluorescent light inside floated her reflection onto the window: her face was thin and pale, almost gaunt looking. Her shoulder-length hair, which had cascaded in voluminous waves of vibrant red when she'd left for work in the morning, had turned to dull frizz. *I need a vacation,* she thought.

On the other side of the door, facing her, were two women sitting next to each other. Two uncovered cardboard boxes—now holding framed photos, coffee mugs, and various papers—sat at their feet. Judging from the passive and resigned looks on their faces, she suspected that, just like the employees she had helped to terminate earlier that day, they were the casualties of the massive financial and economic meltdown happening across the country. She felt the knot that had been twisting in her stomach all day tighten further.

Will is right; a drink may help. She closed her eyes and visualized the drink that literally had her name on it, something she and Joe, the owner and bartender, had concocted years ago, ever since she and Will had started going there to relax, to confide, and to celebrate.

By the time she got off at the Old Town Alexandria station, the rain had stopped, and gusts of wind had blown open the grayish sky, revealing streaks of blue, orange, and yellow. She walked toward the pub and pretty soon saw the American and Irish flags flapping in the wind above its black-and-red facade.

"Hey, Sage, haven't seen you for a while. Where have you been?" Joe greeted the moment she stepped inside.

"Hi, Joe," Sage said, happy to see the always-cheerful bartender with his signature ear-to-ear smile. His deep, steady, yet gentle voice often reminded her of a veteran TV news anchor, trustworthy and full of authenticity. He was big boned with wide shoulders and reddish-blond hair tied back in a ponytail. His broad face, ruddy and framed by a trimmed reddish mane, made him look like a cross between a lion and a large stuffed bear, majestic and cuddly at the same time.

"It's been a bad day. Need a one and one-half today," Sage said, using their code language for one and one-half parts of vodka instead of the regular one part.

"Coming right up."

Sage and Will's usual table in the corner next to the front window was empty. She took off her long khaki trench coat and hung it on one of the dark wooden hooks near the entrance. Walking over to the table, she unbuttoned the jacket of her black skirt suit. Once she reached the table, she sat down and discreetly kicked off her heels. With pointed toes, she nudged the shoes against the baseboard of the wall. By the time she'd finished stretching her legs under the table, Joe was there with the designer drink.

"Knock yourself out, Sage; hope it calms your nerves." Joe winked, his grin mischievous yet comforting. "Let me know if it's too strong. I don't want your brother to give me the third degree for getting his little sister bombed."

"Don't be silly. One drink is not going to do me in. I'm not that little; remember Will is only ten minutes older than I am. Besides, it's not a bad idea to get bombed today. I broke my professional record." She looked around, making sure nobody was listening, and then whispered, "We let a dozen employees go in less than eight hours, not a record I should be proud of. Worse yet, more to come tomorrow."

"Yikes," Joe said. His eyes narrowed, and a scowl deepened the fine lines on his forehead. "Well, you just relax and let me know if you need anything."

"Thanks." She sat down and turned to her namesake drink on the table, the Sage martini: fiery raspberry liqueur at the bottom, a band of faint orange of shaken vodka and pineapple juice in the middle, and a thin layer of vanilla-colored foam with a silver-green sage spear afloat on top. Each layer gradually faded into the next, a fleeting sunset captured in a frosted eight-ounce martini glass. She raised the glass carefully, taking in all its beauty before drawing the first sip. Instantly, tingling warmth traveled from her throat all the way down to the pit of her stomach, loosening the knot that had stubbornly settled there for days. After a few more sips, the tingling surged upward, radiating a buzz to her head, reminding her that she had not had anything to eat since early morning.

The martini relaxed her temporarily, but it could not ease the dread she had for tomorrow, having to let more employees go. Terminating anybody's job was never pleasant, even if she held no illusions that businesses should be forced to guarantee everybody a job forever. She had always approached the uncomfortable task by providing terminated employees an honest, although sometimes painful, assessment of the situation and offering advice she thought would be professionally beneficial to them. She did her best helping them with résumé revision or obtaining outplacement services, all in the hope that sometime down the road, they would land in a new position they would be happy with. She seldom heard from them once they were gone, but occasionally news would reach her regarding former employees who had achieved great professional advancement. It was comforting to her that all her efforts were not in vain. She had accepted the firing aspect of her job as part of the gig, but recently it seemed to have become her only job. The worst part amid this mass layoff was to witness the not-so-pretty aspects of human nature when everybody thought their jobs were on the chopping block. As the HR director and perceived as closely involved in the corporate reorganization and streamlining effort, she and her office had been the center of drama unfolding and playing out on a daily basis. Some confronted and badgered her regarding how secure their jobs were. Some shed tears and bemoaned the big mortgage and student loans they had been shouldering. Others babbled incessantly about the heavy workload they had been carrying and about their colleagues' incompetence. Then there were the very few Sage considered the worst kind. They usually held jobs that didn't require much actual work, and they often gossiped and chitchatted away their workdays but then insisted they did not have time to go to the bathroom or to lunch. They came into her office and declared that the company was lucky to have them as employees, for they could have had better-paying jobs somewhere else. But they were also quick to drop hints that they would take legal action if they were not treated fairly in the layoff process. To her disappointment, a few seemed to have been able to stop or delay their deserved termination so far.

When she had been a young girl, Sage had imagined growing up just like her mom, a woman of elegance and artistic flair with a heart of gold, always ready to help her fellow human beings—qualities best obtained through higher education and a liberal-arts degree. Later, she would meet and marry her soul mate, her Prince Charming, somebody just like her dad, a good provider and a loving husband. Together they would raise a beautiful family that was the envy of the community.

The young Sage had wanted her parents' life.

Human resources management was an area she'd fallen into almost two decades ago, not that she'd planned for it. She'd simply realized that her double-major degree in art history and psychology, which had cost her parents close to six figures, was not likely to land her a self-supporting job.

Life didn't turn out exactly as I planned, she thought.

"Hey, how are we doing here?" a voice asked.

Sage looked up and saw Will's blue eyes and dimpled smile, a combination that reminded her of the little boy Will buzzing around in their grandparents' bakery in Montauk, excited and pleased with himself because he had helped their grandpa carry a tray of fresh-out-of-the-oven rolls to the storefront or assisted their grandma with kneading bread dough.

"Relaxing," she said, taking a sip of the almost-faded sunset. Will was holding a sweating beer glass in one hand and a gym bag in the other. "Good news?" she asked.

"Yeah, something quite big." He took a gulp of beer, dumped his gym bag on the floor, and put the glass on the table. He was wearing faded blue jeans and a cobalt-blue cotton sweater that accentuated the blueness of his eyes, just as a deep-green sweater would have brought out the emerald green in those same eyes. He must have just worked out and showered. His muddy-brown hair, with pepper-and-salt tinges at the temple, had that just-shampooed fluffiness. A three-day-old stubble densely covered the sides and lower half of his face and obscured the small horizontal scar on his chin, the result of an injury earlier in his life from his lifelong passion—surfing, a sport he still mastered, making guys half his age drop their jaws in awe. Year-round, any chance he had, even if it was just a few days, he chased the tidal waves on sun-kissed beaches around the country and abroad. To maintain that ability and proficiency, his dedication to running and strength training equaled his devotion to his company. At age forty-seven, he and his six-foot-tall body had been rewarded with a successful business and a chiseled physique.

"Well, before I tell you my news, do you want to talk about the tough day you had?" Will sat down, the intense electric blue in his eyes softening to a mild sky blue.

"Not very pleasant to talk about. We fired a bunch of people, and I have to go back there tomorrow to do another group. My job is depressing these days. Why don't you tell me something to cheer me up? I could use some good news." Sage looked at her martini glass; the sunset was gone.

"Okay. I received an unsolicited phone call today from a big telecom company, Matrixtech. They expressed interest in buying my company. They are big and publicly held, so I guess, financially, the deal means you and I both could retire now." Will's voice was cool though his eyes glinted that intense blue again.

"But …" Sage stopped short and let her word dangle. She knew the potential financial gain was not all her brother was excited about.

"But what?"

"But what's going to happen to you? You are the CEO and owner now. What are you going to do? Cash out and go back to Montauk and sit on the beach? You don't want to end up too young to retire and too old to surf." She regretted her words right away. That would be cruel for Will if it became reality.

"Of course not. They said it's the technology and know-how they are interested in; what I have could complement their business nicely. So I would still be CEO in charge of every aspect of the company. Nothing would change much, except we would be a division or subsidiary of a much-larger, publicly owned company, and I would have more resources to do what I want to do: develop new cybersecurity software and packages." Will sounded confident.

Sage knew that her brother realized this was a big decision that he alone would have to make. "Not that I'm not happy for you, Will, but the company is your life, and I know how much you always wanted to be in charge of your own destiny. Just make sure you won't lose control in the long run," Sage said, trying not to sound doubtful. She was not an expert in mergers, acquisitions, and business valuations, but she had been in the postmerger, postacquisition, or reorganization situation often enough to know that promises were often made in order to push those deals through, but they were seldom implemented exactly as they were promised. At minimum there would be hurt feelings, and if ego and power struggle were the true motivators behind those deals, somebody always ended up being screwed.

"Don't worry, Sis." Sensing Sage's doubt, Will reached across the table and patted her arm. "I'm not stupid. A lot of due diligence will have to be done before I make the decision. Right now I think another drink is called for."

"Another one of this would be nice." Sage picked up the almost-empty glass in front of her. "After all, your news calls for celebration."

"Hey, take it easy on the vodka; you don't want to get in trouble," Will teased.

"With whom? Stop being so controlling. I am forty-seven years old and having a drink or two with my brother. What kind of trouble can I get into? If you are really worried about me, why don't you also order me a salad. I haven't eaten anything since this morning." She faked annoyance at his overly protective instinct.

"Okay, okay, a Caesar salad and a Sage martini coming up." Will shook his head and walked toward the bar where Joe was attending to an increased number of customers.

Watching Will ambling toward the bar, his gait confident and self-assured, Sage could not help but marvel at how far he had come in building his business, from a one-man IT contractor to the technology company of $100 million in annual revenue and about two hundred employees in multiple locations. She was often envious of her brother, the fact that he'd seemed to know what he wanted to be at a very young age, ever since he had first become conscious of what was going on in their grandpa's bakery shop. Of course he'd loved Grandpa's sweet cinnamon buns, but he had been more fascinated by the process of how a loaf of bread or a cinnamon bun came into being, from bags of flour in the basement to the loaves and buns on the counter ready for sale. He'd been excited to see that customers came in and exchanged their money for the loaves and buns. At the end of day on Sundays, he would help Grandpa clear the cash register and get all the bills sorted and coins rolled, ready for deposit. The reward for his work had been a dollar for his piggy bank, which he'd accepted with sparks in his eyes and a dimpled smile. Soon the family had started calling him a "little capitalist pig." It had not been a surprise when he'd announced at age eight that he would have his own business like Grandpa when he grew up.

"Here's your drink. Your salad should be here in a minute." Will returned from the bar with a fresh Sage martini and sat down at the table.

Sage pushed aside the empty glass and took a sip of the new one. It was not as strong as the first. "Will, it's terrible; it tastes like fruit juice." She dramatized her dislike of the drink with a big frown, casting a look at Joe at the bar. Anticipating her protest, Joe had been watching her, and their eyes met. He shrugged as if saying, "Hey, it's not my fault."

Smiling, Sage gave Joe a nod and then turned back to Will. "Remember how we used to call you a little capitalist pig in the bakery shop? Ever thought what Dad would say if he were still alive?"

"He would still call me a capitalist pig, but I can hear him saying 'I told you so' on this college thing. I guess he was right; a college degree isn't everything, but it sure gets you in the door if you're lucky. I just didn't do it according to his time line." Will's jubilant mood seemed to give way to pensiveness.

"No matter what, I think Dad would have been very proud of you," Sage said. She knew what Will was thinking. She herself could not help but recall that long weekend in late summer when she and Will had taken their last vacation with their dad on the beaches of Montauk.

• • •

AFTER YEARS OF BEING an account executive at a large advertising firm in New York City, Will and Sage's dad uprooted his family from

37

Montauk to Washington, DC, to lead a large public relations agency. At the time Sage and Will were about to enter middle school.

A year after the family settled in DC, one of the agency's clients, a Detroit auto maker, had a series of tire-explosion accidents that triggered congressional investigation and class-action lawsuits. Dad's agency was charged with the responsibility of launching multiple campaigns to control the damage and handle the public relations crisis. For months, Dad and his team worked night and day to roll out the campaigns as effectively as they could under the circumstances. But in the end, neither the client nor Dad's boss in New York was happy with the perceived outcome. When the crisis was finally over, so was Dad's job, and his marriage was on the rocks.

Their trip took place a few weeks before she and Will were to start college. After a couple of days visiting childhood friends and tidying up the beach house that had been home to their grandparents before they had moved south, the three of them went to the beach together in the afternoon of their last day in Montauk. Sitting in the warm sand under the late-summer sun near Montauk Point, the tip of Long Island, Sage watched her dad and Will chase whitecaps on their rainbow-colored surfboards. The glaring sun was descending over the horizon, a giant fireball. No other humans were in sight on the miles of white sandy beach stretched right and left of her, only seagulls posing in one-footed stances or nestling comfortably in the warm sand and a couple of pelicans diving for their supper. The rhythmic sound of lapping waves was interrupted only by occasional bird cries and the intermittent wailing of the foghorn from the lighthouse at Montauk Point.

She drifted asleep.

She was awoken by voices, a heated and passionate discussion.

"No matter what you are going to do, finish college first. It's the only way you will have a chance to make a decent living and support a family. You plan to have a family someday I assume." Dad was talking at Will.

Will, who was lying on his back in the sand and staring up at the sky, did not seem to hear Dad at all.

"Do you hear what I am saying?" Frustrated, Dad was even louder.

"I hear you, Dad. I am willing to give it a try. I am starting college in a couple of weeks, aren't I? But it doesn't mean I can't consider getting

38

into some kind of business on my own down the road," Will answered in a tone that was half-appeasing and half-protesting.

"Some kind of business? When you figure it out, we'll talk, but now you'd better study hard and try to graduate college first." Dad's voice softened a bit.

Will rolled his eyes slightly. "I hear you, I hear you, Dad. Now shall we give it another go before it gets dark?"

For the last time Sage watched her dad and brother, with the same gait, walk toward the shoreline, still arguing about the merit of college education. A moment later they were bobbing in and out of the tidal waves of the Atlantic Ocean. The horizon was a vista of deep violet streaked with orange, red, and gold.

Less than a month later, Dad died of a heart attack. He was only forty-six. For a long time, Will tortured himself for spending his last hours with Dad arguing and fighting about college. Driven by guilt, he coasted through his first couple of years of college education, never quite sure what he wanted to major in. One day he told their mother to keep the money their father had put aside for his college tuition, joined the navy, and left town.

● ● ●

Breaking the dead silence that had fallen over their table in the bar, Sage tried to prevent Will from sinking deeper into his self-imposed guilt. "Will, it was a long time ago, and you didn't mean to hurt Dad's feelings. I'm sure he would be very happy up there knowing where you are today."

"I know, but it still hurts to think that with the burden of supporting the whole family, the constant pressure he was under at work, and Mom's nagging of not enough money saved for our college, I was so stupid that I didn't even appreciate what he had done for me."

"Hey, if anybody is to feel guilty, it should be me. I ended up spending Dad's money on an expensive college education and don't have much to show for it." Sage lightened her tone, hoping a little self-mocking would pull Will out of his melancholic mood.

"You are independent. I am sure that's what Dad wanted you to be, and he would have been proud of you too," Will said matter-of-factly.

"I doubt he would, not for what I have been doing recently," she retorted. "Besides, you really think Dad would have been proud of me? Single and alone at forty-seven?"

"You are not alone; you have me. I will always take care of you," Will said, half-jokingly.

Sage often heard people say that everyone grew up just like their parents or exactly the opposite of their parents. But her brother had turned out to be so much like their father and so much unlike him at the same time. Like their father, Will believed a man was the provider for his family; unlike their father, having a family of his own was his choice—a choice that, at forty-seven, he had not made yet—not an obligation dictated by society. His father believed college education was a man's passport to becoming a successful provider; Will had his own ideas of what the passage to prosperity should be. When it came to Sage, though, she knew both her father and brother held the same old-fashioned view: she could study for a degree in liberal arts if she wanted, but it was more important for her to find a husband who would provide for her family and for her to be a good wife and a loving mother.

Deep down, what her dad and her brother hoped for her was not far away from what she had secretly desired as a girl and young woman. She had dreamed of having her parents' life, the life before they had separated of course, when they had truly been in love with each other and, together, had been a perfect family.

After her parents had separated, she'd stubbornly held on to the hope that sooner or later her parents would work things out and get back together. It did not make any sense to her that the man and woman who, from ever since she could remember, had often looked into each other's eyes and kissed like the couples on "Every Kiss Begins with Kay" commercials could suddenly be so disappointed in each other and harbor so much resentment toward each other. Where had their love gone? Then a heart attack had taken her father away, and the question would remain unanswered forever.

After her dad's death, Sage had pried her mom many times, hoping for some closure: Had Mom ever considered reconciling with Dad?

Regardless of what had happened, did she still love him? But her mom's cloistered heart had revealed nothing; her spirit, her love of life that could light up an entire room, had forever left her. She'd died of leukemia a few years later. To Sage, her mom seemed to have died from lack of joy or the inability to experience life's joy. But again, Sage had been brought up an eternal optimist. The belief that people who loved each other would stay together happily ever after had been instilled in her since she was a little girl. So she'd answered the questions her parents could not answer: Yes, her parents would have gotten back together had the heart attack not claimed her dad; yes, no matter what, her parents had still loved each other until the day they'd died.

She'd told Will her thoughts, but he, however, had never been quite sure.

Then Sage the young woman had grown up and matured after tasting the sweet elixirs and bitter concoctions life had to offer. At forty-seven years old and with a few not-so-happily-ended relationship behind her, her fiery desire for a happily-ever-after life had burned down to a warm ember, glowing softly in a deep corner of her heart. People who were close to her knew, given an all-stars-aligned chance, she still had the ability to rekindle the ember into a blazing fire. But on that particular day, faced with her brother's well-intended offer of taking care of her, she felt the ember cooling and extinguishing.

She sighed. "I think Dad would have been disappointed in his little princess. I didn't turn out exactly as he would have liked, just like Mom."

"Eh ..." Probably knowing Sage was right, Will struggled for words for a moment. Diverting from the subject, he said, "But you are doing well, aren't you? Even in this hell of an economic meltdown, you still have more work than you can handle."

Sage failed to see the humor in what he said. "Yeah, more work that's literally driving me to drink every day. One day the karma will turn around, and the firing will be the fired."

"No worries. I know you don't like me to say this, but you can always come and work for me. Hey, no matter what, we can count on each other, right?" Will was genuine and serious.

Looking into her brother's now-tender blue eyes, Sage knew he was offering emotional support the only way he knew how. She sighed.

"Well, each other is all we have in this world. My chances of hitting the love and marriage jackpot are looking dim at my age. I guess in that sense we would have both driven Dad nuts if he were still alive today. But I don't think it's a good idea for family members to get involved in the same company. My first cardinal rule of work is to not go into business with family members. Nothing good will come out of it."

"Okay, okay, you don't have to get all HR on me, but I do need your help on one thing." Will's effervescent enthusiasm returned. "Remember years ago you mentioned a colleague who was from China? What's her name?" Will squinted his eyes, trying to remember. Before Sage could answer, he beat her to it. "Was it Lu or Li?"

"You mean Lu Li." Sage chuckled.

"You guys still keep in touch?"

"Yes, but not as often as we both want. She moved to New York City a long time ago. We exchange e-mails and have dinner together if our paths happen to cross in DC or New York. Why are you asking about her?" Sage was surprised that her brother remembered the name. He'd never met Lu, and Sage had only mentioned her in passing a few times in the past ten years.

"She speaks Chinese?"

"Of course, she was born in China and grew up there."

"She is in finance, right?"

"Yes, high finance now on Wall Street. What are you up to, Will?"

"Perfect! Anyway, could you give her a call to see if she is willing to provide some advice?"

"I don't know. Why would you be interested in her? You've never even met her before."

"Well, Matrixtech, the company that is trying to buy me out, may be bought itself by a large Chinese telecommunication company. This could complicate things on our end. I need to talk to somebody like Lu, who can not only speak the language but also understand the culture and business."

"Will, you're asking me to break my second cardinal rule of work. Lu and I haven't been spending much time together since she moved away, but we do have a history together, and it's the kind of friendship I think we both would like to keep. I don't think it's a good idea for her to give you advice. What if things don't work out? I would be in the middle, being hit from both sides. It could ruin my friendship with her or at least make it awkward," Sage protested.

"Relax, Sage; don't get ahead of yourself. It's not like I'm going to hire her or anything. I just want you to arrange a meeting with her quickly so I can pick her brains a little. Give her a call to see if she is willing to talk to me. I could go to New York to meet her." After a brief pause to gauge Sage's reaction, he continued, "What's wrong if somebody like her comes to work at a company like mine? Are you saying my company isn't good enough for somebody like her?"

Sage was glad that, at that moment, the food they had ordered arrived—chicken Caesar salad for her, a grilled cheese sandwich for Will, and a plate of fries to share. Both hungry, they consumed almost everything on their plates in silence. Perhaps it was the food, but by the time they were nibbling on the fries, their conversation had become less edgy.

"One phone call is all you have to do. Briefly describe the reason of the meeting, and we will go from there." Will was businesslike.

Sage gave in, even if in the back of her mind she was still searching for plausible reasons why she should not involve Lu in her brother's business. "I guess it won't hurt to just call and see if she would like to meet," she murmured to herself.

"Good, let's do this quickly." Will took the last swig of his beer, pleased that he had fulfilled his mission that evening.

"Now it's your turn not to get ahead of yourself." Sage was not ready to fully give in. "I will call her in the morning, but I will make it clear that this is strictly a professional arrangement between you and her. And if the deal doesn't work out, it will in no way affect my friendship with her. Also, don't ever think you could make her come and work for you; nothing good will come of involving a friend in your family business."

"Deal. Now, you want anything else?" A broad smile deepened his dimples. The blue in his eyes was brilliant. "And give her a call this evening if you can," he said.

CHAPTER 3

· · · · ·

It was past six in the evening when Lu opened the door to her apartment in Midtown. She had lived in the same building ever since moving to New York City. It was an old building, and the rent was reasonable compared to newer apartment buildings in the area. She'd signed an initial lease for a one-bedroom unit on a lower floor. Her windows had faced a dark alley, but she had not minded. She'd liked the fact she was close to all the sounds and sights that could make her rejoice: musicals on Broadway, classic concerts at the Lincoln Center, the impressionist masters' paintings at the Metropolitan Museum of Art. She had never forgotten that these same life-enriching sounds and sights had once been considered mind poisoning and thus off limits to her in Communist China. And she often marveled at how privileged she was to be surrounded by so much beauty all at the same time.

Then there had been the window-shopping. Back then she'd had neither the money nor the time to throw around in those luxury shops dotting the city's iconic shopping districts. But she'd had a weakness for well-tailored designer clothes. She'd imagined that one day she would be comfortable enough to dress herself in the elegant garments showcased in those shops' windows and would not feel guilty or apologize to anybody who would accuse her of being a clothes horse. She would only be making up for her years in China and her time spent in the orphanage in Hong Kong, wearing only hand-me-downs from her mother or donated clothes that often made her look like a tattered rag doll.

As her career at Lehrer & Schuler had advanced, she'd considered buying a condo but did not think the timing was right. Real estate prices had been skyrocketing, and her instincts had told her it was a bubble to burst sooner or later. Then she'd found that a two-bedroom unit was available on a higher floor in the same building. It had more space than she needed, but off of the living/dining room was a small terrace from which she could see a big patch of water of the Hudson River a few blocks away. She'd signed a lease after one visit and had never considered leaving since.

At the entrance she flipped on the light switch, instantly filling the sparsely decorated interior with soft incandescent light. The decor was clean and simple, neutral and earth tones mixed with occasional black. The furnishing was designed with style and comfort in mind, with minimal lines, a fusion of mission and Asian style.

She kicked off her shoes and changed into her favorite James Perse soft cotton pants and sweatshirt. She cracked the sliding door to the terrace to let in the cool air of dusk, unfurled a yoga mat on the floor, posed in a half-lotus position, and started deep breathing, a trick she had mastered to ease her busy mind and relax her tense body.

Ten stories below, the Manhattan rush-hour traffic hissed and whizzed. As her breathing deepened and slowed, the high emotion stirred up by China eased. She drifted into a familiar feeling, a curious and hopeful feeling that often had descended upon her unexpectedly in recent times.

Despite of her painful childhood in China and the promise she'd made to her father shortly before he had been shot in the Shenzhen River, her heart had never been completely closed to the hope that one day she would see China again. Since the early nineties, China had slowly been lifting the iron veil that had shielded the country from the rest of the world for more than four decades. Economically, it had developed and advanced by leaps and bounds, although politically, the country was still under Communist government control. The temptation of money from the West and the prospect of profit and financial gain were hard to resist, even to the most-hardened Communist party members. So under the Communist banner, the country had embraced capitalism with unbridled passion. The rapid economic growth had undoubtedly lifted the living standards of millions of Chinese people who had been living in dirt-poor and deplorable conditions, but those who had profited most were the same party members who used to condemn and prosecute people like her father.

In recent years, as the whole Western world vied for investment opportunities in China and chased the elusive dream of profiting from the 1.2 billion customers of the country, Lu had avoided being pulled directly into any business deals that had anything to do with China. To her colleagues, her lack of enthusiasm and nonchalance toward China was befuddling. Professionally, she was on top of her game on Wall Street, so why wouldn't she capitalize on her language ability and cultural background to make some easy money?

But to her, money would never be the reason if she decided to go back to China. Privately she had been following news on China, reading articles and reports about the country, wondering all along if she dared to hope that the time had come for her to go back to her roots and reconnect to her blood ties and also wondering, if she did so, whether her father would have forgiven her for breaking the promise she'd made thirty-some years ago.

After her breathing exercise, she retreated to her bedroom. She propped herself up comfortably on a pile of pillows and then grabbed her laptop and turned it on. The headboard and footboard of the bed were made of black wrought iron, similar to the bed she'd shared with her grandma when she was a little girl. She stared at the intricately designed curves of the footboard. They looked like ocean waves with curled tips and evoked her childhood imagination: the bed was a big boat, carrying her and floating out to sea ...

• • •

She was awakened by a raspy voice, from a person who had smoked too many cigarettes. "Grandma, who is out there?" she asked in the dark but realized her grandma was not there in bed with her. Scared, she slipped out of bed and tiptoed to her bedroom door. Gingerly she turned the door knob. The glaring fluorescent light in the hallway seeped through the cracked bedroom door. She rubbed her eyes to adjust to the light. Several strange men were standing in the hallway, surrounding her father. They were all in yellowish-green uniforms with red bands on their upper left arms. The raspy voice came from a man in a navy-blue jacket. He said, "You are antigovernment; you need to come with us to answer some questions."

"I am a doctor. I haven't done anything that's against the government," her father said defiantly.

"Take him away," the man in the blue jacket said to the yellowish-green-uniformed gang. Two of them grabbed her father's arms and dragged him out the front door.

"Papa, Papa!" Forgetting her fear, she came out from behind the bedroom door and ran after her father.

"Shut up, you little shit." The man in the blue jacket grabbed her pajama collar from behind and pushed her to her grandma, who was standing next to the front door, dumbfounded.

With her grandma's arms around her, Lu looked up at the man in the blue jacket. He bent down toward her, his pockmarked face sneering, exposing his crooked yellow-and-black teeth; his eyes, like two black marbles, staring at her venomously, unblinking, got bigger and closer, until they turned into two black holes, ready to swallow her up. She started to run away from the man, but her legs were like lead. She could not run fast, and the man in the blue jacket was getting closer and closer …

• • •

LU WOKE UP SCREAMING. She was half propped up by two pillows on her bed, her laptop still sitting on her lap. *That explains why I wasn't able to run in that ugly dream,* she thought. She must have dozed off while reviewing the two due diligence reports.

She sat up, and her eyes swept around her bedroom. In photos on the dresser next to her bed, her father and grandma smiled at her. The faded black-and-white photos had been taken many years before Lu had been born. Her father was in his surgeon's gown, smiling confidently. A nurse had taken the picture right before he'd performed his first surgery in his own country, after completing his medical degree and residency in America. Her grandma's photo had been taken on her fiftieth birthday. It was a portrait shot from a forty-five-degree angle: her hair, still black, was coiled into a chignon secured by her favorite single-pearl clip. The photos often stirred up nostalgia and fond memories of the happier days with her father and grandma when she had been a little girl. But at the moment, the photos reminded her of how alone she was in this world.

She sighed and got off the bed. Taking off the work earrings and necklace she was still wearing, she walked over to the jewelry box on the dresser, next to her father and grandma's photos. The approximately one-foot-square box was made of black-lacquered wood, with a single white mother-of-pearl lotus flower inlaid on the lid. She'd found it in a shop that sold Asian-style trinkets in Chinatown years ago. She removed the lid and put her earrings back in the top detachable tray for rings and earrings. Then she lifted the tray out of the box to put her necklace in the bottom compartment. A small notebook, its stained cardboard cover frayed at the edges, lay next to strings of necklaces. Hesitantly, she picked up the notebook and flipped open the cover, revealing a small black-and-white photo, a photo of baby Lu sitting on her parents' laps. On the back of the picture, her father's familiar writing read, "Lu's first birthday."

In the picture, both her parents were smiling. Lu often wondered if they were actually happy together back then, for in her memory, her mother had a gloomy disposition but possessed extraordinary beauty. Even in the faded picture, she was beautiful: oval face with high, regal cheekbones, her brows shaped like delicate leaves of a willow tree, almond-shaped eyes set slightly wider apart than normal. Her hair was short and wavy, set in the style popular with Hollywood actresses in the Jazz Age, the Roaring Twenties.

Decades had passed since Lu's last communication with her mother. The few memories she had of her mother were as faded as the only family photo she had locked away in her jewelry box.

After Lu's grandma had died with her father still in labor camp, her mother had continued her hospital administrator's job but had often been away for business reasons. For days, sometimes a week, at a time, she'd leave Lu alone in the apartment, with their next-door neighbors checking in on her here and there. On the evenings her mother was home, she was often sad and distant. They often had dinner in silence, and then her mother would sit in front of the vanity in her bedroom, brushing her hair and examining her image in the mirror.

"Mommy, are you sad?" she asked her mother one evening.

Her mother turned away from the mirror and faced her. "Mommy is not sad. Mommy is tired because she has to work all the time or you won't have anything to eat."

"But Papa works too, right?"

With a faint but icy smile, her mother turned back to look at herself in the mirror again. Then she said, "Your papa is making zero money. People being reformed in the labor camp do not get paid. Mommy married the wrong person."

When Lu started grade school, her dad was transferred to a duck farm to continue his reform but was allowed to come home on weekends. By then her parents seemed to be completely estranged. She seldom heard them talk to each other and found the silence uncomfortable and awkward. She was more relieved than happy when her dad suggested one day that she could learn to take the bus and visit him at the duck farm on weekends. So at age eight, Lu became a little adult. She walked to school and back home on her own, and with her neighbors' help, she managed to cook rice and vegetables on the days her mother was not home. She looked forward to Saturdays, when school was finished at noon and she would hop on the bus to the duck farm.

Lu and her dad developed a routine on the duck farm. She would complete whatever homework she had, which was hardly any, before bedtime on Saturday. With most teachers being persecuted and kicked out of school, teaching and learning were limited to reading and reciting Chairman Mao's *Little Red Book*, in which he preached his communist ideologies. On Sundays, they would get up at dawn and let the ducks out to roam around while they cleaned the pens, about twenty of them. In the afternoon, if the weather was warm and decent, they would sit by the river, watching the ducks floating on the water or taking a swim with them. When dusk descended, they shooed the ducks back into their pens, and then it was time for her to take the bus back home to the city. Being able to spend time with her dad every week made her content and happy. She somehow accepted her mother's absence and disinterest in her. Her dad would often tell her, "Your mother is just tired, being the only one to support you. I am sure she resents me for being away from home for so long. Things will get better when Papa gets to go home every day again."

But things did not get better.

When Lu was twelve, her sister was born. Though surprised, she was happy to see her mother becoming a warmer person, often smiling and giggling at the baby, something she had never seen her mother do with another human being before. For a while, her dad came home more often over the weekends to help out. He did grocery shopping and cooked meals, but Lu knew the ice between her parents never melted.

After escaping from China, she often wondered how her mother felt or reacted when news arrived that her husband was dead trying to escape to Hong Kong and that her elder daughter was missing, most likely never to return. She imagined her mother heartbroken, mourning her husband's death while seeking any information leading to her elder daughter's whereabouts. But deep down, she was afraid that reality was not the same as her imagination.

When Mao finally died in late 1976, the Communist government began to allow the country to open up to the rest of the world, although in a controlled fashion. Communications like mail and packages in and out of China, once forbidden, flowed more freely, even if they were constantly checked or confiscated by the government. Lu tried to reconnect with her mother and sister, but her letters were either not answered or returned with the disappointing postmark of "Return to Sender." Later, she tracked down a phone number of a public telephone booth close to the old apartment building where she thought her mother and sister still lived. After repeated dialing, she finally got through. The telephone messenger on duty confirmed that her mother and sister indeed still lived there and said he would deliver her message to them to call her back immediately.

Fifteen minutes later, her mother called back.

"Please do not call us. I don't want anybody here to know I still have ties with the West. God knows I have suffered enough for that, having been married to your father for that many years. Your sister and I are doing fine now. Our life is stable, so please do not bother us again," her mother whispered, as if afraid somebody could be listening in on her.

Since then, Lu often wondered if her mother's unwillingness to reconnect with her was because she was afraid of possible persecution by the Communist government. So she left everything alone. But as the country further opened up, most Chinese people were glad to have family members or relatives in Western developed countries and would try anything to reconnect with them. So every time Lu had relocated, she had dutifully mailed her mother the new address, but no reply had ever come. By the time she'd moved to New York, she'd decided to let things go. After all, she could not force her way back into her mother's and sister's lives.

Now, almost three decades later, she found it increasingly difficult to keep her promise to her father. She had risked her life to flee China, the motherland void of a mother's nurturing love that had robbed her of the only people she'd loved before she'd had a chance to grow up. For the longest time, she had been a lone ship, drifting bravely but aimlessly in the sea of life. When she'd moved to New York City for the job at Lehrer & Schuler, she'd known that, for the first time, she'd found a place that could be her permanent home, with its energy and vitality constantly coursing through her entire being, offering her endless possibilities, and giving her courage and confidence to continue down life's path, even if she was alone.

Shanghai, though it still came into her dreams every now and then, seemed to have become only a place she once knew, where nobody would be around to welcome her with open arms if she chose to go back. It was a fact she'd thought she had accepted and resigned herself to until recently. Whether she was willing to admit or not, China seemed to be asserting its psychological ownership on her. Her heart was like the lotus flower on her jewelry box. She thought she had severed it from its roots long ago, but the wispy, almost-invisible, silky threads between the flower and roots were never disconnected. Now her heart, tugged by these tenuous threads, had become restless and curious.

China was calling; Shanghai was beckoning.

Lu inserted the photo back in the notebook. Her head told her to put the notebook back and close the jewelry box, but her heart directed her fingers to flip through the pages that had kept her away from China for over thirty years—her grandma's journal from January to September 1966. The entries made during the first few months of the year were about events Lu had no memory of. She had not quite been five years old. But she did remember what her grandma wrote about the Chinese New Year's Eve that year.

New Year's Eve, 1966

Xiao Lu and I had the best time together this evening. I taught her how to make rice balls stuffed with sweet sesame paste. She is a funny girl, always asking questions. "Why can't we just make wonton with sesame stuffing? Why does it have to be a perfectly round ball? Why do we only have sweet rice balls around New Year?" She is a little kid with a busy mind. I told her that eating round rice balls around New Year is for good luck. A perfectly round rice ball means wholeness. So if we eat round rice balls on the first day of the year, our family will stay whole and together throughout the new year.

Lu smiled, comfort enveloping her as she went through more entries describing days when her grandma had obviously been happy and content with her life. As Lu continued on, the tone of the journal entries darkened. Lu knew revisiting the events her grandma had recorded during that time bordered on self-torture, but something in her that evening compelled—*demanded*—her to read on.

May 25, 1966

Strange things are happening these days. Our peaceful and quiet neighborhood is invaded by men and women in blue jackets or army-green uniforms. They all wear red armbands, and they call themselves the Red Guards. They march up and down the streets all day along, some of them beating on red drums tied around their waists, some carrying large red banners with gold slogans like Launch the Cultural Revolution! or Down with the Capitalist Class! And the chanting, "We love Chairman Mao, we love Chairman Mao! Long live Chairman

Mao!" Whenever the government launched a revolution in the past, bad things happened to ordinary people. I hope this is not going to be like that.

June 18, 1966

Everyone was asked to go to the neighborhood meeting hosted by the district party secretary. We were told that our great leader Mao has declared that the goal of the Cultural Revolution is to reform and eliminate the capitalist bourgeoisie. I am afraid bad things are going to happen to a lot of people and their families in the building. Most people living in this building are professionals like doctors and engineers. I don't understand why the government is labeling them as part of the capitalist bourgeoisie who have lived off the working class of the country. They told us that most of us will need to be reformed by the working-class factory workers and farmers. What does that mean? What's going to happen?

July 3, 1966

Things are getting worse. The daytime marches in the street are now extending into night. Red Guards are breaking into apartments in the building and confiscating our property. They told us they wanted to "borrow" some furniture for the headquarters they were setting up down the street. Tables, chairs, writing desks, and lamps have disappeared, never making their way back. Now they just barge in at any hour day and night, taking jewelry, watches, porcelain, whatever catches their fancy. This country has descended into chaos and lawlessness.

Lu paused. She was at the end of a page. To continue meant to face the pain, the agony, the despair, and the hopelessness so many people had suffered and to witness again the brutality and cruelty people were capable of inflicting on their fellow human beings. All her blood flooded upward. Her head was throbbing, her heart pounding fiercely. With one quivering hand, she flipped the page.

July 16, 1966

They took my son away last night. They said he had engaged in antigovernment activities and needed to be interrogated. I don't know where they have taken him. I've heard a lot of people like my son have been thrown in jail, tortured, and died. What's going to happen to us? If he doesn't make it back, what's going to happen to Lu, without a father at this young age? I hope God will keep him safe and bring him back to us soon.

July 30, 1966

Almost two weeks now that I haven't heard from my son and don't know where he is or if he is alive. Lu's mother has been busy at work and often is away from home. She says she's trying to find her husband but doesn't seem to be overly concerned. Poor Lu, she has to be home alone during the day when I attend the reform meeting at the district party office. We're required to read Chairman Mao's *Little Red Book* every day until we can memorize some of the essays. I think I am old; my memory is not as good as it used to be. I hope I won't be quizzed tomorrow; I won't be able to recite the entire essay.

August 23, 1966

The seemingly harmless group sessions of studying Chairman Mao's *Little Red Book* have come to an end.

All of us at the meeting today were led into separate rooms for individual reform and confession sessions. The man who interrogated me was the district party secretary with a pockmarked face. He let out several puffs of cigarette smoke in my face before he opened his mouth, exposing his crooked, smoke-stained teeth, and said, "Listen, lady, we want to make things easy for you. If you tell us your husband's and son's antigovernment activities, we won't bother you anymore, and maybe your son can come home."

Before I could say anything, he took out a piece of folded paper from his chest pocket and continued, "I know, I know, your husband has been dead for years. But our records show that he worked with Westerners in a university run by American and British missionaries. And your son, he received his education in the US, didn't he?" He unfolded the paper on the table and smoothed it with his palm.

I held my head high and answered in as steady a voice as I could manage, "You are right: my husband was a math professor in a university where there were foreign professors. But he taught, nothing else. And my son, yes, he got his medical degree in America. He could have stayed there, but we wanted him home. After all, this is his country. My husband and my son are decent and patriotic; they would never engage in any antigovernment activities."

"I see you are a stubborn old lady, just like your son. Yes, he came back, but that is the whole point. Don't think we don't know that he is a spy for the imperialist Americans," the party secretary hissed. "I am going to give you a few minutes by yourself to think about it. If you don't confess, don't blame me, but your life is going to be hell." He exhaled another puff of smoke in my face, picked up that piece of paper on the table, and left the room.

God knows what's waiting for me tomorrow ...

August 24, 1966

What happened today was pure horror in hell. How can we human beings do such evil to each other?

When I arrived at the district party office this morning, I saw a tall wooden platform had been erected in front of the three-story brick building. Stepping inside, I was horrified to see that huddling at the far corner of the dark room, the men and women in my study group had their arms twisted backward and tied at the wrists. All of them had been forced to wear tall, pointed paper hats with black labels classifying them as Capitalist, Bourgeoisie, Counterrevolutionary, Exploiter & Bloodsucker, or simply Monster & Devil. I was terrified. All I wanted to do was to run away. But there was a dark form blocking the door.

"Where do you think you are going, you old whore? You are one of them. Go over there and put your hat on." I looked up, and the party secretary's swine-like eyes stared down at me. Two Red Guards grabbed me from behind and tied my wrists. "I have a pretty hat reserved just for you." The party secretary snickered. Grabbing my chignon, he pushed a tall paper hat down on my head. The hat read Whore of the Counterrevolutionary.

Minutes later we were herded outside and lined up on the tall wooden platform, which by then was surrounded by hundreds of people, most of them wearing the red armbands. "Kneel down, all of you!" one Red Guard barked at us. We looked at each other; most of us had too much dignity to obey.

"Kneel! Make them kneel down!" the mob around the platform roared. Several of them jumped up on the platform and kicked us in the shins. One by one we all fell into kneeling position.

"Make them confess their sins!" The mob was frenzied.

For hours, we kneeled while the mob threw trash and garbage at us and the guards whipped belt buckles against our backs, but we had nothing to confess. We had never been against the government. Our families all worked for a living. God must be blind to let this kind of injustice and brutality to go on ...

Tears dropped on the frayed page, blurring the already tear-smudged words. She knew there would not be another entry after this until a month later, on the night her grandma had died. Lu vaguely remembered that during the days leading up to that horrible night, her grandma had limped a lot. She had asked if her grandma was hurting, but the answer had always been a faint smile and sigh. "Grandma is fine," she had said. "She is just old, can't run around like you do."

The truth was the interrogation and torture must have escalated during the last month of her grandma's life, and she had been too hurt and weak to continue recording the unspeakable horror. Yet she had tried desperately to hide all of it from her granddaughter. Lu wished she had been there for her grandma and been able to offer the slightest comfort. But she had been too young to do so. She sat down on the edge of her bed and read the last entry in the journal.

September 21, 1966

To my dearest granddaughter, Xiao Lu:

If you are reading this journal, it means you have grown up. I hope the nightmarish days your grandma and your papa endured are gone forever. I am sorry that Grandma has to leave you, but I hope you will understand and be able to forgive me.

You soon will realize that your papa is not on business and is not going to be home soon. He was accused of being antigovernment and taken away by the Red Guards months ago. Grandma does not know where he is or whether he is still alive.

I am sorry Grandma had to leave you alone in the apartment so often. But I had no choice. They wanted me to confess your papa's antigovernment activities. I told them your papa is a decent person and a good doctor, that he never did anything against the government, and that I have nothing to confess. But they don't believe me, so they had been torturing me for weeks now. I have recorded the nightmare as much as I can in this journal so you will know one day what Grandma went through. I have prayed to God every day for the strength to endure the atrocities and crimes committed by my fellow human beings. But after today, I give up. I am not able to and do not want to go on in this cruel world.

Today we had a choice for our punishment. We could either kneel on broken glass or eat live cockroaches. To keep our last shreds of dignity, most of us choose to kneel on the broken glass of smashed beer bottles. To make it more painful, the Red Guards ordered us to keep our bodies straight from knee up so our body weight pressed our knees deeper into the knifelike glass bits. Minutes into the torture, the elderly man kneeling next to me started to shake and attempted to lower his hips to rest on the back of his ankles. "You want to sit down, old man?" a Red Guard said as he jumped in front of the man, holding a long, thin bamboo stick. "You have a choice: you eat this, and we will let you go inside to rest." Grinning, the Red Guard waved the stick in a circle in front of the man's face. Pinned on the tip of the stick was a reddish-black cockroach, its legs still twitching. Body shivering, the man closed his eyes and opened his mouth. As the Red Guard shoved the reddish-black bug into the man's mouth, the mob cheered and clapped. That is the last I can remember. I think I blacked out after that.

Remember the moon-fairy story Grandma told you tonight? Just think that Grandma is like the moon fairy. I am so disappointed in this world where so many bad things are happening, so I am leaving to live a lonely life on the moon, but I will always be thinking of you …

Lu fell back in bed. In what felt like an eternity, she closed her eyes and let the tears flow. Slowly she drifted back inside the canopy bed in the apartment in Shanghai on that autumn night. The moon lingered at the window, so big and close, bathing the room in silver light. A gentle breeze stirred up the silk panels of the canopy bed. Lu saw her grandma standing at the bedside, bending down, kissing her on the forehead. When her grandma stepped back out of the canopy, the silk panels cascaded down and shielded Lu inside.

At the window, the moon was beckoning. Lu saw her grandma walking toward it, serene and peaceful, arms stretched forward as if trying to reach the moon. From inside the canopy, she called to her grandma, but her grandma kept walking toward the moon until she was completely immersed in the ethereal light.

CHAPTER 4

. . . . .

From the pub in Alexandria, Will dropped Sage off in front of her apartment building in Rosslyn, a mini metropolitan area in Virginia. After her decade-long relationship with her boyfriend and then fiancé had fizzled, sputtered, and finally died, she'd searched for a temporary apartment of her own, and the search had led her to this building. It was an old ten-floor brick building that sat on the bank of the Potomac River. The moment the landlord had opened the door to the unit, she'd instantly fallen in love with the wall-to-wall window overlooking the nation's capital across the river. It had been home for her for the past three years, and the best part was her rent was much more reasonable than those new apartment and condo buildings mushrooming up in the area, though her window showcased the best panoramic scenes each season had to offer—cherry blossoms hugging the tidal bay in spring; white sailboats dotting the glistening Potomac River in summer; and the green oasis of tress and foliage chameleoned into an impressionist landscape of vibrant red, gold, and deep purple as summer slipped into fall. Even in the more somber season of winter, Sage found her window offered a painting of serenity. The sky, the Potomac, and the bare branches and boughs along the riverbanks all blurred into a multitude of gray, highlighted only by milky ice patches floating on the water. It was like a muted Chinese watercolor, Zen-like.

She opened the door and saw her cat's silhouette sitting on the windowsill against the star-speckled midnight-blue sky. She flicked on the light, and the silhouette turned into a fur ball that trotted over to circle and rub against her panty-hosed legs.

"Hi, Milo." She bent down and scratched his head. Green eyes looking up, he meowed in return.

She fed the cat, took a shower, and settled in bed quickly. Milo jumped up in bed with her, purring and kneading before plopping down and balling up against the pillow. She turned on the TV, surfed all the nightly news channels, and decided nothing eventful had happened that day, not that she was unaware there were terrible things happening somewhere in the world all the time. But she'd had a mentally exhausting day, full of unusual events that had stirred up many emotions—the mass layoff at work, the good news about Will's business and yet the uncertainty down the road, her reflection on her own life ... She wished she had somebody to talk to. In times like this, she wished Lu were still living in the DC area. Will was a loving brother, and Sage knew she could always talk to him, but he was a man. He would die trying, but he would never understand certain feelings and emotions of the female persuasion.

It would be nice if I had a sister, Sage thought, remembering the evening when her mother had announced that her twin children, Will and Sage, were about to have a new sibling.

The whole family had just sat down at the dinner table, their plates piled with Schweinebraten (roast pork) and potato dumplings, both prepared according to Bavarian recipes handed down by Sage's maternal grandmother from Germany. "Honey, don't we have good news for the kids?" Sage's mom had coyly asked her husband.

Sage's dad, ready to wolf down what was on his plate, looked up as if caught by surprise. "Why don't you tell them, dear." He began to dig into the pile on his plate.

"We are having a baby," Sage's mom softly exclaimed, as if she would have burst were she to hold back the news for one more second.

Sage looked at her dad. He was trying to wear a smile and chew his pork at the same time. Will, Sage thought, was just a clueless teenage boy. Staring at the small piece of pork on the fork in his hand, between his plate and mouth, he said cheerfully, "That's great, Mom." Sage wanted to be happy and say something congratulatory to her mom, but certain memories held her back.

She and Will had expressed their innocent wishes of having little sisters or brothers, but each time their parents had been firm on sticking to the plans they'd had from day one. Two kids were enough. "Dad can't afford another baby. Do you know how expensive you are? I would send one of you back if I could," her dad had joked affectionately. And now both teenagers, she and Will had long given up on their wishes. They would not want a toddler sibling following them around when they were in high school; it would be embarrassing.

"You are quiet, Sage. Aren't you happy you're going to have a little sister or brother?" Though the question seemed lighthearted, the pitch of her mom's voice was slightly higher than usual, a sign she was nervous or agitated. Sage looked up and met her mom's intense gaze.

"I thought you and dad didn't want another child," Sage almost blurted, the thought dancing at the tip of her tongue.

But her mom's glowing face and beseeching look made her swallow the words. Instead she smiled and said softly, "It's great, Mom." Sage knew her smile must look as doubtful as her dad's looked somewhat forced. Yet her mom seemed to be satisfied with everyone's reaction to her news. She chirped throughout dinner about possible baby names and her plans for the baby room. "You know what, Bill," she said to her husband, "I have a doctor's appointment late tomorrow afternoon. Why don't you come with me? We can go crib shopping afterward."

"I'm not sure I can get away early. The Detroit account is not doing well, and if the account goes, I'll lose my job." Dad hesitated.

"You worry too much. You've been with them for how long? Everything will work out." Mom was determined not to let anything spoil her good mood that evening.

"I'll try," Dad said tentatively.

The next day, Sage's dad didn't make it to the doctor's office. After the doctor gave Sage's mom and the baby a clean bill of health, Sage's mom was confident she could take care of buying the crib by herself. As she stood on the store escalator descending from the second floor to the first, a young boy accidentally pushed her from behind while trying to catch up with his mother, who was already at the bottom of the escalator. Sage's mom crashed headfirst down the escalator and rolled over a dozen steps before she hit the floor at the bottom. Sage's dad had rushed to the hospital. By the time he'd gotten there, the baby had been gone. And her mom could never have babies again.

A sudden surge of decibel from a commercial on TV interrupted

Sage's thoughts, followed by a bell tone from her cell phone on the nightstand, signaling a new text message. Next to Sage, Milo's green eyes peered up for a second and quickly disappeared again into the fur ball.

Sage picked up the cell and read the message from Will: "Don't forget to call Lu." Sage shook her head, turned off the TV, and dialed Lu's cell number.

CHAPTER 5

• • • • •

WILL DONOVAN SAT DOWN at the bar of American Brasserie, a popular restaurant on Pennsylvania Avenue. Waiting for his favorite German beer, a Hefeweizen, he went over the whole day's events in his head one more time. He had spent the day sitting in meetings and conference calls, trying to see clearly the pathways to becoming a public company. But toward the end of the day, everything had seemed to be more uncertain, convoluted, and murkier than before he'd walked into his office that morning. He was frustrated.

He welcomed the frothy, ice-cold beer and the friendly, chatty bartender, who temporarily distracted him from his deep thoughts on the future of his company. In between sipping the beer and carrying a casual conversation with the bartender, he constantly peered at the entrance of the restaurant.

A couple of days ago Sage had called Lu regarding his situation of to be or not to be a public company and potentially deal or not deal with a Chinese company. To his sister's surprise, Lu had readily agreed to come down to DC for a girls' weekend visit and had suggested meeting with Will over dinner to see if she could be of any help in turning his state of dilemma into a process of decision making. Sage had suggested this particular restaurant because she and Lu used to come here often when they had been working together in DC. Sage would pick Lu up when she got off the train from New York City, and the two of them would meet Will at the restaurant.

He checked his cell phone for the time, almost seven o'clock, still time to kill. Restless, he unbuttoned the collar of his light-blue dress shirt and wriggled his legs to shake off the onset of itchy-pants syndrome, a condition that had begun early in his life when his parents had forced him to wear dress pants to go to Sunday Mass.

That morning, he had forced himself to put on his formal business attire for the dinner occasion. After all, he was to meet a lady from Wall Street, a place where everyone wore confining suits and strangling ties. And his sister, she had no choice. He often teased her about the proper and prim dark-colored dress suit her profession in human resources management required. He figured his blue blazer and gray dress pants should conform to the ladies' conservative dress code. He casually flipped through the thick menu and found the food a bit fancy for his taste. Everything seemed to have a fusion twist to it: grilled salmon with wasabi crust, mashed potatoes with turnip puree and seaweed, roast pork with baby bok choy sautéed in sesame oil, and beef steak in ginger sake sauce.

He found the East and West fusion menu amusing. Just like the business deal he was trying to put together, he was not comfortable enough to jump right in yet was too intrigued to just walk away. He was not uncomfortable with the general road map of a successful merger, but trying to understand the intricacies and complexities of the proposal to merge his company with a publicly owned US company, which could become a part of a Chinese telecommunication outfit, which was trying to raise capital on the New York Stock Exchange, was, he hated to admit, a bit daunting. He had been looking forward to the meeting, hoping Lu might be able to help cut through some of the Wall Street high-finance mumbo jumbo so he could grasp the uniqueness of the deal and see clearly if it was indeed right for his company.

Everyone around him probably thought he had it made. At age forty-seven, he owned a profitable Internet technology company with over $100 million in annual revenues. Once a one-man shop in his studio apartment, he had become the commander of over two hundred loyal managers and technicians who were the envy of the industry. Under his leadership, they were a group of highly trained, technically well certified, and experienced team players that had brought the company robust growth for over a decade, consistently winning multiyear, multimillion-dollar system management and maintenance contracts from a number of federal government agencies.

The business world attributed his success to his being a talented technology whiz kid with a pleasant personality and a disarming smile, a combination of traits rare in the nerdy technology field. But Will knew his success was largely the result of adhering to a set of rules he'd learned from his commanding officer in the navy.

After high school, Will had reluctantly enrolled in a community college in suburban Washington, DC, a compromise he'd made to appease his parents' displeasure about his desire of skipping college all together. A few weeks into his college life, his father die of a sudden heart attack. Grief stricken and feeling guilty, he coasted in college for a while hoping he might stumble onto something that would interest him. But that never happened. As time went by, he became miserable and aimless. Only one thing could temporarily energize his listless body and sharpen his dull mind—surfing, the feeling of trepidation and triumph as a mighty tidal wave swept him into dark undertow one moment and glided him to a glistening crest the next.

One day, riding on the white waves of the Atlantic Ocean in Montauk, his native town, young Will found his calling: he was to join the navy and be part of the sea forever.

But quickly he learned that navy life was not close to how he had romanticized it, free surfing on the sea all the time. At the beginning, learning to abide the regimental rules and disciplines was not easy for Will, and he hated his commanding officer, Wesley Trant, a football-loving, Wagner-opera-listening, and foul-mouthed disciplinarian tyrant. But quitting was not an option. Will knew he had nowhere to go. Gradually, Wesley Trant's foul-mouthed barking was no longer "degrading" to Will; instead, it became the impetus for him to be the best he could be. He'd completed the degree and technical trainings required to become a technician in the navy's cyber-warfare division. In the process, Wesley Trant's commanding style had imparted a set of tried-and-true rules to Will, and Will had been living by those rules ever since.

Trant Rule #1
If you want to be a leader of anything (e.g., captain of a ship, a football coach, or a symphony conductor), you

have to be able to pick the right people on your team. Never be afraid that they might be better than you are. Each of them should be doing their jobs better than you can; you can't do all those jobs by yourself, and that's what you have them for.

Trant Rule #2
The people on your team cannot all be megastars on their own. The team has to be successful before you are successful. Each person needs to not only be good at doing his or her own job but also good at complementing the team as a whole. This means he or she has to have the capacity of stepping back once in a while to play a support role and let his or her teammates shine.

Trant Rule #3
You have to be able to identify the weak links of your team and fix them decisively. If you don't, your entire ship will sink, your team will collapse, and your symphony will be cacophony.

For over a decade of building and growing his business, Will had diligently adhered to those rules and attributed his success to them. Now his business had reached a high point, and people told him he was standing on the apex of a mountain. But it was from there Will could sense the dangers and perils lurking below, threatening to stymie his business.

Will was fully aware of the importance of retaining talent for a growing technology company like his. He had always compensated his employees well, though not beyond the extent that it affected his ability to reinvest profit for growth. But recently he'd found his once-competitive compensation structure not so competitive anymore compared to what the big fish like Google were offering to attract top-rated computer engineers and technicians, particularly those who were experts in the cybersecurity area. It was an area Will wanted to develop and grow, but he had not been able to, because his small technology company simply did not have the financial resources and appeal of large companies to attract the right talent.

So he was tempted by the potentially huge financial gain that would result from Matrixtech buying his company, as well as the promise of being able to retain full control of his company after the buyout. If things were to turn out the right way, Will Donavan would have the resources, financial and human, to develop the cutting-edge cybersecurity technology he had planned. For days, except for his sister Sage, he'd kept everything to himself, tossing the pros and cons of selling in his mind and quietly conducting research on what the road to being a part of a large, publicly owned company entailed. But the more he dug in, the more he realized that the complexity of the deal would not make his decision quick or easy.

"Do you need to order anything?" the bartender asked. Will seemed to have been staring at the menu in front of him forever.

"Oh no, I'm just waiting. They should be here soon." Will smiled and shut the menu. He glanced at the entrance again and was glad to see Sage in her black dress suit, waving at him as she walked toward the bar, her wavy red hair bouncing around her shoulders. He waved back, and his eyes quickly caught the woman right next to his sister.

She was a bit shorter than Sage and wore a beige lightweight sweater dress and a pair of knee-high black boots. A small black leather messenger bag hung across her slender body. Her straight, shoulder-length black hair was shiny and lustrous under the overhead lighting as she stepped briskly toward him.

Will knew the woman had to be Lu, but she did not look like the forty-seven-year-old Wall Street high financier he had imagined. He did not have time to second-guess, though, as Sage introduced them. "Will, this is Lu; Lu, this is my big brother, Will."

"Hi, Will, nice to finally meet you. Your sister has told me a lot about you and your business," Lu said airily, extending her hand.

Will quickly hopped off the bar stool and reached for Lu's hand. "Nice to meet you; I heard a lot about you too." Her handshake was solid but not aggressive, and he responded with a grip he considered to be appropriately firm.

"Okay, you two can talk business later, but we need to take our seats before they are given away. This place is especially popular on weekends," Sage said with mock impatience.

A few minutes later, the three of them were sitting at a table on the second floor of the restaurant, next to the floor-to-ceiling window overlooking Pennsylvania Avenue. Sage suggested a glass of champagne for everyone to celebrate the girls' long overdue reunion. "Go ahead; I'll stick to beer, though," Will said, raising the half-full beer glass he'd carried over from the bar.

"Okay, let's see if they still have that champagne we like so much." Sage opened the wine list that had been lying in the middle of the table.

As the ladies busied with the wine list, Will sipped his beer and quietly observed Lu with great curiosity.

He had expected a slightly uptight, middle-aged woman, like some of the businesswomen he had encountered in his professional life who consciously or subconsciously felt the need to act like hard-charging guys. But the woman in front of him struck him as being at ease and comfortable with herself. Granted, she was not in a formal business setting, not wearing a boring business suit; she had a glowing, sun-kissed complexion that made her look as if she'd just come back from a long, relaxed beach vacation. But it was more than all that. It was her eyes; they were the color of black onyx and liquid like, radiating a smile before a smile turned up the corners of her mouth.

"They still have that champagne we both like so much. Shall we order that?" Sage asked Lu.

"Definitely," Lu said cheerfully.

A few moments later, the waiter came back with two sleek flutes of sparkly effervescence. The three of them raised their glasses and said cheers almost at the same time.

After a couple of sips of champagne, Sage said to Lu, "My brother's been harassing me to no end to drag you down here. Thank God you are here. I can now relax."

Will apologized, businesslike, "Sorry to drag you down here on short notice. I don't know if Sage has told you anything about the situation my company is in these days. It's kind of urgent, so I really appreciate it."

"It's okay. I didn't make this trip entirely without selfish reasons." Lu shot a we'll-talk-later look at Sage. "There is some girl stuff I need to discuss with Sage, but that can wait until later. So where are you on your deal?"

"Frankly, it's a hard decision, perhaps the hardest decision I will ever have to make. If we were only talking about money, the decision would be easy. The financial gain from selling my company to a large, publicly owned US company would be substantial. But money is not the only factor for me ..." Will paused and rubbed his hand through his hair.

"I guess you want to make sure you continue to have control over your company after the buyout," Lu said.

"Right. They've promised me so far that my company would remain a fully owned subsidiary and that nothing would change much organizationally. But I'm not naive. Promises like this are often made to push the deal through; it's never guaranteed how things will turn out after the dust settles."

"If money isn't the main reason and you're afraid of losing control, then why are you even considering selling it?" Lu asked. She took a sip of the champagne, but her eyes remained on Will's contemplative face.

"For the long-term survival of the company, shall we say?" Meeting Lu's slightly puzzled gaze, Will continued, "I know everyone seems to think my business is flourishing, but I think it has peaked. From here on, I'm afraid it will stagnate and decline unless we branch into newer and more-cutting-edge technology."

"What is your bread-and-butter service now?"

"Well, we have large network-maintenance contracts with the government and the business of hardware maintenance of routers, switches, and servers. More and more companies out there are able to do this and do it cheaper."

"And what type of new technology do you want to branch into?"

"Network security. That requires highly skilled engineers to come up with codes and software to play the never-ending cat-and-mouse game in cyberspace."

"Do you have someone who is knowledgeable in the area?"

"Yes, myself and a few staff. But we need more to make it successful. A company of our size does not have the resources to attract the kind of talent and skill we need. Those people are more likely to go work for companies that are much bigger than mine, like Google."

"So you think a large company will be able to provide the resources you want," Lu said. "But you are worried you won't have the autonomy to do what you want. Has the buyer given you any indication why they are interested in your company?"

"Yes, they are a network-design company and have a few large network-system-management contracts with mainly private-sector companies. They reached out to us because they know in the past we developed an antivirus software that was widely used on many key government network systems. So I gather they want to buy us mainly for our small pool of cybersecurity talent while also getting on the long-term government-contract bandwagon."

"That sounds reasonable." Lu took another sip of champagne. "So why is it a difficult decision for you?"

"Well, my sister says I'm the kind of person that if I don't have one hundred percent control of the business, I may just quit completely. Then I'll be in a situation of being too young to retire and too old to surf." Will shot a glance at Sage, who was flipping through the enormous dinner menu.

Laughing, Sage shot back, "I think you'll give up surfing before you give up your company; you're married to it. Now, I think we should decide what to order before the restaurant closes."

After a few minutes of perusing the menu, Sage and Lu decided on the wasabi-crusted salmon, and Will order the pork chop with sautéed bok choy, a dish he considered the least unconventional.

The waiter took the order and disappeared behind the door leading to the downstairs kitchen, and Will picked up the conversation where Sage had left off, teasing him about being married to his company. "To a certain degree, Sage is right. A lot of the employees have been with me for a long time. They are hardworking and loyal. Having been in the navy, I feel like my job is like being the captain of a ship, responsible for the lives of the whole crew. I don't want to steer the ship into hidden icebergs."

"Yeah, yeah, yeah, please don't bore us with your navy talk," Sage interrupted with feigned annoyance, while Lu seemed to regard Will with heightened interest.

Sensing Sage might be a bit bored with the business talk, Will changed the subject. "So what are you ladies up to this weekend?"

"Girl stuff, lots to catch up on. Haven't seen each other for almost a year," Sage said.

Lu readily agreed. "It was last summer when Sage came up to New York City. I remember the city was vacated. Everybody was at the beach or out of town except the tourists. But it was less crowded everywhere, so we had fun. Next time you come up, we should get out of the city and go to the beach."

"Maybe before summer or in the fall when everybody is in town, so we can have the beach to ourselves. Although I am so ready for a vacation now. Work has been crazy lately," Sage said longingly.

Turning to Will, Lu said, "Sage told me you both practically grew up on the beach in Montauk. She and I have talked about going to Montauk together for a long time but haven't been able to do so yet. It seems our schedules are never on the same page. I heard you still go there surfing often."

"Yes, I love it there, rugged and quiet, even in summertime. Not much of the hustle and bustle and congestions you'll find in the trendy Hampton towns. The problem is you have to get through the bumper-to-bumper traffic on the Long Island Expressway to get there in the summer. So I try to go in early fall, after the summer crowd has vacated."

"Me too. I often go there in October. It's breathtakingly beautiful that time of year," Lu said enthusiastically.

The lively conversation about Montauk continued for a while before it was interrupted by the arrival of their meal.

After first taste of his pork chop and declaring it quite good, Will said to Lu, "There is something I am hoping you could simplify for me. Selling my company to Matrixtech sounded relatively simple initially until I was told we all could become a part of a Chinese telecommunication company. That could complicate things. No offense, Lu; you know what I mean."

"None taken. I know exactly what you mean," Lu responded matter-of-factly. "What is your gravest concern if you end up having a Chinese parent company?"

"I think there could be political risks? Last time I checked, they are still a self-proclaimed socialist country. But after a bit research, it seems to me the Chinese have embraced the capitalist system on the economic-development front." Will paused, searching for proper words to describe his concern.

"True. But you are concerned culturally how the Chinese would handle reorganizing or streamlining issues if suddenly part of their company ended up in the US," Lu said, voicing what was on Will's mind.

"You're right; the last thing I want is to go through all the trouble with the buyout, only to be forced to operate in a culturally mismatched environment." Will was impressed that Lu had zeroed in on part of his concern so quickly.

Sensing how important control of his company was to Will, Lu asked, "Do you know anything about this Chinese company?"

"A little. All I know is they plan to buy a few US technology firms, including Matrixtech, so they can establish their presence and raise capital in the United States more easily. Back in China, they are a manufacturer of telecommunication parts and equipment, but they seem to have the ambition to become a full-fledged telecommunication company, from manufacturing parts to integrated network design and management."

"What's the company's name?"

"Great China Telecom."

"Interesting," Lu said, her eyes widening with vigilance. "I've heard the name, and I think they might be already making their intentions known to Wall Street underwriting firms. But I think they have a lot to do before they can prove to be a worthy investment."

"Is that so!" Will was startled; the Chinese company was moving forward faster than he expected.

"Like many other Chinese companies who want to list their stock here in the US, they have a lot of paperwork to provide and regulation hoops to jump through. Believe it or not, though, one of the reasons the Chinese want to come to the US capital market is that there's less red tape to deal with here. But back to your concern. The Chinese are quite shrewd when making investment decisions. They usually don't buy things if they don't consider them truly valuable. So if they do end up buying a US company, other than it helping them establish presence in this country, the target company must have something they don't have. If they are a telecom-parts manufacturer, I don't think they would want to acquire another parts manufacturer here; they are pretty much manufacturing everything for the world already. What you need to be really careful about and think through is that the Federal Trade Commission and the Department of Justice have quite strict rules regarding foreign investment in US telecommunication companies, mainly for national-security reasons."

"Boy, never have to worry about that when you're just a small private company," Will said, looking a bit despondent.

"It doesn't mean it can't be done, just that those deals will be subject to more regulatory scrutiny," Lu said apologetically and added thoughtfully, "Sometimes, to simplify things, other forms of partnership could be considered instead of a complete merger of two companies. I've seen that quite often."

"Maybe Kevin could help in this respect," Will said to himself, using his fork to push the few remaining pieces of bok choy leaves around on his otherwise-empty plate.

Lu shot him a puzzled look. "Who is Kevin?"

"Oh, Kevin is my chief operating officer. He has a friend in Congress, so he might be able to get some information for me when it comes to rules and regulations regarding national security and the cyber industry."

"Oh my God, not that politician friend!" Sage exclaimed.

"Sage, I know you don't like politicians. But this friend of Kevin's happens to sit on the subcommittee of national security in congress. It won't hurt talking to him." Will tried to appease Sage, regretting he'd even brought up the subject.

Sage glared at her brother. "Oh, yeah, tell Lu his name and whom he is related to." Sage was not going to let it go. Before her brother could respond, she said, "His name is Rob Kessler, sound familiar? He's the nephew of our former boss, Earl Kessler, who conned investors out of hundreds of millions and ran the company into the ground ten years ago, and then he had the nerve to blame you for not informing him of the company's spending problem soon enough." Angrily, she turned to her brother again. "You are naive if you think that Rob Kessler could be a better character then his jerk of an uncle. They are both politicians, and they have the same weasel blood in their veins."

Seeing Will being backed into a corner of total embarrassment, Lu cut in to neutralize what felt like a potentially explosive situation. "I agree. Most politicians don't put their country first these days; all they care about is getting reelected."

Will understood the lifeline Lu was throwing him. "That's what all politicians do these days. Name one who is not out there hustling for his or her reelection," Will said, grateful to Lu for helping him get off the Rob Kessler issue.

Sage checked her emotions and said to her brother, "You do what you want, but if I were you, I wouldn't get too involved with him. Nothing good will come of it."

"I think I can handle it. You can come with me to make sure I don't get hustled and weaseled if you want," Will teased his sister.

"Don't push it," Sage said, looking at her brother in a way that said, "You're lucky I'm dropping the subject."

The waiter came to clear the table and asked if the meals had been cooked to their liking. "I don't know; we're not sure," Will said, gesturing at the empty plates and feigning doubts. Everybody laughed; the tension at the dinner table eased, giving way to a more casual and relaxed ambiance.

The waiter asked about dessert, but all three of them turned it down and opted for coffee. It was going to be a long evening ahead for everyone. Will had to finish some work before bedtime, so a strong coffee would help. Lu and Sage decided to make an exception to their usual one-cup-a-day rule and catch up on girl talk.

As the three sat and sipped coffee, the three-way conversation gradually became a communication between only Lu and Sage. Will realized he was about to become a third wheel at the table. *Time to excuse myself and leave the ladies alone,* he thought. Reaching for his jacket on the back of his chair, he said, "I'd better get going. You two enjoy your chat and the weekend. By the way, where are you staying Lu?"

"At the Hyatt in Rosslyn, almost right across the street from Sage's apartment. Convenient for Sage and me to meet for brunch tomorrow morning."

"That's great." Will stood up and put on his jacket.

"It's nice finally to have met you. I hope everything will all work out," Lu said cordially. Neither woman tried to convince Will to stay; they were eager to catch up.

"Likewise." Will extended his hand to Lu. "Thanks for your advice, very helpful."

"Anytime, if I can be of some help." Shaking his hand, she held his gaze for a prolonged moment.

• • •

"That's my brother; he thinks he is in charge of his company, but sometimes I think the company is in charge of his life," Sage said to Lu as she watched her brother step away from the table.

"Well, there are people whose whole beings are defined by their work. They become restless and lost if they're not on top of everything all the time. Sometimes I wonder how they got into that mode in the first place," Lu said. "Then again, I'm the kettle calling the pot black here. I can't say I'm not guilty of that either. I guess it's okay as long as your brother enjoys what he does; that's important."

"He sure does. He knew he wanted his own business when he was a boy. Although back then his first passion was surfing, having fun and not a care in the world. Now, of course, business comes first, but he keeps himself in shape so he can go and conquer the waves any chance he has."

"No argument there; he certainly is in great shape, cute too, those blue eyes and the dimples when he smiles …" Lu tried hard to maintain a serious look but broke into laughter before finishing what was on her mind.

"What's with the blue eyes? The women who have dated my brother always seemed to be obsessed with blue eyes. Although I have to say, Will's eyes are so changeable, depending on what color he is wearing and what mood he's in. They can be blue or green or in between."

"I like green eyes too. I find colorful eyes fascinating. I've told you what my grandma said about Western people."

"Yep, we Westerners look like devils, with our green eyes and red hair." Sage giggled. "I think the feeling was mutual on Will's side when he first saw you. I believe he was expecting to see an uptight, middle-aged corporate high roller with a fancy MBA degree. Sorry, that's how my brother describes corporate executives in general. I could see the way he looked at you when you showed up, not fitting into that preconceived image," Sage said, trying to control the volume of her laughter.

"You mean just as I preconceived in my mind that he must be a bit nerdy and chubby, somebody sitting in front of a machine, developing those esoteric computer programs and having pizza delivered to his desk for lunch?"

They had officially started girl talk, something they had not shared for quite a while, a time when they could be silly and trivial, laughing about their comical and sometimes bizarre dating experiences or lamenting over the end of what they'd thought was a meaningful relationship.

"Talking about preconceived notions ..." Sage caught her breath after a good belly laugh. "Seriously, my preconceived notion would be for you and Will to get together."

"You're kidding, right?" Lu started laughing again.

"Hey, I just said it's my preconceived notion. Just think, according to logic, you and Will are both workaholics; you understand each other on the first and foremost level of your lives. You are both fitness fanatics, so you spend the tiny bit of downtime from work the same way. You may insult each other with name-calling like uptight corporate bitch and pizza-eating IT nerd, but we've all know since we were kids that when boys and girls call each other names, they actually like each other," Sage concluded in an I-rest-my-case tone and took a sip of her coffee.

"But you've forgotten that opposites attract," Lu said. "The fact that we are very much alike works against that old adage."

"I know, I know, I'm just joking. Plus I think my brother is not good at handling long-term relationships. He tries, but he doesn't believe he'll be lucky enough to have a lifetime relationship. With Will, when things are going well, he seems to find a way to self-destruct." Sage sighed.

"Well, we all have our quirks and eccentricities and get settled in our ways as we get older, I guess. Over the years, one thing I've learned is that being successful at a relationship is kind of like financial investment. You ever heard the saying that money is the ultimate attention seeker? You have to constantly pay attention to it. If you don't, you will wake up one morning and find it gone. Well, relationships are the same way; you have to pay attention on a day-to-day basis, always on alert so you won't be inconsiderate and insensitive to the other person or take the other person for granted. But both sides have to make the same effort in order for the relationship to stay in balance. If one side slacks often, as I think we are all prone to do, that balance will tip," Lu said with resignation.

"So your theory is still that, sooner or later, we become lazy and give up. But I still believe what my dad said: 'You have to keep trying, hoping this time is different.' Otherwise we are all merely lonely souls wandering aimlessly in the world."

"That's why I love you, Sage: you are the eternal optimist. You really believe in what you are saying. Me, I quit investing in relationships seriously since the Sunday-football, quickie guy fifteen years ago."

"Oh, I remember you telling me about him—the guy who wanted to spend every Sunday during the entire football season drinking beer, watching football, eating pizza, and having occasional halftime quickies," Sage said, laughing out loud.

"Yep, he said I was not cool and was selfish because football games only last four months out of a year. Maybe I am selfish, but I don't think I can live up to that kind of standards of being a cool girl anyway. So now I am officially an old, cynical woman."

Both were silent for a while. When Sage spoke again, she changed the subject. "You know, I meant to e-mail you about that politician my brother mentioned, but I kept forgetting. Dealing with mass layoffs seems to be all I do these days." Sage's eyes glinted mysteriously.

"Rob Kessler, Earl Kessler's nephew—the world is small, isn't it?"

"Well, he has been a congressman since the beginning of this year. I found out while meeting Will for a drink at the pub. Kevin, Will's COO, happened to be there. He told us how his friend Congressman Rob Kessler could help with Will's business. It didn't take long for me to realize this Rob Kessler was related to our former boss, the once-noble Earl Kessler who was going to deliver quality education to the whole world. I looked Rob up as soon as I got home, and you know, they look like father and son, instead of uncle and nephew."

"Sounds like another family of career politicians." Lu seemed amused.

"I just hope it's not going to be like uncle, like nephew, with this Rob Kessler being another weasel."

"Would you ladies like another cup of coffee?" the waiter interrupted.

"Could you please just send us the check?" Sage asked. Turning to Lu, she said, "Don't you think it would be more fun to continue our talk in my apartment? There's a bottle of chilled champagne in the refrigerator with our names on it."

"That would be super."

A minute later, the waiter came back, without the check. "Ladies, Mr. Donovan already took care of the check."

C H A P T E R 6

. . . . .

THE INTERIOR OF SAGE's apartment reminded Lu that it had been quite a while since she'd last been there. It was fully decorated with comfortable furniture made of driftwood. The walls were painted in soft green, a color that was the namesake of the woman who lived there. The lighting of the apartment was gentle and soothing. A potted lavender plant sat on the windowsill, its fragrance subtle and calming. Lu felt she had just stepped into a Zen spa.

"You've done a beautiful job with this place. Come to think about it, it's been at least a couple of years since you moved in, right?" Lu said, admiring the place.

"Almost three. Feels like it was just yesterday," Sage said, unbuttoning her jacket and kicking off her shoes. "Can't believe it's been that long."

"I know. It's easy to be bogged down by the day-to-day demands of work, and before you know it, a chunk of your life is gone. We should really do this more often."

"In that sense, we're both guilty. I'm going to get rid of this suit. Go open the champagne if you would like, and I will be only a minute," Sage said as she walked to the bedroom.

"Okay." Lu lingered in front of the large window for a few seconds, taking in the panoramic night view of the nation's capital before she headed toward the kitchen. On the way, she saw a neatly rolled-up yoga mat standing in a corner of the L-shaped dining room. "Still practicing yoga?" she asked in a slightly raised voice.

On the other side of the small apartment, a thump came from the bedroom, followed by a loud meow. "Religiously," Sage said as she emerged from the bedroom in a pair of black capri yoga pants and a boxy sweatshirt. Leading the way was a gray cat with white paws and emerald-green eyes, its tail straight up in the air.

"Oh, hey, it's Milo," Lu said tenderly. His green eyes looking up at Lu, Milo meowed louder, as if saying, "I am happy to see you too," and proceeded to bunt his head against Lu's boots.

"How old is he now?" Lu asked, gently stroking Milo's velvety coat.

"I guess around ten. The vet said he was between one and two years old when I adopted him nine years ago," Sage said from the kitchen. She sprinkled a few treats in Milo's bowel and took the bottle of champagne out of the refrigerator.

"Oh, yes, I remember you adopted him when we were both working at GlobalReach.com. No wonder we're all middle aged."

"Yep, let's toast to middle age. We are older but hopefully wiser too." Sage came out of the kitchen, two champagne flutes in one hand and a sweaty bottle of sparkly in the other. She laid the flutes on the dining table and handed the bottle over to Lu.

"Agreed. To the age of wisdom." Lu twisted the cork, and a loud pop sent Milo scurrying to the kitchen.

A minute later, each with a glass of champagne in hand, the two women perched on the ends of the roomy canvas couch. Milo, after emptying the treats in his bowl in the kitchen, joined them, circling and kneading before curling up and settling down between them. As the champagne bubbles slowly fizzled, the effervescent and celebratory mood gave way to introspective reminiscing.

"You know, when I was a young girl, my mom often lamented how a woman could end up being a spinster with only a cat as companion if she didn't get married at a certain age. Look at us; we've turned out exactly that." Sage gestured with her champagne flute at Lu and the cat next to her. "Better yet," she continued, "I've had Milo longer than any relationship I've had with any human, except for my family, of course; that's a given."

Lu shot Sage a questioning look but remained silent.

Sensing Lu's unspoken disagreement, Sage clarified, "I meant relationships with men."

"You are being too hard on yourself," Lu said, taking another sip of champagne. "I've come to realize that spinsterhood is a state of mind.

Some people say it's sad when one ends up alone with no family. On the other hand, you could say it's rather liberating if it's by choice."

"Hard to imagine anybody would deliberately choose to be alone. I understand nothing is guaranteed these days, marriages or relationships. But just because they may not last forever, we shouldn't choose to shut everything out either. I know it's a complicated issue, but I guess I am my father's daughter, still trying and hoping the next time will be different," Sage said softly, knowing the two of them had never seen eye to eye on this one.

"Maybe not deliberately, but as you go through life, you are bound to fall into many types of relationships, be it love relationships or relationships with friends, colleagues, family members, and relatives. You find sooner or later that they all run the risk of ending in disappointment. It doesn't matter if you are the disappointer or the disappointed. After a while, you become more careful with relationships in general ..." Lu trailed off.

"Wow, Lu, I guess we haven't changed. We both are not good at relationships, though for different reasons. You are too guarded going in, while I open my heart too quickly. End result: we scare men away. The only people we haven't scared away are each other. I hope we haven't disappointed each other yet."

"What do you think? You know better than that, don't you?" Lu chided with a smile.

"Of course I know. I'm just kidding," Sage said, reaching for the champagne bottle on the coffee table. Refilling both flutes, she continued, "I have come to realize the wisdom of the saying that you are indeed lucky if you end up with one true friend in your life. I guess we both are lucky." She raised the brimming flute.

"Agreed," Lu said. "And I am so glad we liked each other right away the first day we worked together."

"I remember; we went to lunch together that day," Sage said, taking a sip of champagne. She knew that no further elaboration was needed when it came to their friendship. It was a friendship shaped by character-testing events, sustained through hard times by just being there for each other, and relished over countless sessions of carefree, silly, occasionally soul-baring girl talk. And it all had started on a spring day in 1999.

• • •

IT WAS THE GOLDEN age of the dot-com era. It seemed everybody could become rich overnight by betting on any business with a name ending in .com. Dot-com companies did not need to rat-race to cash in on the commercialization of the Internet. They were more like a bunch of fat cats; the race was about who could become fatter faster. When a new dot-com company appeared on the capital market, investors opened their wallets with manic exuberance, and millions and millions of dollars gushed into the dot-com treasury.

GlobalReach.com, formerly Capitol Communications Inc., had just reinvented itself from a beltway government contractor with $10-million-a-year revenue from putting together training materials for the federal government to a dot-com sensation. It had raised more than $100 million through its recent initial public offering on NASDAQ. Its CEO, Earl Kessler, a former high-ranking bureaucrat in the State Department, was touted by the investment community as a man with a vision, a vision to spread knowledge over the world through a to-be-developed e-portal. The portal would initially focus on educational materials about American democracy as well as American know-how in economic development. Later the portal would offer an assortment of educational and academic courses to the underserved developing world.

While Mr. Kessler was promoting his company on national TV, a financial reporter asked him who the customers of the portal would be. Mr. Kessler said with great confidence, "My vision is to make basic education available to everybody in the world, especially people and children in developing countries who cannot afford to go to school or who live where there are no school systems available. My company is not just about revenue and profit; we are doing our world-citizen duty to spread American democracy throughout the world."

"That's very noble, Mr. Kessler," the reporter said with a cordial smile. "But to access GlobalReach.com's portal, customers would need a computer. In developing countries, many people may not be able to afford—"

"I understand your concern perfectly," Earl Kessler interrupted, speaking with a slightly increased tempo. "This is where my dear friend

Mr. Stolle comes in. You must have heard: he has pledged to donate one hundred million dollars to support the launch of GlobalReach. com's portal. We will work with the right organizations and government entities to ensure computers purchased with this money will reach people around the world who need it most. Of course, we are confident that additional donations will follow."

"Yes, Mr. Kessler, we have heard about Mr. Stolle's generosity. But it still leaves us the question, how is GlobalReach.com going to make money?" The reporter looked directly at Earl Kessler as the camera lens advanced for a close-up of both of them.

The question seemed to surprise Kessler. After a slightly uncomfortable pause, he continued, his right hand raking through his slick, side-swept, unnaturally black hair, a gold cuff link on his shirtsleeve glinting under the studio light. "Well, we have reached out to a number of foreign governments regarding our portal. The feedback was overwhelmingly positive. They are all willing to pay a subscription fee so their citizens can have access to the wealth of knowledge our portal has to offer. I am just grateful that my years of service at the State Department have enabled me to reach out to friends and officials across the world who have in turn helped us get to where we are today." Kessler looked directly into the camera and spoke with a voice that gushed gratitude.

On that day, had all the world's fortune tellers gotten together for a convention and looked into a crystal ball, none would have been able to foretell that in less than a year, Mr. Stolle would have pocketed hundreds of millions of dollars from cashing in on the stocks of his two-year-old dot-com company and would be officially charged for cooking the company's books to deceive investors. His company's value would plummet to less than one-third of what it had been before the burst of the dot-com bubble. And GlobalReach.com, after its stock had soared to over one hundred dollars a share, would be defunct. But on that day, after Kessler's appearance on national TV, he and his buddy Stolle were catapulted to the status of not only visionary businessmen but also saviors of the world. And it was on that day Lu started her job as the chief financial officer at GlobalReach.com.

After Kessler's TV interview, which Sage and Lu had watched at

GlobalReach.com's Washington, DC, office, Sage, on behalf of Kessler, took Lu to a welcome-aboard lunch. They decided on sushi at a restaurant on N Street, a block away from their office. The restaurant was on the first floor of an old townhouse-style building. It was tiny but inviting, with soft cream-colored furnishings and black-and-white paper lanterns above the sushi bar area.

"I am sorry nobody on the management team is able to greet you today. It's hard to get everybody in the office at the same time these days," Sage said after they settled in comfortably at a table in the back of the restaurant. A waiter with a boyish face rushed over and asked for their drink preferences.

"Iced tea for me; make it strong if you could," Sage said automatically.

"Hot green tea for me, not too strong please," Lu answered without giving it any thought.

"Okay, one cold and strong, one hot and light," the waiter said in a heavily accented monotone as he wrote the order down on a notepad, "I'll get your drinks and be right back for your orders."

After glancing through the menu, Sage said, "I think I'll stick to my favorite, tuna and yellowtail sashimi."

"You are more authentically Japanese than I am. I'll stick to what I usually have at Japanese restaurants, salmon teriyaki and miso soup. I can't eat raw food; everything has to be well done for me." Lu made a face. Then something dawned on her. "Hey, have you noticed that so far we are completely on opposite ends, iced tea, hot tea, raw and well done?"

"You're right," Sage laughed. "Maybe that's because we are from two ends of the world. When I was little, I truly believed it when my parents said that if we dug a hole in the backyard, we'd end up coming out in China."

"That's what my grandma said too. I remember there was a dry well in the back of the apartment building where I grew up. It was covered with a wooden top for safety reasons. I was fascinated and tried many times to pry the top open. To scare me off, my grandma said that the hole led all the way to America, where everybody looked like the red-haired, green-eyed devils in the cartoon books she and I read together.

If I opened that top, those devils would come and get me. I never tried to open it again."

They burst into laughter.

The waiter was back with two teas of diametric temperature. He took the orders, repeated the orders monotonically, and went away.

Sage leaned toward Lu and lowered her voice. "You know, the waiter seems robotic, but the Zagat review said the sushi is very spirited here, always fresh and flavorful."

Sensing the humor in what Sage had said, Lu said lightheartedly, "Spirited sushi? Interesting critique. A piece of raw fish on a gob of white rice—how spirited can it be?"

As Sage had said, the food did not disappoint. The fish, raw or well done, was succulent and tender.

"You know, when I was little, my parents often took me and my brother to a Chinese restaurant on Long Island for Peking duck. It was so delicious. Then we moved here, and we couldn't find any good Chinese restaurants," Sage said as she masterfully prepared a piece of sashimi with chopsticks. She dabbed a bit of wasabi sauce on the fish and then dipped the whole piece in the little dish of soy sauce.

"Well, it used to be better. But over the years Chinese food has been Americanized, becoming salty and greasy—a recipe for developing high blood pressure at minimum." Lu stopped to pick up another piece of salmon teriyaki.

Sage grinned. "You know, talking about Chinese food has reminded me of the Chinese moon-fairy story Mrs. Wong told me then I was a kid. She and her husband owned that restaurant we used to go to on Long Island."

"Really! Are you talking about the story that has something to do with the Chinese Mid-Autumn Festival?" Lu asked, her eyes widened.

"Exactly," Sage answered with a controlled exclamation. She then recounted the moon-fairy story Mrs. Wong had told her at the Autumn Moon restaurant when she'd been a little kid.

Lu listened with great interest, her eyes following every gesture Sage made. Normally she would consider what Sage was doing a bit showy, although with good intention. She had encountered quite a few people in her professional life who had never been to China but would impart to her their knowledge of everything China nonstop as soon as they found out she was originally from there. It bothered her sometimes, but she convinced herself that their intentions were good, that they wanted to make her, the only female among a group of high-finance professionals, feel comfortable and not ignored.

With Sage, it was different, the moon-fairy story obviously had left a great impression on her as a little girl. But Sage had grown up. She was a thirty-some-year-old American woman narrating a Chinese folklore with the innocence and sincerity of a five-year-old.

"So did I tell the story right?" Sage asked when done, anxious to verify the story's authenticity.

Lu did not answer the question directly. She asked instead, "Did you really believe it when you were a little girl?"

"Absolutely. At that time, I was five but well versed in the happily-ever-after stories like Snow White and Cinderella. I lugged all those storybooks everywhere I went, to the beach, to Grandma's house. But the moon-fairy story was a little different. The fairy left the earth and her husband because she loved him. Later they could only be together on the moon, when he had time to visit her, but they were happy when they were together. It leaves the story open to everybody's interpretation. From then on I always thought the moon was a beautiful and happy place." Sage stopped to drink the last bit of her iced tea. Then she said, "Oh, I forgot to tell you about the mother-of-pearl motif covering the entire wall in that restaurant. I thought it was gigantic, maybe because I was little then. The way it was done, it was like the fairy was in a beautiful silk gown floating between the blue sea and the moonlit sky. It was the kind of sea and sky I was familiar with growing up on the beach in Montauk. My parents became quite good friends with Mr. and Mrs. Wong. So for years, they invited us to go midautumn moon watching on the beach and to eat moon cakes made of red-bean paste. I would stand on the beach, imaging the moon fairy rising from the sea and flying to the full moon above. Sometimes Mrs. Wong would say to me, 'Look carefully, Sage. Do you see the shadows in the moon? Those are the shadows of the moon fairy and her husband, eating moon cake together.' I have to say I was really impressed by this whole moon-fairy thing. But enough from me. Is this the same story you were told when you were a little girl?" Sage paused, feeling a little embarrassed that she might have been too chatty.

"Well, there are many versions of the moon-fairy story. The version I know is a little different from yours," Lu said pensively. She remembered well the moon-fairy story her grandma told her on the last night of her life, but the image that came to her mind had never been a fair lady flying to the full moon in the midautumn sky. It had always been her grandma, standing by the window in her white silk gown, her arms reaching out as if she were trying to touch the silver moon hanging right outside the windowsill. Lu had never shared this image with anybody in her life, so she only told Sage her grandma's version of the story.

"Wow, interesting," Sage said when Lu finished telling the story. "It's the complete opposite of what I was told. In my version, the moon fairy leaves because of love; in your version, she leaves because of hate? Maybe that's too strong a word—disappointment maybe?" Her voice trailed off, her mind still searching for the proper words to describe the reason the moon fairy left the earth in Lu's story.

"Disappointment seems to be a good word," Lu said, her mind still on how her grandma had died that night. "I think it's fair to say that in my version the moon fairy is disappointed with what's going on in this world, so she leaves. But then she's condemned to a lonely life on the moon forever. The moon in my version is a sad place."

"I wouldn't go that far." Sage turned more serious. "All of us are capable of disappointing each other at one time or another, but it doesn't mean we just condemn ourselves to go off and live lonely lives forever. My dad used to say, 'You just have to keep trying.' He meant trying to be a better person who doesn't disappoint, I guess."

"Well, I guess you and I have our own different moons, one happy, one sad. Maybe it's because, as you said, we are from opposite ends of the world," Lu half joked, knowing a perspective on life discussion required more time than a quick lunch and should be reserved for friends who knew each other well.

Sage seemed to know that Lu would prefer to conclude the discussion, and she said cheerfully, "You're right; we are indeed from opposite ends of the world."

When they left the restaurant, the impressions they'd formed of each other were just as opposing. Sage later told Lu that she thought Lu was serious and a little guarded, and Lu thought her new colleague was delightful but a bit naive. But they both knew intuitively that somewhere in between the opposite ends of the world, there was affinity.

• • •

"CAN YOU BELIEVE IT's been ten years since the GlobalReach.com debacle?" Sage said. She finished the last bit of champagne in her flute and continued, "You know, I still see Kessler's and his wife's pictures appear now and then in some local papers and magazines. They're busy rubbing shoulders with the DC social elite."

"That's the impression I got the first time I saw him on TV. He is better at holding cocktail glasses at philanthropic fund-raising events than running a business, except his motive is not to raise funds for noble causes but to ingratiate himself to the rich and elite and enrich himself in the process. I still can't believe he blew over seventy million in investors' money in less than a year—all his globe-trotting, first class all the time, and charging five-thousand-dollar Armani suits, three-thousand-dollar Montblanc pens, and thousand-dollar dinners on company credits cards, claiming they were business related when they didn't bring back a single dime of revenue."

Putting her champagne flute down on the coffee table, Sage nodded. "And don't forget the exorbitant fees he'd doled out to his crony circle of so-called international consultants. Everybody was drunk, spending like no tomorrow. You are the only one who nagged him about those ridiculous expenses. Then when the money was almost gone, he had the nerve to run to that jerk of a board chairman to complain about you, saying that you didn't bring the company's cost issue to him early enough."

"Oh yeah, I wonder what happened to Kessler's buddy John Smith, the most comical board chairman I've ever met. Remember that board meeting you and I attended?" Lu laughed reflectively, replaying the meeting in her mind.

The meeting had been held at a lunch where cocktails had been followed by a lavish buffet and an assortment of wine and liquor. John

Smith had been in his sixties, short, portly, and completely bald. His small beady eyes had blinked constantly behind the rimless spectacles, his stubby, round nose red and veiny. After gulping down a couple of gin and tonics, Smith began the meeting with long-winded opening remarks. He praised Kessler as a noble warrior who had sacrificed what could have been a much more lucrative career somewhere else to fight against global illiteracy at GlobalReach.com. He paused for a round of applause and motioned the server standing behind him to fill his wineglass. After taking a long draw, he expressed his gratitude to the management team, mentioning each of them by name, and thanked them for their dedication to GlobalReach.com's noble cause. Lu couldn't tell if it was because of the booze or if he was truly caught in the moment, but there was actually a tremor in Smith's voice, as if he was truly touched by the abundant altruism in the room that day.

After another round of applause died down, Smith bestowed his adulation on all employees and associates of GlobalReach.com, whose undertaking would surely change the world, and he said that, as chairman of the board, he would make sure their compensation would be the most competitive.

The meeting was a blur to Lu, with everybody around the table paying more attention to the food and booze than how GlobalReach.com was performing operationally and financially. Nobody asked what the company had to show for its burning of the bulk of the $100 million raised less than a year ago.

After the conclusion of the meeting, Kessler had introduced Lu to Smith. Standing up tipsy, Smith had put one of his hands on Lu's shoulder as he'd said, "I like your presentation." He'd laid his other hand on Lu's lapel and said, "I love your suit."

"What did you call him? The touchy-feely liberal who ..." Sage said.

"Who touched and felt liberally!" Lu said, finishing Sage's sentence.

Laughter burst out between them.

"Ever run into somebody like Kessler or Smith at your current job?" Sage asked.

"Of course. Plenty of greedy weasels like those two are out there. In my line of work, you don't run into dirty politicians like Kessler and Smith often, but on Wall Street, there are often people willing to throw ethics and morals out the window when it comes to money. Why do you think we had the financial market meltdown less than eight years after the dot-com bubble burst? I just try my best to avoid directly working for people like that. I do my best to work around people like that and make a living while still being able to look at myself in the mirror every day."

"Yeah, you know, this reminds me of my brother. I hope he never has to involve himself with the next generation of Kessler because of his potential deal with China. It makes me nervous."

"Well, your brother is an intelligent businessman, don't you think? Otherwise he wouldn't be where he is today, so give him some credit." Lu gently nudged Sage on the shoulder. Then she turned serious. "Now, sorry to change subject, but speaking of China, there is something I want to talk to you about."

Sage reached out for the champagne bottle on the coffee table and filled both flutes. "Okay, spill," she said.

CHAPTER 7

· · · · ·

AT 5:00 A.M., WILL'S alarm clock emitted a single soft, high-pitched noise. Then all was quiet again. A minute later, more high-pitched noises sounded, becoming rhythmic and increasingly distinct until there was no mistake that the master of the bedroom was awake. Will switched on the bedside lamp. The alarm clock, punctual and reliable, was Louis, the Doberman pinscher Will had rescued years ago.

"Come on, boy, time to get up," Will said to the dog lying on its blue-and-green flower-patterned mattress at the foot of the bed. In return, Louis jumped into Will's bed and slobbered wet kisses all over his master's face.

In the kitchen, Will let Louis out the back door. He made coffee and poured Louis's favorite crunchy kibbles in a bowl secured in a wooden feeding tray tucked in the nook next to the kitchen door. By the time he'd poured coffee into a large mug, Louis was back in the house, gulping down his breakfast. The bowl was vacuumed clean in less than a minute. His docked, stubby tail waggling with content, Louis trailed behind Will into the living room like a bluish-gray shadow.

Louis was what the breeders called a blue Doberman, a diluted version of the standard black-and-tan Doberman pinscher due to a mutation of the skin-color gene. Four years ago, while jogging on the trail near his house in Great Falls, Virginia, Will had found Louis scampering around in the shrubbery, flea ridden, with only skin on his three-month-old frame. Will had scooped him up and taken him to a local veterinarian. Careful medical examination and blood tests had revealed no serious illness other than the puppy having had little to eat for days, perhaps weeks. The vet thought the poor little thing, with docked tail but floppy ears, might have been deserted by a local

Doberman breeder because nobody was willing to pay hundreds of dollars for a dog with genetic skin defects. He further explained to Will that blue Dobermans' hair tended to get thinner as they matured into adulthood.

What others saw as defective, Will saw as unique and exceptional. He kept the puppy and gave him an authentic Doberman name, Louis, after the first Doberman breeder, Louis Doberman of Germany. Under Will's care and with proper training, the skeletal puppy blossomed into a loyal and affectionate companion. When Will took Louis for runs, passersby would often stop and admire the lean, compact, yet powerful creature, his dark-chocolate-brown eyes exuding intelligence and his smooth short hair shining blue. They would say, "What a magnificent dog!" Ever since then, Will was Louis's leader, and Louis, Will's shadow.

The living room was more like an open space, merging several rooms in a conventional house into one with multiple functionalities: dining, watching TV, doing serious and leisure reading, surfing the net, working to solve network technical issues, or simply lounging around and doing nothing.

In the center of the living room, Will settled into his roomy easy chair in front of the massive stone fireplace soaring into the vaulted ceiling twenty feet above. It was his favorite time of the day, leisurely drinking coffee in the quiet and tranquility of his home while Louis snoozed at his feet.

Will had bought the property years ago when his business had been starting to take off. It was a cottage house located in Great Falls, Virginia, about twelve miles outside of Washington, DC. It had been built in the 1950s and had been uninhabited for years. Its exterior had been overrun by vegetation, and the interior had clearly been home to many field animals. But it sat on the high point of five acres of secluded woodland, gently sloping all the way down to the Potomac River in the back. The Realtor had told Will that the house was considered a teardown and that the asking price was really for the land. Will had bought the property with the intention to build a brand-new house, the way he wanted. But as he'd walked around the property with an architect to decide a design plan, he'd realized the foundation of the old house was rock solid and its stucco structure not too different from what he had in mind for the house he wanted to build. In the end, it had taken over a year, but the worthless old cottage had been transformed into Will's home with its foundation and structure more or less intact.

From outside, Will's home looked like a cross between an English cottage with a gabled entry and a New England saltbox with the back side of the roof sloping nearly to the ground. The shape reminded Will of his grandparents' house in Montauk, sitting high on Old Montauk Highway, overlooking the Atlantic Ocean. He had recoated the stucco exterior in light cement gray and shielded the roof with dark-gray composite slate. At the center high point of the back slope of the roof was the tip of the stone chimney hoisted from the living room more than twenty feet below. The design of the interior broke the rule of the conventional layout of a New England saltbox, which was usually two stories in the front and one story in the back. Will did not want a McMansion, but he wanted his house airy and spatial, so he had traded square footage for height. Every inch of living space was on the same level, under vaulted ceilings with exposed dark wood support beams. The living room and the bedroom were in the front of the house, separated by the entry foyer in the middle, both with ceilings vaulting to twenty feet high. The ceilings then sloped down into the kitchen and bathroom in the rear of the house. Will wanted the house to be filled with light, so he'd had only windows the size of french doors installed and had light-obstructing trees and shrubberies near the house removed, replaced by lush green turfs. After the landscaping had been completed, the house sat on an acre of green meadow surrounded by four acres of woodland.

Will had the house exactly the way he wanted, a place he could step back to after a day's work in the outside world. Sage had teased him that he had built a man cave fit for a recluse, with no room for anyone else. Will had thought about this and then added a structure to the side of his man cave. It had the same shape of the main house, only smaller. It could house two cars downstairs, and upstairs was a dormer with a ten-foot-high ceiling and a bathroom with a white cast iron tub. He'd decorated it with more-feminine furniture made of driftwood, the kind Sage had in her apartment. In addition to the large windows, he'd installed two skylights in the roof. They became Sage's favorite feature of the house. When she stayed over her brother's house, if it was a clear night, she could lie in the bed and look through one of the skylights, gazing at the bright moon and stars.

After his first mug of coffee, Will's mind got busy, making noises that drowned out the peace and quiet around him. It was Saturday. Usually he would lounge around with Louis until his second mug of coffee was gone before he tackled the tasks and projects on his calendar. But his mind could not wait that morning; it started barraging him with questions, as it had been for the past several days. *So what are you going to do with your business? Are you going to sell or not? Are you sure what you are doing? What would it be like to be part of a Chinese-owned company?*

He got out of his easy chair and decided to get a refill of his coffee before mulling over those questions again. Immediately, Louis's head popped up from his snooze. In a split second, he was on his feet and followed Will into the kitchen.

After the previous evening's dinner with Lu and Sage, Will had come home and jumped right into research on rules and regulations regarding foreign ownership of US telecommunication companies. Prior to meeting Lu, his concerns about potential Chinese ownership of his business had been more cultural than political and legal, more about what would happen to the control and autonomy Matrixtech had promised him. But Lu had pointed out some issues he had not considered, including rules on foreign ownership and potential national-security implications. He'd spent hours trying to find something on the Internet that would provide him with some basic education on these issues, but nothing was of much help. Finally, at midnight, mental exhaustion had caught up with him, and he'd drifted into a few hours of restless sleep.

Will carried his second mug of coffee back to the living room and sank back into the easy chair, planning in his head what he needed to do next to eliminate some of those question marks that had been boggling his mind. He sipped his coffee and made a couple of decisions as Louis snoozed at his feet.

First, if the Chinese were out of the picture, he would say yes right away to Matrixtech. This would be the best-case scenario for him, no political or legal complications. He felt comfortable, from meeting

Matrixtech's senior executives, that they would indeed keep his company intact after the buyout.

Second, he decided it was time for him to lay everything out on the table with his two right-hand men, Frank Holt and Kevin Jagger. He needed to tell them of his intention to sell the company. He was fully aware that without these two, his company would never have gotten where it was. And his loyalty to them was unconditional.

Then he would also ask Frank and Kevin to consider the more complicated scenario if the Chinese decided to get involved with Matrixtech through merger or joint venture or some other form. Frank and Kevin might have their own take on that. Three heads collectively would be far more effective than his lonesome one.

Will gulped down what was left in the coffee mug and picked up the cell phone lying on the end table next to his easy chair. He texted Frank and Kevin, "Meet me at the pub at noon?" He stood up and said to Louis, "Come on, boy, let's go for a run."

Will changed into a dark-blue jogging suit with neon-green stripes that ran horizontally across the chest and back of the jacket. In the kitchen, he double knotted the lace of his running shoes while Louis tugged at the ends of his leash hanging from a wooden hook on the wall next to his feeding station. Will grabbed the leash and opened the back door. Like a streak of light, Louis darted out.

It was mid-April, and outside, the sky was twilight gray, the air moist and warm. A light fog, like wispy white smoke, floated in and out of the surrounding trees and shrubberies. Will followed Louis and crunched his way down the narrow gravel trail toward the Potomac River. Dew droplets falling from budding tree branches peppered him along the way.

At the foot of the trail, Will put Louis on the leash and slowly jogged onto a hiking trail of Great Falls Park. They meandered along the bank of the Potomac River, swift and swollen with abundant April rain. Less than half a mile upstream, the trail curved out closer to the riverbank, becoming part of a vantage point. There, in front of him, torrential white water tumbled over juxtaposed rock cascades that seemed to ascend all the way into the twilight sky in the distance. Will paused, taking in the panoramic view of the great falls. It was this very scenery that had captured his imagination when he'd roamed along the Potomac River years ago, looking to buy a home. It was like something straight from the imagination of a boy who worshiped the ocean and a man who romanticized the sea. The white water of the Potomac River, tumbling down seemingly from the sky, often brought him back to his childhood days in Montauk, where his father had taught him to stand up on his rainbow-colored surfboard and let the white waves of the Atlantic Ocean carry him ashore. Other times, like on this morning, the hovering fog, the roaring waterfall, and the twilight sky seemed otherworldly. He imagined himself out on the deep sea, where Captain Trent had introduced him to Wagner's opera *The Flying Dutchman*, which Will initially had thought was dark and gloomy. Then the captain had told him the folklore-like story of the *Flying Dutchman* and made Will listen to the music again. This time, out of the dark and gloomy tone had sprung notes of masculinity and romanticism. The story was that the Dutchman, the captain of the ghost ship, made a deal with Satan and was thus condemned forever to float on the dark sea. However, every several years he was allowed to come on land to find a woman, a woman who could stay true and faithful to him forever. If he could find her and marry her, then the curse would be broken, and the Dutchman would be able to bring his ship back to land …

A buzz came from the Blackberry in the back pocket of his jogging pants as he watched a couple of kayakers bounce in and out of narrow passageways between gray rock cascades. Reaching for his cell phone, he kept his eyes on the kayakers until they paddled far downstream and then out of sight. He glanced at the Blackberry screen; both Frank and Kevin would be at the pub at noon. He put the phone back in his pants pocket and found Louis sitting up straight and looking ahead, as if absorbing the view of the waterfall. At a gentle tug of the leash, the dog was on his feet and resumed trotting alongside his leader.

As they picked up speed, Will's brain automatically switched to a different gear, where his mind would just wander. Most of Will's best business ideas came from this wandering state of his brain while his feet pounded the ground. On that morning, his mind drifted back to the previous evening's dinner meeting with Lu and Sage.

Prior to the meeting, Will's preconceived notion of Wall Street analysts, people like Lu, had been quite simple: they were a bunch of arrogant narcissists sitting in their fancy Manhattan offices enclosed by walls paneled with their Ivy League diplomas and certifications from fancy finance boards. They dispensed their mathematic-formula-based stock ratings and blabbered their predictions of companies, good or bad, with a myopic three-month horizon. Yet a lot of them had never worked a day in the real business world. Being the owner of a private company, Will felt fortunate that he'd never had to go through these so-called analysts' inquisition on a quarterly basis like the CEOs of the public companies listed on the stock market. But with the prospect of his company being part of a large, publicly owned company, complicated by the potential Chinese ownership, Will had decided that seeking advice from a professional like Lu had become a necessary evil. He'd decided that he needed somebody who could provide the guidance he needed to navigate through the maze of rules and regulations if he decided to go through with this buyout, merger, acquisition, or whatever they wanted to call it. And he'd thought that Lu's Chinese background could potentially make her very useful to him in case the Chinese ended up having control or even partial control of his company.

Then he'd met Lu the person. He'd immediately noticed her black liquid and smiling eyes, but he had also noticed how quickly those eyes had turned vigilant and guarded when they'd touched on sensitive business subjects, like how Great China Telecom was seeking an IPO on Wall Street. He had been able to see in those eyes that she knew more about this Chinese company than she had admitted. Will had sensed she was an ace at her profession yet morally capable of staying out of trouble, as well as capable of not getting anybody around her in trouble. Then there had been her attire, luxurious cashmere sweater dress, supple leather boots, and the long strand of iridescent pearls adorned with a silver interlocking-Cs Chanel logo around her delicate neck. Her clothing and jewelry had all been a bit expensive for Will's taste but not as boring as he had expected. And as fancy as her clothing and accessories had been, she had not let them wear her; she'd only let them add a touch of sophistication that had made her classically sexy.

As for his preconceived notion of Lu being an arrogant Wall Street narcissist, it had dissipated quickly. He had been impressed by her mergers and acquisition knowledge and her ability to anticipate his doubts and concerns for his company's future. To Will, it was obvious that she knew very well what it took to run a business, and like himself, she understood the importance of always staying a step ahead. She was someone who did not have to prove anything, and if she were the boss, all her staff would feel they were working with her, not for her.

A sudden pull of the dog leash yanked Will's mind out of its wandering state. Louis sprang and pounced in vain at a squirrel scurrying across the trail and disappearing into the woods. Will stopped and lengthened the leash, letting Louis sniff the ground the squirrel had trod on. "You'll never catch it, boy," he said. The dog looked up at Will and whimpered, as if accepting his defeat.

• • •

Will arrived at the pub in Alexandria a few minutes before noon. After what had seemed to be weeks of nothing but gray clouds and chilly rain, the sky had turned azure blue, and the sunshine felt warm. Spring, although late, had finally arrived. There was a tight metered parking spot right in front of the pub. Will managed to squeeze in his blue Mustang. After inserting a few quarters in the meter, he walked toward the pub and, through the front window, saw Frank sitting at their table, busy with his Blackberry.

"Hey, Will, how are things?" Joe, the bartender, said from behind the bar. He fetched a tall glass from underneath the counter and filled it with Will's favorite Hefeweizen beer.

"Pretty good, how about yourself?"

"Not bad." Joe laid the beer on the counter. "Hey, how's Sage? Hope things are better at work for her. She was really down last time she was here."

"She's fine. Hey, if you're so concerned, why don't you give her a call? You have her number, don't you?" Will said mischievously. He'd known for a while that Joe liked his sister but did not want to admit it.

"Nah, I won't bother her. I was just wondering if that layoff stuff had slowed down." Joe deflected Will's question, his ruddy face turned a shade redder.

"I'm just saying that if you'd like to chat with her, there's nothing wrong with giving her a call and inviting her here for a drink," Will said in the most encouraging way. He and Sage had known Joe for years, since he'd bought the rundown pub from the previous owner and turned it into one of the most popular bars/restaurants in Alexandria. Nothing would make Will happier than if Joe and Sage became more than just friends. But the aftermath of Sage's last serious relationship seemed to be long lasting, and Will knew that, under the surface of perpetual optimism, Sage was afraid of getting involved with another guy. For that reason, Will did not want to push either of them too much.

"Hi, boss, what's up?" Frank tore his eyes away from his Blackberry and greeted Will with a smile noticeable only to Will and a few who really knew him well.

"Hi, Frank, sorry to drag you out on a Saturday. There's something I need to talk to you and Kevin about, and I think it's better we do it here."

Quiet, Frank nodded and waited for Will to say whatever he was going to say. Frank was in his early thirties, about five feet ten, of medium build, and quite fit. But his pale complexion, icy-gray eyes, and platinum-blond hair rendered him the appearance of being cold and aloof. He disliked being around too many people for too long, particularly at social functions that involved small talk and chitchat. When forced, he would utter words in the most-economical quantity, as if each syllable would drain his energy unnecessarily. Most people either misconstrued him as withdrawn or branded him as antisocial. But to Will and a few who knew him well, Frank was one of the main reasons that the company had won numerous multimillion, multiyear network-maintenance contracts. His ability to develop customized network-security software and tools that fended off anticipated and real cyber breaches had won clients' trust and made him invaluable to Will's business. Ironically, Will had spent tens and thousands of dollars over the past decade to fight the US immigration bureaucracies so that Frank was not deported back to Finland.

Frank had entered the United States legally, paying his own tuition to be educated at the University of Michigan, one of the nation's top schools for computer science and engineering. But the country's immigration laws dictated that he go back to Finland after graduation if no US company was willing to spend money on his behalf to fight for his permanent residency in the United States.

"So how is the testing going?" Will asked. He knew Frank had been testing some new security software just installed on a client's network, making sure it had minimum vulnerabilities to potential hackers.

"Okay," Frank mumbled, looking a bit sullen in his usual black jeans and a charcoal-gray sweatshirt.

Will knew exactly what Frank was going through. Frank wanted to devote 100 percent of his time to developing security software. He believed he could be the chief cat of cybersecurity, outsmarting the hacker mice out there. And Will believed him too. But that meant he would have to get Frank off a number of network-maintenance projects where he was considered as the key personnel. Will's clients would not be too pleased. This had been one of the main reasons Will knew a merger with a larger company might help, so someone with talent like Frank's could be better used and bring the company much-needed growth. Knowing Frank was not about to say much, Will decided to just drink his beer and wait for Kevin before he broke the news.

A few minutes after noon, Kevin Jagger rushed into the pub. He knew he was only a little late, but he hated being late. A former marine and the chief operating officer of Will's company, he ran everything like clockwork. When he called for a meeting, staff knew they'd better arrive five minutes early. Kevin never delayed his meetings because somebody was a few minutes late, and he had various punishments for tardy people. His favorite was to make them wear ties to work the next day. Kevin's personal weekend schedules were a different story. With three kids, the oldest being ten and the youngest being three, he was always behind, running around for his children's soccer practice, softball games, and karate lessons. His wife was a stay-at-home mom, which, Kevin had confessed to Will, often was no easy job. Over weekends, Kevin did the lion's share of house chores so his wife could get away for a manicure or get together with girlfriends. Everybody considered Kevin a model father and husband, but Will also saw his own father, William Sr., in Kevin in the way he carried the responsibility of providing for his family on his shoulder alone.

"Sorry I'm late," Kevin said as, still in his early-morning running outfit, he whirled toward Will and Frank. At forty-eight, Kevin was wiry and edgy. He had long given up on his "shitty hair," according to his own words, and shaved his head. And that accentuated his angular face and piercing blue eyes. He could pass as the twin brother of Ed Harris, the movie star.

"Had a good run?" Will asked.

"Yeah, sorry, haven't had time to change."

"Planning for another marine marathon in the fall? You have run how many of those, by the way?" Will knew Kevin had been running the Marine Corps Marathon in DC every year for years and had no plans to quit. But he asked anyway, just to put Kevin in a more relaxed mood. Long-distance running was in Kevin's DNA, no matter how demanding his schedule was. He would get up at three in the morning if necessary to get his training done. That kind of discipline was carried over to the way Kevin ran the day-to-day operation of the company. Like running, he put one foot in front of the other until he ran, dragged, or crawled to the finish line.

"Lost count, but I'll go on as long as my body holds up. So what's up?" Kevin knew Will had something important to say; otherwise he would not have dragged them out on a weekend. He took a sip of the beer Joe had sent over and waited for Will to speak whatever was on his mind.

"Okay, this hasn't been easy for me, and nothing is set in stone yet. You guys have been with me for a long time, and whatever we are going to do, I need your help, and I need you to feel comfortable," Will said, surprised of the nervousness in his own voice. But Frank's and Kevin's anticipating yet reassuring faces calmed him, and he told them about potentially selling the company to Matrixtech but held off mentioning the Chinese part.

Frank seemed intrigued and stopped his habitual checking of the Blackberry next to his beer on the table. Kevin, meanwhile, remained quiet. Will kept gulping down his beer as if he did not notice the awkward silence at the table. After what seemed to be forever, Frank spoke first. "Is it going to affect my citizenship process if you sell out, boss?" Although annoyed by the seemingly selfish question, Will understood where Frank was coming from. It had taken years and a bundle of money for Will to get a green card for Frank. It had been a long, uphill battle to convince the government that Frank's technical skills were unique and crucial to the success of the company. Frank had been happy to remain a citizen of Finland while residing legally in the United States, but that had changed quickly when Will's company had begun to win large government contracts that required security clearance and US citizenship. So it had been back to the attorneys and naturalization office to start Frank's citizenship application. That had been months ago, and the process was supposed to come to a successful end soon.

"Don't worry, Frank; it's not going to affect your citizenship. But watch your English; you keep that up, and you won't be a US citizen. I'm not *selling out*; I'm selling the company, merging with Matrixtech," Will said, trying to lighten the mood.

"Sorry, boss, bad English," Frank said sheepishly, pushing his Blackberry away from the spreading puddle of water around the bottom of the beer mug in front of him.

"Kevin, what do you think?" Will turned to Kevin, who, with both hands cupping his glass, seemed to be watching the frothy head of the beer inside disappear.

"I am happy for you, but I wouldn't be honest if I said I'm not worried about the postmerger consolidation. It's bound to happen," Kevin said without looking up.

"Well, I told them one of the conditions that has to be met is that I get to keep all key employees," Will said confidently. He knew Kevin was too proud to admit he was worried about his job. Will also knew Kevin had reason to worry. Unlike Frank, whose technical skills were easily transferrable in the exploding cybersecurity world regardless of his perceived antisocial personality, It would be a little trickier for Kevin to find a perfect fit as the chief who planned and oversaw a company's day-to-day operations. Kevin had been with Will when the company had had only a handful of employees, most of them with military backgrounds. They had not had much trouble getting used to Kevin's no-nonsense and sometimes-regimental management style. Time had changed that. As Will's company had continued to grow, the size of the workforce had grown larger but younger. Although most staff sooner or later had accepted and respected Kevin as their boss, the process had not been without glitches. Will had tactfully broached the subject with

Kevin, reminding him he was no longer directing a group of ex-navy men or ex-marines and suggesting a firm but softer approach might be more effective with the millennial generation. Kevin had responded, "I don't give a rat's ass about your millennial generation, or generation X or Y, whatever you call them. They seem to be a generation of softies to me." Will had thought he'd meant it figuratively until he'd heard some staff complaining that Kevin had called them soft as the Pillsbury Doughboy and ordered them to go to the gym instead of the pizza parlor at lunchtime.

Will shot a glance at Kevin, who still seemed to be brooding over his half-emptied beer mug. Trying to be as comforting as he was confident, Will said, "Hey, guys, cheer up. You're both my right-hand lieutenants. I can't do this without you. This should be good news."

"If you say so." Kevin seemed to have decided to move on to other aspects of the potential deal. "So why does Matrixtech want to buy us?"

"They are mainly a telecom network-system-design company. They have a few large management contracts with private-sector companies, but I think they'd like to get in business with the feds too, which might not be the most lucrative, but once you're in, you could stay on for decades. We're a good way for Matrixtech to get in the door."

"What can we get from them? Stay as a maintenance contractor? What is the difference between doing it by ourselves or with Matrixtech?" Kevin seemed puzzled.

"Remember I told you guys that I would love to get into the business of developing web-security products and tools? Well, Matrixtech might just afford us the staff and financial resources needed to get into that business. They have a small group of software engineers already working on network-security stuff. Together with the few expert staff we have, people like our Frank," Will said, pausing to look at Frank, whose face was beaming and eyes twinkling, "we could grow the business big time, and we will have the financial resources to hire more top-notch software engineers if we need to."

"Cool!" Frank blurted with great excitement.

"Congrats, Will, sounds like you've got everything all figured out, your dream coming true. So what's the timeline?" Kevin said matter-of-factly.

"Well, it could happen very quickly if it were not for one potential complication. Tell me what you think."

For the next half hour or so, Frank and Kevin listened intensely without interrupting as Will explained in detail the possibility of Matrixtech being a business partner with a Chinese telecommunication-equipment company that was trying to list its stock in the US stock market, his conversation with Lu the previous evening, and his research so far on rules and regulations regarding foreign ownership of US telecoms. When he finished, Frank was completely confused and lost, his icy-gray eyes staring at the void under his nose. Kevin knitted his brows and squinted his eyes, an expression he often took on when he was trying to process large quantities of information quickly and figure out how to ask questions coming into his mind at the same time.

After a few moments of silence, Kevin took a deep breath and exhaled. "Wow! Didn't see that coming, but I don't think it will fly," he said firmly, like a judge rendering an absolute verdict.

"Why?"

In a clipped tone, Kevin said, "Because there is no way the US government would let red China maintain the United States' secured network system, which last time I checked is still our business, isn't it? This means we could be spun off or sold to some Beltway government contractors. What would happen to the staff who had been on those projects for years? You can't control what would happen to their futures, but you would have bigger and fancier technologies to play with." Kevin picked up the beer glass and slugged it empty, the blue veins around his temple bulging.

"You're right, Kevin. I don't mean to get everyone upset," Will said calmly. "You and I both want our business to last, although our approaches might be a little different. You prefer everything stays the same as long as it's not broken, but I think, in our line of business, we need to constantly renew and rejuvenate in order to thrive. We have to be able to see where the next growth will be coming from. This scenario with the Chinese may not play out at all; it's in a very preliminary stage, and for all the national-security reasons you have just mentioned, Kevin, it may never happen. The Chinese may settle with a simple joint venture with Matrixtech, so they can sell their telecom equipment and raise capital here in the US more easily. I told you guys about this possibility, even if remote, because I thought you ought to know."

"Assuming there won't be a full merger or any involvement with the Chinese, you still have to give Matrixtech an answer soon, don't you?" Kevin asked logically, now calmer.

"Yep, I think I need to be very direct with them to see where they are with the Chinese. Either yes or no, it will make our decision much easier. I will call the contact guy at Matrixtech Monday and get an update on this." Will decided it was time for them to stop arguing and speculating about something that might not happen in the end. "Come on, guys, let's have another beer and enjoy it this time." He signaled to Joe at the bar.

• • •

WILL GOT BACK HOME later that afternoon. In the living room, he turned on the flat-screen TV inlaid on a six-foot stone partition wall next to the giant stone fireplace. He settled into his easy chair, aimlessly flipping through over one hundred channels without finding anything interesting to watch, all the while going over in his mind Kevin's reaction to the potential Matrixtech and Chinese partnership idea. He had not expected Kevin and Frank to embrace the idea with open arms, but he had not expected such a negative reaction from Kevin, who, for more than a decade, had always provided him with unconditional support and who was a disciplined officer and risk-taking entrepreneur at the same time. But he seemed to have changed over the years; a decade was a long time. Kevin was no longer the happy-go-lucky bachelor; he had a wife and three young kids to support and a big mortgage to pay. Naturally he was more risk averse and did not want to rock the boat.

His phone dinged loudly from the side pocket of his cargo pants. He fished it out and read an e-mail from his contact person at Matrixtech.

"Hope this is good news for you. We have been informed that the Chinese have decided not to pursue any relationship with Matrixtech at this time for undisclosed reasons. Although this is somewhat disappointing to the management of Matrixtech, we hope it will help with your decision regarding the merge of your company with Matrixtech in the near future …"

Will did not finish reading the e-mail; he knew he had gotten what he had hoped for. The Chinese were finally out of the picture, although the wording "not to pursue any relationship with Matrixtech *at this time*" sounded as if they could come back later. But Will did not dwell on it. He was relieved that he would not have to go through the Chinese argument with Kevin again. He would sell the company to Matrixtech, no Chinese, no complications, and everybody should be happy.

But strangely, the relief he felt did not push him into the celebratory mood called for under the circumstances. Instead, he felt a mild sting of disappointment. He found himself cursing the Chinese for withdrawing so abruptly. He almost wished they had stayed on the scene for a bit longer, complicating everything for him so he could arrange to meet Lu again for obvious reasons, her business advice. It was a fleeting feeling, and Will almost laughed at his silly thoughts. He would be very busy for a while, taking care of his business. He texted the news to Frank and Kevin. But his mind, uncharacteristically, drifted to Montauk instead of being laser-focused on the next steps and plans for his business. Lu had mentioned she loved to go there in summer. Summer was only a couple of months away. He thought, *I think I can coax Sage to ask Lu to spend a weekend in Montauk. After all, they are best friends.*

CHAPTER 8

• • • • •

"LADIES AND GENTLEMEN, WE have begun our descent and will be landing in Shanghai Pudong International Airport in about thirty minutes. The local time is approximately 2:00 p.m., and the sky over Shanghai is mostly sunny with a mild temperature of seventy-two degrees Fahrenheit, twenty-two degrees Celsius." The gentle announcement from the captain of the Boeing 747 nudged Lu out of her conscious dreaming state, a state in which she was conscious enough to know she was dreaming yet, when awoken, not conscious enough to know immediately where she was. It took a few moments for her to be fully aware of her surroundings, realizing she had reached the end of her almost-twenty-four-hour journey to Shanghai, China.

She adjusted the seat to a sitting position and looked over across the aisle, where Dick Witherspoon, her counterpart at the largest investment banking firm on Wall Street, was lying flat on his back, his body completely wrapped in a gray flannel blanket. He appeared to be sound asleep, but the fitful heaving of his chest and the faint gurgling sound from his gaping mouth suggested to Lu that the euphoria from the little magical white pill he'd popped with vodka hours ago had worn off and Dick was now officially in the zombie zone. "Have one; it helps you relax and makes you happy," Dick had said, offering her the pill when they'd gotten on the plane.

Looking at the pill bottle suspiciously, Lu had turned him down. She'd seen Dick throw one—or was it a couple?—of those pills in his mouth as the plane had roared off the runway. Happy hours had followed, during which Dick had giggled at the TV screen with miniature vodka bottles lined up on the tray in front of him. At least that was how Lu had last seen him before drifting into her conscious dream state.

With the anticipation of finally returning to her native city after thirty-three years, Lu reached for the window shade next to her. She realized she was about to see for the first time the landscape of the city from thousands of feet above—the city that she'd risked her life to flee yet that often had come to her dreams as a wistful ghost during the past thirty-three years of her life.

She lifted the shade. Nothing greeted her eager eyes. The windowpane was just a hazy, yellowish sheet. No blue skies, no bright sun shining, and, above all, no city. She wiped the window with her palm, hoping it was just dust blurring the view. "It's not dust; it's smog," the man sitting next to her said expertly. Lu turned to face him. "You look surprised," the man continued. "Have you been to Shanghai before?"

"Yes, but it was a long time ago," Lu said with a smile and turned back to look outside the window. She stared down, hard this time, hoping to make out something resembling civilization beneath. But there was nothing, only the feeling of the plane rapidly descending. "So when was the last time you visited Shanghai?" the man next to her persisted. Without waiting for Lu's answer, he said, "Depending on how long ago, you may not recognize it. I have been coming here for the past ten years. Every six months, it's looked more developed, but the pollution has gotten worse."

Politely, Lu smiled and nodded as the man told her his full résumé and the knowledge and experience he had accumulated in the city over the years.

Minutes later, the drone next to her was fortunately drowned out by the captain's prepare-for-landing order. The flight attendants buzzed around the cabin to enforce the "Adjust seats in the upright position" rule. Lu turned to face the window again, casting her glance into the now slightly dissipated fog outside. The old yet unfamiliar city faded in like the ghost in her dreams; Shanghai reluctantly unveiled itself, revealing muffled silhouettes of skyscrapers and blurred construction structures adrift in an eerie stratosphere of haze. Then the landing gears were clanking out of the belly of the jumbo jet, and with a jolting thump, Lu touched the ground of the city she had vowed never to return to.

It was early afternoon. The interior of the Shanghai Pudong International Airport was not too crowded. Going through customs and baggage claim in the modern yet unremarkable terminal was relatively hassle-free. Lu felt she could be in any airport in the United States if it were not for the people around her, most of them speaking Mandarin or her native tongue, the Shanghai dialect. She gathered her luggage and walked expectantly toward the exit to the main terminal, a bleary-eyed Dick Witherspoon dragging next to her.

Stepping outside the double sliding door into the main terminal, they were greeted by a throng of people standing behind roped walkways, most of them holding cardboard nameplates. "I guess they're drivers sent to pick up important guests," Lu said to Dick as they wound through the walkways toward the exit.

"In that sense, you can say we're important guests too," Dick said, lightly elbowing Lu to look ahead. At the end of the roped walkway stood a man in a dark jacket, white shirt, and red tie, holding a cardboard sign with Lu's and Dick's full names written on it in black Magic Marker. As they got closer, he waved the sign at them. Lu recognized him. They had met during a videoconference. He was one of the managers of Golden Seafood.

"Welcome, welcome." Now sure the guests he was expecting were in front of him, the man oozed enthusiasm. "I am James Chan. So glad we finally meet in person. Let me help you with the luggage." He trotted a few step forward and grabbed Lu's Tumi rolling suitcase.

He then offered to take over Dick's luggage, but Dick mumbled, "Thanks, I can manage."

"My car is right outside. Let's get out here," Mr. Chan said, guiding Lu and Dick toward a small inconspicuous side exit door. All the way he showered Lu and Dick with questions about the conditions and comfort of the long flight.

Outside, the afternoon sunbeams high above labored to pierce the smog shrouding the lower atmosphere. In the opaque air, Mr. Chan set down the luggage on the curbside. Snapping his fingers, he called out in Chinese to the other side of the exit lane, "We are here. Pull the car over, pull the car over."

An engine started, and the shadow of a car materialized.

Minutes later, the shiny black Audi sedan was cruising smoothly along the Pudong Airport Expressway toward Shanghai. Dick sat quietly in the seat next to the driver. He had not said much since getting off the airplane, which Lu believed was probably due to the residual effect of the little white pill he'd taken.

"I am sorry you came on such a bad day." Mr. Chan broke the silence, figuring his guests were now in a relatively settled state in the comfortable car. "It was never this bad until recently, actually shortly after the 2008 Olympic. Yes, we've had mildly hazy days here and there for years due to air pollution, but since we're on the sea, a little wind used to blow the pollutants away. But things are getting worse. A day like today is becoming more frequent, so bad we can't see anything clearly on the other side of a street."

Leaning closer to the window, Lu watched patches of yellow fog swish by and said, without turning to face Mr. Chan, "I was told that Beijing is the smog place, but mainly because of the sandstorm in the desert close to the city. I never expected Shanghai could be this hazy."

"Sandstorm, fog, haze, whatever. It's pollution, and it will slowly kill everything. Anybody who doesn't want to admit that is in denial; I know the government is," Mr. Chan said, his tone a mix of sarcasm and resignation.

"Where does the pollution come from?" Lu asked.

"They say we have too many cars on the road. So the government is restricting approval of new car registrations and license plates. You will laugh when I tell you this, Ms. Li: the license and registration fees, plus *incidentals* to *expedite* the process, can equal to half the price of an average car," Mr. Chan said in a tone of mockery. Lu interpreted his emphasis on *incidentals* and *expedite* to mean corruption and bribery. She looked at the back of Dick's head in the front passenger seat to gauge his reaction; the top of his pale head was ruffled but still. She nodded at Mr. Chan to indicate she'd gotten his joke.

For a short while, they continued west in silence. Leading the way was the afternoon sun. The ashen sky had choked off its brilliant beams, reducing it to a mere orange-red aperture, gaping down suspiciously at the earth activities below.

Soon they were approaching Pudong, the eastern district of Shanghai. Mr. Chan leaned forward and tapped on the back of Dick's seat. Dick remained still and quiet. "Mr. Witherspoon, look ahead; there is the Jin Mao Tower, where your hotel is."

The pale head stirred this time, followed by Dick's groggy voice. "Are we close?"

Lu inched to the center of the back of the car so she could have an unobstructed view through the front window of the car. Straight ahead loomed the silhouette of the skyscrapers she had become familiar with through pictures on many websites. In real life, the Oriental Pearl TV Tower—or the Brilliant Oriental Pearl TV Tower, if translated word for word—named so mainly for the two giant spheres linked by a tall antenna column, looked more like a colossal pair of pregnant spiders pierced on a metal rod. The square aperture capping the Shanghai World Financial Center did live up to its nickname, the Bottle Opener. As for the rest of the skyscrapers lining the shore of Shanghai, they were just big, tall, and blurred.

Dick turned around and asked Lu, "Sure you don't want to stay at the Grand? It has the most breathtaking view of Shanghai." Though still bleary eyed, he was much more animated.

"No, thanks. I can always join you for drinks and the view later. I prefer the west side. The view may be less breathtaking, but hopefully the air is easier to breath." Lu felt guilty for poking fun of the city she had not seen for over thirty years.

They dropped Dick off at the Grand Hotel and wound out of the skyscraper area and entered the tunnel under the Huangpu River, linking Pudong to Old Shanghai in the west. With Dick gone, Mr. Chan switched to Chinese, and the conversation took on a more natural flow. "So, Ms. Lu, I remember you said it's been many years since you last saw Shanghai. Everything must be new to you."

"Yes, I left when I was still a young girl. I remember the only way to cross the Huangpu River to Pudong was by ferryboat. My father took me there once, and there was nothing much in Pudong back then. The whole area was a stretch of marshland, giant weeds everywhere, although I thought the wild geese were beautiful," Lu answered in Chinese, surprised some of the words she wanted to utter did not come easily to her. "You have to excuse me; I think my Chinese is a bit rusty. I haven't had too many chances to speak it for so many years."

"No, no, it sounds perfect. If you don't have the opportunity to speak Chinese in the United States, then you'll just have to do more business with us, so you can have more excuses to be back here to practice your Chinese," Mr. Chan said good-humoredly. Thinking he was making good conversation, he followed with questions more personal in nature. "So how old were you when you left China? It's easy for us Chinese to go anywhere in the world now, but many years ago, it was not that easy. How did you get out? Do you still have family here?"

The questions, though a bit too familiar and nosy according to Western decorum, were harmless and socially acceptable in the Chinese cultural environment. But on a subconscious level, her keen awareness of being inside red China prevented her from indulging in too much chitchat that could lead to revealing too much personal information. She had gauged Mr. Chan's age at close to sixty years old. He was a seemingly affable man but old enough to have been one of the teenage Red Guards during the Cultural Revolution who had raided 'capitalist' homes like hers.

A few seconds later, she heard her own voice, as hazy as the surrounding atmosphere. "Oh, my mother still lives here … Thank you so much for coming all the way to the airport to pick us up, Mr. Chan; it's a long way. Dick and I could have just taken a taxi."

In the semidark tunnel, the expression on Lu's face was vague, but Mr. Chan could hear the uneasiness in her voice. He chattered on, as if completely unaware of Lu's avoiding his questions, "Not at all. We could have just sent a company car and driver, but you and Mr. Witherspoon are our honored guests. I am delighted to do this myself. Besides, my boss insisted it too."

As they emerged from the tunnel into the west side of the city, Lu expected that they would go through the Bund, or the waterfront of Shanghai, a mile-long shoreline along the Huangpu River lined with dozens of century-old magnificent commercial and banking buildings in styles ranging from Gothic to Baroque to Romanesque and Renaissance. Once the center of Shanghai's politics, economy, and culture before the Communist government had taken over in 1949, the Bund had been in desperate need of repair and renovation when Lu had left the country. In recent years, she had seen pictures in newspapers, magazines, and on TV of the Bund returned to its old glory, and now she was curious and itching to see the real thing. But the circuitous exits and entrances they took offered only a few brief and clouded glimpses of segments of the famous landscape before they entered what seemed to be another expressway.

Looking around in confusion, Lu asked, "Where are we?"

"We are on the Yan'an elevated expressway, miss," the driver said in the Shanghai dialect, his eyes skimming the rearview mirror. "It's not quite rush hour yet, so it's faster to get into the city on this road. Wait until after four thirty, and we could be crawling on this so-called expressway."

"I guess we are on Yan'an Road then." Reflexively, Lu responded in the same dialect, familiar yet strange sounding at the same time.

"Yes, we are on Yan'an Road, the top level, though," Mr. Chan chimed in. "The old Yan'an Road you are familiar with is right underneath."

"Ah" was the only word to softly escape her as memories of the painful past began to surge within. In silence, she let her eyes dwell on the left side window for the next several minutes, wishfully searching for the four-story art deco apartment building—42 Yan'an Road—that had only existed in her memory for the past thirty-three years, all the while fully aware it may have ceased to exist in reality a long time ago.

"Up here, you can hardly see anything that resembles the old city. The way it is going, I don't see anything different between Shanghai and New York." Mr. Chan's now-tour-guide-like voice, tinged with a touch of pride, retracted Lu's eyes from the left side window. Leaning her head against the window next to her, Lu gazed at rows of concrete buildings flanking the once French-plane-tree-lined Yan'an Road. She noticed most of the skyscrapers were apartment buildings faceted with tiny windows and small balconies. From a distance, shrouded in the smog-plagued air, they looked like colossi of concrete beehives truncated at the top. But sensing Mr. Chan's national pride, Lu concurred matter-of-factly, "I would say the roads are much more modern and developed than New York, which does not have so many expressways going into the city. But all these buildings, are they all apartments?"

"Most of them around here are. They are quite expensive, though; average people in Shanghai cannot afford them. If you drive by at nighttime, you will see a lot of the windows are dark. But somehow they keep springing up like bamboo shoots in springtime. As you will learn, a lot of things happening in China cannot be explained by logic," Mr. Chan said with regret, the mild glow of his pride seconds ago now extinguished.

"If average people are priced out of the market, where do they live? I believe there are at least twenty million people in the city?"

"My generation is lucky; we were able to secure some housing back in the nineties. Although old apartments like ours are very small, the prices back then were more reasonable. My wife and I both worked, so we could manage. My son's generation, it's a different story. We paid his college education, and he now has a decent job, but with the sky-high real estate market, we've calculated that he'd have to work thirty years before he could afford the fifteen to twenty percent down payment on an eighty-square-meter apartment, a little over seven hundred square feet in America. So many young people—well, some of them are not that young; my son is almost thirty years old—but they can only afford to stay with their parents these days, even if they have decent-paying jobs." Mr. Chan sighed.

"But it doesn't make sense," Lu said, questioning Mr. Chan's illogical explanation. "If people with decent-paying jobs have to work thirty years to save enough for a down payment on a small apartment, either the real estate market is just a bubble, or the jobs they hold are only paying slave wages."

With a sly smile, Mr. Chan said, "You bring up a good point, but as I said, certain things in China cannot be explained by logic. You will see it yourself if you stay here for a while."

Based on her cultural background and research before the trip, Lu had suspected that, on some levels, China's much-touted rapid economic development and growth could have encrusted the country in a layer of golden veneer—beautiful to look at, but if one scratched the surface, what lay underneath was not all pretty. "So what's the market price of a little apartment like you've mentioned?" she asked with the instinct of the businesswoman she was.

"About two hundred thousand to half a million dollars depending on location."

"Chinese dollars?"

"No, American dollars."

"If I may, what is considered a decent salary for an average person in Shanghai?"

"About ten to fifteen thousand."

"A month?"

"No, a year, in American dollars also."

The numbers were shocking and totally unexpected, piquing Lu's interest to a curiously high level. She was keen to continue the discussion, but the Audi suddenly veered right, toward an exit from the modern elevated Yan'an expressway to the old Yan'an Road beneath. One of the multiple exit signs indicated Hilton Hotel. In a few seconds, the Audi turned onto the intersecting Huashan Road and slid into the circular driveway in front of the forty-two-story Shanghai Hilton.

Her breathing irregular and her heart thumping violently, Lu stepped out of the car. She realized instantly that she was standing on the same ground that used to house a three-story government building, where the Red Guards and mob's shouting and yelling at the kneeling capitalists and counterrevolutionaries, like her father and grandma, could be heard in her home, the art deco apartment building a block away. She looked across the street. The familiar rows of sand-colored stucco houses she used to walk by on her way to grade school were visible. She'd always loved those quaint-looking houses with pointed roofs and arched front doors.

"Welcome to Hilton." A young man rushed down the steps in front of the hotel to greet her. He was wearing a red uniform that reminded her of a cross between a nutcracker and a guard in front of the Buckingham Palace.

"Ms. Li, check in and rest. I know you are tired, but try to stay up until it's regular bedtime. It will make the ooziness of the twelve-hour jet lag go away faster. I will pick you up around nine tomorrow morning in the lobby," Mr. Chan said, his voice drifting from the other side of the car.

"I don't want to trouble you, Mr. Chan. I can grab a cab to your office on my own; I have the address."

"No trouble. My house is not far from here. I will see you tomorrow."

Mr. Chan waved and lowered himself into the car before Lu could utter a few words of appreciation.

• • •

OPENING THE DOOR TO her room on the thirty-eighth floor, Lu was greeted by a wall-to-wall and floor-to-ceiling window, fanning out like a 180-degree semicircle. The lady at the front desk had said something during check-in about her room having a panoramic view. The real thing in front of her certainly lived up to the name. She dropped her Tumi roller case and duffel bag at the door and proceeded to the views the window had to offer.

The window was almost directly above the circular pedestrian overpass at the intersection of the Yan'an expressway and Huashan Road. She cast her eyes straight ahead, across the expressway. About a block away was the famous Jing'an Temple, which meant Temple of Peace and Quiet in English. Lu had been there many times with her grandma when she was just a little girl. She still remembered the pungent smell of the burning incense and the solemn chanting of the bright-yellow-robed monks. Back then, it had been a small Buddhist temple. From the front, it looked like a miniature Tiananmen Gate from Tiananmen Square in Beijing, with a gold-tiled pagoda-like roof and burgundy facade. But the temple in front of her seemed to have multiplied. Several structures similar to the original but varied in size had been erected behind the almost eight-hundred-year-old temple, taking up an entire block once densely filled by local open-air food markets, restaurants, and shops. *The Jing'an Temple should be called Jing'an Temples,* she thought as she surveyed the towering glass, concrete, and metal structures around, casting noisy shadows over the Temple of Peace and Quiet, making its pollution-dulled gold roofs even duller.

"Temple in metropolis," she murmured.

From the temple, her eyes traveled along Huashan Road back to the pedestrian overpass right beneath the hotel. She mentally mapped spots with sights and scenes that now existed only in her childhood memory. At the corner on the other side of the expressway, a small patch of green made her eyes linger. In the middle of the green, a few sad-looking weeping willows hunched around a tiny body of water. It was the park, the temple's namesake, where she used to follow the chirp of crickets in autumn until she caught a few and brought them home in a paper box. But unlike the enlarged Jing'an Temple, Jing'an Park had been eaten into a mere remnant; its once-expansive green, with stately French-plane-tree-lined walkways that had stretched over several street blocks, had been concreted over by designer stores ever-present in the modern commercial world.

Lamentingly, she scanned across the tiny green patch to the view beyond the right side of the panoramic window. It was late afternoon, and the traffic had picked up. Cars inched in slow motion eastward on the elevated Yan'an expressway. The haze seemed to have thinned slightly, affording her a longer range of visibility. She turned to face the right side of the window and looked down. To her surprise, the sand-colored stucco houses she had visually reacquainted a minute ago were not the only ones that had survived the invasion of skyscrapers. Behind them, century-old Western-style row houses crouched low and sprawled more than half a block eastward, parallel to the hovering Yan'an expressway, until they converged with a narrow strip of construction debris. Her eyes stretched farther ahead. On the other side of the rubble, a lone small building came into view. Its once-light-gray exterior had taken on a blackened hue, but its art deco form, with rounded corners and curved balconies, was instantly recognizable.

For weeks, she had imagined this moment, the moment she returned to see the building she once had called home. She had imagined how the moment would unfold: she would be walking down Yan'an Road, getting glimpses of the building at first from a block away. As she got closer, the building would come into full view, until she could see the stacked balconies that rounded one corner of the building. She'd had no clue how she would feel emotionally at that moment, but she'd thought of an old Chinese saying that might describe her would-be mental state: she'd thought it would be like mixing bitter with sugar, vinegar, and chili pepper.

But the visual she had played in her mind so many times was instead a sudden aerial view from the thirty-eighth floor of the Hilton Hotel. And the mixed emotions she had anticipated were not that mixed after all. There was only a deep sense of loss and the feeling that it was better to let the past stay in the past.

"The same blood runs through you; it's your family, your mom and sister," Sage had told her upon hearing Lu's almost-truthful account of her estranged relationship with her mother and sister for the first time, during their recent late-night girl talk in Sage's apartment.

The kind of friendship Lu had formed with Sage was the kind where she could talk to Sage just about anything in her life, past and present. But she had kept her nonexistent relationship with her mother and sister to herself. Whenever the mother subject came up, which was not very often, Lu found herself using the words *infrequent communication* to cover the haven't-heard-from-them-for-decades reality. She'd convinced herself that there was no reason to dwell on a puzzle for which she had racked her brain but could not solve.

But then, faced with the hard-to-refuse work requirement, she'd confessed to Sage the nonexistent relationship with her mother and sister and the dilemma she was in, whether to contact them or not when she arrived in Shanghai.

"Oh my God." Sage had been shocked by the revelation. "No matter what, they are family; they are forever when everything else in the world can come and go. Whatever happened in the past most likely was because of the circumstances at the time. We are all capable of being disappointing once in a while, but you always love your family. After all, you have only one sister. I always wished I had one. Think of all the fun, girlie things you can do together."

Sage's argument had not been convincing, for Lu was keenly aware of the black-and-white difference in their backgrounds and upbringings. But Sage's love for her family was contagious and had reminded her of what her grandma once had said about the bond between siblings: it was like that between one's hands and feet; if you severed one limb, the entire body would be off balance.

During her journey across the Pacific Ocean, Lu had managed to hold on to the kindred feeling invoked by her grandma's wisdom and Sage's family values. Now, overlooking her childhood apartment building from a hotel room a block away, she realized she was not ready to go in, to face the past.

The telephone on the desk behind her rang. She picked it up. Dick, sounding self-assured and wide-awake, said, "Hey, have you checked in yet? I'm sitting on the top floor of the hotel here, having a drink. If it weren't for the smog, the view would be spectacular. Maybe you should come over for dinner this evening, and we can talk a little about tomorrow's meeting and then enjoy the view."

Lu was actually grateful for Dick's phone call and invitation. She now could put off thinking about the visit she would be making a block away. But it did not mean she could not walk around her old neighborhood by herself before dark. So she suggested, "We do need to touch base for tomorrow's meeting, but if you don't mind, can you come over to the Hilton here? It'll give you an opportunity to see what the former French Concession in Shanghai looks like and gives me a bit more time to unpack and get ready."

"Okay, I can do that. See you around seven then?" Dick pleasantly agreed. Being his first time in Shanghai, he was enthusiastic to see everything he could during the short stay.

Lu clicked off the phone and glanced out the window one more time. *I'll figure out a good time to visit when all the meeting appointments are firmed up tomorrow,* she thought, justifying her procrastination to herself, and went about unpacking her luggage.

CHAPTER 9

· · · · ·

THE NEXT DAY, WHILE Lu was conducting her first round of meetings on the top floor of a glass skyscraper overlooking the Bund, Shanghai's waterfront, her mother, Mrs. Lin, spent the day packing in the two-bedroom apartment on the fourth floor of the old art deco building on 42 Yan'an Road. Soon she would be moving into one of the most prestigious apartments in Shanghai's most prestigious and sought-after areas, in the heart of the old French Concession.

The government had ordered her apartment building torn down to allow for expansion around the Yan'an elevated expressway. She would leave everything except for clothing, jewelry, and personal effects behind. Her new apartment would be furnished with brand-new furniture in the style to her liking and equipped with the most-modern appliances. She did not need to bring a single piece of old furniture that would only remind her of the life she had wasted. As far as she was concerned, it was about time they vanished together with the soon-to-be-torn-down building.

She was in her early seventies and physically well preserved. Her body, free of age-related bulges and bumps, was clothed in a black fitted turtleneck and a pair of loose-fitting black silk pants. Her once-raven-black hair had turned silver gray. Cut short, it was meticulously set in a bob with high volume on top and tapered at the sides and back of her head. Age had etched fine lines on her face but left its structure more or less intact. Her regal cheekbones, almond-shaped eyes, and delicate eyebrows, all features of classic Chinese beauty, were still evident. The only noticeable change was her mouth. The once-cherry-shaped lips had thinned considerably, adding a touch of harshness to her otherwise still elegant face.

Mrs. Lin was in an unusually good mood that day. Overnight, bursts of spring breeze had blown away the choking smog and brought back a milky-blue sky. She had cranked all the windows in the apartment open, letting in the warmth of spring and the fragrance from the magnolia trees around the building.

She moved unhurriedly from room to room, collecting clothing from closets and drawers in the bedrooms and sorting through them in the living/dining room, where several cardboard boxes had been filled and taped, ready for the upcoming big move in a few days.

Midday came, and she decided to take a short rest to drink a cup of tea and eat a piece of fruit. She would move on to sorting out family photos and jewelry in the afternoon.

In the kitchen, she boiled some bottled springwater and poured the hot water into a small jade teapot with the jasmine tea leaves she had deposited in there earlier in the morning. She put the teapot and a matching teacup on a rosewood tray, added a plate of mixed fruit from the refrigerator, and returned to the fan-shaped living room with a view of the skyline of the waterfront in the distance. At the dining table, she poured a cup of tea and set it next to the fruit plate. Waiting for the steaming hot tea to cool slightly, she sat down and looked out the window. A faint smile softened her pursed lips as her eyes leaped toward the silhouettes of the tall buildings lining the far-away horizon, as if acknowledging that destiny was finally smiling on her, though belatedly. She would soon be living in a place matching the status she deserved, envied by everyone who knew her.

She was the only daughter of the last foreign minister of China's Nationalist government, before it had been defeated by the Communist Party and banished to the little island of Taiwan to the south of Mainland China. She had been raised in luxury fit only for a princess of princesses but groomed according to etiquette and decorum designed for a top-notch diplomat's wife. She had been expected to possess supreme grace, sophisticated style, and persuasive charm, capable of influencing the outcomes of negotiations of treaties with foreign dignitaries to her country's favor by raising glasses at cocktail parties and waltzing at lavish state balls. At the age of five, when she had still been learning her native tongue, a British governess had incorporated English lessons into her daily routine. When she had been eight, she had been conversant in the hauteur vocabularies of French cuisine. Then as a young lady of fifteen years of age, she had routinely attended diplomatic banquets and balls hosted by her father, the foreign minister of China. On those stately occasions, she'd stood demurely by her parents' side, greeting a long line of politicians and foreign dignitaries dressed in gowns made of Chinese satin, Italian silk, and French lace, fabrics that had aroused her feeling of luster, opulence, and female sensuality. She had been sure that her life was destined for nothing short of luxury, fame, and glamor.

But the life she had been accustomed to had ended abruptly. First her mother had been killed in a car accident, on her way to a cocktail party at a foreign embassy on a stormy evening. Six months later, in the fall of 1949, on the eve of the National government's total defeat by Mao's Communist Red Army, her father had fled to Taiwan in fear of being persecuted and executed. Before leaving the country, he'd sent her to live with a remote relative in Shanghai. "It's temporary, Xingxing," he'd said, using her nickname for her first name, Xing, which meant "star." "The Americans will help us to defeat the Communist Party. Daddy will be back in no time."

But she had never seen her father again. Shortly after fleeing to Taiwan, Mr. Lin had developed an illness, of which the cause could only be described as deep regret for leaving his daughter on the mainland and the hopelessness of never being able to see her again. After languishing for a few years, he'd died one night in a hospital bed, alone.

After a few moments of gazing at her invisible new dwelling somewhere in the distance, Mrs. Lin decided the jasmine tea had cooled to an appropriate temperature. She took a sip. At that exact moment, a warm spring breeze drifted in, infusing the air around her with subtle jasmine fragrance. For her, it was a scent of the glorious past, for jasmine tea was the customary tea her mother would have served to her lady guests in the stately residence of the noble and famed foreign minister of China. It was in that mood of nostalgia that Mrs. Lin sat and drank her tea while scanning the photos affixed on the wall and displayed on the rosewood credenza in the room.

Many of the pictures were yellow and faded. They were formal portraits of her family, her father always in a Western suit, her mother mostly dressed in the traditional Chinese *qipao*, a long, form-fitting dress with high mandarin collar and midthigh-high slits on both sides. She herself was always in the middle, held by her parents when she was a baby and standing or sitting in between her parents as a girl and young lady. Here and there a few photos in vivid color were mixed in with the old family pictures, including wedding pictures of her younger daughter and son-in-law and photos of them standing in front of world-famous landmarks like the London Bridge, the Statute of Liberty, and the Eiffel Tower. Then there was the one black-and-white photo at the far end of the credenza. It was a picture of herself and her late husband and their one-year-old daughter Lu. It had been taken at a time when she had been addressed as Mrs. Li by her friends and neighbors yet had still been Xing Ling at work and on her Shanghai residency papers.

She had never taken her husband's surname after the wedding. To everybody around her, she had merely conformed to a social custom commonly observed by most Chinese women. But in her heart's secret compartment, it had been a decision of her own volition, for she never had considered her husband's family name, Li, good enough for her pedigree breeding and superior upbringing.

After her father's sudden departure, she had gone to live with a remote relative in Shanghai's French Concession area. Time had seemed to inch forward while she waited for her father's return. Days, weeks, then months crept by. She did not hear from her father—no letters, not even a postcard. She began to worry. Soon worry turned into disappointment, and disappointment turned into resentment and even hatred for everything around her. It took her a while to address the relative and his wife as uncle and aunt. She considered them boring people who taught middle school during the day and sat at home reading or making small talk with each other every evening. No parties or even small get-togethers. She disliked their cooking, bland with ingredients fit only for poor peasants. She detested the high school she was forced to attend, for the brassy Shanghai dialect her classmates spoke often escaped her and left her with a headache if she listened to them for a prolonged period of time. She became withdrawn and depressed and often locked herself in her little bedroom for hours at a time, lamenting over the miserable conditions she was in, pitying herself for the princess life she so deserved but that had now slipped away from her forever.

It was not until a year later, when she graduated from high school, that she finally gave up the last bit of hope that her father would ever come back for her. She could point out on a map where the small island of Taiwan was but was fully aware she would never be able to go there. Somebody like her father was an enemy of the Chinese people, according to the Communist government propaganda. He was forever banished from the country and would be annihilated in the near future. Her adopted uncle and aunt had instructed her to keep quiet about her father. "Just say your father passed away when you were a baby, and don't talk about what he was and did if anyone asks. It's for your own good," they told her, in their attempt to protect her.

She finally resigned herself to fate. The dream of Xing Lin, once the daughter of China's foreign minister, was blown away by the Communist tempest sweeping through the country. The young lady groomed for no ordinary life, fluent in English and French, with impeccable decorum and etiquette, was assigned a mediocre job as a hospital administrator after high school, checking patients in and out at an emergency room. She got up at dawn, what she used to consider as an ungodly hour, elbowed her way onto the smelly old trolley bus that took her from the west to the east side of the city, sat at the emergency check-in window for nine hours in a yellow uniform that was supposed to be white, and then fought her way back to her little room on the west side at dusk.

Yet amid the ever-present feeling of hopelessness, a deep-rooted sense of superiority she had developed since early age sustained her. It had something to do with her breeding, her upbringing, the blood coursing through her. Nothing could take that away. And people around her took notice. Words like *elegant, graceful, dignified, poised,* and *exquisite* were often used to describe her, the young clerk at the emergency window. Male colleagues often found themselves lingering around the area she worked, hoping to be noticed by her. But they were lucky if she bothered to cast a cold and dismissive look at them.

As she progressed into her midtwenties, the number of young men who crowded her workstation dwindled significantly—not because they no longer desired her, but because they realized their efforts were like trying to touch the beautiful moon by reaching for its reflection in the water. She was not touchable. Most of them gave up and married women who considered their blood less noble. She began to feel the sting of social stigma delivered with falsely sincere advice: "How old are you now? Aren't you setting your standards a tad high? Don't wait too long; you don't want to end up a spinster or too old to have kids." But she held on, refusing to consider proposals and fix-ups she thought to be beneath her social standing.

Then she met Dr. Pei Li, a surgeon in his thirties who had received his entire medical training in the United States but had returned to China right around when the Communist government had taken control of the country. She and a coworker happened to sit down at the same table in the hospital cafeteria where Dr. Li was lunching with the head of the surgical department. It was his first day at the hospital after being transferred there from a smaller hospital in Shanghai. After they said hello, she quietly inspected the doctor from across the table. He was wearing a standard doctor's coat, brand new and gleaming white, making his naturally dark skin appear darker.

The skin tone of a peasant working in the rice field rather than a respected surgeon performing delicate operations in the largest hospital in Shanghai, she'd thought regretfully. From the way he'd filled the coat, she'd judged that he was at most an average-sized man, and she could only describe his appearance the same, average and forgettable.

After that day, she indeed had forgotten about the doctor quickly. And she should have left it that way.

Mrs. Lin took her last sip of tea and started to take down those photos. One picture frame at a time, she dusted and wiped the framed photos with a felt cloth, wrapped them with paper tissues, and packed them in separate boxes according to chronology—her childhood pictures with her parents in one box, the ones of her younger daughter and son-in-law in another. She performed this task peacefully, her good mood sustained by the wafts of spring breeze blowing in continuously from the waterfront, until she reached and grabbed the last photo on the credenza, the photo of herself, her late husband, and baby Lu.

Her first thought was the picture could stay in a box forever from now on. She would be saying good-bye to her long-time neighbors in the building soon, and it would not make any difference to her new neighbors at her new apartment building whether she continued to display the picture. They had never met her late husband and did not know of her elder daughter's existence. She had only kept the picture in a noticeable place for all these years to maintain her image as a grieving widow who had stayed faithful to her late husband by never marrying again. She would not have to worry about that image anymore.

Pondering over a good place to leave the picture permanently, her eyes lingered on it a few seconds more than she was willing. Her husband and daughter both smiled at her, but they were the kinds of smile that chilled the warm and cheery mood she had been in all day. She felt ill at ease, like being caught naked in broad daylight. She wanted to look away, but Lu's dark eyes commanded her attention that day. She was surprised to see for the first time how her daughter's eyes resembled her own. But even at only one year old and in a black-and-white photo, Lu's skin tone was clearly dark, unlike the flawless porcelain-white skin she herself had possessed at that time. It was her husband's skin shade, a shade that reminded her of the lowly peasants working on rice paddies and a shade that had made her already-dark living darker on the day Lu had been born.

• • •

IT WAS 1961, ON an oppressively hot day in July. Weeks of constant rain mixed with one-hundred-degree heat had left yellow mildew in every nook and corner of Shanghai, where the sun did not shine directly.

Xing Lin, more than nine months pregnant, was lying in a non-air-conditioned hospital ward with several other women, all like her, waiting to give birth at any minute. The ever-closer waves of contraction pained her, but she did her best to refrain from groaning and grunting like her fellow mothers-in-waiting. It was degrading enough to be lying in a hospital room of such pathetic condition; she was determined to preserve the few shreds of dignity she still possessed after this long and undignified process of pregnancy. It was a torturous and sleepless night. The air was stagnant, and the heat of the night was thick and heavy, enfolding her like a wet, hot blanket.

As dawn approached, her contractions curiously lessened. There was slight movement in the air. She succumbed to exhaustion and drifted into a semiconscious state.

A cold but refreshing sensation revived her; it was like cool rivulets trickling over her feverishly hot face. She exerted her eyes on the figure bending over her, dabbing her face with an ice-cold wash towel. It looked like a doctor, in a white jacket, but the head was covered in a pale-blue hat, the kind of hat surgeons put on before they went into the operating room. She found the touch and mannerism of the figure standing by her bedside as welcoming and comforting as the cooling towel grazing her face. She murmured, "Thank you."

"How are you feeling?" he asked.

She realized it was her husband's voice. He must have completed the minor surgery he'd had scheduled for this morning and come to check on her. She remembered what he'd told her the previous evening when she had checked into the hospital's gynecological and obstetrical ward. He had cleared his calendar for the rest of the day to be with her.

"It's hellishly hot and stuffy here. Are you sure the baby is coming today? I don't feel as much pain now. Maybe it was a false alarm. I'd rather go home and come back later when I am ready," she said quietly and then felt herself drifting away.

A wave of sharp pain shocked her back into consciousness. She heard herself scream. She felt her husband's arm wrap around her contorted body. "What's wrong? Can you tell me what's wrong?" he whispered.

Then everything was black again.

When she opened her eyes again, she was lying on a birthing table under intense operating-room lighting. Her body was in immense pain, but her brain was lucid enough to loathe her life, a life she did not seem to be able to control. She had no love for the man she'd married, had only gone ahead and married him for fear she would forever be laughed at as an old spinster nobody wanted. Though she loved to be admired for her beauty and elegance by the opposite gender, sex repulsed her, and motherhood was not her natural propensity, yet she had let herself become pregnant because being gossiped about as a barren and infertile wife was potentially more dreadful. Not a single fiber in her body had developed the slightest maternal instinct toward what had been living inside her for more than nine months, yet soon she would be burdened by the overwhelming responsibilities of being a mother.

She heard the obstetrician say something about a breech baby, and then he told the nurse to prepare for a cesarean. They must have administered a heavy dose of sedative. She felt somewhat relieved. The baby could die, or she herself could die. If either or both happened, it would be okay with her. She closed her eyes, fully prepared to submit herself to fate.

Moments later, she heard someone say, "Here we go."

The baby must be out, she thought, *but it's not crying.* She kept her eyes closed, but she could hear the conversations around her.

"I am sorry, Dr. Li. It was a girl. She didn't make it, but your wife will be okay," the obstetrician said.

"I'm sorry, Dr. Li. I think she was gone before we took her out. Breech babies often die of lack of oxygen," a nurse said.

"Anybody checked her over yet?" It was her husband's voice. "May I have a towel or something so I can clean her up?"

"The baby is dead, Dr. Li. Look at the poor little creature. She might as well be a blue baby," the obstetrician said.

"A blue baby, a blue baby," her husband murmured, his voice trembling. She struggled to open her eyes. Her husband flipped the baby upside down, holding her by both ankles, and patted her bottom a couple of times.

Nothing happened.

He repeated the action a couple of times.

There was a single faint gurgling sound.

He gave the baby's buttock a few more spanks.

Suddenly, a loud cry followed. It was Lu's cry, at the top of her lungs.

• • •

In her soon-to-be-torn-down apartment, Mrs. Lin looked away from the picture she was holding, away from the gaze of her daughter's large, dark eyes. Just as she had on that day in the hospital, after seeing her daughter for the first time, she closed her eyes. She could still feel the pain and despair that had filled her entire being on that day, the day she'd realized her childhood life, the life she had dreamed of living, had forever slipped away.

She opened her eyes at the telephone ringing from the hallway. She left the picture on the credenza and hurried to answer the phone.

"Mama, how is the packing going?" her younger daughter, Mei, asked. Her voice was girlish and high-pitched, a voice like the chime of a silver bell, seasoned with slight breathiness to affect feminine vulnerability. It was a voice many Chinese men found irresistible.

"Coming along, coming along," she said.

"Don't overdo it, Mama; leave the big things to the movers. Juin and I will be back in a few days to help."

"Where are you now? Are you having fun?"

"We're in Paris. Spring is beautiful here, Mama. You should come with us next time."

"Mama is too old to make long trips like that. Maybe after I settle in at the new apartment, I will take a short trip with you."

"Okay. I've got to go. Juin and I are going to dinner now. We are meeting someone Juin said is good for his business. I will see you in a few days."

"All right. Remember—be nice; a pleasant and gracious wife can do wonders for her husband's career and business," she reminded hurriedly before Mei hung up.

Mrs. Lin went back to her task at the credenza in the living room. Mei's call had fully restored the cheerfulness she had been feeling earlier that day.

When she'd found out she was pregnant with Mei, more than a decade had passed since her first daughter, Lu, had been born. The thought of enduring another difficult pregnancy and labor had made her wince. She'd considered abortion at first. But to her surprise, she had not experienced the nausea and dizziness that had plagued her the first time around. Months had gone by, and she had not been overwhelmed by the gloom and sadness that had crippled her during the first pregnancy. She'd considered the gentle pregnancy a lucky sign. As the fetus had grown inside her, so had her realization of being a mother again, the realization that this baby would truly be hers, raised, influenced, and molded by her. It would grow up exactly the way she wanted it to grow up. She alone would have to shoulder the burden of raising the child, but she would find a way to manage.

She had been right; Mei had brought nothing but good luck and now good fortune. Mrs. Lin sighed softly and dropped the black-and-white photo in the box that contained other items she had decided would be stored away forever.

A knock at the door startled her, as she was not expecting any visitors that afternoon. It could be the next-door neighbor, she thought, checking on her, the old lady living alone, to see if she needed any help getting ready for the big move.

"Coming, coming," she said as she headed toward the front door, her voice at a higher pitch than normal. She unlocked the dead bolt, slid the security chain off its track, and twisted the doorknob.

The light from the slanting afternoon sunshine inside the apartment made it difficult for her to see clearly the person standing in the dimly lit hallway.

"Yes?" she asked quizzically, straining her eyes to get a good look of the visitor.

For an instant, the person at the door remained silent and motionless. The person's general features appeared unfamiliar, except for the eyes. Those were the eyes that gazed at her in the mirror every day, the almond shape, the upward slant at the outer corners, the liquid-like sheen.

"Lu? Is that you?" she asked in a voice inaudible to her own ears.

"Yes, Mother, it's me."

CHAPTER 10

• • • • •

IT WAS A FRIDAY afternoon in June. The sun sprinkled its dazzling particles from above the blue sky, infusing the air with a hint of the fragrance that promised the heat and fervor of summer ahead.

Inside the pub in Alexandria, Virginia, high summer had already arrived. The clinks of glasses were constant, vibrating cheerfully through the air thick with assorted scents of beer and warmed by the body heat of a noisy and enthusiastic crowd. Will Donovan and his headquarters staff were having a party, celebrating their company's successful merger with Matrixtech, of which they were now officially executives, employees, major stockholders, or minor stakeholders. No matter what, everybody had come out with either a thicker wallet or a promotion or both.

Will, his team, and a few close friends occupied just about every inch of the cozy pub. Joe, the owner, had removed a few tables temporarily to accommodate more standing space for the crowd. After his speech of no more than two minutes, expressing his gratitude for his employees' hard work and toasting to an even brighter future, Will nudged his way through the crowd to his usual table at the window, where Frank and Kevin were sitting. With them at the table was a man in his forties, dressed in a salmon-colored polo shirt and khaki pants. His muddy-blond hair had a clean-cut but highly styled look, long and fluffy on top and short and tapered at the back and sides. He had a complexion almost the same color of his shirt. It was hard to tell if it was due to natural sun exposure or to sunshine in a tube. If you wrapped a pastel-green or blue sweater around his neck, he would be a middle-aged man with the perfect prep-boy look.

"Hey, Will, allow me to introduce Congressman Kessler. He was in the area today, so I invited him to stop by," Kevin said cheerfully.

Will hardly had time to extend his hand before the congressman greeted him with the charm and enthusiasm of a politician on a campaign trail surrounded by supporters and numerous cameras. "Ah, Will, congratulations on the merger. Kevin's told me a lot about you. Glad we finally meet." He shook Will's hand violently.

"Glad you could stop by, Congressman," Will said courteously, casting a mildly surprised glance at Kevin, who responded with a slight shoulder shrug.

"Oh please, call me Rob. Kevin and I have known each other since high school. I was just telling him that I am so proud of him, a successful business executive, while I am just a politician without any particular skills. At least that's what people say about somebody like me these days," Congressman Kessler said in a seemingly self-deprecating tone.

Detecting a slight awkwardness on Will's part, Kevin cut in and said, "Will, Rob is currently sitting on the House Committee on Homeland Security. He has traveled extensively to foreign countries, working on technology and cybersecurity issues, issues that could have impact on our federal network-systems business."

"Well, I think cybersecurity is important to any kind of business these days, and understanding where the threat is coming from is critical in winning the constant cat-and-mouse game of the cyber world. Any advice or guidance, technically or legislatively, would be greatly appreciated," Will said matter-of-factly.

"Agreed—we all have to work hard and stay a step ahead all the time. As I have told Kevin, you guys, don't hesitate to contact my office if you think I might be of any help to your business. After all, it's my job, being the representative of the great Commonwealth of Virginia," the congressman said with enthusiasm and then quickly checked his wristwatch. "I'd better get going—don't want to take too much of your time, just stopping by to offer my congratulations."

Will waited until he could see the congressman outside the window and then turned to Kevin and asked, "What's this all about? You didn't tell me he was stopping by."

"Sorry, boss, it was a last-minute thing. He texted me saying he was in the area, so I invited him to stop by. No harm done, I hope. You don't have to like him, but trust me—he could be useful to our business with his position in Congress," Kevin answered, a bit defensively.

"I don't dislike him. I just don't like to be surprised like this." Will's tone softened a bit. "Not that I don't trust you, Kevin. I just can't help being a bit cynical and suspicious when it comes to politicians."

"This Rob guy is quite slick," Frank, who had been drinking beer quietly the whole time, chimed in.

"Cut it out, Frank." Kevin threw Frank a reproachful look. "I know politicians are not a likable species, but in our line of business, they are a necessary evil. They could potentially give us a leg up against our competitors or help with our decision making." Looking at Will smugly, he continued, "You almost wanted to consult with the congressman regarding the potential Chinese buyout of Matrixtech. Luckily, it's not an issue for us anymore, but remember things like this could happen again, and you'll all be glad we have ties to someone like Rob."

Not wanting to spoil everybody's celebratory mood, Will said quietly to Kevin, "I know, I know; you have rested your case. Now let's forget about the business and politics for a while, go get another drink, and mingle with the staff. After all, it's as much a big day for them as it is for us."

Frank jumped on Will's suggestion in a hurry, probably feeling uncomfortable with Kevin's argumentative attitude. "Okay, boss, time for another beer." He left Kevin and Will and elbowed his way toward the bar.

After Frank was reasonably out of hearing distance, Kevin said to Will, his tone softened considerably, "Sorry, boss, got a little excited there, but you know I have the best interests of the company in mind."

"I know, Kevin, but this is not our company anymore; we are now part of Matrixtech, a much larger, publicly owned company. The decision-making process may not be as simple as back in the days when it was just you and me, shooting from the hip just to get our business off the ground. You may want to make sure people around you are on the same page or at least informed about whatever you will be doing. Remember you are not working with me on a day-to-day basis anymore."

Staring into the beer mug in his hand, Kevin said, as if to himself, "That might be the case with you; now you are on the senior-management team of Matrixtech. But for me, I am still the guy in charge of our old federal network-system-maintenance business. It might not be as glamorous or cutting-edge as your new endeavors, but it's part of the reason Matrixtech bought us. I have run this business for over a decade, and I'm pretty damn good at it. I'm not about to change my style and play politics simply because our company has a new name."

Kevin's internal-monologue-like speech might have seemed strange to people who did not know him well, but Will was used to Kevin speaking this way whenever confronted with tough issues, usually work related. It was Kevin's way of thinking possible solutions out loud, expressing his defiance against anything that dared to prevent him from doing a perfect job. But what Kevin had said this time hit Will differently. Kevin's defiance was not directed at an operational problem but at his own fear of some kind of failure. Concerned, Will asked, "Is everything okay, Kevin? You're not stressed out about something, are you?"

"Of course everything is okay." Kevin diverted his eyes away from the beer mug and looked at Will. "Why wouldn't I be okay? I am the boss of Matrixtech's Federal Network Systems Division—more responsibility for sure to make it bigger, but I can't complain about the stock options and generous pay raise. Wife is happy; kids get to go to private school; life is good. Congratulations, boss, here's to us!" He clinked his glass against Will's and slapped Will's shoulder. "Let's go and get another beer." He turned around and headed toward the bar.

Watching Kevin disappear into the crowd at the bar, Will smiled and shook his head. Kevin would forever be Kevin, unpredictable yet dependable, confident yet at times insecure, gregarious as a colleague yet autocratic as a manager. But Kevin had been there for him from day one, a fearless risk taker, pounding the pavement and holding out the tin cup 24-7 to get the first contract. It was undeniable that without Kevin, Will Donovan would not be where he was that day. But what Kevin had said that day was worrisome to Will. Maybe Kevin had had a few more beers than usual, but under the cheerfulness of his congratulatory words lurked self-doubt and fear. It was as if all the successes he had achieved so far in life—having a well-established career and being a devoted father and a loving husband—were burdening him and preventing him from walking tall.

Will thought of Kevin's resistance not long ago when first learning of the plan to merge with Matrixtech, of the unexpected anger Kevin had exhibited when he'd thought the Chinese might take over Matrixtech and therefore the federal network-systems business Kevin knew could so easily be spun off or sold. All these were signs to Will that Kevin, close to fifty years old, with a stay-at-home wife and three young kids, a mortgage, and future college tuition costs, was duty-bound as a husband and father. Network-system maintenance was what he knew and what he did well, and working for Will's small company in the premerger environment was what he felt familiar and comfortable with. He was not willing or did not think he could afford to be the risk taker he used to be. Somehow Will could see a bit of his own father in Kevin, or was it the other way around?

"Hey, what are you thinking? Didn't you see me passing right outside the window? It sure is crowded here," Sage said.

Will had been so engrossed in his thoughts about Kevin he had not realized Sage had walked past the window and waved at him from outside on her way into the pub. Now she was standing in front of him, in blue jeans and a light-green long-sleeve shirt that matched the color of her eyes.

"Hey, Sis, glad you are not in your banker's outfit today. It wouldn't have fit in with the crowd here today." Will grinned.

"Well, I simply followed the dress code of your celebration party: jackets and ties not allowed," Sage said while looking in the direction of the bar. The crowd had thinned a bit. She could see Joe busy slinging beer mugs to people sitting around the bar counter. Then he looked her direction, and a beaming smile flashed across his ruddy face. "Coming right up," his baritone voice boomed at her.

"So how's it going so far?" Sage sat down, scanning the room.

"Everybody is having a good time, though some of the young staff have left. It's Friday night, date night for them."

"Where's Kevin and Frank? I haven't seen them for a while; hope to say hello." Sage studied the crowd, searching for familiar faces. It did not take her long to spot Frank's conspicuous platinum-blond hair. He was standing in the corner across the room, in his usual dark sweatshirt and jeans, busy talking to a circle of four or five people.

"There's Frank," Sage said, nodding in his direction. "I can see everybody must be happy about the merger. Even Frank, didn't you say he usually doesn't like chitchat too much? He looks like he's having fun, talking to several people. I don't see Kevin, though. Did he come?"

"Oh, he was here earlier. I don't know if he's left. It was very crowded for a while, hard to track who was coming and who was going," Will said casually. He looked around, but Kevin was nowhere to be found.

"I'll go say hello to Frank and get my drink; be right back." Sage stood, about to hasten away.

"Okay, so I don't forget, remind me to tell you later about Kevin's politician friend who paid me a surprise visit today," Will said, suddenly remembering Sage and Lu once had worked for Congressman Kessler's uncle. As much as he was suspicious of politicians and a little perturbed that Kevin had surprised him by bringing Rob Kessler to the party without any prior notice, he had to admit that Kevin was right; a congressman sitting on the House Committee on Homeland Security was a worthwhile contact, for the sake of the business they were in. But Will wanted to find out a little more about the congressman's background.

Sage stopped in her track. She whirled around, her soft and easygoing eyes suddenly intense. "What politician?"

"Rob Kessler, the nephew of your old boss—what's his first name?"

"You mean the honorable Earl Kessler who cheated investors for millions and millions of dollars and then ran the company into the ground?" Sage asked. Her voice, though controlled, blared mockery and derision.

"I guess that's the one. Boy, you're scary, Sage. I've never seen you hate somebody that much."

Sage reddened. She lowered her voice, but her words hissed and seethed through her teeth. "That's because he is the biggest lowlife scum I've ever known. Just think, for a while I looked up to him as a selfless god, endeavoring to rid mankind of the disease of illiteracy. Then I found the only thing he was endeavoring for was to squander away company money to rub shoulders with the rich, powerful, and famous and to pad his own bank account, all in the name of the noble cause of educating the poor and disadvantaged."

"Okay, okay, I got it. I don't mean to get you upset. Why don't you sit down, and I'll get your drink? Then I'll tell you about his nephew," Will said coolly. Then with perfect timing, Joe brought Sage her martini and Will another frothy Hefeweizen.

"Sorry, guys, don't mean to neglect you, but it's been quite busy—thanks to you, Will. I was afraid I was going to run out of beer," Joe said with his famous ear-to-ear smile. Noticing the now-fading flush on Sage's face, he continued casually, "Hey, Sage, haven't seen you for a while. How are things at work?"

Joe's voice seemed to soothe the last bit of irritation caused by the name of Kessler. And a sip of her Sage martini relaxed Sage further. "Thanks, Joe. I've been busy, but things have stabilized at work; the mass layoff has died down. I guess your business is good?" Sage said, reclining comfortably against the back of her chair, her eyes a natural soft shade of silver green again.

"Glad to hear that. Do stop by more often, whenever you have time. I'd better get back before a riot starts for lack of beer over there. Catch up with you guys later."

Watching Joe going back to the bar, Will said with feigned jealousy, "Hey, how is it that Joe can always put you in a good mood better than your own brother?"

"Because all you do is irritate me, not deliberately but still irritating," Sage said without thinking.

"So is it Joe the man, his martini, or both that always seem to put you in a good mood? I guess he is good for you. I know he likes you, very much," Will said mischievously.

"Of course I like him. How many years have we known him now?" Sage said. Noticing her brother's wicked smile, her eyes widened. "Oh no, I like him as a friend, but he's not my type in that way."

"Yeah, yeah, I hear women say that a lot, not their type, just a friend, but honestly, I don't think many of them know what their type is," Will screeched to mimic a female voice.

"Cut it out. You sound like an idiot." Sage reached across the table and jabbed her bother in the shoulder. "Now, seriously, what was Rob Kessler like?"

"He struck me as one of those Ivy Leagues who thinks he puts on his pants differently from the rest of us," Will said with a chuckle, thinking about the pastel-pink—or was it salmon-colored?—polo shirt the congressman had been wearing.

"You mean a phony elitist. Must take after his famous uncle. Stay away from him. Nothing good can come from somebody like that," Sage warned.

"I know what you're saying, but Kevin seems to think he could be a good resource person when it comes to legislative policy and regulation on telecom businesses. Kevin actually got a little ticked off when I hinted I don't like surprise visits from politicians like Kessler."

"Why? Where is he anyway?" Sage looked around, but there was still no Kevin.

"He might be gone. I think he might have had a little too much to drink today. I've been a little worried about him recently."

"Worried about Kevin? The tough guy who has it all? Beautiful kids, beautiful wife, nice house. This merger has made him the head of your old company."

"I don't think he's really happy, and I sensed he is a little insecure about this whole merger thing," Will said tentatively.

"Has he said anything to you? You guys have gone through so much together. Don't you think he would tell you if something is bothering him?" Sage asked, serious now, affected by her brother's thoughtful tone.

"Not really, but he seemed to be irritable and edgy. Small things have been setting him off easily, like he's angry with the whole world."

"Kevin is always edgy; being edgy is his trademark. Didn't you tell me that's part of the reason he's so good at what he does, being edgy keeps him on his toes?"

"Well, maybe you're right. I guess this whole merger has turned everything upside down, even if it's in a good way, and everybody still has some adjustments to make." Will decided not to dwell on Kevin, as he had something important to accomplish before the evening was over. It was a delicate subject, and he had mulled over the best ways and the best time to bring it up. He decided the timing couldn't be better than on a day when the successful merger had put everybody in a festive mood and celebratory spirit, so he braved the question. "So why don't you like Joe? I think you guys would make a good couple."

"So you're serious. Did Joe set you up to this?" Sage asked, eyes stirred like a calm pond agitated by the throw of single pebble.

"Nobody set me up to this. It's so obvious that he likes you. Every time I'm here, the first thing out of his mouth is 'How is Sage? What is she up to?' I see the way he looks at you when he thinks nobody is watching ..."

"What way? You make it sound as if he is a shy schoolboy, but he's an adult. He could ask me out *if he really likes me*," Sage said.

"All right, I thought I should mention it to you. Since you have always accused me of being clueless when feelings are involved, shouldn't you be glad that I'm trying to be sensitive and observant for once?" Will said good-humoredly.

"But I've told you, Will: Joe is a good friend, and I don't see myself in a relationship with him other than being a friend. Actually, with my track record and forty-seven years of age, I have officially stopped seeing romance through rose-tinted glasses."

"Maybe it's because you've been looking for the wrong man. You said Joe isn't your type, so honestly, what exactly is your type, or what do women usually look for in a man?" Will was full of surprises that day, even to himself.

Sage seemed to be equally surprised by Will the practical businessman playing Will the deep-thinking life philosopher, and she decided to be serious. "I believe women want a man to be ambitious, successful, a good provider, and a family man. Of course, good looking never hurts."

"Somewhat like Dad," Will said.

"Um ..." Sage hesitated for a second but said quickly, "You could say that."

"I'm no psychiatrist, but I think those criteria are contradictory."

"How so?"

"Have you ever considered that extremely ambitious and successful men are often selfish and self-centered, because they are first and foremost driven by their ambition and dreams of success? They simply are not capable of devoting themselves all the time to their families. Quite frankly, extremely ambitious and successful men do not make good family men at all. But women often want them to be both, not realizing their desire is a catch-22."

Sage appeared to see her brother's point only vaguely. "Okay, but Dad wasn't like those guys."

"Well, Dad belonged to another category."

"What do you mean?"

"Dad worked hard to be a good provider to his family because family was indeed the most important thing in his life. I think his ambition, or his dream, was, after his kids were grown, to live a quiet but comfortable life with his wife back on the beach in his hometown of Montauk. But he was not able to do that."

"Because?"

"Because he was supposed to be ambitious in making as much money as he could to meet life's demands."

"What demands?"

"The demand of providing for his family, buying a bigger house, putting away money for his children's private school and college. I think those demands became burdens that he alone carried. So he worked harder in order to meet those demands but instead was blamed for not being there for his family all the time. Not exactly a life he had planned for himself." Will winced, imagining himself in his father's position.

"So what you are saying is Dad did everything while Mom just sat around and had fun with us?" Sage turned defensive; she had always believed that being a stay-at-home mom was a full-time job.

"I didn't say that. Of course Mom spent her life raising us, but she also held the same criteria that you have for a man who should be Donald Trump, the high financier; the father who knows best; and a one-woman Casanova when it came to romance—all at the same time and all the time."

"So you think that's why he walked out on Mom? Oh Will, your theory is both quirky and chauvinistic." Sage almost laughed.

"I simply defined yours and mom's criteria from a male prospective," Will said smugly.

"According to you, Will, women are evil then."

"No, I didn't say that. Only most of them hold illusions that often lead them to guys who are not a good match for them to begin with. Just listen to yourself; you said Joe is not your type. Why?"

"I don't know why. Chemistry maybe?"

"That's a teenager's argument." Will the practical businessman reemerged. "You would agree if I say Joe is a reasonably successful man. He's not setting the world on fire, but he does well running his business. Using your own words, you love him as a friend, a friend who is hardworking, honest, warm, and comforting. Am I right so far?" Will sounded as if he was setting premises for a business case.

"Agreed."

"Then why is he not your type?" Not waiting for Sage to answer, he said, "I think it's because Joe is so different from the wildly ambitious men you have dated so far. You don't think he's driven enough."

"Now you're saying I'm a snob?"

"Get off your high horse, Sage. Just think, the corporate attorney, the partner of a financial services firm, the pilot who flew his plane to the glamorous cities of the world. All great for a while, but either you dumped them, or they left you. The chief complaint I heard from you was they were not around for you or focused enough on you. Just think how you would feel if you were actually married to one of those guys and had several kids," Will said with a need-I-say-more look.

Sage opened her mouth but then paused, as if swallowing the words she was about to hurl at her brother. When she spoke again, she did not sound as if she was ready to accept her defeat. "Maybe I am attracted to a certain type of man, so what? Sometimes, it's chemistry, not logic, that determines whom we fall in love with or not. Come to think about it, Will, you have never even half-committed to any relationship in your life."

"True, maybe I haven't met the right woman, but I haven't been hurt either. We're not talking about me; we're talking about you. I think you and Joe could be good together, other than being friends."

"I think I've sworn off serious relationship since Howard, the attorney. Now at age forty-seven, why would I want to start all over again? I am way beyond the kids, husband, and family thing," Sage said softly, talking more to herself than Will. Will knew what she was thinking. The memory of her ex-fiancé, Howard, still pained her.

A few years ago, Sage had fallen sick and ended up in the emergency room, waiting for doctor to rule out what could be a heart problem. Howard had been out of town on a business trip. When she had stabilized enough, she'd called him. He'd said, "Let me know if it is your heart; I will try to come back." Fortunately, it had been a case of anemia, but she'd called it quits with Howard right after she'd come out of the emergency room.

"Precisely," Will said. "I'm not talking about husband, kids, and big family either. Just you and Joe, companions in life, nothing wrong with that. Also, I don't think Howard and Joe are the same." Allowing Sage to think over what he had said, Will glanced at the bar. "Looks like everybody is leaving. I'm going to say good-bye and ask Joe to get us something to eat. Shall I get you your favorite, chicken Caesar salad?"

"Thanks, that will be good."

At the bar, Frank and a few technical staff were getting ready to leave, saying good-bye to Joe. Seeing Will approaching, Frank said, "Thanks for the drinks, boss. But I need to get going, need to test a new idea that just came to me a moment ago."

Will had noticed that, since the merger, Frank had become uncharacteristically cheerful and enthusiastic. Compared to the antisocial nerd he was before the merger, he was almost a social butterfly, often calling brainstorming meetings with his staff for the new cybersecurity software he had been developing in his mind for quite a while. And Will was not surprised by the metamorphosis. Frank now had more time and resources to do what he wanted to do, to shape his ideas into new, cutting-edge products. And above all, Frank had become an American citizen. Will was happy for Frank; he wished he could feel the same for Kevin.

"It's Friday, Frank; go home and relax. Work will always be there waiting for you." Will poked a soft fist in Frank's shoulder and wished everyone a good weekend as they dropped out of his sight and into the warm, summery evening air.

"Did you talk to Kevin today?" Will asked Joe as the last of his staff disappeared out the door.

"Very briefly, but I think he left quite a while ago. He seemed to have had a little too much to drink today. Can't blame him; it's something worth celebrating," Joe said. Glancing at where Sage was sitting, he asked, "Shall I make you guys another drink and some bar food maybe?"

Will was going to ask Joe if he had noticed anything different about Kevin recently, but Joe's beaming smile stopped him. *No sense in spoiling the day,* he thought, so he said instead, "That will be great, Joe; the usual please, for both of us."

But Kevin's earlier remarks, tinted with sarcasm and borderline bitterness, nagged Will as he headed back to Sage at their table, doubts and questions swimming noisily in his mind. *Am I too close to Kevin to see everything about him clearly? Maybe I need to have a one-on-one talk with him next week. Maybe I'm being overly sensitive and nothing is really wrong.*

At the table, a more serene Sage raised her empty martini glass and waved it in the direction of the bar, a warm smile on her face. Will looked back and saw Joe nodding at Sage, smiling from ear to ear.

CHAPTER 11

· · · · ·

TEN MINUTES BEFORE ELEVEN in the morning, Lu stepped into the fishbowl conference room on the top floor of Lehrer & Schuler's building in Lower Manhattan. Again, she was the first one to arrive for an impromptu meeting called by Fred Armstrong, the Wall Street giant.

Less than an hour ago, her boss, Jack Earnest, had stopped by her office with a smile. "Fred is going to be in the neighborhood later this morning. He wants to stop by to discuss some new deal he's been working on. He has specifically asked for your presence at the meeting. I know you're trying to get out early today, but can you stop by for half an hour or so?"

"What's it all about?"

"He didn't say on the phone, but he sounded urgent and excited. It's got to be something pretty big for Fred to be excited. So can you come?"

Tilting her head slightly to one side, Lu had affected a theatrical tone and asked, "Do I really have a choice?"

"Okay, see you in a little while in the fish bowl upstairs." Jack had gulped the last bit of his morning Starbucks coffee and tossed the cup into the wastebasket next to Lu's desk. "Good shot," he'd congratulated himself and gone on his way to his own office.

It was a Friday in mid-July, sunny, dry, and hot, like a perfect subtropical Mediterranean beach day. And the beach was where Lu had planned to be for the next two and a half days. A week ago, she'd accepted Sage's invitation to spend a long weekend at Will's beach house in Montauk on Long Island. She'd only stopped by the office that morning to take care of a couple of minor tasks before heading out to pick up a rental car. Other than a few e-mails and a couple of phone calls, she and Sage had not had time to conduct a heart-to-heart girl session since she'd come back from her trip to China back in April, so she had been looking forward to this weekend.

She glanced at her watch, already eleven. But knowing Fred, it could be another ten to twenty minutes before she would see him dragging his enormous body into the conference room.

Lu was already dressed for the beach, wearing a pair of high-waist, wide-legged white linen pants; white wedge sandals; and a sky-blue cotton T-shirt. With her deep skin tone and slightly tousled black hair, she looked as if she had already spent two weeks on the beach. She glanced at the time again and murmured, "Come on, Fred, let's get whatever it is over with." Outside the fish bowl, a patch of Hudson River dazzled in between two skyscrapers, seductively testing her patience.

"Sorry to drag you into this. Let's try to wrap this up quickly," Jack said apologetically as he glided into the fish bowl. He was in an even better mood than usual. He would be retiring in a couple of months. Nobody had pushed him; it was his decision. Jack Earnest had had his day. He had set the world on fire many years ago, and now it was the younger generation's turn. It was time for him to bow out, with the respect he had earned intact and his legacy, if any, untarnished.

"What's Fred up to again? The IPO of Golden China Seafood has just gone through successfully. Shouldn't he be lying around on the beach somewhere just like everybody else around him at this time of year?" Lu said jokingly.

"You know Fred; he didn't get to be the king of Wall Street by lying around all day. He is like a lion on the prowl; the minute he sniffs out something, he pounces for the kill."

"What kill? What lion? You guys talking about me?" a voice boomed gaily at the door, its frame once more filled horizontally and vertically by Fred Armstrong's giant form.

"Hello, Fred, you're surprisingly early." Jack turned around and checked his watch. "Lu and I weren't expecting you for another fifteen minutes."

"Well, you told me Ms. Lu wants to leave early for the beach, so here I am to accommodate her wishes." Fred smiled jovially, removing himself from the door frame and revealing a lightly tanned, polo-shirted Dick Witherspoon. Peeling off the jacket stretched on his hulky body, Fred said, "Dick, why don't we get started so everybody can get out early today."

"Yes, sir." Dick nodded at Jack and Lu across the table and pulled out a stack of paper from his compact Montblanc briefcase. "Here is some new information we asked for several months ago from Great China Telecom when they first came to us for an IPO deal back in April. For a long time, they were very quiet and didn't produce what we needed to go forward. We thought the deal was dead." Dick paused to slide two copies across the table to Jack and Lu; then he continued with a tone of high confidentiality and exclusivity, "But it seems they have come back with an even bigger and more ambitious proposal."

With great curiosity, Lu glanced through the two-page document. When she looked up around the table again, her eyes were charged with both bemusement and vigilance.

"I know, I know, it's an unusual proposal. But it's a multibillion-dollar deal. Sure, the Chinese will have to go through a lot of regulatory red tape, but hey, this is what we are here for." Fred Armstrong resonated assurance and confidence.

"Let me try to understand this." Peering at Jack, who was still marking off the paper in front of him, Lu said with deliberation, "Great China Telecom is currently a telecommunication-equipment manufacturer in China. Sure, they export a large portion of the routers, modems, and phone jacks they produce worldwide, and they are the dominant telecom equipment manufacturer in China."

"That's correct," Dick Witherspoon affirmed with strain of impatience.

"Thank you, Dick." Lu shot a fiery look at Dick and continued, "According to this document, the reason they want to raise additional capital is to upgrade and expand their production technology and capacity. And they choose to raise capital here in the US because, presumably, the process here is simpler and entails less red tape. Well, I could agree if this was all it was."

"In essence, that is all it is," Dick injected eagerly.

"I'm afraid not. They also briefly mention in here that they intend to use a portion of the funds to be raised to acquire or form joint ventures with a number of telecom network-system-design and network-management companies here in the United States. Their goal is to become a global and fully integrated telecommunications company."

"Well said, Lu. So besides potentially generating us more business down the road because of their ambition, this concerns us how?" Fred said with authority and flattery.

"Normally, nothing, nothing wrong with a company that has a long-term plan of growth," Lu said calmly. Pausing for an instant, she went on methodically, "My concern is this is, after all, Communist China. We may view them as a business and trade partner, but we are naive if we don't think they view us as political and economic rivals. Telecommunications is a sensitive area; it involves cyber- and homeland-security issues. We have to be careful and fully understand the rules and regulations before we get involved in a deal allowing the Chinese to come here for a shopping spree of sensitive US technologies."

"I have to agree with Lu on this," Jack said, taking off his black wire-rimmed reading glasses. Turning to Fred, he stated more than asked, "I am sure you have people working on it already, Fred?"

"No worries, leave the legislative and regulation hurdles to us," Fred said airily and moved on to the more important subject. "I am hoping once we receive the details we've asked for from the Chinese that Lu can devote a substantial amount of her time to work with Dick on this deal?"

Both Lu and Jack noticed Fred Armstrong now said "work with Dick" instead of "assist Dick," as he had when he'd asked for Lu's help in the Golden Seafood IPO. It was an admission, though a grudging one, that Lu was just as important, if not more important, than Dick in the upcoming multibillion-dollar deal with the Chinese telecom company. Not wanting to appear to be pressuring Lu, Jack asked tentatively, "Do you need to check your schedule before getting back to Fred?"

Knowing well that any investment banking firm would rejoice to get in on such a deal, including Jack, Lu asked, "Do I have a choice?" While everybody at the table laughed, she said seriously, "But I will check what's on my plate and get back to you regarding how to best coordinate the whole thing."

"Okay, it's settled then." Lifting himself up, Fred Armstrong said, "You know, Lu, we'll need the best of the best to ace this deal. Based on what I saw and heard about you on the Golden Seafood deal, you are the ace; everybody loved you. Now enjoy your beach days, and we'll talk soon."

After bidding farewell to Jack and Lu, Fred Armstrong lumbered out of the conference room, mumbling something to Dick Witherspoon, who was walking a few steps behind him. A few seconds later, their laughter and giggling echoed up through the descending elevator. Jack and Lu looked at each other and shook their heads at the same time.

• • •

AN HOUR LATER, LU was cruising at a reasonable speed on the Long Island Expressway in a rented BMW M3 convertible. Anticipating what could be bumper-to-bumper traffic along Interstate 495 on a Friday afternoon, when it seemed the whole world had decided to race to the beaches in the Hamptons for the weekend, Lu had decided to remain fully enclosed in the car—no sense in breathing in the gas fumes and car exhaust. The top could come off when she got on NY Route 27 and closer to the beach towns in the Hamptons. But the traffic on the Long Island Expressway was thinner than usual. Perhaps it was still early and the rush would come later, or perhaps everybody had abandoned the city a day earlier since the forecast had called for a fantastic beach weekend. Whatever the reason, Lu was happy her journey on the expressway concluded rather expeditiously.

Soon after she got on Route 27, she pressed the control button of the convertible top. The roof popped open right above her head and retracted, rose, and reclined at a forty-five-degree angle before clanking itself into the trunk seconds later. She glanced up. The sun was high and burning white. She looked ahead. Dazzling white pavement stretched before her until it blurred into the cloudless electric-blue sky in the distance. For a moment, she fancied herself in a spaceship, launching into the universe of light and air. The sun embraced her feverishly, and warm breezes whirled by, whimsically shaping her hair into a wafting patch of black clouds one second and a fluttering swath of black satin the next.

Her body, encased in glass and concrete and deprived of light for too long, took to the sun with sheer abandon, every fiber of her being tingling as she absorbed the sun's rays. Her mind, constantly on alert and jam-packed with numbers, data, and statistics, began to ease and unclutter as the fitful breeze, carrying the scent of seashore air, played about her face. A familiar sense enveloped her, the sense of being intoxicated and cleansed at the same time. It was the scent of Montauk—the water, the air, and the sun. Whether it was for real or psychological, she could smell it every time she got close to the Point, as the locals called it, or, according to her own imagination, the tip of the world. It was a smell from the fusion of the ocean and sun, briny and aseptic, the smell of nature, unadulterated. *I wonder what the air quality index is here in Montauk,* she wondered, recalling the air pollution index reported on TV in the Shanghai Hilton every morning during her visit there two months ago. On a bad day, the pollution could be ten or twenty times worse than what was considered a hazardous level. On those days breathing the air was like breathing cement. The sun could be dazzling and the sky electric blue in the upper stratosphere above the city, but Shanghai was invisible. The thought of the Shanghai pollution made her lungs heavy. She drew a deep breath and slowly blew it out, imagining whatever impurities within her being drained away. Reflexively, she pressed down the accelerator, and the electric-blue BMW seemed to fly toward the electric-blue sky in front of her.

Her soaring exhilaration was interrupted by the tepid female voice of the GPS from the car's dashboard, alerting her to prepare to take exit 27 for her final destination. Soon she was the only traveler on quiet side streets with residential houses on large lots screened off by shrubberies and foliage rustling and flowing in the playful ocean breeze. She could not see the ocean yet, but she could hear its familiar sound in the near distance, rhythmic and hypnotizing. She glided on. After a couple of more turns, Lu found herself coasting along the precipice of Old Montauk Highway. On her right side, a thirty-foot drop below, white waves of the Atlantic Ocean thrashed against the shoreline, exploding into a million pieces of dazzling crystal in the air before disappearing into the glistening sandy beach.

The female voice from the GPS announced robotically, "You have reached your destination; your destination is on the left." She looked to her left. A couple of hundred feet ahead, on the unpaved curb, stood a white wooden mailbox in the shape of a country house, with a raw cedar shake roof and black trim. As she inched up farther, she could see clearly the black street number on the white post of the mailbox. She had reached Will Donovan's beach house on Old Montauk Highway.

Slowly she climbed up the short but steep gravel driveway that leveled into the front yard of a white saltbox with a large front porch that ran the entire width of the house. She pulled the BMW into one of the three parking spots to the right side of the yard and shut off the engine.

"Oh, hello, welcome to Donovan's oceanfront resort and spa!" The cheerful greeting seemed to have popped out from the flock of golden sunflowers hugging the white latticed base of the porch. Lu jumped out of the car, and there was Sage, standing on the porch, at the front door. She was in a bright-yellow T-shirt and blue denim shorts. Her wavy auburn hair appeared more golden. The smile on her tanned face was as bright as the sunflower blooms that rose to brush the white porch railing she was leaning on.

"Hey, how are you? Thanks for inviting me here." Lu waved and turned to the back of the car to get her luggage. By doing that, she found herself facing the ocean, or the distant ocean where the blue water blurred into the blue sky. To gaze at the beach of Montauk, she had to lower her eyes and stretch her vision slightly across the narrow two-lane Old Montauk Highway where the sand sparkled at her feet. "Wow!" she exclaimed, stunned by the view the house commanded.

Flying to Lu's side, Sage said with excitement, "Let me help you with your bags. Wait until you see the view from the room upstairs." She grabbed Lu's large duffel bag and led the way to the house.

• • •

Half an hour later, having unpacked, showered, and changed into a sleeveless black cotton dress that fell a bit below her knees, Lu came downstairs. "Make yourself comfortable. I'll bring our drinks out on the porch," Sage called from the kitchen in the back.

"Okay, don't trouble yourself; water will be fine for me. Want me to give you a hand?" Lu asked and wandered toward the back of the house.

"No, no, go enjoy the view. I'll be out in a minute," Sage insisted adamantly.

So Lu turned around and wandered into the living room in the front.

It was a small house, befitting the name of its architectural design—saltbox. Living/dining room in the front, a stone fireplace in the middle, kitchen in the back. The decoration was minimal with an airy color scheme—white walls, simple wood, wicker beach house furniture in shades of white to neutral, and a few white-and-blue-striped cotton area rugs here and there. Off to one side of the living room was a separate room with its door open. Lu glanced inside. It was set up like an office, with a couch and desk with printer and computer equipment. She stepped out onto the porch and descended into the front yard. It was approaching midafternoon, and the sun had slanted toward the back of the house, casting the entire front flower bed in shadows. She stepped away from the house, turned, and looked up. Three windows with black shutters lined the second floor. The ones on the sides belonged to the two dormer-like bedrooms separated by a bathroom in the middle. She had left the window on the right side open a few minutes ago. She could see the opaque white curtains rousing to the gentle, warm ocean breeze. She imagined lying down in bed behind those curtains at night, in a room painted frost white by a moon suspended in the midnight blue of ocean and sky, her body blanketed only by the warm breeze drifting in from the window, the sound of cascading ocean waves lullabying her into a deep, sweet sleep.

She smiled, and the sunflowers smiled back.

"Here we go, a taste of local delicacy."

Lu raised her eyes as Sage laid a large tray on the round wrought iron table on the right side of the porch. "Come on, eat and drink while they're cold," Sage urged.

"Coming." Lu hopped back on the porch and examined the display on the table: on the large sandy-colored rectangular wooden tray were two flutes of champagne in blushing pink. Embedded in a crystal layer of crushed ice, on a white porcelain plate, clusters of pearly oysters on half shells shimmered against a bright center ring of lemon wedges encircling a seashell-shaped dish of burgundy-hued vinegar with purple-red sprinkles of chopped onion. "Wow, they look like they just came out of the ocean a few minutes ago." Lu was amazed by the freshness of the oysters.

"You got that right—harvested, shucked, and delivered an hour ago."

"Good to know. Who here in Montauk has this kind of service?"

"We're in luck. My brother, Will, knows a couple of local surfer dudes who run an oyster farm at Lake Montauk. They started the farm less than a year ago, but their oysters have already made their way to five-star restaurants in New York City. No way we could have gotten our hands on these if it weren't for Will." Sage handed Lu one of the champagne flutes and raised the other. "Well, welcome to Montauk, cheers!"

After their lips touched the pink sparkle, Sage and Lu each picked up an oyster, spooned a tiny burgundy liquid on top, then slurp, slurp, and a pause for another sip of champagne. The bubbles danced on their tongues, and the plump meat slid down their throats smooth as velvet. It was salty; it was sweet; it was dreamy; it was heavenly.

"When is Will going to be here? I need to thank him for such a lovely treat," Lu said several oysters later.

"Tomorrow afternoon. He's been even busier after the merger, practically lives in the office. Well, as least we will have the house to ourselves for a whole day," Sage said, excited like a teenager ready for a pajama party with her parents gone.

"I'm glad you invited me out here. This is such a cozy house, on such a beautiful spot." Lu gazed at the ocean in the distance, as if etching the view in her mind permanently.

"Technically, it's Will's house now, but it belonged to our grandparents, and they lived here for decades before they moved south. My dad planned to move back here had he lived long enough. Mom wanted to sell it, but Will begged her not to. Somehow he believes he will be back here one day when he's had enough of the business world, but I don't see that happening anytime soon." Sage sighed. "When Mom passed away a few years ago, the house was in bad shape. Will spent a lot of money to renovate it, but he doesn't get to use it often."

"It would have been a shame to sell it. I can't get over the view from here," Lu said admiringly.

Standing up, Sage changed the subject. "Well, enough about the house; you need to tell me about your trip to China. How was your visit with your mom and sister?" She hopped back into the house and, a few seconds later, reappeared with a sweaty bottle containing enough champagne to fill both flutes.

Lu took a sip and remained thoughtful for a moment. "I guess it was okay, maybe better than I had expected," she said, her voice wary and tentative.

"What do you mean?"

"Well, my mother was cold and reserved initially, but she seemed to warm up a bit after we got to talk for a while."

"And your sister?"

"I didn't get to see her. She was abroad on vacation with her husband."

"So what did your mom say?"

"She asked me if I was married and seemed disappointed that I was not. She did ask how I support myself without a husband, so I told her what I do for a living. After that, she became less reserved, telling me what happened to some of the relatives I knew."

"That's good, isn't it? After all, you haven't seen each other for thirty years. Conversations are bound to be awkward at first. Give it some time, and everything will come together naturally. It's too bad your sister wasn't around, but I guess you will have opportunities to go back there again," Sage said with great optimism.

But Lu was a bit pensive. "I hope you're right. But if anything good came out of this trip, it was getting to be in the apartment I lived in for the first thirteen years of my life one more time. It's been torn down by now, to make room for the ever-widening highways and new skyscrapers in the area."

"I'm sorry to hear that. Where is your mom going to live?"

"She said she was about to move to an apartment in a good area; she seemed excited about it." After pausing to allow herself a faint smile, Lu continued, "But I still feel sad for the old apartment building. I can hear the wrecking ball hitting its soot- and pollution-covered wall as we speak and imagine it's century-old brick, mortar, and plaster crumbling down amid the glass and concrete skyscrapers that seem to have taken over the entire city. I know it was old, but like a lot of old buildings in

Shanghai, it had character and unique architectural design. It's a shame so many of them have been torn down."

"But at least you got to say good-bye ..." Sage said softly, trying to lighten the mood, but she stopped short. A few seconds later, she continued quietly, "You've told me what you've gone through, but I guess I'll never really know what it was like to live through what you lived through then."

They sat quietly until a group of noisy surfers blended into the panorama of pure nature. Their rainbow-colored surfboards effected a lighter mood. "Sorry, I don't mean to work myself into a gloomy mood," Lu said and pushed aside the image of the debris of the apartment building that had piled up in her mind during the past few minutes. "Enough about my trip, no more sappy talk. How's everything going with you? How is Will doing at Matrixtech?"

"I think my brother is over the moon these days. He is now in charge of everything that has something to do with the company's technology innovation and development, a.k.a., cyber cat-and-mouse games of hacking and antihacking, things he wanted to do but didn't have the resources to do when he was on his own. I guess he is in total control of his professional life—no danger of being too young to retire but too old to surf."

"I guess he was relieved that the Chinese decided not to acquire Matrixtech, at least not for a while," Lu said casually, but her mind went back to the document Dick had given her only hours ago. Great China Telecom's IPO proposal had identified a few acquisition targets in the United States, and Matrixtech was one of them. For confidentiality reasons, she was not going to mention it to Will unless he was already privy to the information.

"Oh yes, Will seems to be happy that the Chinese went away. I'm not an expert in this kind of thing, but it's just too complicated for everyone."

"Good, I'm glad everything is going well for your brother." Lu decided to put the brakes on the delicate subject and deal with it when it became necessary. After all, she had not come here to conduct business or be haunted by the unpleasant memories of the past. So she switched the subject, confident that Sage's inherent optimism of the world would guide her into a weekend of lighthearted fun. "So how is everything with you at work? Or life in general?"

"Not as bad as a couple of months ago, I guess. At least the layoff has slowed down, so I haven't had to go to work every day with a knot in my stomach," Sage said, holding the champagne flute closer to her chest for an instant.

"I know what you mean. Telling people they no longer have a job, especially when it's good employees, is probably one of the hardest things to do." Lu sympathized.

"Tell me about it. But you know what the worst part is? The worst part is seeing people you thought you knew well turn themselves into people you hardly know—I mean when they feel their livelihood is being taken away or their self-interest threatened. Though some people cope reasonably well in the end, I've seen loyal employees become backstabbers or legal liabilities overnight. We humans are so unpredictable in hard times, or maybe we don't really know ourselves until times get tough and testing," Sage lamented with a soft sigh.

Lu had often admired Sage's willingness to be more accepting of people's flaws and to focus on the good of humankind. She often wondered if it was because they came from opposite ends of the world, where their worldviews had been formed in environments as contrasting as black and white. Whatever the reason, Lu was thankful for having Sage as a friend, a friend whose trusting nature and eternal optimism often helped soften the edges of her guardedness, helped her live the life she loved, only with more vivacity and effervescence.

Meeting Lu's introspecting gaze with a mysterious look, Sage said, "I do have something interesting to report on the personal side, thanks to my brother. It proves my theory that sometimes people close to us may know us better than we do ourselves."

"You're dating someone! I know that look. Who is it? I want details," Lu exclaimed.

"Not *dating* dating; we've just gotten drinks a couple of times," Sage said with a coy smile and rosy cheeks. "You know Joe, the owner of the pub in Alexandria? I think we went there once when you visited a few years ago."

"I remember vaguely. Was he the one making you the famous Sage martini at the bar, with the thick red hair and scruffy red beard?"

"Yes. Anyway, I just found out a few weeks ago from my brother that Joe has some kind of crush on me, but somehow I never noticed. I just never thought he was my type. Will said it's because I've been a snob, dating only egotistic highfliers in the past. He thought Joe and I might hit it off. So I relented and met Joe for coffee a couple of times." Sage chattered with the excitement of a schoolgirl new to the dating scene.

"So how did it go?" Lu eagerly asked.

Thoughtfully, Sage picked up the champagne flute and drank the remaining pink liquid inside. "So far, interesting," she said and put the flute down on the table.

"Not good enough, details please." Lu chuckled.

"Okay, but since neither one of us has had any lunch, let's get ready for an early-bird seafood dinner first. Let me go upstairs to put on something more presentable." Sage rose from the chair and gathered the plate and flutes now lying empty on the table.

"You're trying to be suspenseful, aren't you?" Lu teased, mocking impatience.

"No, but we have the whole weekend to be silly." Sage hopped back into the house, her laughter as feathery as the clouds sailing by in the distant sky.

CHAPTER 12

· · · · ·

IT WAS PAST EIGHT o'clock on Saturday evening when Will Donovan pulled his blue Mustang convertible onto the gravel driveway in front of his beloved saltbox beach house. As soon as he came to a full stop, Louis, his Doberman, who had been sitting on the bucket seat next to him, hopped out of the car and went straight for the front porch. Will got out of the car, circled back to the trunk, and fished out his gym bag. By the time he stepped up to the porch, Louis was sitting squarely on his hind legs by the front door, waiting for him to unlock it.

Bending down to pat Louis's head, Will whispered, "I know, I know, we're late, and you're hungry."

They entered the house together. As Louis darted from one room to another, putting the house under his sniffing test, Will went into the office at the side of the living room. He switched on the light, dropped his gym bag on the couch, and automatically turned on the power switch that controlled every piece of equipment of his workstation. Then he headed to the kitchen in the back. He took out a can of dog food from the cabinetry, popped the lid open, and used a soup spoon from the flatware drawer to scoop the contents into one of the two bowls in the feeding station by the door to the backyard. Within a second, a streak of blue lightning flashed and twirled into the kitchen. Another second later, the food bowl was empty and as clean as if had it just come out of the dishwasher. Will shook his head and laughed. "Easy, Louis, easy," he said as the dog kept licking his empty bowl. For a dog who had been left on the roadside, almost starved to death, Louis always ate his meals as if he had not eaten for days and would not have the chance to eat again for days.

Will filled the dog's water bowl and went for the refrigerator. The food in the refrigerator was mostly for breakfast—eggs, milk, juice, and bread. But Sage had stocked a few bottles of his favorite Hefeweizen. He grabbed one and took a tall, hourglass-shaped beer glass from the open cupboard. A moment later, Will was sitting on the front porch, a frothy beer in hand, with Louis playing by his feet.

Will had been looking forward to this weekend. He was rather eager to see Lu again, but not like when he'd first met her months ago, in a rather-formal restaurant and businesslike setting. He wanted to know Lu the person better, and Montauk was the perfect place—a casual and relaxing location where Lu and Sage should feel familiar and comfortable and a territory where he could be in his natural element. So as not to appear too anxious, he'd waited for a reasonable amount of time to pass after the restaurant meeting before he'd casually asked Sage how Lu was doing. Luckily for him, Sage had said Lu had just come back from Shanghai and had showed him a picture on her cell, an image of Shanghai shrouded in foggy pollution. "She'll need to clean her lungs after breathing in this junk," Will had said with honest alarm.

"I was thinking of inviting her to your beach house in a few weeks. Don't you think that's a good idea?" Sage had said, eyes still on the blurred image of Shanghai on the phone.

"Of course, great idea," Will had blurted, glad Sage had initiated the invitation first. All he'd had to do was invite himself. "I'm actually thinking of going up there myself," he'd said casually.

"Why don't you join us then?"

"Well ..." Will had allowed himself a moment of hesitancy, as if he had never considered Sage's suggestion up till that moment. Then he'd laid out his plan rather quickly. "I don't want to be a nuisance at your girls-only party. How about this, if everybody's schedule works out, you and Lu can go first, and I can meet up with you there a day or two later."

Will remembered how Sage had teased him mercilessly about his premeditated scheme. "Well, well, well, you have everything all worked out, don't you? I think somebody has a crush on somebody."

As the weekend had approached, things had seemed to be working out nicely according to his plan. Sage had texted him Thursday evening after she'd arrived the beach house first to get the house ready for the weekend. Then Friday evening before she and Lu headed out for dinner, she'd texted, "We are having fun, see you tomorrow."

He had planned to arrive in Montauk no later than late afternoon on Saturday so the three of them could all go out for dinner together. But an unexpected last-minute conference call with the top management team had detained him at his Great Falls house until after noon. *There goes dinner with the girls,* he'd thought. Reluctantly, he'd texted Sage to go ahead without him, feeling as if he had missed out on a big date. He had not been expecting Lu and Sage at the house when he arrived, but he was nevertheless disappointed that they had not waited for him.

The sun had sunk below the western horizon, leaving the dusk sky with faint streaks of pink. On the eastern horizon above the sea, a pale almost-full moon threaded in and out of clusters of lacy clouds. Quietly, Will waited for the ladies to return. *"Somebody has a crush on somebody,"* Sage's tease echoed over the murmuring tide. *At my age, I don't have crushes,* he thought. *But then why do I think about her so often?*

Will Donovan was forty-seven years old, and he was not inexperienced when it came to the ritual of dating women. He was, however, principled in upholding criteria he had established over time for the women he had relationship with—their personality traits, professional training, career goals and achievements, and most importantly, their trustworthiness. So far, neither his experience nor his principles had netted him any serious and long-term relationships. His mother used to tell him he was too picky, had set his sights too high. His own sister had accused him of commitment phobia. Most of his ex-girlfriends whom he'd broken up with regarded him as an arrogant ass who had broken their hearts, destroyed their self-esteem, and moved on to conquer a younger and prettier face. To the few women who left him, he was a chauvinistic pig and self-centered jerk who had not devoted any time to their relationship.

To all this concern, accusation, blame, and anger toward his perceived attitude of the opposite sex, Will's usual reaction was a wave of the hand and a dismissive chuckle. In the business world Will Donovan was not afraid of making instant decisions on whether to seize an opportunity that could later turn out to be a blunder. The ability to make decisions and not regret but instead correct if a decision turns out to be a bad one was the secret to his success as an ambitious and competitive businessman. To his colleagues, business partners, and employees, he was loyal and honest, sometimes to the extent of being detrimental to himself. Friends and relatives described him as affable, gentle, and easygoing. But when it came to making a commitment to a woman, there was a hard, unbendable core in him. It had taken shape as early as his teenage years. It was a secret he kept to himself; not even Sage knew it.

The truth was contrary to his parents' and sister's belief; young Will had not been completely clueless about what had gone on around him other than the excitement of playing on ball fields and the thrill of riding waves on beaches. He'd overheard adult conversations he was not supposed to hear and observed grownup interactions he was not supposed to notice. Good or bad, interesting or boring, trivial or consequential, he absorbed the information quietly. Like a camel storing food in its stomach for digestion later, his brain stored the information sequentially for future processing. In between, he went about just being a young boy.

As a young boy Will considered his dad a superman who took care of everyone's needs and had no needs of his own. Every so many days, his dad handed over a piece of paper to his mother at the dinner table. And his mother would say, "I'll go to the bank tomorrow." Soon Will figured out the power of that piece of paper. It fed him, clothed him, and bought him school supplies, baseball bats and gloves, and colorful surfboards. It provided the family everything they needed in life, all because Dad brought it back home first. The only thing Dad asked for was "What's for dinner?" often as soon as he stepped in the door after a day's work in the office.

Then they moved to Washington, DC. Will began to notice that Dad the superman had a regular guy's needs, or more like desires and dreams. So many times, he heard his dad mention to his mother that he would like to go back to Montauk one day and run a bakery or a bed-and-breakfast after retirement. But his mother often met the idea with comments like "You have a long way to go before retirement, Bill, dear. The house needs to be renovated so it's more presentable when you entertain your boss and colleagues. And there is the kids' college education; we need to put away as much money as we can so they can go to the best ones if they can get in, don't you think?" To that, Dad's response was usually silence or a sigh followed by "What's wrong with in-state colleges?" Just like that, the conversation that had begun with Dad's retirement dream ended with Dad needing to work harder and make more money. The same conversation, hushed and controlled, though more intense and argumentative as time went by, would travel through the wall that divided Will's bedroom from his parents'. He empathized with his dad, who, in his mind, carried the burden of supporting his family alone.

One night, Will awoke to muffled crying and weeping on the other side of his bedroom wall.

"It was nothing, just entertaining a couple of clients," his dad mumbled.

"Don't lie to me," his mother hissed. "Who was the slut you were with? A girlfriend of mine saw you."

"Shi, calm down. You're making something out of nothing."

Then his mother's wet voice became fainter and fainter. Will soon drifted back to sleep.

The next morning, Will had almost forgotten what had seeped through the wall from his parents' bedroom. *It might have been a dream,* he thought, brought on by his sister's constant prattling to him about how she was worried about their parents' not getting along with each other recently.

Back from school in the afternoon, he walked past the kitchen swinging door, directly to his room. "Have another baby. That'll settle things down a bit. You know—" A woman's voice drifted out from the kitchen but stopped midsentence.

"Will? Sage? Are you back from school?" his mother asked in a startled voice.

"It's me, Mom," he answered and went into his room. What he had just heard, plus what he'd heard through the wall the previous night, went to his mind's storage compartment. He did not give it too much thought.

A few months later, his mother announced she was pregnant. Young Will happily congratulated his mother. It was not until after his dad moved out of the house, when the only communication from his mother to his father was by phone asking for money—"Where's the child-support check? We've got to eat here."—that a lightbulb suddenly went on. All the bits and bytes in his brain began to process and make sense.

As a young boy, Will adored his mother. She was the comfort when he was sick and the safety net he ran to when his dad became too much of a disciplinarian for him. As a young adult, though he knew he would always love his mother, the mother who had devoted her entire life to worrying about her children's future, well-being, and happiness, he began to see his mother the woman, the woman who had prodded her husband to work harder, make more money, until his spirit had broken and his body had buckled under the load of weight he had been carrying. Was his dad a flawless human being? Of course not. Though his dad never admitted to having extramarital affairs, rumors of him being seen with unsavory female characters at questionable clubs were numerous. His defense was if a client wanted to be entertained in a strip club, then he needed to do so—it was the way of the advertising industry. The alternative for him was to switch to a career where no exotic client entertainment was required. "Are you willing to accept half the salary I am paid now?" he asked his wife. Not long after that, he left the house he had worked so hard for and then died of a heart attack at age forty-six. *Was that fair?* young Will often asked himself.

The dots had continued to connect—his mother's surprise pregnancy, the crying and weeping at night on the other side of his bedroom wall, the advice he'd overheard from his mom's girlfriend to have another baby. Had his mother gotten pregnant deliberately for fear of losing her husband, to cure their troubled marriage? Will had never had the courage to ask his mother for the truth during her final years of joyless life.

So young Will had taken a course in life, consciously or subconsciously, to avoid the path his father had gone down. *Tragic* was the word that came to mind. He'd vowed never to be chained by a job he hated, simply because he had a family to support. It went the other way around too. He wanted a family only with someone who was honest and trustworthy, willing to share life's responsibilities, obligations, and burdens together. So far, he'd had no problem not being beholden to somebody for a paycheck. In that department, he was his own master, conquering and setting the world on fire in a way his father could never have imagined. But finding the right woman to start a family was risky business for him. A wrong business partner could derail his business, but a wrong partner in marriage could not only make him lose a big chunk of what he had worked for but also cause tremendous emotional toll. He could lose his kids, and in general, dads were always the losing person in a divorce situation. As his business grew, his fear of ending up like his dad grew too. Now, at age forty-seven, the idea of a conventional family with a wife and several kids had long ceased to visit him, even during the wee hours of those lone sleepless nights. The thought of traveling down life's path by himself did not easily invoke melancholy or sentimentality in him anymore.

The beer glass was almost empty. The gray and pink of dusk had turned into the deepest midnight blue. The moon, like a platinum pendant, dangled from the sky, casting a pool of brilliance on the dark water.

A shaft of high-beam light arced across the dim driveway entrance, and a car glided in, its tires crunching the gravel surface. In a split second, Louis jolted up to a standing position. He barked a low, broken bark, a mix of alertness and excitement.

The little two-seater convertible pulled into the last parking spot on the side of the front yard. The engine turned off, and the blinding headlights dimmed. His sister stepped from the passenger seat. He knew the woman who had been driving was Lu, but even in the faint light diffused from the front porch lamp, she did not look like the Lu he had met months ago. She wore a long, dark tank dress, and the straight and sleek black hair he remembered was now tousled and flowing about her shoulders tempestuously.

"Good evening, ladies." He stood, both palms planted on top of the porch railing. Louis, who had pranced around Sage and received his pat on the head, was now swirling and sniffing around Lu at the bottom step to the porch.

"Hello, Louis." Standing still, arching slightly forward, Lu greeted the dog. "Sit, Louis, sit, good dog."

Louis circled around his guest one more time and then sat facing Lu and licked her outstretched hand.

"Sorry, I guess you passed the inspection and have his permission to enter the house," Will said apologetically as he walked down the steps to greet Lu, wondering whether he should greet her with a hug and a peck on the cheek.

"No problem. He is so friendly." Lu withdrew her hand from the dog, straightened, and then extended her hand to Will. "Nice to see you again, Will. Thanks for inviting me. It's absolutely beautiful here."

"Glad you could come," Will mumbled awkwardly. He was relieved that Lu had solved his dilemma over whether to shake hands or hug and kiss.

"We brought you back a chicken salad and some dessert," Sage said, taking out two boxes from a plastic bag and setting them on the porch table. "We decided not to have dessert at the restaurant, so we can eat with you if you're hungry and want the salad."

"Thanks, actually I haven't had anything since I left DC, except a beer a few minutes ago. I could eat something." Will looked at the transparent plastic boxes on the table.

"Okay, I think Lu and I could use champagne with the chocolate cheesecake. Do you want another beer?" Sage asked as she headed toward the kitchen in the back of the house.

"Yes, please," Will said.

"Just one glass," Lu said. "I already had two glasses of wine; that's a lot of drinking for me."

"You're on vacation. Relax!" Sage shouted cheerfully from inside the house, followed by the clink of flatware and pop of a champagne cork.

"So what have you guys been up to today?" Will asked Lu, who was now sitting at the table with Louis next to her, his chin on her lap.

"We lounged all day at the beach, almost had the entire beach to ourselves. Isn't it amazing? It's so quiet here yet crowded everywhere in the Hamptons just a few miles away," Lu said. She glanced up at Will for a second before stretching her eyes longingly to the water across the other side of Old Montauk Highway.

"They say Montauk is the Hamptons without the crowds, though this may be too scruffy and rugged for the Hamptons crowd."

"Well, I don't want to sound snobbish, but I do like some of the restaurants in the Hamptons. When it comes to beach, though, I like it here in Montauk. I've always thought of the place as the tip of the world, far away from the noise and crowd." Lu glanced up at Will again before she lowered her eyes to the head resting on her lap.

"I know exactly what you mean," Will said.

With nightfall descending, Lu's black eyes were bottomless. The light in them came and went, like the moonlight shimmering through dark passing clouds. Her black hair cascaded around her shoulders, and her face, neck, and shoulders glistened an olive hue. Her lips were glossed in papaya red, and her fragrance smelled like mix of ocean mist and coconut water. She reminded Will of nightfall in the tropics.

"Here we are, one beer and two bubblies." Sage emerged from the house carrying the same tray that had presented the pearly oyster platter the previous day. "Too bad you couldn't join us. Lu and I really enjoyed the dinner and the view of the ocean at Sunrise Restaurant."

"The food was great, but the view was overrated. The view of the ocean from here is just as good," Lu said, raising the champagne flute.

"Sorry I missed it. It was this damn conference call, right before I was ready to leave. Looks like the Chinese have not totally given up on some sort of partnership with Matrixtech," Will blurted, regretting right away having mentioned anything to do with China. He did not want Lu to mistake his inviting her out here again for business reasons. He laid both of his hands palm down on the table and said, "No big deal, forget I even mentioned it." He slid his hands off the table, as if sweeping away the subject of China.

Without taking a single sip, Lu set the champagne flute back on the table. "I've heard similar news," she said, glad Will already knew Matrixtech remained an acquisition target by the Chinese.

Seeming to sense where the evening conversation could be heading, Sage cut in and said, "Hey, Will, Lu is here to relax, not to be your business consultant again."

"It's okay," Lu said to Sage. Turning to Will, she continued, "Actually, it's good you know this early. I think Great China Telecom is dead serious in pursuing acquisition of a number of US telecom companies, Matrixtech being one on the list. These are complex deals. Lots of research and due diligence work will be needed, and both companies can expect to jump through numerous regulatory and political hurdles—that is, if Matrixtech is willing to explore the possibility of a merger or some kind of partnership with the Chinese."

What Lu said reminded Will of Kevin, who had been visibly upset when the subject of potentially being acquired by a Chinese company had first come up. How would Kevin react once he found out the Chinese were back again? "Well, I'm not the sole owner of our company anymore. In the end, the board and the senior-management team will have to decide what's best for the company. If it was entirely up to me, I would stay clear of any partnership with the Chinese or any other foreign company, too complicated, especially when it comes to regulations in the area of cybersecurity."

"We'll see what happens then," Lu said.

"Okay, enough of that." Sage raised her champagne flute. "Cheers."

"Cheers," Will and Lu said simultaneously. They all clinked glasses and drank.

• • •

When Lu came downstairs the next morning, Will and Sage were drinking coffee on the porch, facing the ocean in front of them.

"Good morning, sorry I overslept. It must have been the wine and champagne. Three drinks in one evening is more than I'm used to," Lu said sheepishly. She had checked her cell phone upon waking to find it was past nine.

"Relax. You're on vacation. Eat, drink, and sleep—that's what we're here for." Sage was as bright and cheerful as the sun shining above the horizon. "Do you want some coffee? Will made a large pot in the kitchen. I'm going to have another cup." She stood to head to the kitchen.

"Desperately. I'll go with you," Lu said.

"I hope you slept well," Will said before Sage and Lu stepped back in the house to fetch their coffee. He had just finished checking something on his cell and had decided there was nothing important enough for his immediate attention. It would be a lazy Sunday, a day at the beach, maybe some surfing. He would suggest dinner with the two ladies, as an apology for not being able to make it the previous evening.

"Very well, thanks. And sorry you have to sleep in your office because of me." Lu beamed, brushing strands of wet hair away from her face. She had just showered and was wearing a navy-blue T-shirt and a pair of khaki shorts.

"No problem. The upstairs bedrooms seldom get used anyway. I actually usually fall asleep on the couch in my office when I'm up here." Will set his cell down on the table and picked up the coffee mug in front of him. Whiffs of ocean mist and coconut water drifted over from where Lu was standing, mixing with the aroma of his coffee.

"So what's everybody's plan for today?" Will asked after Lu and Sage were back at the table, each holding a mug of coffee.

"Lounging on the beach sounds good to me," Lu said, squinting at the white sun in the cloudless blue sky.

"Agreed," Sage said. "But I have to head back later today."

Lu's eyes widened, and Will put his coffee mug down on the table.

"I know, I know, I'm not supposed to leave until tomorrow. But my boss e-mailed me last night. Something's come up, and my presence is required at the office tomorrow morning."

"Are you sure, Sage? Why? I'm sure they'll survive without you just this once." Lu regretted saying it the moment she said it. "I'm sorry. I don't mean your job isn't important—"

"It's okay. I know what you mean," Sage said. "You guys can relax and have fun without me here too. Besides, I have been here since Thursday. It's not like it's a wasted trip or anything."

"Too bad. It would be nice if you could stay until tomorrow, but if it's urgent stuff at work, I guess you have to go," Will said calmly, the initial surprise on his face gone.

"Maybe I should leave today too, so Will can relax in his own house and catch up with his friends," Lu suggested. The idea of spending another afternoon on the beach was appealing, and one more night under the same roof with Will alone did not bother her, but she did not want to create an awkward situation for Will.

"I can go have a beer with my friends in town if you want to have the house to yourself for a while," Will joked. "But I think I at least owe you dinner since I couldn't make it yesterday."

"It's settled then," Sage said. "You guys have fun." A sly smile appeared on her face as she excused herself to get more coffee.

• • •

At seven that evening, Lu and Will sat down at a table in the flagstone courtyard of a French bistro in Bridgehampton, about fifteen miles away from Will's house in Montauk. A handful of small tables dotted the courtyard, which was surrounded by all-white trellises covered with mature wisteria vines. Will had insisted that Lu pick a restaurant for dinner. "I promised Sage I'd buy you both dinner. I am fulfilling a gentleman's promise even if she is not here." So Lu had picked her favorite, the Bistro on Main Street in Bridgehampton. Every time she vacationed in Montauk, she ate at least once at the Bistro. It served fresh, local seafood but was also famous for its classic steak and fries. She remembered what Sage had said about Will when it came to food: meat and potatoes kept him happy.

Earlier that day, after Sage had left to head back to DC, Lu and Will, plus Louis, had gone to the beach near a popular surf site, where Will had introduced her to his buddies who owned the famous oyster farm. After that, Lu had spent the afternoon lying on the beach with Louis at her side, watching Will and his friends go in and out of the waves a few hundred yards away. Every now and then, Will would get out of the water and come back to check if she was comfortable or if the dog was behaving. It had been an afternoon of bright sunshine, warm sand, and pleasant breeze in the company of a water-phobic but otherwise fearless Doberman. She'd watched the ocean waves turn Will, the forty-seven-year-old businessman, into a happy-go-lucky boy without a single care in the world. Lu could not remember the last time she'd felt so relaxed and at home. Her whole life so far had seemed to be always leaving— leaving Shanghai, leaving China, leaving the orphanage house, leaving Hong Kong, leaving Washington, DC. On that afternoon, Lu had felt Montauk was a place she could leave but also come back to.

"So did Louis behave today on the beach with you? He's a little weird when it comes to water; he won't get near it. You'd think he'd love water, being a dog. I hope he didn't bother you too much."

"No trouble at all; he was very well behaved. I had a great time," Lu said. Her eyes smiled before the corners of her mouth turned up. "Thanks again for letting me stay at your house. I don't think there is a single hotel or bed-and-breakfast in the Hamptons that offers a better view than your place. I had a great time." A voice in the back of her mind asked, *Did I just say "had a great time" twice? I hope he doesn't think I am babbling. Why do I care? It's not like I'm on a date or anything.*

But she cared.

After they had gotten back from the beach, she'd showered and washed her hair. She'd debated what she should wear, the shorter black cotton jersey dress she'd worn the first evening at dinner with Sage or her long white maxi dress. She tried them both on and was impressed by the effect of the white one, the way it set off her sun-bronzed face, neck, shoulders, and arms, stunningly radiant after two days on the beach. *Good God, I would be considered black back in China.* She thought about young women in the streets of Shanghai carrying flowery umbrellas to protect their porcelain-white skin even on days the sun's ultraviolet rays had trouble penetrating the particles that cemented the air and domed the sky.

She opted for the white maxi dress. She twisted her hair in a relaxed bun and secured it at the back of her head with a single pearl hairpin, leaving a few loose strands around her face. She always wore her hair up with long dresses. She put on some light makeup and applied a deep-red lipstick she often used dining out in the evening, the color of smooth, velvety Bordeaux, though she was not a big red-wine drinker. Satisfied with the look of the woman in the mirror, she stepped into a pair of white wedge sandals and went downstairs. She walked toward the front door as Will came out of his office to the side of the living room. He had changed into a sky-blue polo shirt and fitted khaki pants. His skin was tanned, and his medium-brown hair seemed a shade lighter from being in the sun for the better part of the day.

His intense blue eyes had locked with hers for an instant before he'd said, "You look great."

"Thanks, ready to go?" she'd murmured, trying to remember if she had seen bluer eyes than the ones in front of her. She'd felt excited but nervous at the same time, a moment she had last experienced many years ago on the first date with a guy she really liked.

"Nice little place. The menu looks great," Will said, glancing at the menu.

"I come here every time I'm in the area. The food is pretty good."

"I think I'll have a Caesar salad to go along with my steak. Glad Sage isn't here; she would have accused me of being predictable," Will said with a smile. "I've never been to this place before, though I've driven by countless times and seen the sign in front of the building."

"Sage told me you always find time to come here to surf. Louis and I had a good time watching you and your friends this afternoon. It was funny: every time you got out there in the water, Louis would stand at attention and bark. It was like he was worried you wouldn't come back."

"Come to think of it, that was the first time he's watched me surf. He's afraid of water, and I don't want him to run loose on the beach. So every time I go surfing, I leave him at the house. It was a treat for him today to sit with you on the beach for the entire afternoon, although I didn't mean to have you up here to dog sit."

"It was no bother. He sat next to me like we were best buddies. Funny how some people are intimidated by Dobermans, but they are the most loyal breed."

"So you know Dobermans. Have you ever had one?"

"Not really, but the orphanage in Hong Kong where I stayed for years had a house dog that was part Doberman. She was red with all the correct tan markings of a Doberman, but she had a white spot on her chest the size of a quarter, and her ears were a bit too floppy and long for a Doberman. Maybe she had a little bit of hound in her. We called her Spot. She was so affectionate yet a great watchdog …" She paused when a waitress brought the drinks they had ordered.

After they ordered dinner, Caesar salad and steak for Will and watercress salad and grilled sea bass for Lu, Will picked up where Lu had left off. "What happened to Spot in the end?"

"A friend wrote me years later and said she stayed there until she died of old age. But I will never forget the day I left the orphanage. A cab came to pick me up. Spot and some of the girls saw me off at the gate. As the cab drove away, I looked back. Spot pounced around in circles for a while; then she stopped and sat down, still as a statue. I watched her until she was out of sight." Lu paused to steady her slightly trembling voice. "I'm sorry. This is embarrassing. I still feel sad about a dog I knew thirty-some years ago," Lu said, trying to smile.

"Hey, it's okay. I know exactly how you feel. Dogs are funny in that way. They can get to our hearts and stay there forever. If something happened to Louis, he would take a piece of me with him. I bet my waterworks would flood uncontrollably." Will's voice was comforting, almost soulful.

"Thanks. Here is to our loyal friends then." Lu raised her champagne flute. They clinked glasses and took the first sip together.

"Now let's talk about something more cheerful," Lu said. "Surfing. I don't know too much about it. But from what I could see today, watching you and your friends, it's a physically demanding and sometimes-frustrating sport. But when everything all comes together, the wave, the wind, the position of the board, the surfer himself, it can be magical. I guess that's how you feel when you're out there on the sea."

For a few seconds, Will was quiet, his blue eyes twinkling at her, his tanned face beaming. "You got that right. Imagine," he said dreamily, gliding his left hand from right to left in the air, as if a cinematic scene was unfolding in front of him, "being out on the ocean with multiple overhead swirls, a fiery sunset background, and perfect off-shore winds. Everything is lined up, like destiny and fate."

It was Lu's turn to be speechless. "Wow, you should have been an artist, the way you describe it."

"I wouldn't go that far. According to my sister, I'm just an IT nerd who happens to be good at managing boring stuff like revenue, profits, and growth." Will chuckled in a self-deprecating way.

Their salads came. The Caesar salad's baby romaine leaves were creamy green, topped with several flat anchovy fillets and egg-yolk shavings. The delicate watercress salad was assembled with diced avocado and julienned golden mango.

After his first taste of the salad, Will switched subject. "So enough about surfing. Sage told me you're a good swimmer. She said you actually escaped from China by swimming across the river dividing China and Hong Kong when you were young."

"I wouldn't call my kind of swimming a sport. When I swam across the Shenzhen River, it was more like doggy-paddling for my life. I've developed a love-hate relationship with water. Every time I get into a river, sea, or ocean, I think about how the water pushed me to a new life but killed my father in a sense." The smile in her eyes dropped off, lingering precariously on the corners of her mouth.

"I'm sorry; I didn't mean to stir up bad memories."

"It's okay. I have accepted what happened. It was such a long time ago. But it's something I think about when I see bodies of water."

"So how long were you in the water?"

"I don't really remember. One minute my father and I thought we were going to make it; the next minute bullets were splashing across the water. I ducked down to the bottom of the river and kind of crawled to the shore on the other side. All I know is from where we entered the water it was about a mile and a half to the other side if we stayed on a straight line. I don't think I can make that distance anymore."

"That's quite a distance for an adult, and you were only what, thirteen years old?" Will was incredulous.

"Yeah, thirteen years old. Can't believe it was that long ago."

"Do you still have family in China?"

"My mother and sister are still living there," Lu said. She then quickly diverted the conversation. "So you and Sage both grew up around here. She told me your beach house used to belong to your grandparents."

Will seemed to sense that Lu did not want to talk about her past, and he answered her question instead. "Yes, my father's parents lived in the house almost all their life. I guess Sage told you my dad died early, so the house got passed down directly to Sage and me. I was in the navy at that time, often out on the sea for months at a time, so the house was neglected for years. After I got out the navy and finally got my business up and running, I had it renovated. Sage and I often joke that the two of us may come back here later to make a bed-and-breakfast out of it. Meanwhile it's a good beach house."

"So your love of surfing must have something to do with you joining the navy?"

"That was what I thought at age nineteen. Once I got in the navy, though, I realized I got more than I bargained for. I naively thought being in the navy was as exciting as surfing, but the training and months on ship floating on the sea could be mind-numbing, especially to an undisciplined nineteen-year-old like me, who laughably considered himself free-spirited."

"So how did you get through it?"

"It took a while for the navy to beat some discipline into me. For a while I was stubborn about not giving in to the training command officer, but he was determined not to give up on me. It was a test of wills, and in the end he succeeded in molding me into the person I am today, for my own good of course," Will said fondly.

"So what exactly did he do?"

"Shaming, a lot of shaming, in front of the whole crew, a lot of profanity." Will laughed.

"So you tried harder to avoid being shamed again?" Lu asked with great interest.

"You can say that, but don't tell Sage. She is all about encouragement and self-esteem—you know what I mean." Will grinned.

"I know what you mean. That's actually something Sage and I don't see eye to eye on sometimes. It may have something to do with growing up on opposite ends of the world."

"What do you mean?"

"In China, academic achievement is considered the foundation for building a successful career and prosperous life later, but sometimes it's a prestige thing for parents. Having smart kids makes them look good in front of other parents. So from very early on, kids are taught to strive to be number one. I remember one time I went home with a report card of mostly As and a couple of Bs. My father asked who had done better than me in class, and my mother asked why I had lost the other two As. So many kids today, and myself back then, have what I call a never-good-enough complex. As a result, we all try harder to be number one so we won't feel ashamed because somebody else beat us. My father once said that being second is being a loser."

"I can see why you disagree with Sage on this. She grew up believing everybody should get a medal or trophy for just showing up," Will joked.

"She doesn't go that far. When we worked together years ago, I think Sage and I complemented each other because of our disagreement. We both agree that I became more empathetic, and while she was still trusting, she verified more often."

"Well, we all knew Sage was a very trusting girlie girl when she was growing up."

"Don't be fooled by Sage the woman. She was tough enough to walk out on her job in defiance of that weasel Kessler after he handed me my two weeks' notice. How many so-called friends in our lives would do what Sage did for me?"

"I think she did it for herself too. I remember she told me it was a moral choice she made so she could face herself in the mirror every day. You've seen how she reacts every time the name Kessler comes up," Will said reflectively.

Lu did not want to let the name Kessler spoil her dinner, so she decided to circle back to Will's life as a young man. "So in the end, your navy training officer's shame tactic worked on you."

"Believe it or not, I came to love him. He was a tough SOB—that's what we used to call him behind his back—loved whisky, football, and yelling profanity constantly, but that's not what comes into my mind when I think of him every now and then. What I remember is how his toughness pushed me through college and training to become a navy cyber-warfare engineer, and I remember the evenings when he forced me to stay with him in his quarters, listening to Wagner's opera *The Flying Dutchman* as the ship floated amid the pitch darkness of the sea." In the dimmed light, Will's eyes turned a deep, dreamy blue.

"That's the opera based on the story of the ship captain doomed to sail the ocean forever unless he could find a woman who would forever be faithful to him, right? Or something like that?" Lu asked, fascinated that their conversation had turned from an SOB navy commander to classic opera.

"So you're an opera buff?" Will was as surprised as Lu was fascinated.

"Not really, but I like some of the lighter opera music. Wagner is too heavy for me. So did he convert you into a Wagner lover?"

"No, I liked *The Flying Dutchman* for the story, not the music. But again, what music could be more suitable for a young man and an old drunk deployed at sea, fantasizing about a nice woman waiting for us when we got back to land?" Will laughed.

Lu laughed too. She got the humor in Will's words, but she also saw sensitivity within the man Sage described as a boring workaholic and saw romanticism underneath the raw masculinity he exhumed while conquering the white waves of the Atlantic Ocean.

"He sounds like an interesting man," Lu said after their laughter subsided a little.

"Yep, but the whisky finally caught up with his liver. He died a few years ago. He never really seemed to be truly happy with his life, though. I could feel the gloominess in him when we were listening to Wagner together. For a while I thought it was because the music was gloomy. He kept his personal past to himself. All I knew was he was divorced and never remarried again."

"I guess he had inner demons to fight, but who is really happy all the time in this world? Many people say all they want in life is to be healthy and happy. I understand the health part, but there is no such thing as constant happiness. There are only highs and lows in life; to be happy is to love one's life enough to best manage the lows."

"That's an interesting way of looking at life. Actually, my dad used to say we humans would never achieve permanent happiness, because we have a natural tendency to self-destruct when everything is going fine and dandy. We screw up and then try to right things again, going in circles forever ..."

"But hopefully we learn in this circular process so we don't screw up the same way time and again," Lu said.

Will cast Lu a knowing look and was about to say something, but he was interrupted by the arrival of their main course. The lanterns under the wisteria vines came on, shining a soft yellow light around them. The pale moon climbed above the tall brick wall of the courtyard in an unfathomable sky of the deepest blue.

"We should order more champagne and some wine," he said, looking at Lu.

Lu held his gaze and nodded enthusiastically. But she was more intoxicated by Will's changing eyes. Under the soft lantern light, his crystal-blue eyes had taken on a gentle hue of teal green.

So they ordered more champagne and wine, and they talked. They talked about Sage, as a sister, as a friend. They revealed more of their childhood memories to each other, choosing to stick with the happy and pleasant ones.

And they did not for one second touch on anything that was business, and Great China Telecom became the farthest thing on their minds.

• • •

At 5:00 a.m., Lu woke up to "Romance" from Dmitri Shostakovich's *The Gadfly Suite*. It was her favorite classical music. She had programmed it as her alarm on her cell. It took her a few moments to be fully conscious of where she was and to remember what had happened during the past weekend. She got out of the bed and tiptoed to the bathroom in the hallway, wincing and frowning every time a floorboard squeaked under her feet. Will's office, where she hoped he was still sleeping, was directly beneath her bedroom.

In the hallway bathroom, she decided not to take a shower. She brushed her teeth and washed her face in the sink and then went back to the bedroom to change into her travel clothes, the blue shirt and cotton pants she'd worn last Friday. Carrying the duffel bag, she glided downstairs quietly. In the kitchen, she tore a piece of paper from the notepad sitting on the counter and wrote Will a note:

> Thanks for a fantastic weekend. I had a great time. Hope everything will work itself out with the Chinese telecom. Lu

She pinned the note up on the refrigerator door with a magnet in the shape of a sunflower. From the kitchen she slipped into the living room, heading to the front door. She heard a squeak from the side door in the living room that led to Will's office. She turned, ready to apologize for her premeditated leaving-without-saying-good-bye departure. In front of the half-opened door, Louis's curious eyes looked at her, his head cocked slightly to one side as if asking, "Where are you going at this early hour?" She put her index finger on her lips. "Shh … Quiet." Louis trotted toward her, his stubby tail waggling in circles. She patted him on the head. She could hear Will's deep, steady breathing from behind the partly opened door.

She continued to walk to the front door, the dog following her until she turned the knob and stepped outside. She turned around to close the door. On the other side of the doorway, Louis stood in a Doberman forward-lean pose, his dark-brown eyes looking up at her longingly, as if saying, "You are going to come back, right?"

• • •

All the way from Montauk to her Midtown apartment, she tried to focus on questions she needed to ask at the 10:00 a.m. meeting that morning in Fred Armstrong's office downtown. Her boss, Jack, had e-mailed her the meeting schedule on Saturday. "It's going to be a big deal for Fred and for all firms involved in the potential Great China Telecom IPO. Don't miss the meeting," he'd said in the e-mail. But her mind was playing a trick on her, playing back the moment when she and Will had stood at the foot of the staircase in the beach house the previous night, after they'd gotten back from the Bistro.

"Good night. Dinner was fun. See you in the morning," he'd said.

"Thanks for dinner; it was great," she'd said softly. She had not been able to decide if she should give him a hug or just a handshake.

He'd leaned forward and kissed her cheek. "Good night," he'd said again. His lips had been warm, and his breath had smelled of red wine.

She shook her head swiftly from side to side a few times. "Focus, Lu, focus," she told herself. "Okay, let's try again. First things first, I need Great China Telecom's detailed financial statements."

Will's kiss, his warm lips, and Bordeaux-scented breath, her mind played back the moment again. It went on until the elevator door opened on the top floor of the headquarters of Wall Street's most elite investment firm. She stepped out and walked into the conference room at 10:00 a.m. sharp.

CHAPTER 13

. . . . .

THE ELEVATOR DOOR DINGED open. "Eighth floor," a soft female voice announced. Lu stepped out and looked right then left. She still could not quite believe her mother's new apartment was in the Grosvenor Tower, the historically famous art deco luxury apartment building in the most prestigious location in Shanghai, the old French Concession. There were only two units on the floor, one to the right and one to the left. Her mother's unit, 8A, was on the left side. She walked to the door and tapped on it a couple of times, only spotting the gold dome-like doorbell on the door frame afterward. She heard footsteps approaching and held her breath.

The dead bolt clicked, and the metal chain lock slid. The door popped open, and a young woman stood in front of her. For an instant, they stared at each other with the same intensity and curiosity, siblings who might as well had never met. One had been thirteen and the other hardly one when they had parted decades ago.

"You must be Mei."

"You must be Lu."

They spoke almost simultaneously.

"Come on in, come on in." Mei's voice was softly high-pitched, almost childlike.

Lu followed her sister into the expansive living/dining room area, facing the front courtyard of the building. Along the way, Lu noticed the original structures of the apartment had been preserved sensitively—high ceilings, parquet floors, stained glass windows, and curvaceous niches and shelves.

"I am so glad you left your business card with Mother. I wanted to contact you so badly over the years, but we didn't know where you were,"

Mei chirped and gestured Lu to sit down on the circular leather couch in the center of the room. Lu's impulse was to challenge immediately the "we didn't know where you were" part. She had forwarded her address to her mother every time she'd moved. But she held her tongue and examined her sister carefully instead.

Lu gathered Mei was about five feet six inches, a couple of inches taller than herself, and painfully thin. She was wearing a pink silk sleeveless dress; her arms and legs were sticklike. Her feet were adorned with a pair of white two-inch-heel pumps, with the universally recognizable Chanel logo in black on top. She had a round face, slightly too large for her delicate body, round eyes, a short snub nose, and a small cherry-shaped mouth glossed with cherry-colored lipstick. Every feature on her face came together to make her look like a cute bunny. Her black hair was thick and chin length, blunt cut, and streaked with a curious color of terra-cotta. Her skin was void of any trace of color or pigment, smooth white porcelain, the hallmark of female beauty in China.

"I'm sorry I wasn't around when you first visited. I was out of the country with my husband." Mei asked cheerfully, "Would like to have some tea? I'll ask the maid to make some tea."

"Ice water will be fine. It's hot out there," Lu said.

"Auntie Li," Mei called in the direction of what looked like a kitchen door, "could you bring us a glass of ice water?"

No answer.

"She must be out," Mei said. Then she leaned over and lowered her voice. "You know she's not our auntie. She's the new help Juin and I hired for Mother. Mother has been complaining that she is getting old and can't take care of housework anymore. In Shanghai all housemaids are called aunties."

"Is that Lu?" Lu's mother's voice preceded her from the hallway leading to the bedrooms on the back side of the apartment. Seconds later, Mrs. Lin glided into the living room, her wide-legged silk pants fluttering gently around her legs. She wore a fitted white silk blouse, with emerald piping around the stand-up mandarin collar and capped sleeves. A pair of jade earrings dangled around her cheeks. Her short silver hair was set in a stiff and voluminous bob, more like a white helmet.

"I am glad business has brought you back to Shanghai again." Her face broke into a faint smile, but her eyes narrowed slightly as they scanned up and down Lu's clothing, a pair of beige linen capri pants and a white T-shirt.

"How are you, Mother?" Lu asked, ignoring her mother's what-the-hell-are-you-wearing look.

"Good, good, just settling in. The move has taken a lot out of me, especially in this hot and humid weather." She looked out the window and dabbed some imaginary sweat off her forehead with a white handkerchief.

"Your apartment is beautiful," Lu said, looking around and noticing the room's mix of modern and classic furnishing. The scallop-edged wood mantle over the restored fireplace in the living room had been painted and glazed gleaming white. Tanned kid-leather couches encircled a glass octagon coffee table, and a mahogany Howard Miller grandfather clock stood in a corner, next to the built-in bookshelves. In the dining area, a rosewood dining set was complete with a double pedestal table, six chairs with black leather cushions, and a black marble-topped side buffet table.

"It's comfortable. I was thinking of buying a new apartment unit somewhere else, but then I thought, *I'm old, don't have much life ahead of me. What's the difference between buying and just renting a place, as long as it's comfortable?* This one came fully furnished, saves everybody running around buying new furniture and everything," her mother said with a wave of her hand, as if she'd just settled for the place.

"Mother, Juin said he would have bought you a new apartment if you would consider the newer ones out there for sale. This building is a historic landmark; it's not for sale." Mei pouted, looking anxious that her mother was not 100 percent happy.

"I know, Mei; you and Juin have helped me a lot. You are good kids. Mommy wouldn't know what to do without you." She circled one arm around Mei's shoulders and pulled Mei toward her while casting a look at Lu, a look of a guilt master saying, "What have you done for me?"

The gesture of endearment made Mei happy. She smiled and looked at her wristwatch. "It's past noon. I made reservations at Apricot Garden. Shall we go now?"

"Good," Mrs. Lin said cheerfully. "It's something to celebrate, mother and daughters, after thirty-three years. Let me go and put on a pair of shoes, and we can go."

"I'll go and use the bathroom before we go," Mei said to Lu before heading toward the powder room in the hallway.

In her mother's and sister's brief absence, Lu went to look out the living room window. Downstairs, in front of the building, men were working on the meticulously kept pastel-green lawn. The open wrought iron gate, rusty and dirty the last time she'd seen it, had been restored to its glory, with a shining coating of black and gold. Across the street, the five-star Garden Hotel tower hovered forty stories high behind its century-old baroque-style facade. The building had been designed by a French architect in the early 1920s as a luxury French sports club. The garden area of the hotel stretched over the entire block and was dotted with lotus ponds and lined with Japanese cherry trees.

She turned away from the window, feeling a little overwhelmed, oozy. Maybe the jet lag was setting in. She had only arrived the previous day, a day earlier than everybody else on the due diligence team for the Great China Telecom IPO deal.

When she'd visited her small apartment in the now-torn-down building a few months ago, she'd thought her mother's reaction lukewarm and her emotions detached and remote at best. But somehow Lu had known that she would be back in Shanghai, and she had wanted try to reconnect with her sister. So she'd left her business card with her mother and asked her to tell Mei to contact her if she wanted to. She had not had great expectations, not after she had been rejected and ignored for thirty-some years.

To her surprise, Mei had e-mailed her, apologized for her absence, and invited her to visit if she ever came back to Shanghai again. And here she was, having lunch with her mother and sister. It was something worth celebrating.

Lu went over to the couch to get her handbag. The framed photos on the mantle caught her eye: her mother as a little girl with her parents, Mei in a Western-style wedding gown standing next to her husband in a black tuxedo and white bow tie. He looked quite a bit older than Mei and had slicked back black hair and a bony face, a face Lu thought she had seen somewhere, a long ago time, in a faraway place.

"Ready to go?" her mother asked from behind her. "Oh, you're looking at the pictures. That's Mei's wedding picture; she just got married less than two years ago. You know I was kind of worried that she was going to be an old spinster, but she was lucky. The son of a friend of mine, now Mei's husband, Juin, had gotten divorced several years ago, so we set the two of them up, and here they are, married and happy. Juin is an extremely smart and successful businessman."

"That's great, Mother," Lu mumbled as she heard Mei's heels clicking in the hallway.

· · ·

They arrived at Apricot Garden, one of the most famous Chinese restaurants in Shanghai. It had a golden pagoda facade supported by two round red columns with gold phoenix and dragon etchings. The restaurant was inside an old brick duplex with dividing walls knocked down to allow for a spacious dining area. They were greeted by a young hostess in a red traditional Chinese *qipao*, a form-fitting, mandarin-collared dress with high side slit. "Mrs. Lin, how are you today?"

"Not bad. Is our table ready? Please sit us away from all this smoke," Lu's mother said, waving both her hands, fanning away the cigarette smoke that had infiltrated the entire dining area.

They made their way to a private dining room in the back. The decor, if not for the lingering smell of acrid cigarette smell, could have evoked a Zen- and nature-like atmosphere. A straight-legged square black table sat in the middle, a chair with satin-upholstered seat on each of the four sides. Against the wall next to the door was a matching serving table. Two black-and-white reproductions of famous Chinese watercolor paintings, *Koi Pond* and *Galloping Horses*, adorned the two side walls.

The three of them sat down around the table already set with chopsticks, napkins, plates, teacups, and wineglasses. After laying the menus on the table and wishing her guests an enjoyable meal, the hostess quietly retreated.

"I guess this is okay," Lu's mother said, her eyes dancing around the room. She then fumbled in her handbag and fished out her gold-rimmed eyeglasses. "Let's see what we have here." She put on the glasses and focused on the menu.

Two young women, Lu was sure they were no more than twenty years old, entered the room, one with a large teapot and the other with a notepad, ready to take the order. As the teacups were filled, Lu's mother read out the dishes she wanted: bird's nest, sea cucumbers, prawns, shark fins—all things the Chinese considered delicacies and the most-expensive items on the menu. Lu winced when her mother ordered shark fins, and without giving too much thought, she blurted, "I don't think I like shark fins, Mother."

"Oh, why?" Her mother lifted her glasses slightly and let them rest on the lower part of her nose bridge, looking at Lu from above the upper rim.

"I read a report that too many sharks have their fins cut and then are left to bleed to death in the sea. And for what? Nutrition?" Lu said matter-of-factly.

"But it's a century-old delicacy. I thought we are celebrating today." Her mother looked surprised.

"You order what you like. I just think the way they are killed is inhumane, and all so we can chew on something that tastes like big needles."

"You eat meat, don't you?" her mother asked.

"Yes, occasionally."

"Those animals have to be killed first too, so what's the difference?" Her mother rolled her eyes and then looked back at the menu in front of her. "Okay, no shark fins," she announced without looking at the waitress taking the order.

Lu remained quiet during the rest of the elaborate order. Her stomach was unsettled. It could be jet lag, the nervous anticipation of seeing her long-lost sister, or the anxiety of facing her mother again. Whatever it was, she had no appetite, even though the menu looked delicious at first glance.

"So exactly what do you do at the company in New York, Sister?" Mei asked after their mother had ordered at least a dozen courses and both waitresses had left the room and closed the door behind them.

"I conduct research on companies that sell their stocks on the US stock market, making sure they are reasonably good investments to whoever buys the stocks."

"Oh, what kind of companies? American companies or any companies? Do you talk to them, or do you write articles?" Mei asked.

"You could say both." Lu smiled at her sister's earnest effort to comprehend exactly what was involved in her job.

"Well, I heard my husband saying something about helping one of the companies he manages to sell stock in New York. Maybe they will come to you," Mei said innocently.

"Do you know the company's name?" Lu asked. Somewhere in the remote back of her head, she heard a siren.

"I don't remember. Juin is the head of so many companies."

"Well, make sure Juin has time to meet your sister. Didn't he say he would like to meet Lu the other day?" their mother chimed in.

"Yes, Mother. But Juin is always so busy. Sometimes I don't see him for weeks at a time. But he did promise he would be back this weekend," Mei said softly, looking at her mother. Lu noticed for the first time that her sister's eyes, though large, lacked light.

The cold appetizers came. Small plates of smoked fish, smoked duck, wine-marinated chicken, and pickled vegetables were spread on the table.

"So what do you do, Mei? You haven't told me where you work," Lu said.

For a moment, silence hung awkwardly around the table. "Mei doesn't do work in the office like you do," their mother said, breaking the silence, "but she is plenty busy helping her husband, entertaining clients, accompanying him on business trips, and so on. I don't think Juin could be this successful without her, right, Mei?" She reached over and touched Mei's arm.

"You are exaggerating, Mother. I'm not that important, and sometimes it's lonely all by myself when Juin is away on business." Mei reddened slightly.

"Lonely? What nonsense. Go shopping; go out to eat; go to the theater or concert with your girlfriends. You are lucky to have a husband who is so capable of providing you with all these nice things, and you can't expect him to be around you every minute of the day, you know." Their mother sounded shocked that her daughter could be so unreasonable.

Sensing her sister was uncomfortable with their mother's remarks, Lu changed the subject. "So, Mother, do you like your new apartment so far?"

"So far so good. But if it turned out to be not acceptable later, I am sure Juin and Mei would find me something better," her mother said casually.

For the first time Lu thought, *You mean Juin will take care of it for you.*

Shallow and trivial conversations dominated the rest of their meal. Mei stayed relatively quiet. Lu compared Shanghai August weather to New York August weather, and their mother judged the quality and taste of each dish (usually not good enough) and complained about the high cost of living in Shanghai and her measly pension.

The bill came on a black-lacquered tray, inside a check holder embossed with the restaurant's name and apricot flower petals. Not sure who was the host of the meal, the waitress set the tray in the middle of the table, together with a plate of orange wedges. "Dessert on the house," she said.

Mei reached out for the tray, but her mother gently pushed her back. "Mother, let me pay for this. I invited both you and Lu," Mei argued.

"I didn't say I was going to pay for this." Her mother pursed her thin lips. Turning to Lu, she said with a smile, "Now, Lu, I know Mei invited you, but she is your younger sister. She has been taking care of Mommy for all these years. Perhaps it's time for you to do something nice for Mommy?"

"I am glad to do this for you, Mother," Lu said. She quickly turned to grab her handbag hanging on the back of her seat and fished out her wallet. She slid her credit card inside the check holder without examining the bill. A voice inside her said, *Just pay the bill, get this lunch over with, and get out.*

CHAPTER 14

• • • • •

WHEN LU WOKE UP, the clock blinked 3:20 at her in the darkness. It took her a few moments to collect her memories of the previous day. She'd had lunch with her mother and sister, come back to Hilton, worked out, taken a shower, and checked her e-mail. She had been exhausted and feeling oozy, so she'd decided to lie down and just close her eyes for a few minutes. That had been around seven o'clock on Friday, and now it was almost three thirty in the morning Saturday. She had slept over eight hours in a white cotton hotel bathrobe on a bed that was not turned down.

She turned on the bedside lamp and got up. Through the panoramic window partially covered by heavy draperies, neon signs flickered blue and silver on top of an office building across the street. Her stomach growled, reminding her it had been over twelve hours since her last not-so-appetizing meal. Nothing was open for breakfast yet. She could order from the twenty-four-hour room service but decided to force herself to go by the local time, waiting until six thirty to have breakfast in the executive lounge.

She went over to the individual-cup coffeemaker in the room, popped a small coffee pod in the machine, poured bottled water into the brewing compartment, and pushed the On switch. With the coffeemaker hissing, she walked across the room to the window and pulled back the draperies on both sides until her view of the city was maximized. It was a city well lit, illuminated by a network of skyscraper neon lights, department-store billboard lights and storefront decorating lights. But the illumination was dull, blurred by humidity and pollution. She cast her eyes downward. There was hardly any traffic on the Yan'an expressway, but come daytime it would be puffing toxic exhaust like a dragon breathing out smoky fire. She leveled her eyes; the expressway sprawled into the hazy darkness ahead. Close by, less than a block ahead of her, a nebulous hole crouched not far away from the base of the elevated expressway, where her childhood home had stood less than three months ago. She had walked by the empty lot a day ago and had seen a large construction sign that had been erected in the middle of the lot with a sketch of what looked like a neighborhood green with French plane trees, wooden benches, and arced streetlamps. *At least it won't be another metal-and-glass monstrosity,* she'd consoled herself at the time. But now it suddenly hit her that during the past thirty-some years, the little old building had been one of the last few threads connecting her to the city, a place she still considered home despite how many of her childhood memories there were painful. "You can break a lotus root in half, but its delicate, silky threads still connect the two halves together," her grandma used to say. The black hole in front of her reminded her that at least quite a few of the delicate threads were now forever severed.

The coffeemaker stopped hissing. Lu turned away from the window, fetched the mug of coffee at the machine, and sat down in front of the desk. She checked her cell phone and found it had run out of battery. She connected the phone to the charger and powered on her computer to check e-mail. Dick Witherspoon had sent a message from the airport saying he would be arriving in Shanghai Saturday evening and was wondering if they could touch base sometime on Sunday. Other than that, work e-mail traffic had been light during the past couple of days.

Lu smiled when a message from Sage popped up on the screen. Since they'd seen each other in Montauk, they had hardly talked or even e-mailed. Lu had been swept into the Great China Telecom frenzy the minute she'd come back from the beach and had been trapped in meetings and drowned in a myriad of data, analyses, and reports. She clicked the message open.

> Hope all is well. Just want to let you know Will has been invited by the Chinese to visit their plants in China. He might leave as early as this weekend for Shanghai. The Chinese are still very much interested in working out

some deal with Matrixtech. I told him he could call you
if he needs help. Hope you don't mind …

The news of Will's visit was a surprise but not completely unexpected.
She and Will had not communicated with each other since she'd
pinned a thank-you note on his refrigerator and then sneaked out of
his Montauk beach house. Sure they'd had a great dinner together and
had some interesting conversations, and yes, his good-night kiss had
stirred up some emotions she had not felt for a long time. But she knew
better, and she and Will both knew their professional paths might cross
again sometime down the road; it was prudent to leave their personal
relationship the way it was. She was Sage's best friend, and Will was her
best friend's brother. She just had not anticipated that they would be
bumping into each other for business reasons so soon.

She replied to Sage's e-mail, telling her she was actually in Shanghai
for two weeks and provided her hotel information in case Will needed
to get in touch with her after his arrival.

Her cell phone ding-donged. A quick glance told her there was a text
message. It had come in late last night to her dead cell. She was glad to
see it was from her sister. "Juin is not coming home until Sunday. Let's
have dinner Saturday evening?"

"Great, tell me when and where. Or you could come to the hotel,"
she replied. *This weekend is turning out to be interesting,* she thought,
and she began to look forward to it. She decided to go for a run first in
the gym downstairs.

• • •

In the lounge-style bar on the Hilton Shanghai hotel's thirty-ninth
floor, Lu was sitting at a table next to a floor-to-ceiling window with a
view of the entire west side of the city in the dusk. A pink watermelon
martini sat on the table in front of her, and a man in a black tuxedo was
playing a baby grand piano at the far end of the room. In the step-down
center lounge area, two cocktail waitresses in bright-red *qipao* wound
their way around the couches, chaises, and cocktail tables, bringing
guests drinks, cigars, and light refreshments.

She and Mei had agreed to meet here for a drink first and then have dinner at the Sichuan Chinese restaurant on the other side of the same floor. At 7:00 p.m. sharp, Mei appeared at the entrance, where she lingered for a brief moment. Her eyes danced across the room and quickly spotted Lu by the window. She wore an A-line white floral lace dress, knee length and sleeveless. Her straight chin-length hair had been curled and tousled slightly to complement the feminine flair of the dress. A pair of teardrop pearl earrings danced around her face as she swayed toward her sister. A gold clutch bag and a pair of three-inch-heel gold-toned pumps completed her ensemble.

"What are you drinking?" she asked, examining the pink drink Lu had ordered.

"Watermelon martini, a popular light summer drink, according to the waitress," Lu said.

Mei frowned slightly at the drink. "I think it's more like fruit juice. I'm going to have something a little stronger." She waved at one of the waitresses.

A few minutes later, two glasses of Veuve Clicquot arrived at their table.

"I am sorry Mother made you pay for lunch yesterday. It's my treat today. I am so glad we get to see each other after over thirty years." Mei raised her glass of champagne.

"Me too. In that sense, I'm almost glad Juin is not home today. He must be very busy," Lu said.

"Honestly, he is away too much. We've been married for two years now, and we're still trying to have a baby. Mother said I will soon be too old for that," Mei said with a chuckle.

Surprised by her sister's directness and the personal nature of the subject, Lu diverted slightly. "So how did the two of you meet?"

"It's a long story." Mei stared at the bubbles in the champagne glass for a moment, as if gathering her thoughts about how to best tell the story. "Juin's mother died when he was only a baby. And Mother and Juin's father used to be friends because they worked in the same hospital together. When Juin was a little boy, his father often brought him to the hospital on days when school was out, so Mother literally watched Juin grow up. When Juin was fourteen years old, his father passed away, and

Juin went to live with his father's best friend, who was a general in the army. Mother knows him too because he was sick once and stayed at the hospital for quite a while. When Juin got divorced, his stepfather, the general, and Mother set us up for a date."

"So Juin's stepfather is still alive. He must have retired from the army."

"Oh yes, he is very healthy. He, his wife, and Mother often play bridge together."

"If he was a general in the army, he must be very powerful and very connected with high-ranking government officials," Lu said, surprised her mother had been long connected to people in high places.

"I think so. That's why Juin was sponsored by the government to get his education in the US and Europe. Mother said Juin is very smart and studied hard, and that's why he is so successful now."

"Have you asked him the reason for his divorce?"

"Well, just once. He said they were both young and she soon became resentful because he was too busy with his business. He didn't really want to talk about it," Mei said, not once looking at her sister. "What's funny is I think his ex-wife was right. I feel like I'm now in the same situation as she was before."

"They say couples are closer when they don't see each other every day," Lu said.

"But he's never around. Sometimes I forget I have a husband. Mother said an old maid like me should feel lucky to find somebody like Juin, rich and powerful. My girlfriends' eyes have all turned red with envy because I have everything, a big house in the suburb and condos on the waterfront, big cars and fancy jewelry. So I never get to talk too much about Juin's absence from home. I don't get any sympathy from my friends." Mei forced a smile, as if convincing herself she was just being too needy.

"But?" Lu fixed her eyes on her sister's pale face.

Mei remained quiet.

After a moment of silence, Lu said, "How could Mother say you were an old maid? You were what? A little over thirty when you married Juin?"

"I was almost thirty-three."

"In that sense, I'm ancient," Lu said, smiling. "Look at me: I am forty-seven and have never been married. What would Mother say about that? I practically belong with the extinct species like the dragons and dinosaurs."

Lu's self-deprecating humor seemed to defuse Mei's self-doubt. "You're right; I should not take Mother too seriously, but sometimes it's hard to be around her. She complains and nags constantly. For a while it was about me turning into an old maid. Now that Juin and I are married, all she asks is when we're going to have a baby. She even said that if I don't have a baby with Juin, somehow my future is not guaranteed. I think she worries too much."

What Mei said troubled Lu. She had the feeling that her mother was pressuring Mei to have a baby with Juin to secure a certain lifestyle for herself. She did not think it appropriate to voice her concern directly to Mei, so she said instead, "Mother is lucky she has you and Juin to be around to help her. Anybody would say that she is living very comfortably, even according to the living standards of the well-to-do in the United States."

"You could say that, but Mother doesn't considered herself an average person. She thinks she deserves better after the sacrifices she made to raise me all by herself. I'm not blaming you or anything, but I think it was horrible our father deserted Mother when I was only a baby. It must have been very hard on her. Juin and I are doing our best to make her old-age life more comfortable." Mei's voice was small and childlike.

Lu was about to say something, but the cell phone Mei had left on the table buzzed. She glanced at it and picked it up immediately. "Sorry, I'd better get this; it's Juin."

Lu nodded. Lifting her champagne glass, she gazed outside the window. Darkness had fallen. An orange half-moon hung low in the hazy sky. The city beneath was lit up like a fluorescent spiderweb. For a moment, she was back in the little apartment just a block away. She heard herself ask, "Why are you always so sad, Mommy?" And she heard her mother say, "Mommy married the wrong person."

"All right. Bye," Mei said and shut off the cell. "Sorry, Juin told me he is coming home tomorrow and wants me to be with him at a business dinner next week."

"It's okay. I'm glad we at least have this evening to catch up."

"We should move to the other side now," Mei said, taking a last sip of champagne. "The food should be pretty good; it's supposed to be the best Sichuan-style cuisine in Shanghai. We can stay as late as we want tonight, to catch each other up on what we have missed out on for thirty-three years."

"Agreed," Lu said.

They stood up and walked out of the bar side by side. A big part of the past thirty-three years seemed to have already dropped away.

• • •

Kevin Jagger was furious. With his elbows on the desk, his chin resting in his palms, and the blue veins in his temples bulging and throbbing, he had been staring at his computer with narrowed eyes for a while but did not seem to be aware that the screen in front of him was black.

It was Saturday. He'd gotten up at five, just as he did every day, gone for a long run, told his wife he had business to take care of, and left the house for his office at Matrixtech. He had hoped a long run could help him see some logic in the recent chaos in his professional life. But it had not helped much. An inner voice, clipped and curt, had kept talking to him.

It all had begun less than five months ago, when Will had told him he was planning to merge with Matrixtech. To him, Will's status of being the boss and the owner of the company was only a technicality. In reality, Kevin Jagger was the one who had built, managed, and pushed the company to the success it had achieved. Granted, the profit margin of their business was not high, but it had provided guaranteed revenue year in and year out for over a decade. A paltry few percent of net profit, even after taxes, had netted Will a seven-figure personal income every year for years. Kevin could not deny the fact that Will had already been in business for a couple of years before he'd joined the company, and he admitted that he had been making a good salary and receiving generous bonus payments in recent years. But the facts were the facts. He was the key person responsible for winning the company's first multimillion-dollar long-term contract. Because of that, other similar contracts had followed. Without him, without his personal connections to certain government agencies, Will Donavan would still be scrambling for chicken feed and pittance.

His cell vibrated in the back pocket of his cargo pants. He took a deep breath, puffed his cheeks, and blew out with a *pooh* before reaching back for the phone. It was a message forwarded from Will, asking him to attend a client meeting with Frank next week. "Surprise, surprise, good old Kevin is always there to help," Kevin murmured to himself as he responded to the e-mail with two letters: "OK."

Ever since Will had revealed his intention of merging with another company and branching into what he considered as more-cutting-edge technologies, Kevin had seen a growing gap between the two of them. After the merger with Matrixtech, the gap had become as wide as the Grand Canyon. Will was now the hotshot senior executive of a billion-dollar company, wheeling and dealing globally to build a company focusing on fancy new technology products and services, while he, Kevin Jagger, was the person overseeing what was viewed as the boring, low-margin government-contract business. He felt insignificant and inadequate at the same time but was willing to put up with it as long as he could keep his rather lucrative compensation package he and his family had gotten used to for many years.

He had always been proud of his planning, organizing, and executing skills. They were the key factors in his success. Will Donavan might be the face of the company, personable and charismatic enough to be awarded those long-term contracts. But managing and executing the contracts well so they got renewed again and again was a different matter. It required control, order, and discipline. Kevin was good at that, and he had succeeded.

In his personal life, the same principles applied. He'd waited until he'd been almost forty to get married, when he had finally been comfortable with his financial condition. He would never have started a family knowing he did not have sufficient means to afford them a comfortable life. Until recently he'd thought he had planned his life and executed his life plan flawlessly.

But the life he had planned and worked hard for was now threatened.

He might be considered inflexible, regimental, and resistant to change, but one thing he was not was stupid. He did not have to be in those high-level meetings with the senior executives and board members to figure out what could happen to him if Matrixtech formed any sort of business relationship with the Chinese. There was no way the federal contracts he managed would continue to stay with Matrixtech, due to national-security reasons. The US government would never allow the Chinese to get close to contracts that required secret or top-secret clearance from each and every one of the project staff. Most likely, they would be spun off and swept under some stodgy large defense contractor who had been managing similar projects much longer than Kevin had. In that case, Kevin Jagger would perish. The amount of revenue his contracts garnered would be a drop in the bucket within a large defense company that had annual revenues in the tens and billions of dollars. His current position would become an administrative redundancy, streamlined and eliminated.

What would he do then? He was close to fifty years old. Where was he going to get another similar job at his current pay?

For the first time in his life, he was worried and afraid. He put his cell back in his pocket and turned on the computer. He tried to focus on a dashboard project report, a statistical summary of the performance of the network his staff had been maintaining for one of the government agencies. He found it difficult to insert just a few numeric numbers into his one-page report. The numbers muddled his mind and taunted him, whispering, "What if you can't afford the huge mortgage anymore? What if your children can't go to private school or college? What if your wife has to cut down on expenses like spas and salons, housecleaning, babysitting, and nannies while she's out on girls-only parties and retreats? What if, what if …?"

He paused and gulped on the lukewarm Starbucks coffee he had bought on his way in. He could not just sit around and let them destroy the business he had spent almost his whole career to build. And he would not go down without putting up a good fight. But this was going to be different. It was not the kind of fight like when he had been in the marines. He would have to be patient, plan carefully, and execute the plan artfully so he would survive everything in the end but not be viewed as a villain, at least not by the public. He thought about Will for a minute and quickly concluded that he no longer had an obligation to stay loyal to him. Why? Will Donavan would have never had today if it were not for him. And it was Will Donavan who had breached the brotherly bond between them by rocking the solid boat they both had been on to merge with Matrixtech, and now he wanted to collude with the Chinese and did not seem to give a damn what would happen to the buddy who had been nothing but loyal to him.

He drank the last bit of coffee and somehow felt better. Then he thought of Rob Kessler. *I'll give Rob a call; he should be able to help,* Kevin thought, a grin appearing on his face.

• • •

Will was in the airport lounge at Dulles airport when Kevin's reply e-mail came through. "OK" was all Kevin replied to Will's request asking him to attend a client meeting on his behalf while he traveled to China. He shook his head. *Kevin is being Kevin again. I'll have to have a good talk with him when I come back from the trip,* he thought.

Ever since the merger with Matrixtech, Will's day-to-day interactions and communications with Kevin had been greatly reduced. Kevin's team had moved into the basement level of the Matrixtech building (for security reasons) while Will had joined the senior-executive team on the fourth floor, the top floor of the company's campus-style office building. The four-story physical distance between them seemed to have driven them apart, threatening to fracture the solidarity they had maintained for over a decade. Socially, they had not had a beer together for months. Will had invited Kevin once or twice to happy hours at the pub, but he'd always had excuses for not coming. When they did interact, at meetings or via e-mail, Kevin's style and manner had been curt, even temperamental.

At the beginning, Will had not thought too much about it. He'd known that Kevin, whose personality and work style sometimes could be considered rigid and inflexible, might need some time to adjust to the different working environment of a much-larger company. Will also blamed himself for being not as available, being pulled into all sorts of strategy and reorganization meetings all the time. Recently Will's close involvement in the potential deal with Great China Telecom and intense negotiations with the Chinese had kept him behind closed doors for days at a time. When a preliminary understanding had finally been reached between the two companies, it had been decided that both parties would present the memorandum of understanding to the higher-ups, Matrixtech to its board of directors and Great China Telecom to its holding parent company, Great Wall Holding. At the same time, it had been mutually agreed that Matrixtech would benefit from a visit to a number of Great China Telecom's manufacturing plants in China to increase "mutual understanding," as the Chinese called it. After an internal discussion among Matrixtech's senior executives, it had been determined that the Chinese were most interested in Matrixtech's telecommunication network design and security expertise and that Will, with his strong knowledge in cybersecurity and antihacking products and services, was the best candidate for the trip.

Immediately after the China-trip decision had been made, Will had gone to see Kevin in his office. "Welcome, boss, to our bunker," Kevin had greeted with a contrived smile, his tone acrid.

"Sorry I haven't had time to keep you updated on what's going on with the Chinese, knowing how you've always felt about having a Chinese company as our boss."

"You're right there. I prefer not to have anything to do with them at all," Kevin had sneered.

"Well, there might be a compromise. Their interest in us seems to be really focused on our network-security products and services. They are willing to consider a joint-venture partnership. They have invited me to visit a number of their plants to get firsthand knowledge of what they are all about."

"Good for you, Will; have a good trip." Kevin's tone had been curt and clipped.

"I just thought you were interested in being kept in the loop, having invested a lot of your life in the company. And I know we wouldn't be where we are today if it weren't for the hard work you put in at the beginning."

Kevin had seemed to be touched by Will's nostalgic reassurance. "Good to know you still remember the good old times."

"Neither one of us will ever forget. But times change, and technology changes. We're in a field where if we don't keep up, we could languish and disappear."

"I understand, boss. As I said, have a good trip to China," Kevin had said, the glimmer of softness in his eyes fading. "Excuse me, boss, I have a network to maintain." He'd walked away without saying anything else.

That had been the last communication Will had had with Kevin, not counting the two-letter e-mail of "OK" he'd just received. He looked at the time on his cell; he still had about an hour to kill before boarding. He scrolled down the e-mail list and came to the e-mail he'd received from Sage the previous evening.

"Just got a message from Lu. She's actually in Shanghai for about two weeks for business. She is at the Shanghai Hilton. She said you can call or e-mail her if you have the need to."

"... call or e-mail her if you have the need to." Will's eyes went back and forth a couple of times on those words. It was obvious to him that Lu was pretending that the evening they'd spent together in Montauk had never really happened. To her, he remained her best friend's brother, nothing more than that. The fact Lu had sneaked out of his beach house that morning without a face-to-face good-bye had made her let's-just-stay-friends intention clear. So logically, what she had written in her e-mail to Sage should not have been unexpected. But he still felt his heart sink with disappointment.

"Got it. See you when I get back," he replied to Sage's e-mail. Then he opened his last unread e-mail. It was from Great China Telecom regarding what they had planned for his visit. He would be meeting the company's senior-management team in Shanghai the first day. He would spend the next couple of days touring a manufacturing plant outside Shanghai and another plant in southern China, near the special economic development zone of Shenzhen. On the last day, he would be meeting the senior executives of Great Wall Holding, the parent company of Great China Telecom, followed by an evening banquet. Will and a team of Wall Street investment bankers would be the guests of honor.

The last day's activity made him think of Lu again, and her reason to stay as friends with him suddenly seemed to be clear. In Montauk, she had already known she was going to be working on Great China Telecom's IPO and had been privy to the Chinese's interest in Matrixtech. Being a good friend to Sage, whose brother was an executive at Matrixtech, Lu was exercising care to stay objective and avoid the perception of any conflict of interest. But now they were both in Shanghai. Whether he had the need to contact her for business reasons or not, they would most likely bump into each other. Besides, Sage had already told Lu he was going to be in Shanghai. It would only be proper for him to personally let Lu know he would be arriving in Shanghai soon.

"... We could meet for a drink if we can find some free time." He completed his short message to Lu and hit the Send button.

CHAPTER 15

. . . . .

FOR THREE DAYS LU had conducted on-site reviews at four of Great China Telecom's eight manufacturing plants in small cities and towns of Guangdong Province. When presented with a list of the names, sizes, and locations of the eight plants, Lu had picked the four plants in the south, all in places away from the metropolitan areas of Guangdong Province. She'd left the flagship plant in Shanghai and a couple near the Shenzhen special economic development zone to Dick Witherspoon. Those were not the ones that concerned her; they would be every bit modern with up-to-date facilities and even state-of-the-art equipment and machinery. The workers there would be wearing clean, crisp uniforms like in the photos shown in business and financial newspapers and magazines back in the United States. But those plants would not reflect Great China Telecom's real operating environment and cost structure—just like Shanghai, with its omnipresent skyscrapers and high-rise condos, the streets lined with designer stores and congested by Mercedes and BMWs, the neon lights and gigantic commercial billboards emulating those in Time Square in New York City, the restaurants filled with Marlboro smoke and Bordeaux-drinking crowds. All that did not represent the real China, where the majority of the people still lived on a couple of dollars a day.

Her three days on the road had been grueling to say the least. In the subtropical Guangdong, she'd traveled from one plant to another, riding in a small van for hundreds of miles a day, and then had spent hours inside the ninety-plus-degree manufacturing plants, most of them without air-conditioning and sometimes without proper ventilation.

She was grateful to be back in the five-star Hilton in Shanghai. She wanted desperately to shower, order room service, and crash into bed for a good night's sleep. But she only had time to shower and maybe close her eyes for an hour before she had to go downstairs to meet Dick and Will for a drink and to exchange notes on their respective plant visits of the past few days. It was Thursday, the only evening they would all be free, without yet another Great China Telecom–hosted banquet to go to. At least that was the case for Dick and Will; they had been wined and dined every evening after their visit to the plant in suburban Shanghai and in the special economic development zone of Shenzhen. Friday would be the last official workday for Lu and Dick, a day of meetings with top executives of Great China Telecom's parent company, Great Wall Holding Company, during which they would iron out a last few details regarding the IPO. As for Will, he'd told her in an e-mail that he would be engaged in separate meetings with Great China Telecom to work out a more detailed partnership agreement between Matrixtech and Great China Telecom. The grand finale of the day would be an evening banquet, to celebrate the successful cooperation and promising business relationships between Wall Street, Great China Telecom, and Matrixtech. It seemed to be an "all's well that ends well" situation for everybody.

After a quick shower, she wrapped herself in the hotel cotton robe and sat on the edge of the bed to check her e-mail. An e-mail from Sage made her smile again. She and Joe had had a few dates now, and things were going really well between them. "Joe is sweet but a rock-solid man. I know I can always trust him, and I feel secure being with him," Sage wrote.

Both Will and Dick had also just e-mailed her, asking if she had made it back to the hotel and confirming their meeting at 7:00 p.m. in the lobby bar of the Hilton. Both men had been gentlemanly, offering to meet her at Hilton so she did not have to travel across town to the Grand Hotel in Pudong, the hotel where Dick had stayed the first time he'd visited Shanghai. The Grand Hotel was located in the newest and tallest building in the city and was highly recommended by the managers of Great China Telecom since their parent company held a part ownership in it.

As much as she would love to see Will again, to get to know him better, she had been hesitant at first to accept his e-mail invitation for a drink together. Her work in the Great China Telecom IPO was coming to an end. She would have preferred to wait until the deal had gone through so she could say honestly to herself that her personal relationship with Will did not in any way affect her professional objectivity. But their being in Shanghai at the same time had made it impossible for them to avoid each other. She felt relieved that Dick and Will obviously had been introduced to each other while she'd been in Guangdong Province and that they were coming together to meet her mainly for business reasons, though deep in her heart, she considered Dick a nuisance intruding on a get-together she would rather attend alone.

• • •

At seven, Lu stepped out of the elevator on the lobby level of the Hilton. The bar area was on the other side of the expansive lobby, off to the left side of the hotel entrance where the four wings of the revolving door were briskly sweeping in mostly evening dining guests. Their sense of relief from the sweltering heat outside was likely quickly overcome by the chill generated by the full-blast air-conditioning inside. They probably wished they had brought a jacket or sweater.

Lu had come downstairs prepared. Dressed in a pair of long linen pants and a long-sleeved white cotton sweater, the chill in the lobby was nice and pleasant, especially compared to the steamers she had left earlier that day in Guangdong Province. She passed the front revolving door and noticed Will and Dick sitting on a black leather sectional couch tucked in a corner at the far end of the bar. Sitting on the glass coffee table in front of the couch were a half-full beer glass and an almost-empty white wineglass. Both guys were wearing polo shirts, Will in navy blue and Dick in powder blue. At the opposite corner a few yards away stood a baby grand piano. A man in a black tuxedo and black bow tie had just sat down on the bench and began to play the theme song of *The Godfather.*

The start of the piano music seemed to interrupt the conversation Will and Dick had been engaged in. They looked away from each other and looked around. They saw Lu approaching them and stood up simultaneously to greet her.

"Good evening, gentlemen," she said as she got closer to the two men.

"Welcome back, our road warrior. When did you get back?" Dick leaned forward over the table to extend his hand.

"A couple of hours ago," Lu said as she shook hands with Dick and quickly turned to face Will. "Hi, Will, nice to see you here in Shanghai."

"It's been a while, Lu," Will said with a broad smile.

For a second, they looked at each other, hesitating about what to do next. Then almost at the same time, they both extended a hand to the other.

"How's your visit so far?" Lu asked.

"Please sit down. Would you like to have a drink?" Will gestured for Lu to sit down.

"A watermelon martini would be nice," Lu said and waved at the cocktail waitress standing at the entrance of the bar area.

The waitress came and took Lu's order. Dick asked for another glass of white wine while Will continued the conversation. "So far, everything has been very pleasant except for the heat and pollution. People are friendly, and hotel services are first class—not to mention the twelve-course banquets every evening. I think I'm officially a real Chinese-food connoisseur now." Laughing, Will turned to Dick. "And our friend Dick here has just shown me around the west side of the city, once the French Concession, right?"

Dick chimed in, "Don't forget we also visited Great China Telecom's plant right outside the city. Everything there was cutting-edge, very modern, no different from most of the plants in developed parts of the world." Then, as an afterthought, he asked, "By the way, how was your trip? What's the condition of the small-town plants in Guangdong?"

Lu was about to say something when the cocktail waitress showed up with their drinks on a silver tray. Her work uniform was a full-length bright-red *qipao* with midthigh-high side slits. She bent to lay the tray on the table before picking up the drinks and setting them in front of Lu and Dick. Lu thanked her and noticed Dick peering at the waitress's leg peeking through one of the side slits. As the waitress straightened up to retreat from the table, she cast Dick a coquettish sideways look, which Dick readily caught and acknowledged with a flirtatious wink.

As she turned away, Dick's eyes followed her, as if raking the *qipao* off her slender torso.

Lu took a sip of the watermelon martini and cleared her throat slightly, to divert Dick's eyes away from the waitress as she swayed back to stand at the center of the bar, a vantage point where she could scan the entire area for thirsty guests.

She waited until Dick was mentally back with her and Will and said, "The working conditions in the plants I visited were deplorable; imagine no air-conditioning or even adequate ventilation in ninety-plus heat with high humidity. Some workers told me they often work for long hours and weeks at a time without a day off."

"That's not what we saw at the plant here and in Shenzhen." Will seemed surprised. "A lot of workers were wearing white lab coats and working in clean, modern, air-conditioned facilities."

"I think it all depends on whether a factory owner can get away with it. The workers at the plants I visited came from poor and remote areas of the country. They were happy just to have jobs. One worker told me she'd left her two children back at home in some mountain area to take care of themselves so she and her husband could work at the plant. The child who is twelve years old has to take care of her nine-year-old sibling."

"That's unbelievable considering how developed this city is," Will said.

Lu smiled faintly. "Well, this is China. Peel back the surface glitz and glamor, and what's underneath is not too pretty. The worst I've seen so far was at a small city. They told me the area is a major e-waste dumping ground in the world. I wonder whether it's a coincidence that a telecom equipment-manufacturing plant is sitting right next to container after container of old computers, cell phones, and all kinds of electronic devices shipped from the US, Europe, and even Japan. The plant I visited employs about five hundred workers, but the city hires over one hundred thousand people, a lot of them children, and pays them next to nothing to do the so-called e-waste recycle work, recovering every bit of metal and plastic that has a ready market."

"Is that legal?" Dick's eyes widened, finally coming out of the trance induced by the cocktail waitress.

"Not based on the books of rules and regulations, but nobody seems to care about the air and water pollution the e-waste recycling shops have caused. They said the lead in the blood of local people there is almost fifty percent higher than normal. The sad thing is that the government doesn't seem to have any intention to crack down on it, and the people are just happy that they at least have jobs." Lu paused to swallow. She turned to Dick. "I think what I saw is part of the reason Great China Telecom's costs are lower and its profit margin higher than most of its competitors in the world. Yet the developed world often accuses the Chinese of dumping; most of those countries just don't know the kind of hardship people here are willing to endure so they can continue to just live."

They sat drinking. Not a word was said for a few moments. After the last drop of wine was gone, Dick asked, his tone tentative but defensive, "But you have to agree that what you heard is hearsay, and it's not our job to investigate China's pollution problems, is it? We are here to verify Great China Telecom is financially sound and investment worthy."

"I understand what we're here for. You asked me how my trip to the plants went; I'm telling you what I saw and heard," Lu said, her voice soft but firm. "From a business perspective, I am sure nobody can deny Great China Telecom is awash in cash and not lacking new market prospects for its products."

"Good." Dick smacked his hands palms down on his lap. "In that case, it's safe to say that all is clear for Great China Telecom to launch its IPO."

"Your firm is the lead on this; the decision ultimately is yours. My duty is to present you analyses and evaluations based on the facts, data, and information available to me to support your decision making," Lu said calmly.

"Well, you have fulfilled your duty excellently."

"Thank you." Lu accepted the praise with a smile.

Happy in his mission-accomplished mental state, Dick's eyes began to wander around and a few seconds later landed squarely on the cocktail waitress standing languidly at her usual spot at the center of the bar.

"Well, guys, I'm afraid I'll have to leave now; got to finish preparing for the final meeting tomorrow. The head of Great China Telecom's parent company is going to be there. I hope you don't mind," Dick said, rising from the couch.

"I'd better get going too." Will stood and said to Lu, "You need to rest after a long day like this."

"Oh, no, no, no," Dick almost shrieked. "Don't let me spoil your fun. You don't have to leave with me. Stay, have another drink, or have some dinner. I'll see you guys tomorrow."

Before Will could say anything, Dick hurried away from the table and headed toward the front entrance. Halfway there, he stopped and said something to the cocktail waitress. She smiled and nodded and then watched the revolving door sweep Dick outside.

Lu and Will stood speechless and watched Dick disappearing into the darkness beyond the well-lit hotel entrance. "I think Dick is spellbound by that waitress," Will murmured humorously.

"You can tell too?" Lu laughed.

"Isn't that obvious? Did you notice him stripping her naked when she brought our drinks?"

"That's Dick." Lu shook her head. She thought about the first time she and Dick had been in Shanghai. The manager of the seafood company had taken them to a karaoke bar one night. Halfway through the evening, Dick had mysteriously disappeared and hadn't been seen again until the following day at a meeting, eyes bloodshot and exhausted. The manager later had told her that Dick had had fun in a back room with a female staff member of the karaoke bar and had not left until early morning. "Some businessmen in America like to be entertained in strip clubs; we do it here in karaoke bars," the manager had said, finding Lu's embarrassed expression funny.

"Have you had dinner?" Will asked.

"No, have you?"

"No. I thought we would all have a bite together before I found out Dick had other plans." Will grinned.

With just a few steps, they were in the Atrium Café behind the lobby area that served breakfast and casual lunch and dinner. The entire dining area was under a glass domed ceiling, immersed in natural light during the day and illuminated by flickering candle-like LED lights in the evening. As they sat down and looked at the menu, a summer storm churned up and large raindrops splattered the glass dome above. Soon the splattering turned into thumping as the rain came down in sheets and buckets.

Having had two beers in the lobby bar and an earlier ten-course lunch at one of the restaurants near Great China Telecom's flagship plant in Shanghai, Will was not that hungry and ordered a small smoked salmon sandwich. Lu, on the other hand, had not eaten since she'd gotten on the plane earlier that day to fly back to Shanghai. By the time she had gotten back to the hotel, the desire to get away from the sizzling heat and out of her sweat-drenched clothes had suppressed the gnawing sensation in her stomach. Now the twinkling fairy lights, the soft piano music, and the pleasantly chilled air all reminded her she was hungry, actually ravenous. She ordered an Asian salad and a large bowl of Chinese noodle soup topped with thinly sliced meat and seafood.

"Somebody is hungry," Will said when Lu's mixing-bowl-sized noodle soup arrived.

"Yeah, I'll finish it," Lu said, twirling a few strands of noodle on the soup spoon. "Here we usually slurp our noodles, loudly; that means you really enjoy it. But I'm not going to gross you out, so I'll eat it the American way." With a mouthful of noodles, she looked at Will, who was watching her with great amusement. With one hand over her mouth, she swallowed as quickly as she could. "Sorry," she said, embarrassed by her overly enthusiastic table manner.

"No, no, good to see somebody really enjoy her food. You can slurp; I don't mind," Will said. His blue eyes sparkled, and his dimpled smile flickered under the shimmering fairy lights.

"Okay, I'll leave the noodle slurping for later. How's your visit been so far, fruitful or dragging?" Lu asked.

"You mean the deal between Matrixtech and Great China Telecom. I think it's most likely to be a joint venture; they will have a fifty-one percent stake, and Matrixtech will have the rest. Money didn't seem to be a problem for them. They're interested in the network-security products and services we've developed. They want to market them together with their network equipment to their clients worldwide. I didn't know how big they are until recently; they're not far behind the biggest telecommunication-equipment manufacturers in the world. The routers, modems, and switches they make are used on just about every continent, and they are making billions every year."

"But they're not satisfied to remain just an equipment manufacturer; they have the ambition of becoming a full-fledged telecommunication company, with design and management and risk-containment capabilities too. That's why they want to partner with Matrixtech so badly," Lu said, twirling more noodles on the spoon with chopsticks.

"If it were up to me, I'd prefer Matrixtech stay as a domestic company. A partnership with a foreign company, particularly a Chinese company, just complicates everything. But the huge cash infusion is too much temptation for us to resist. You know, they promised me just yesterday that they would infuse up to a billion dollars into the joint venture for R&D purposes, like a billion dollars is just chicken feed. Then they introduced me to Dick, who told me you guys are in the final stages of Great China Telecom's IPO preparation. What I don't understand is they could buy a couple of companies like Matrixtech if they wanted, so why would they go through the trouble of doing an IPO in the United States?"

"Because being listed on the New York Stock Exchange gives them legitimacy, the perception that they are truly an independent business enterprise and not in any way influenced by the government. I guess perception is just as important here as in the US, whether the system is capitalism or communism."

"So you're saying the government still has influence on it. I somehow suspected that," Will said thoughtfully.

"I haven't lived in China for a long time, but from what I've seen and what I've studied, the Communist government still has control over everything; it's just not as overt as it used to be." Lu smiled at the irony.

"So Dick told me this is the second Chinese IPO the two of you have worked on together." Will changed subjects; the talk of the Communist government seemed to make him uneasy.

"Well, it's all about networking and contacts on Wall Street or anywhere else. Dick and I work for separate firms, but his boss and my boss have been doing deals together for ages, so my firm was invited to join the underwriting team for the now-ever-popular Chinese IPOs. The first deal was for a frozen seafood company; it went quite smoothly, and the company's stock has held up nicely, thank God. Even though Dick's firm was the lead firm and would have to take the good with the bad if things went wrong, I was nervous and afraid that I had missed something during the due diligence study and that the stocks we were trying to sell would turn out to be dogs for investors. You never know; it could happen."

"But I'm sure they consider you the best person for this kind of job; you're not only bilingual but bicultural too. You notice the signs and subtleties people like me and Dick could easily overlook, no matter how much we think we understand the businesses."

"You sure you and Dick are alike?" Lu said and laughed.

"Huh? Oh, not in that way." It took Will a second to get the joke, and he blushed. To cover his bashfulness, he said, "Well, according to Dick, tomorrow is a big day for us. I will be hammering out a draft joint-venture agreement with Great China Telecom, and you and Dick will have a ceremonial meeting with the senior executives of Great China Telecom's parent company. By the way, I almost forgot; I've met the head of Great Wall Holding already, and he told me he is your brother-in-law."

Lu froze; only her black eyes flicked to widen. She laid down the chopsticks and last spoonful of noodles and asked, "What's his name?"

"Whose name?" Will asked, surprised at the shock on Lu's face.

"The name of the head of Great Wall Holding?"

"You mean you don't know him? I don't think I'm making a mistake. He specifically told me that you are his wife's sister. I think his name is Chen Juin, or Juin Chen. He told me his first name means 'soldier.'"

"Juin, it means 'soldier.' Yes, he is my brother-in-law, but I haven't had the chance to meet him yet," Lu said, her voice so low she could hardly hear herself.

"How come?"

"We kept missing each other. When I visited my mother and sister last week, Juin was on a business trip. By the time he'd come back, I'd left for Guangdong Province, so we haven't had a chance to meet each other yet." Lu avoided Will's questioning eyes.

But Will did not press further. He nodded and said, "Oh, then you definitely will see each other tomorrow."

Their dinner came to an end. The storm had passed, and the glass dome framed an ink-blue sky dotted with a few bright stars. Will offered to pay for the dinner, but Lu insisted on paying since he was the guest in her hometown.

"So when you were growing up, did your family live around here?" Will asked as Lu wrote down her room number and signed off the bill.

"You're sitting in the heart of my old neighborhood right now."

"Then we should go for a walk, and you can show me around, if you're not too tired ..." Will said.

"My neighborhood was only a few blocks, hardly recognizable now with all the new roads and buildings, but I could use a walk after a day being cooped up indoors. I just hope the rain has washed the heat and pollution away," Lu said.

"Let's go outside and see. Hey, you saw where I grew up, on a strip of sandy beach; it's only fair you show me the blocks where you grew up."

Outside, the passing storm had reduced the repressive heat and humidity to a bearable level. The hazy pollutants had been blown out to the sea, the opaque air had become more translucent, and the dull lighting of the city had turned more vivid. A three-quarter faint orange moon peeped out now and then from behind clusters of lotus-flower-shaped clouds.

They crossed the street, strolling along the French-plane-tree-lined sidewalk of Yan'an Road. Pretty soon, they came to a stop next to a small lot scattered with concrete debris and dirt.

"This is where our apartment building used to be," Lu said quietly. "It was still here a few months ago when I came to visit my mother. See the picture on the board there? It will be a street green area once the junk is removed."

"It's a shame," Will said pensively. "This reminds me of that movie with Jack Nicholson. I forgot the name, but he was this man who decided to revisit his childhood house after he retired. He drove his RV hundreds of miles to see the house he hadn't seen for decades only to find it had become a Merchant's Tire store. It was quite sad, but I guess changes like this happen in life and are beyond our control."

Lu had mourned the loss of the building only from the windows of her hotel room. She had avoided coming here to stand on the lot that was empty physically but full of memories of her first thirteen years of life. She had thought she would feel sad, gloomy. But strangely, at that moment, she felt calm and accepting. She looked up at Will and met his concerned gaze. "I don't mean to make you sad," he said.

"I was, but I'm okay now." Lu began to walk across to the other side of the lot. "I know you must think it strange that I have been back here a couple of times recently but have not met my brother-in-law yet," she said over her shoulder.

Will followed her quietly.

"Well, the truth is I was not exactly close to my family. Until a few months ago, I hadn't seen my mother and sister for over thirty years. I had no idea what had happened in their lives. I hardly remembered what they looked like after such a long time. And I didn't know I even had a brother-in-law."

"How come?"

"It's a long story, and mostly depressing."

"I would like to hear it," Will said.

"Well, the short version is when I was five years old, the Communist government persecuted my father simply because he was a surgeon who had studied and trained in the United States. He was labeled as antigovernment and counterrevolutionary and sent to a camp to do hard labor for years, during which time he never came home. I didn't even know if he was dead or alive. Then he was lucky enough to be moved to a farm to tend ducks until he and I tried to escape to Hong Kong. The reason they moved him away from the death camp was to preserve him so high-ranking Communist party officials could call on him when they became sick."

"That's awful. So your mom took care of you and your sister by herself?" Will asked from behind her. They were now standing on the other side of the lot, in front of a block of old row houses.

"Not really. My mother had a job at the hospital my father used to work at. She was constantly away on business trips during those years. My sister wasn't born until a year before my father and I left the city; she was still a baby then."

"So you were often by yourself?"

"My grandma took care of me after my father was taken away. Actually, she had been taking care of me ever since I was born because my mother went back to work at the hospital after giving birth. Then my grandma died …" Lu's voice trailed off. She had just realized she was standing where the back courtyard used to be, where her grandma had jumped from their fourth-floor apartment to her death on that moonlit autumn night. "She jumped out of the window while I was asleep and killed herself, right here," Lu murmured, turning to face Will, who seemed frozen in the semidarkness.

"I am sorry." There was an almost-undetectable tremor in Will's voice.

She continued, straining not to blink her eyes, "After Grandma died, next-door neighbors often dropped by to keep an eye on me when Mother was away from home, which was very frequent, and because of that, we never grew close. I grew up quickly, learned how to cook rice and vegetables." She turned to stare at the debris so only her profile was facing Will. Everything became a blur. Her eyes flicked, and two large teardrops rolled down her face. "I am sorry; this is too morbid," she said, struggling to keep her voice normal.

"It's okay." Will stepped next to her. He laid one hand gently on her shoulder; it felt warm. "Hey, what you went through was horrific; it's natural to be melancholy. If Sage were here right at this moment, she would have cried her eyes out by now." Will wrapped his arm around her shoulder and pulled her slightly toward him before letting go.

"I remember that night. I woke up and saw my grandma standing at the window. The moonlight was unusually bright that night. She had just told me a story about the midautumn full moon, an old Chinese folktale, before putting me to bed, so I thought I was just dreaming. Next morning I woke up, and she was not there next to me. I heard noise from outside the window, so I climbed on a stool to see what was going on. I saw her lying on the ground, in a pool of blood. I was only five years old. For a while I didn't understand exactly what had happened." Lu looked down at the ground she was standing on, trying to steady her voice.

"What happened to you after that?"

"The lady next door came and took me to her apartment until my mother came back from a trip a few days later. My mother later told me that Grandma's body was cremated and disposed of. For a while I couldn't understand how Grandma had just disappeared without a trace like that," Lu said, looking around her as if searching for something.

"But why did she kill herself?"

"Because they tortured her, every day. They wanted her to confess her son's crimes against the government and people of China. But there was nothing to confess. My father was a surgeon who could have remained in the US to practice medicine but had chosen to go back to his country. What crime had he committed? She told me she had to go to meetings every day, so I stayed at home by myself during the day. I didn't know that they made her kneel in the hot sun on broken beer bottles in front of those Red Guard mobs and that they beat her with leather belts. But she hid all that away from me until she couldn't endure it anymore. You know, the exact number of people who were murdered or died like my grandma was never made public, but we know it's in the millions. It's not something that is often talked about in the West, like how millions were killed by the Nazis in World War II," Lu said, her voice became more matter-of-fact.

"What you and your family went through is unthinkable to me, but I'm glad you told me, and I'm glad I had the chance to be here," Will said.

"I'm glad you came here with me tonight. It made it easier for me to face the past up close one more time before the whole place becomes unrecognizable when construction is completed." Lu scanned the surroundings one more time before she turned to Will. "Let's get going. I still have some of my childhood neighborhood left to show you."

They rounded the corner onto Prosperity Street, according to the illuminated street sign. It was a narrow residential street lined with mature maple trees, their thick, leafy branches arching out from both sides of the street and intertwining in the middle to form a half-mile-long green arcade.

As they reached the end of the green arcade, Lu noticed an empty lot on the other side of the street, wedged in between two old, low apartment buildings. "Oh, they tore the coffeehouse down. That used to be *the* coffeehouse in Shanghai. My dad told me that a lot of old time movie stars used to go there, and it was a big deal for young people who were dating to go there to sit and have a cup of coffee with a piece of cream cake. It was pricey, so guys usually wouldn't take their dates there unless the relationship was promising."

"You mean if they felt like the woman they were dating would most likely become their wife?" Will said.

"You could say that. I can't believe they tore it down. Of course, it was just a hole in the wall compared to the Starbucks on every major street in the city; they have become the new luxury dating sites for young people these days."

"I'll look at Starbucks differently the next time I go into one."

From there they turned left onto a back road leading to the famous high-end shopping street, Huaihai Road, the center of the French Concession in Shanghai. In front of them stood the Garden Hotel, its modern tower looming above the expansive baroque facade that used to be the French sports club. As they approached the hotel front gate, they heard classic music undulating across the garden from the lobby, beckoning them to slow down, stop, and listen. "I wonder what the occasion is," Lu said.

"We should go in and check it out."

Lu gave him an are-you-sure look.

"We can go in and see what's going on; don't have to stay long. Maybe have a cup of coffee. It's not like we're going to a Starbucks," Will said, smiling at his own humor.

Lu felt her face warm and was glad that nightfall camouflaged her blush.

Through arched double french doors they entered the grand lobby area. A stately tiered crystal chandelier plunged from the soaring center ceiling, shining a golden light on the mosaic medallions inlaid in the marble floors. They followed the music to the left side of the lobby, the lounge area. As they stepped down into the rectangular-shaped lounge, they descended into an oasis of miniature bonsai trees in oval and round containers of onyx black, sapphire blue, and jade green. Each was individually displayed as a centerpiece on a marble pedestal surrounded by minimalist dark-wood cocktail chairs and tables. Johann Strauss's *The Blue Danube* waltzed over from a sixteen-piece orchestra across the lounge area, its rhythm resonating gently in the air.

The hotel was celebrating its upcoming twentieth year in business.

The menus featured special cocktails and a description of live entertainment. They ordered café crème, which Lu explained was the French version of cappuccino with less foam.

"You know what's funny." Lu dropped two cubes of sugar in the coffee. "Chairman Mao, the Communist party leader who started the Cultural Revolution, killed millions of people in order to purge the decadent bourgeois influence. Yet forty years later, the Western decadence has come back with a vengeance. Look around us; what is not Western style? The hotel, the music, the drinks—even the bonsai trees. You could say they are either Chinese or Japanese, but anything Japanese was once considered bad by the Communist government too. I think Mao must be turning over in his coffin seeing all this happening."

"Where is he buried?" Will asked curiously.

"In a crystal coffin on display in Tiananmen, his giant picture still hanging on the front wall, watching capitalism running amok. Does it make any sense?" Lu sneered.

"It doesn't, but better capitalism than communism, don't you think?"

"Yeah, but it's mostly crony capitalism. From what I can see, people who become ultrarich are the offspring of high-ranking party officials and affiliates of Mao's generation. The system is highly corrupt."

"Crony capitalism or not, the same could be said about the rich and powerful in the US," Will countered.

"Hmm …" Considering what Will had said, Lu was silent for a moment before turning serious. "Talking about crony capitalism, I think we need to avoid broadcasting this; everybody knows everybody's situation in the deals we are currently involved in."

"What do you mean?" Will could not tell where Lu was heading.

"The fact that you and I are friends through your sister and that the head of Great China Telecom's parent company is my brother-in-law. Great China Telecom is trying to acquire Matrixtech, of which you are the senior executive. Come on, we may easily have a perception issue if somebody wants to create a problem out of all this."

"Now you've said it, yeah, I haven't mentioned it to anybody, except a few close colleagues at Matrixtech." Will's voice was not quite sure.

"Let's keep it that way, particularly about my brother-in-law, whom I've yet to meet. Perception could turn into reality …" Lu suggested firmly before a round of applause erupted from guests sitting close to the orchestra. The conductor politely bowed to the audience and announced that a short break was in order, but after that, guests could request the orchestra to improvise their favorite music.

"Okay, what would you like to hear? Or I should ask, what kind of music do you listen to usually?" Will asked.

"I don't have that much time during the day to listen to music, but I do carry a portable CD player with me when I run in the morning, mostly exercise music to get my heart pumping."

"You ought to try the newest iPod; it will give you a completely different experience."

"I guess I'm still in the dark ages when it comes to electronic gadgets. It may also be I'm lazy," Lu said sheepishly.

"But you still have to tell me what your favorite piece of music is. They say you can tell a lot about a person based on what kind of music he or she likes. I'm taking a wild guess: you are a classical music kind of woman."

Lu thought for a moment. "You can say that, although I do like certain pop music too. So what kind of person am I?"

"The word sophisticated comes to mind," Will said earnestly.

"In that case, what are you? I know you like Richard Wagner's *The Flying Dutchman*, which according to critics' consensus, is classic but sullen and gloomy. Does that make you sophisticated and gloomy?"

"I don't think I'm a classical music lover. *The Flying Dutchman* is the only Wagner opera I occasionally listen to and only because I was forced into it by my navy boss. I think I told you I like the storyline better than the music."

"How a man needs a faithful woman to rescue him from the curse of the devil?" Lu said playfully.

"You're right," Will said, his dimples deepened by a shy smile. "So tell me what your favorite is, and we can request it when the conductor comes back," he pushed.

"Okay, if you want to marry the music to a storyline, my favorite would be 'Romance,' the eighth movement of *The Gadfly Suite* by Dmitri Shostakovich, a Russian composer."

"Never heard of him in my life, and you need to write it down. I'm afraid it's too sophisticated for a beach bum and bits-and-bytes nerd like me to be able to repeat what you just said."

"Please stop that," Lu almost implored. "I'm not sure they'll have the sheet music, but let's try." She picked up the paper cocktail napkin on the table and tore it in half. She wrote down "Romance," *The Gadfly Suite*, and handed it to a waitress who just happened to pass by. "Please give this to the conductor when he gets back."

"Just joking. Anyway, I am sure the music is beautiful, but what is the story all about?" Will asked.

"It was based on a book written by a female Irish writer in the early or late nineteenth century—I don't remember the exact time period. It was my father's favorite book. I caught him crying while reading it one day, so I read it too. It was about an English Catholic boy who went to Italy to study to be a priest and ended up being an atheist freedom fighter. His transformation was triggered by the deceit of his teacher, a cardinal who was actually his birth father; the betrayal of his friends; and being misunderstood by the girl he loved. There are a lot of political and religious implications in the book, but what I'm most interested in is how Gadfly's pursuit of love was at the same time a lifelong test of his moral strength and integrity. Be it his love for his country, his love for the only woman in his life, his love for his father, or his love for God, they all seemed to conflict and cause him to struggle through despair and hopelessness, enduring tremendous physical and psychological sufferings. In the end he was executed by the government, but he lived a fulfilling and morally honest life because he never stopped loving life itself, even when faced with subhuman conditions, when death seemed the better way out. I still remember the last verse in his last letter to the woman he loved: 'Then am I a happy fly, if I live or if I die.' It's so realistically romantic."

"Sounds like an emotionally charged book. Did you say it's written by an Irish writer?"

"Yes, born in Ireland, lived in England, and later migrated to the United States."

"My dad's family was originally from Ireland; you want to know about emotional struggle and guilty conscience, talk to an Irishman."

"I've heard; we'll need a drink then, not coffee," Lu suggested.

Will gestured to the waitress standing just a few steps away. There was a cacophony of string-instrument tuning followed by taps of the conductor's baton. After a few seconds of quiet, a solo violin began playing a melody, soft but deeply meditative.

"That's it; they have the 'Romance' sheet music after all," Lu said and glanced at Will, who responded with a spontaneous, soft "Oh."

They sat quietly as more string instruments joined the meditation of the solo violin. The music gradually heaved and surged to a crescendo, as if a question about life was asked, reflected upon, and finally answered.

He agrees; this music is soul touching, Lu thought.

CHAPTER 16

• • • • •

THE GREAT CHINA TELECOM headquarters was located on the east side of the Huangpu River, in one of the super-tall skyscrapers in Shanghai. On a lucky day, when the air was clear, any of the high floors in this one-hundred-plus-story building commanded an unobstructed 360-degree view of the city.

It was Friday morning, the morning the head of Great Wall Holding was scheduled to meet Lu and Dick. The previous night's storm had blown the smog out to the sea, and the next batch of pollutants from hundreds of coal-burning power plants and millions of car exhaust pipes had not yet risen to thicken the air. The sky was milky blue, and the 360-degree view from the company's conference room on the eighty-eighth floor (double 8, double luck, according to Chinese superstition), though dizzying, was indeed breathtaking.

Lu was ten minutes early, but most other attendees had arrived before her and were busy helping themselves to an assortment of breakfast pastries and beverages spread out continental buffet style in the back of the conference room. A long, white fiber glass table, curved in an elongated S shape, stretched across the room like a giant python. Multiple videoconferencing screens covered the entire front center wall.

Nobody noticed her come in. She scanned the crowd at the buffet station. Dick, in his light-gray suit, heavily starched gleaming white shirt, and a silver tie, was standing in a circle with a group of men, most of them dressed in darker suits.

Dick was the first to see her. "Morning, Lu, have you had breakfast yet?" he asked, waving from across the room. She wished he had not greeted her in that attention-drawing way. The hubbub paused briefly, and the few seconds it took to walk across the room seemed extra long with everybody seeming to be staring at her.

"Morning, thanks, I had breakfast at the hotel," she said, shaking hands with the guys around Dick as he introduced or reintroduced her.

"And of course you know Will Donovan," Dick said, gesturing at the man standing near a coffee machine.

"Oh," Lu said and turned to face Will with an expression of mild surprise. She had not expected him to be in this meeting. Her instinct took over quickly. *The Chinese want him here to show that they have the capability and means to acquire and partner with foreign companies of their choosing regardless whether they do the IPO or not. It's a Chinese face thing.*

"Hi, Will, glad to see you again," she said. Will nodded at her with a smile, but his gaze was as if she had become a completely different person overnight. Lu was wearing a black crepe jacket over a white fine-cotton dress shirt tucked into a midcalf-length black pencil skirt. Her black pumps had three-inch heels, a comfortable height that also uplifted her confidence when she needed it. Her hair and makeup were also formalized for such an occasion. She had flatironed her shoulder-skimming hair so it was super straight, clean, and sleek. She had found that even moderate application of makeup could make her features angular, even a bit edgy, so she had looped a long strand of pearls twice around her neck to soften the sharpness of her face.

"Wow, you look different," Will finally said.

"Good different or bad? And might I say you look very professional today," Lu said quietly, smiling. Will was in what she guessed was his most professional outfit, the same one he'd worn the first time they had met, the blue blazer over the itchy gray pants, a light-blue shirt, and an open collar without a tie.

Will leaned slightly toward her and whispered, "Sophisticated and elegant as a woman yet imposing and not to be taken lightly as a businesswoman, all in a good way."

"The businesswoman part is a new one to me; nobody has ever told me that."

"Then you don't know yourself very well."

There was a minor commotion at the door; another group of men had arrived, and Dick was the first rushing over to greet them.

"There's your brother-in-law, the big boss; we should go and say hello," Will said.

"You go first; I'll be right behind you," Lu said but remained standing still.

She watched the big boss shake hands with Dick and proceed toward her, exchanging niceties with everybody along the way. He looked very much like himself in the wedding picture Lu had seen in her mother's apartment a week ago. Average height, on the thin side, slicked-back hair, in a dark suit and a deep-red tie. His face was in the shape of an upside-down triangle, hollow beneath the cheekbones, and tapered into a thin and rather long neck. It was a face she had seen somewhere, at a time she could not place.

"There is my sister-in-law. I am sorry I missed you over the weekend." Juin Chen, her brother-in-law, greeted her warmly in perfect English as he quickened his last few steps toward her with both of his arms outstretched. "How was your visit to the plants? I hope they treated you well," he said before she could say anything other than a hello. He held her hand in both of his and gave it a vehement shake. His hands felt moist, and his eyes behind the gold-rimmed spectacles were cold and darting.

"The trip was fine; learned a lot for what we needed," she said, finding the whole situation a bit bizarre, conducting business with a brother-in-law she'd never met before who was acting as if they had known each other forever. And there was Will, her best friend's brother, who clearly at the time was the object of her brother-in-law's affection, in a business sense ...

"Good, let me get a cup of coffee, and let's get started. I know everybody is busy, but this should not take long. I think all parties have more or less come to some kind of agreement," Juin Chen said as he pushed the Cappuccino button on the coffee machine.

Moments later, everybody sat down around the S-shaped conference table. Juin Chen was flanked by Dick and Will on one side, and Lu was seated on the opposite side, directly facing Juin.

After setting down his coffee cup, Juin Chen said, "I want to thank

everybody who has worked hard on this project, or I should say projects."
He smiled and glanced around the table. "As the CEO of Great Wall
Holding, the parent company of Great China Telecom, I am not directly
involved in the projects, but I understand they are extremely important
to the modernization of China's telecommunication system, and I want
to make it clear that you all have my one hundred percent support.
I know the potential partnership between Great China Telecom and
Matrixtech technically is a separate deal from what Mr. Witherspoon
has been working on, that is, to make Great China Telecom a publicly
owned company listed on the New York Stock Exchange." He paused
to look to his right and then his left. "And we all know that these two
deals are mutually independent of each other. That means Great China
Telecom has enough resources—or shall I say, is rich enough—to buy
the proposed fifty-one percent stake in Matrixtech regardless of whether
Mr. Witherspoon is successful in taking Great China Telecom public
in the US." He paused again, relishing the controlled laughter from
around the table in reaction to his humor, "But as the top manager of
the parent company of Great China Telecom, I want to conduct business
the best I can—in a transparent way, according to you Americans—so
I suggested that everybody involved in these two deals come sit at the
same table today to ask any questions you want and clear any doubts
you may have. As some of you here may know, Ms. Li and I are related
through my marriage to her sister, and according to Mr. Donovan, he
and Ms. Li were friends before all this partnership and IPO business
started, right?" He stopped. His eyes darted to Lu across the table and
back quickly to Will next to him. "I just want everybody to know that
there is no corruption or cronyism going on here. Now does anybody
have any questions?"

Silence around the table was the first reaction.

"I would like to say something." Dick cleared his throat. "On behalf
of my boss, Mr. Fred Armstrong, and our firm, I want to thank all the
managers at Great China Telecom, Mr. Chen in particular, for giving us
the opportunity to be the lead underwriter in this IPO deal. Because of
your support and cooperation, everything has been going smoothly, and
the launch should be on schedule when everybody on the Street comes
back from their summer vacations."

"Thank you, Mr. Witherspoon." Juin smiled and turned to Will. "Mr. Donavan, would you like to say something?"

Will thought for a moment. "I want to thank everybody for showing me around Great China Telecom's manufacturing facilities despite the heat and humidity. It helped me better understand the company's operation process and technical capability. As for the joint-venture agreement, we have agreed on a draft, and it needs to be reviewed and approved by Matrixtech's management team and board before it is finalized. On a separate matter, though, I have eaten more delicious and authentic Chinese food in the past week than in my whole life. I want to thank everybody for their hospitality."

"I hope we can finalize the agreement soon so you can come back more often for the food, and I am sure the managers here would like to visit you more often so you can treat them to hamburgers and fries every day," Juin said. He gave a cackling laugh before concluding, "Okay then, I see everybody is happy here; the meeting is adjourned. I will see you all this evening at the banquet. Bring your spouses and loved ones. We will celebrate."

"Sorry, Mr. Chen, I have one point to make; shouldn't take long," Lu said as her brother-in-law half raised himself.

"Of course." He lowered himself into the chair, annoyance flickering in his glassy eyes.

"I understand the joint-venture agreement and the IPO are separate projects, but part of the underwriters' job—that includes Dick's firm and my firm, Lehrer & Schuler, and a number of other Wall Street firms that have committed to this project—is to disclose potential risks to investors, whether it's financial, political, or geographical. I would like to point out to everyone here, including Mr. Donovan, that Matrixtech is currently the owner of several large network operation and maintenance contracts awarded by the US government. Staff who work on these projects have top-secret clearance, and the systems are extremely sensitive to the security of our country. Once the joint-venture agreement between Matrixtech and Great China Telecom is finalized, depending on how it is structured, there is a chance these contracts will have to be spun off and moved to other approved contractors. Therefore, even if the two deals are not directly related to each other, this is a potential risk that needs to be disclosed in our due diligence analyses, I just want to point it out here. And of course I appreciate the help, cooperation, and assistance provided by staff from Great China Telecom so far; they have made our job easier. That's all I have to say."

Around the table there was silence again. Most people seemed to be staring at the blank notepads in front of them. She looked at Will, who in turn was peering sideways at Juin Chen. On the other side of her brother-in-law, Dick's eyes flipped upward at the ceiling and then down at the Montblanc leather notepad holder in front of him.

After moments of uncomfortable silence, Juin took off his glasses and rubbed his nose bridge. "Thank you, Ms. Li, I am glad you pointed this out. But we understand, and we hope you understand, that the joint venture should be mutually beneficial. We provide substantial funds for research, and in turn we get to share the fruit of the research, which is new technology that we can apply to improve our own telecommunication systems here. We will never do anything to jeopardize the national security of the United States. We will all work together to figure out a solution that's satisfactory to both parties and governments, if it comes to that." His eyes rolled around the table until they met hers, like two black glass marbles, chilling, sinister, and unblinking.

Snake eyes. It came to her. She closed her eyes for a second, to shut Juin's eyes out and to remember more clearly at the same time. Those eyes had first shot venomous looks at her one night when she had been just a little girl; those were the eyes that had snatched her father away; those eyes had been haunting her dreams ever since. The room suddenly felt icy cold, draining blood away from her entire body.

"Anybody have any more questions? Ms. Li, do you have anything else to say?"

"No, thank you, that's all I have for now," she said, opening her eyes.

"Okay then, everybody back to work. Oh, one more thing," Juin said, gesturing to everyone to sit still for one more minute. "Regarding this evening's party at my house. We usually hold banquets at restaurants, but obviously, Mr. Donavan and Mr. Witherspoon have had enough restaurant food for the past few days, so I thought it would be more relaxing and comfortable for us to gather at my house. My wife and I will be honored if all of you could come. I will see you this evening."

Everybody stood to leave. Lu remained seated to steady herself, to wait for the blood to flow back to her cold body.

"Are you okay? Are you sick or something?" Will asked, appearing at her side.

"Oh." She looked up at him. "I'm fine, just a little distracted."

Will looked at his watch. It was only a little past eleven. "Dick invited me to have lunch with him later. Do you want to join us?"

"No, thank you, I think I'll go back to the hotel and do some work. I'll see you this evening." She stood up, went around the table, and headed toward the door.

"Are you sure you don't want to come with us?" Dick asked.

She paused and turned around. "You guys go ahead. I'll see you later." She walked to the elevator and pushed the down button. *It can't be, it can't be,* a voice inside her head kept saying, but she knew she could not be mistaken. That face, those eyes, they were a carbon copy of what she had seen that night, the man in the blue Mao jacket, yelling at her father, "You are antigovernment and counterrevolutionary." Then he'd ordered the Red Guards to take her father away. She had told her grandma she would call the man who had taken her father away "Snake Eyes" because his eyes had looked exactly like the eyes of the black snake in one of her cartoon books. They had been scary, creepy, and evil.

The elevator door dinged open, and she rushed in. She wanted to get back to the hotel, maybe lie down for a while. It could just be a dream; it would all go away when she woke up.

• • •

JUIN CHEN'S COUNTRY VILLA sat on thirteen acres of manicured oasis in the famous Sheshan resort area thirty miles to the southwest of Shanghai. At six in the evening, Will and Dick arrived at the front gate in a black Audi sedan chauffeured by a Great China Telecom driver.

The driver slowed as they approached the ornate black-and-gold wrought iron gate and came to a stop for a few seconds before the gate buzzed open. They entered the gate and drove on a promenade lined with emerald-green arborvitae trees. A minute later, the car veered right onto a long, narrower driveway. To their left, tiered, mazelike landscaping zigzagged across a vast garden, all the way to the front entrance of a French country chateau in the distance.

Will thought he had entered the garden of the Palace of Versailles.

At the end of the circular driveway, they curved left and stopped by a gurgling carved marble fountain in front of the mansion-sized house.

Fascinated and dumfounded at the same time, Will and Dick were slow to get out the car until the driver opened the door and announced they had arrived at their destination. At the front door, a man in a black traditional Chinese brocade jacket greeted them. He bowed slightly before directing them to a ballroom-sized reception room in the back, with a wall of double french doors opening to the back veranda, overlooking a long reflecting pool screened by layers of shrubberies in ascending order, dwarf rosebushes, medium-height spiral pines, and giant geometrically shaped green shrubberies.

"What a place," Dick said, walking out of the center french door onto the veranda.

"We must be early; nobody is here yet," Will said, looking around. Long buffet tables covered in white linen had been set up to one side of the veranda. A few uniformed caterers were in and out through a door on the far right side, bringing in silverware.

"Well, Juin insisted we arrive around six for cocktails. I don't think I heard him wrong." Dick glanced at his Rolex wristwatch.

They went back inside and sat down on one of the couches grouped around a rectangular crimson Persian rug. An antique table with delicately curved legs and a marble top showcased a two-foot-tall pedestal crystal vase holding an umbrella-shaped bouquet of white tea roses.

"Welcome, welcome. I am so happy you could come early," Juin's soft voice slithered across from the doorway. To Will, something in his voice welcomed more than the two of them; it welcomed the money and power he and Dick could bring.

"You see, I want to spend a few minutes and have a drink with you before everybody else arrives, and I would like to introduce you to my wife and my mother-in-law; they will be coming down soon. By the way, where is Lu? Didn't she come with you?" Juin asked, turning left and right as if looking for her.

"I talked to her this afternoon and told her we could pick her up on our way, but she said she wasn't feeling too well and wanted to rest for a while, but she said she will be here later," Dick said.

"Oh, hope she is all right. She is family, and it's not easy for all of us to be together like this." Juin frowned to express his concern.

A uniformed female caterer approached them quietly, carrying a cocktail tray with three glasses of champagne.

"Please." Juin took a glass first and raised it halfway to Will and Dick. "Cheers, to our cooperation and a successful partnership down the road."

Will and Dick picked up the champagne, and the three glasses clinked.

"Now, before I forget," Juin said after a sip, "I want to make sure that you both understand that we are only interested in Matrixtech's cybersecurity technology. Once the partnership goes through, we can package it with the network-system equipment Great China Telecom is already manufacturing and market it to our customers all over the world. Matrixtech will greatly benefit from the partnership. I was a little concerned by what my sister-in-law brought up during the meeting this morning. I am sure she is a conscientious worker trying to do a good job for her firm and yours, Mr. Witherspoon," Juin paused to pat Dick on the shoulder. "And I agree we need to address the federal contracts Matrixtech currently holds, for about one hundred million on an annual basis, yes? That's a drop in the bucket considering our two companies' combined revenue of billions of dollars. These contracts could be easily shed and transferred to another government contractor, can't they?" He looked at Will.

"If the partnership is finalized, these contracts may have to be sold for regulatory and security reasons. They are relatively small in dollar amount, but they do affect many people's jobs," Will said, wondering where this conversation was going.

"I appreciate your concern for your employees, but a deal like this benefits both companies' future, and from what I've heard, both parties are eager to wrap it up and make it official. I suggest we take care of the federal-contract issue quietly so we don't raise flags that could trigger bureaucratic investigation and unnecessary delay. We need to make sure that Ms. Li, your colleague and my sister-in-law, does not bring this up in such a public way in the future. Don't you agree?" He took another sip from the champagne glass and waited for a reaction from Dick and Will.

"No problem, Mr. Chen. I'll talk to her. I'm sure she won't mind; it's not like we're asking her to break the law or anything," Dick said airily and guzzled down the rest of the champagne.

"Lu and I have no working relationship in this deal. We only know each other through my sister ..." Will hesitated. A wave of uneasiness surged inside him.

"Friends give friends advices, don't they? Anyway, I am just suggesting that we don't make things more difficult for ourselves if we can help it. I am not in any way suggesting anything that could be viewed unethical," Juin said smoothly. He looked past both Will and Dick and beckoned, "Come on over here; I'll introduce you to our guests of honor."

Will turned around and saw two women gliding toward them. They had to be Lu's mother and sister. The roundness of the young woman's face and every feature on it seemed to be in disproportion to her tall and stick-thin body; large, round eyes; round button nose; and red, small, round mouth. She was wrapped in a long pink dress, fitted and sleeveless. It tapered slightly from her hip all the way down to her ankles. The lack of any front, back, or side slits on such a long dress prevented her from making normal strides. Her steps were short and rapid, reminding Will of a Japanese geisha wrapped in a long, elaborate kimono and stepping in clunky high wooden shoes.

Lu's mother, on the other hand, seemed to float toward them effortlessly in a loose white silk robe dress, closed in the front with black fabric Chinese knot buttons. Contrary to her flowing dress, her silver-gray hair was coiffed in a short bob style, stiff and motionless. As she got close, she said something to Juin in Chinese. Her voice had a put-on breathiness that was too young for her age.

"Mother, Mr. Donavan here is Lu's friend, and here, Mr. Witherspoon, he is Lu's colleague." Juin introducing his mother-in-law in English was a surprise to both Will and Dick, but more surprising to them was the fact that the elder woman switched to English, only sounding more like King's English.

"Oh, how do you do?" She smiled at Will and offered her hand, her eyes scanning him with x-ray focus and intensity.

"Nice to meet you." The second Will took hold of her hand it slipped and dropped off as if her entire arm suddenly had gone limp. At a close distance, he noticed the color and shape of her eyes resembled her daughter Lu's, black and almond shaped, but unlike Lu's, they remained judging, cold, and even superior when her mouth made an effort to smile. Her face, pale ivory from a distance, showed a net of tiny lines around her eyes, mouth, and forehead.

"And this is my wife, Mei." Juin introduced his wife by making a small side step and nudging her to the forefront.

"Nice to meet you," she said bashfully, but exacting proper pronunciation of each word.

"Good, you need to take this opportunity to practice your English; don't be shy," Juin said. "Now if you will excuse me, I need to go and say hello to the other guests. Mr. Witherspoon, would you come with me? There is somebody I would like you to meet."

Within a few seconds, Will found himself standing awkwardly face-to-face with Lu's mother and sister. He looked around the room, feeling self-conscious about his attire, which he considered his most professional and Sunday best—blue jacket, light-gray pants, white dress shirt, and black dress shoes. He had even put on a burgundy-colored tie. But every man in the room was in full suit and tie, and every woman was in an outfit made for evening occasions, like going to dinner at a fine-dining restaurant.

"So you are Lu's friend—friend friend or boyfriend friend?" Lu's mother asked without warning. She laughed, her laugh an octave higher than her speaking voice, as if amused by her own question.

Will could feel his own face reddening; he was taken aback or embarrassed or both. "Actually, Lu is my sister's good friend."

"He is shy," she whispered to Mei. "Don't be shy; she is lucky to have a friend like you. We have a joke here in China: unmarried women above twenty-five are leftovers, and unmarried women of Lu's age are throwaways, beyond spinsters, hee, hee, hee ..." More high-pitched cackling.

Will forced a tiny smile while searching for words to respond to the joke that would be considered borderline demeaning back home. "Your daughter is a very smart and intelligent woman," he muttered.

"Well, the old Chinese saying is women of intelligence have no virtue and morality; I guess times have changed." A sigh of sarcasm. "Where is Lu anyway? Is she coming, or is she doing another business deal somewhere?" A question of acerbity.

Will was at a loss of words. He was a man, and just like many other men, he had never quite understood the mysterious dynamics of the female persuasion. But he could not think of any occasion where a mother had hurled this much negativity at her long-lost daughter in a matter of minutes. As the old woman continued her digs and jeers, he searched desperately for an excuse to get away.

"Ma," Mei, who had been quiet and almost invisible, suddenly interrupted her rambling mother, her hand pointed at the door.

Will looked across the room and saw Lu standing at the door, scanning the crowd, obviously looking for someone she knew. She wore a long white dress, hair tousled in a loose updo. Her eyes met his from across the room. She smiled and wound her way toward him, around and through circles of guests, nodding and smiling back to whoever chose to exchange greetings.

Under the soft light from three Napoleon crystal chandeliers suspended on thick gold chains from the ceiling, her dress shimmered. It was a modified Chinese *qipao* of pure-white satin, sleeveless with a round neckline without the Mandarin high collar and a single thigh-high slit in the front right instead of the traditional two side slits. The dress boldly drew the outline of her svelte yet athletic body; enhanced the deep, warm tone of her skin; and subtly revealed her toned runner's legs as she walked with graceful fluidity.

"You are late, Lu," the old woman reproached, her narrowed eyes sweeping from Lu's feet all the way to the top of her hair.

Mei oohed and aahed something in Chinese, clearly admiring her sister's dress.

"White is not your color; it makes your skin look darker," the old woman critiqued.

"Sorry I'm late," Lu said to Will as if she had not heard her mother's comment. Her smile was faint; it was not warm and joyous as called for on an occasion that was supposed to be a family reunion, and she looked preoccupied.

"Are you okay?" Will asked.

"I am okay, just a little tired. Maybe the past few days of travel have gotten to me. I am sure you have been formally introduced to my mother and sister," she said, casting Will a look that said, "I hope she didn't embarrass you."

"Yes, Juin introduced us. He is over there with Dick. I think you need to go and say hello to him." Will took her cue. "Well, Mrs. Lin, it was very nice meeting you."

"Oh, yes. I hope to see you again soon," Lu's mother said. Will could feel her eyes following him as he and Lu walked away.

"Thanks for rescuing me," Lu whispered as soon as they turned away.

"Same here. I was looking for a way to excuse myself before you got here. Your mother was a little tough to talk to."

"You mean she is critical; just be honest," Lu said. A warmer smile rose both on her face and her eyes.

"You could say that." Will's smile was uncomfortable, but the dimples on his face seemed to deepen and glint. "I guess that happens to old people. They think they can say whatever comes to their minds."

"I don't think that's what you really think; you're just trying to be nice."

Before Will could say anything, Juin spotted them and waved from the couch where Will and Dick had sat earlier but that was now occupied by several dark-suited men, including Dick. "Oh, Lu, you are here; that's great. Come over here. I need to introduce you to several of my very important friends," Juin said.

A rapid succession of introductions was followed by greetings and handshakes. There were VIPs from the telecommunications bureau, high-ranking officials from the city government of Shanghai, and executives of Great Wall Holding, all bowing and presenting their business cards with both hands. When it was all over, Lu had given away the last of the few business cards tucked in her small evening clutch bag.

She was wondering what was next when Juin's soft but slippery voice called from the center of the room, "May I have everybody's attention please?" He briefly raised the champagne glass in his hand to the thirty-some guests in the room. Now all seemed to stand at attention.

"My wife and I want to welcome everybody this evening who came all the way out here from the city." He glanced at Mei standing by his side, looking up at him adoringly. "Our guests of honor today are Mr. Dick Witherspoon and Mr. Will Donovan. As many of you here already know, Mr. Witherspoon will help us raise a lot of money on Wall Street while Mr. Donovan's company hopefully will soon be our partner in the telecommunication business. In a sense we are like a big family, helping each other. Now, because of that, I've invited everyone here so we can have more time to get to know each other in a comfortable and relaxed setting, rather than in a restaurant, where we eat and leave in a hurry. My wife has planned a casual buffet on the veranda, so everybody eat, drink, talk, and get to know each other. Go outside for a stroll in the garden, and stay as long as you like. After all, tomorrow is Saturday." He raised the glass. "Cheers! *Ganbei!*"

Everyone in the room raised their glasses and *ganbeied* (cheered) each other.

"One more thing," Juin said to the crowd ready to stream out onto the veranda, "my wife has just reminded me to say something about the dessert she has special ordered for everyone, the egg-yolk moon cake, a Chinese tradition celebrating the harvest full moon this time of the year. Technically the moon festival is a month away, but that's not to say we can't start eating moon cake now to celebrate today's occasion. Friends, family, and partners, that's what the moon cake stands for, the wholeness of everything, the wholeness of my own family. It's not often that my wife, my mother-in-law, and I can often have Lu, my American sister-in-law, be here with us for a few days." With one arm he pointed at Lu. He wrapped the other around his wife's waist and pulled her in toward him. "To my American sister-in-law, who, no matter what, will forever look like one of us Chinese." He raised his glass again and cast Lu a look she compelled herself to believe was sincere.

"That was nice of him and nice of your sister to think of you that way," Will, standing next to her, whispered.

"Yeah, I only met my sister a week ago, but I like her. I just wish she could be more of her own person."

"What do you mean?"

"I think she is very much under the influence of my mother and very much controlled by her husband. By the way, what do you think about Juin?"

"He is obviously very successful; look at this place."

"Welcome to the home of China's ultrarich," Lu said quietly as they followed the crowd to the veranda.

"He seemed to be friendly and well mannered, but I can't say that about his eyes."

"What about his eyes?" Lu asked, surprised.

"It's like he has two pairs of eyes. One pair looks at me like I'm a valuable business partner, but I always feel there is another pair of eyes behind the one you and I can see. That pair assesses and evaluates everything around him constantly, determining the next best lead to more money and power," Will said thoughtfully.

"I think he is like a snake, lurking in the darkness, waiting for his next prey," Lu said bluntly.

Will did not comment further. Lu had never been this blunt, and her voice never this chilly. Instinct told him it had something to do with what had happened in the meeting that morning when Lu suddenly had seemed to blank out. He concluded it was something off limits, at least for now, and he was not going to push.

They had reached the side of the buffet station. Three large gold-rimmed porcelain trays were spread on a side table, each containing at least a dozen golden, perfectly round, palm-sized moon cakes.

"Sister, you should try one, especially the double-yolk, lotus-paste ones." Mei's delicate voice came from behind them, speaking in deliberate English. "I ordered those for you, for good luck. Juin is right, about how often you can be here with us. I waited thirty years to meet you for the first time. But I am glad we finally get to know how we look today, not in the pictures when I was just a baby and you were just a little girl."

"Thank you. I hope we will be seeing each other more often from now on." Reflexively, Lu spoke in English too. She paused to pick up a double-yolk, lotus-paste cake and took a big bite so the remaining cake looked like a crescent moon. "Mm, I forgot how delicious this is," Lu said and smiled at her sister.

"Now, now." From behind Mei, their mother thrust her helmet head forward. "You need to take it easy. These cakes are fattening; you can easily gain a few kilo the way you are eating it." Derisiveness echoed in her seemingly joking tone. Turning to Mei, she gently scolded, "Mei, don't just stand there. You are the hostess; you need to tend to other guests. You have plenty of time to talk to your sister; we are all going for dim sum together this Sunday, aren't we?"

"Yes, Mother." Mei side-glanced her mother and then turned to Will. "Well, Mr. Donovan, I was hoping you could come with us on Sunday to try the best dim sum in town?"

"I would love to, but my flight back is tomorrow. Maybe next time," Will said politely.

"Okay, see you next time then." Mei smiled and went inside.

"It's a pity you have to go back so soon, Mr. Donavan. I hope business will bring you back more often," the old woman said. She turned to Lu, who was chewing on the last bite of the moon cake. "Now, Lu, I am just an old woman. I don't understand Juin's business very well, but I am glad you can help him. We are all family, and it makes me very happy to see everybody together like this." She smiled, this time not just her mouth; her icy face seemed to have thawed enough to smile too.

"Did I hear my name? Are you talking about me? I hope it was good." Juin had approached quietly and had positioned himself right behind his mother-in-law, resting both his hands on her shoulders.

"Oh, Juin, I was just telling Lu that I am so happy that she is helping you with your business," the old woman said, her hand touching Juin's hand.

"Yes, Mother, Lu knows we are all family, and I take good care of my family. I am sure she will help us as much as she can, right?" His voice was glib, and his black marble eyes gaped hypnotically behind his gold-rimmed, round spectacles.

A grimace shadowed Lu's face before she said with a polite smile, "Juin, I am just an assistant to Dick, gathering data and fact-checking. I see you are a very powerful and successful businessman; you hardly need any help from someone like me."

"You are being modest, Lu." Juin cracked a half laugh. "I have heard that your opinion matters on the Street; people take you seriously. I'm just glad that we have someone like you to give this deal more credence."

"Thank you for thinking so highly of me. I'll do my best," she said and then craned her head at the buffet station. "The food smelled delicious; we should get some before it's all gone." Lu cleverly changed the subject and stepped over to stand at the end of the line.

"Yes, I am very hungry. If you don't mind, I am going to get some food too." Will bowed slightly to Juin and the old woman and joined Lu at the buffet station. He could feel the heat of the old woman's stare and the chill of Juin's look on his back.

Will only had the time to set a few pieces of miniature puff pastry appetizers and a moon cake on his plate before Dick singled him out and dragged him from one circle of VIPs to another group of officials, to fulfill the obligations that came along with being the guests of honor, he said. Will hobnobbed and chitchatted, but every moment he could, he searched for Lu and trailed her movement. Her sullen and preoccupied mood and temperament since that morning were out of character for her. When they had said hello for the first time, it had been her eyes that had caught his attention, how they had seemed to always smile first before the corners of her mouth turned up and her face blossomed like flowers in the warmth of spring. Then there was her disposition; she was content with where she was in life and comfortable with herself yet fully capable of exercising practical and professional acumen in a highly competitive and sometimes cutthroat world. But underneath all that, he also had sensed a touch of sadness in her that had something to do with a secret past. And whatever that secret was, it had come back to haunt her. He could not imagine what he would have become had he suffered the same brutality the Communist Party had inflicted on her family. Would he still have embraced life with the passion and contentment she had? At the age of six or seven years old, she had worried about survival while his biggest complaint or worry had been not getting a new baseball bat or glove. He wished they had more time to spend together as they had the previous evening. But he had to leave tomorrow, so it left him with only this evening, and he wanted nothing more than to spend his last evening in China with her. He would not push her to reveal what was bothering her, but he would like to be there if she was ready to shed the burden of whatever was troubling her.

An hour had passed when Dick finally seemed to be satisfied with the amount of goodwill he believed he had gathered for the benefit of his firm's business. Will set out to look for Lu.

But she was not in the room. He went out on the veranda; she was not there either. He began to worry. Maybe she was gone; she had said she was not feeling well and had not seemed to want to come here in the first place. Disappointment took over, and he stepped off the veranda and wandered aimlessly alongside the reflecting pool.

When he reached the other end of the pool, soft laughter drifted over from a nearby stone bench nestled in a cluster of rosebushes. In the gray light of dusk, he could tell the bench was occupied by two women.

"Hi, Will, having fun hobnobbing with the elite of Shanghai?" Lu asked. Mei was sitting next to her, her tubelike dress rolled up above her knees.

"I thought you were gone," Will said, relief washing over him.

"Oh no, I can't leave without tasting each of the assorted moon cakes my sister had special ordered for me." She pointed at a silver plate on the bench, between her and Mei, where a few pieces of quartered moon cake remained.

"We figured we needed a place where we could pig out in peace and quiet, without being criticized for being too fat or too thin. Do you want one?" Lu picked up the plate and offered it to Will.

"No thanks, I had one earlier, and I think I've had enough to eat for the day. Sorry to intrude; I'll leave you alone," Will said, turning to leave.

"No, no, you can stay. I have to go back to the house anyway." Mei stood and then murmured something to Lu in Chinese and giggled before departing the way Will had come.

"Don't forget to roll down your dress," Lu reminded her.

She turned around and grinned. Then she kept walking toward the house. The bottom of her dressed stayed rolled up to her knees, her stride long and bouncy.

"I think she has livened up a lot since you arrived." Will watched Mei disappear behind a curve of shrubbery.

"Don't say that in front of my mother; she'll think I'm a bad influence."

"I'm sorry; I didn't mean to interrupt. I think I drove her away."

"Actually, we were about to get back to the house anyway. My mother would come looking for her if she found her missing on the scene for more than a few minutes."

"We don't want that, do we? Somehow I have the feeling you don't want your mother coming to look for you either," Will said, eyes stretched toward the sprawling mansion on the other side of the reflecting pool. "You want to get out of here?" he asked.

CHAPTER 17

· · · · ·

IT TOOK THEM A while to get out of Juin's mansion. Lu only said good-bye to her sister, saying she was not feeling well but would be at Sunday's dim sum brunch. Then she sneaked out from a side door to wait for Will at the front driveway. Will spotted Juin on the veranda and simply walked up to him and apologized that he had to leave since he had a morning flight to catch. Juin did not object. He thanked Will and assured him they would meet again soon and insisted that Will take one of the service cars waiting in the front to take guests back to the city. On his way out, Will saw Dick talking boisterously to a man sucking on the butt of a cigarette as vigorously as if his next breath depended on it.

"Dick, thanks for everything; I'll see you back in the States," Will said as he passed by without slowing down.

"Oh, okay, buddy, see you then," Dick slurred, his eyes glassy. Will was not sure if Dick knew whom he was talking to.

At the front door, the man in the mandarin-collared jacket who had greeted Will when he'd arrived opened the door to the car parked right in front of the house, engine running.

He got in, and Lu was already sitting in the backseat.

"How did he know you and I are together?"

"I told him that a *laowai*, that means 'foreigner,' would be out soon and that we both needed to get back to the city. Come on, you and Dick are the only *laowai* at the party this evening. How difficult is that?"

"Where do you want to go, miss?" the driver asked in Chinese.

"Hilton Shanghai please," Lu answered in Chinese, but English would have sounded the same to Will.

"Me too," Will said, grinning.

The ride back to the city was quiet. There was not much to say while the driver was only a few feet away. By the time they pulled in front of the Hilton lobby, it was almost ten.

"We can go to the top for a drink. You can have a snack there too if you are still hungry," Lu said.

"The last thing I want is more food. I've felt like a duck being force-fed these last few days. Do Chinese businessmen eat and entertain like that every day?" Will patted his stomach, said thank you to the driver, and slipped him a hundred-yuan bill before he got out of the car.

"Thank you for doing that," Lu whispered as they walked up the steps into the lobby.

"What?"

"I saw you tip the driver. I would have done it if I were by myself. You know drivers like that are just happy they have a job. In this city, a few dollars are nothing to somebody like my brother-in-law, but you just made that driver's day."

"You are welcome," Will said simply.

At the bar on the hotel's thirty-ninth floor, Lu picked a tall pub table tucked in a corner, directly facing the Yan'an expressway winding eastbound toward the waterfront. "I'll just have a watermelon martini," she said to the waitress.

"I thought you'd have a real drink; you said the watermelon martini here is nothing more than fruit juice," Will said. He studied the menu and was delighted to find his favorite Hefeweizen listed on it. "I'll have one of these. I haven't seen it anywhere else and have kind of missed it."

"Two glasses of champagne with moon cake was enough for me, bizarre paring but quite good. What I enjoyed more was a good chat with Mei, talking about silly things like shoes and fashion, just girl stuff. I think that was the only normal part of the day." A smile thinly veiled the melancholy in her eyes, but only for a second.

"Lu, I'm just guessing, but it seems the past couple of days would have been kind of surreal for anybody in your shoes. Even for me, I'm here for the first time and know little about the country's history, but I feel like I've dropped off the real world for a few days. The only time I've felt real was when we were walking around the city together last night and right now. And don't get mad at me, but I have to include Dick in a sense: it's like you two are the only connection to home, back in the real world ..."

"Oh my God, I couldn't have said it better. That's exactly how I feel too," Lu interrupted, her eyes brightened.

"What I'm trying to say is you must be on an emotional whirlwind, seeing your sister for the first time in thirty years, and so many things here must remind you of the awful past. Who wouldn't be feeling strange?"

Lu did not say anything, only locking her eyes on his for a long moment.

Their drinks came, interrupting the intensely intimate interaction between her black-onyx eyes and his saphire-blue eyes. Will felt warm. He got up, took off his blue blazer, and laid it on top of the extra bar stool at the table. It reminded him of something.

"Well, talking about in a surreal world, let's get back to the real one." He reached into the interior pocket of his jacket and pulled out a small rectangular box neatly wrapped in red paper and tied with a thin red fabric ribbon.

"What's this?"

"Open it. It can't be more real American," he said with a mischievous wink.

Lu slid the ribbon off the box and tore the wrapping off as if it were the first surprise gift she had ever received in her life. A red rectangular device was encased in the transparent box.

"It's an Apple iPod. I think it will make a far superior running mate than the bulky CD player you have now."

She took it out of the box. It was light as a feather, laser thin, and bright red.

"I got it in an Apple store here this afternoon and registered it in your name and your e-mail address. Put the earphones in, and try it out."

She was speechless. Quietly she unwound the earphones and plugged them into the tiny slot on the iPod.

"Put it on, and just push the bottom part of the round button," Will said.

She did. Her face told him she heard the familiar soft flick and tremor of the violin string, the pulsating rhythm, the shimmering variation. It was telling her the story of Gadfly all over again—his romantic quest for all forms of human love, his struggle to make the moral choices that broke him physically and killed him in the end, and yet his triumph in his romance with life, as he put it and she quoted a day ago, "Then am I a happy fly, if I live or if I die."

Whether it was the advanced acoustic technology of the iPod or her unusual emotional state at the moment, or maybe both, her eyes began to water, brimming with tears. She grabbed the napkin on her lap and buried her face in it. She sobbed silently, only her shoulders quivering.

He remembered she'd once said there were not many things in her life worth crying over. He waited quietly until she lifted her face from the napkin.

"Sorry, you must think I am silly to let the music get to me," she said sheepishly, dabbing her red, slightly puffy eyes.

"Not really. I've seen big, tough men tear up over music before. It means you are alive and can feel."

She seemed to contemplate what he said for a moment. "I don't think I was completely honest. There are other things making me sad today. The music just pushed me over the edge."

"Does it have anything to do with this morning in the meeting room? I thought you were fine one minute, and the next, it was like you saw a ghost or something."

"You can say that. And I am sorry that I had to mention the federal-government-contracts issue. I know it might be hard for you because you invested a big part of your life building that business, but I think it's clearly a security risk if the Chinese are to hold a majority interest in the joint venture. Don't you agree?"

"Yeah, no worries, I have been prepared to let those contracts go for a while now, although in a perfect world I'd keep them. I know some staff may lose their jobs once those contracts are transferred. Most of them have worked for me for a long time."

"I know things change, especially in the business world, and we are forced to adapt so we can stay in business and not be left behind. We seldom adapt to change willingly; it's a choice we have to make. I just want you to know that I understand your dilemma in this deal," Lu said.

"It would be my dilemma if I were still one hundred percent in control of the company, not anymore. Whatever we do, it's something the whole management team and the board will have to agree to for the best interest of the company. You, on the other hand, are working on Great China Telecom's IPO; you have nothing to do with the potential joint venture, which in the grand scheme will end up as a footnote on the prospectus. In that sense, neither you nor I should have any dilemma or guilt. What I'm more interested in is the ghost you saw this morning."

"Not just this morning but all day, or since I was a child," she said tentatively, losing some of the cool composure she had just regained. "It's about Juin; he has the exact face and eyes of the man who raided our apartment with a mob of Red Guards when I was a little girl. I remember peeping out from behind the door of the bedroom I shared with Grandma. He was yelling at my father, accusing him of being a spy, and then he ordered the Red Guards to drag my father away. I ran after my father, and this man grabbed me and pushed me on the floor. I'll never forget those eyes. They stared at me, never blinking, stone cold like a predatory snake. The next day, Grandma told me it was all a nightmare, that my father was away on a business trip and would be coming home soon. Of course he didn't for years."

"But that was more than forty years ago. The snake-eye guy could be dead by now—" Will abruptly stopped himself. He thought about the unthinkable. "Are you saying Juin is somehow related to him?"

"That's what's been bothering me all day. I keep telling myself not to let my imagination run wild, but I can't help it. His face, triangular-shaped like a snake's, just like the one that haunts my dreams, and those eyes, the way he stared at me across the table this morning, like shooting venom, obviously displeased with what I said. The only thing different is his voice, slimy and slithery, while the man who took my father sounded like a heavy cigarette smoker."

Will did not know what to say.

"All afternoon, I turned everything in the past few days over and over in my mind. First, Mei told me that Juin's father and my mother used to work at the same hospital many years ago and that when Juin's father died, his father's best friend, a general in the army, adopted him. And my mother seems to have been very good friends with this general

251

too. I once told my father how I thought the man who took him away looked like a snake and how those eyes terrified me. He told me the snake was the party secretary of the hospital where he and my mother worked."

"What did a party secretary do?"

"Back then, party secretaries were everywhere, hospitals, factories, in the military, on the farm, and even in the neighborhood districts. To me they were the eyes and ears of the Communist government, constantly spying on people like my father. I think they are still around today, at most government-owned enterprises."

"This sounds like what Hitler did in Germany, what the Nazis did to the Jews or to people who sympathized with the Jews."

"Exactly. There are so many coincidence here that I just can't dismiss the possibility the two snakes are related; they could be father and son. Juin might not be out there declaring he is a member of the Communist Party, but his wealth and power say he came from that lineage. And my mother, if you haven't noticed, is a sucker for money and power, and she is riding on Juin's coattails through Mei's marriage to him. You should have seen the apartment she just moved into, which I am sure Juin is paying for. All this makes sense yet is so confusing at the same time. I don't want to believe it, but it's bothering me that my mother pushed Mei to marry a man whose father helped the government in persecuting her husband." Lu winced, as if pricked by what she had just said.

"So that almost stopped you from going to Juin's party this evening," Will said, everything making sense to him now.

"You can say that. I know it could just be my wild imagination, but I can't help it. I'm going to try to find out for sure."

"How?"

"I have this dim sum thing on Sunday. I plan to go to my mother's apartment on the early side. I think I'll just ask her about the background of Juin's father or if she has a picture of him. Anyway, I think I need to find out so it doesn't drive me crazy."

"I think you could be treading on dangerous ground. Sometimes it's better to leave the past alone. So what if Juin is related to the old snake? What are you going to do? Does it change the fact that Mei is still your sister and your mother is still your mother?"

"I don't know, I don't know. I guess it's because up until recently I believed that I was done with Shanghai. There was nothing here for me to come back to. Then my work forced me to be here, and I saw my mother and sister, the family again. My mother is still the mother I remember; life is never good enough for her. Even when I was a child, she complained how she had married wrong, so I figured she and my father hadn't married out of love. I can accept that; that could happen in any society. My sister, Mei, I thought she was just a spoiled rotten brat at first, but from talking to her, I think she is a very lonely person deep inside. I think on a certain level she knows her mother is using her to get the lifestyle she wants, but she has no clue about the history, what happened to our father. What if Juin is the son of the man who persecuted our father, and our mother has known that all along and still pushed her to marry Juin? It was only yesterday I thought part of my roots might still be here after all these years," Lu murmured. For the first time, she was baring her soul to him.

"But how you feel about Mei won't change even if you find out who her husband really is, right?"

She looked at him, her eyes questioning his question.

"Okay, you may not agree with me, but I'm coming back to my leaving-the-past-alone theory. Sometimes not letting a secret lie risks breaking a relationship that might have a chance to last for a lifetime."

"That depends on how horrendous the secret is and whether all parties involved know it but choose to pretend not to so they can stay together, but then are they really together?" Lu said, her eyes piercing him like laser beams.

"I guess it's a choice different people will make differently and then live with the consequences." He found himself on a subject he was seldom comfortable talking about with anybody else in his life, not even Sage, sometimes particularly not Sage. But he continued without hesitation, "If it's of any consolation, I think everybody to a certain degree carries some kind of secret in life, or at least part of their life, whether it's about themselves or somebody in their family. People say honesty is the best policy. I don't necessarily find that true all the time."

"Are you telling me you have some dark secrets buried somewhere inside you?" Lu asked, joking for the first time since they'd sat down at the table.

"You could say that, and I have never even told Sage about this. Has Sage ever told you that she and I could have had another sibling but our mom suffered a miscarriage?"

"Yes, she has."

"Sage and I were teenagers when my mom got pregnant again. We were all a little surprised because my parents had made it very clear that the two of us were enough, no more babies. It was a period when my parents seemed to be having some problems. He was under pressure at work and had to travel frequently. Mom was always complaining about Dad's absence but at the same time was worried not enough money was saved for our college education. They argued and fought often in their bedroom, which was next to mine, and the wall was thin. It was always about money or Dad not being home enough. One night they fought because one of Mom's friends had seen Dad with a group of guys in a nightclub, a fancy name for strip club. The next day, I came home from school and heard Mom and her friend talking in the kitchen. They didn't think I heard anything, but I did. They suspected my dad was fooling around. The woman told Mom that the best way to keep a straying husband is to have another baby. And the next thing we knew, Mom got pregnant."

"So you guessed your mom got pregnant deliberately?"

"I'm almost certain that's the case. I think Dad knew the pregnancy was not an accident, but he kept to himself for a while. Mom, meanwhile, seemed happy. Then she fell and lost the baby. She didn't talk to Dad for quite a while. Then the nighttime arguing and fighting resumed. Mom always blamed Dad for the miscarriage because he was supposed to be with her that day she fell, but he hadn't been able to because of some emergency at the office. One night, Dad must have had too much to drink, because his angry voice was louder than usual. I heard him say something about Mom not taking the pill. Shortly after that he moved out. He died a year later before they were officially divorced. I still wonder sometimes if they would have gotten back together had he not died. Sage has always believed our parents had a perfect marriage, that they would have worked things out ultimately, so I've never told her what I know."

"So you let her keep what you might call an illusion."

"We'll never know. It could be either way: illusion or real-world perfect marriage. Dad died too early. Besides, I am not a hundred percent sure what really happened, so the best thing to do is just leave it alone."

"Suppose what you said is true and your dad never confronted your mom, you think they would have stayed together and truly been happy together?" Lu asked.

"We'll never know. Everyone handles life's disappointments differently."

With curiosity, she studied his face, as if it suddenly embodied something she had never expected. "You know, Sage talks about you a lot. She says you are the big brother she can always depend on, a workaholic, an extremely loyal friend and employer, and of course a superior surfer dude and fitness nut."

"Wow, are you sure she was talking about me? Anything bad?"

"She's said that, she also said like most men, you are not very sensitive or observant when it comes to human dynamics and that certain things fly right over your head." Lu let out a chuckle.

"Hey, I'm just a nerd; I'm clueless when it comes to psychoanalyses."

"But I don't think Sage is exactly right here. I don't think you are clueless; you just choose not to talk about things that are uncomfortable, or like you said, you think it's better to just let secrets lie. It's your way to protect the people you care about."

Will thought about what she said. He wanted to tell her that she thought too highly of him and that there were times he chose what Sage considered the generic male traits of being insensitive and clueless to mask his deep-down insecurities and fears in his personal relationships with women. But he was also aware that he loved every minute he had been together with Lu so far. He actually felt comfortable talking to her about uncomfortable memories, and she had revealed secrets that had been obviously off limits to anybody else in her life. It was like their relationship was at a perfect equilibrium.

"It's getting late. When is your flight tomorrow?" Lu looked at her wristwatch, interrupting his inner monologue.

It was close to midnight. Neither of them was tired, and both wanted to linger in the surreal world they were in, but both knew tomorrow would come soon, and then they would be back to the real world to meet life's demands and deal with its deadlines. "Yeah, I'd better get going; have to be at the airport by 8:00 a.m.," Will said regretfully. "Let me take care of the bill."

"It's only two drinks; I'll just put it on my room," Lu said and signaled the waitress to bring the check. After Lu took care of the check, they headed out of the bar.

"Tell you what, it's Labor Day weekend next week. When will you be back in New York?" Will asked.

"I leave Monday morning and should be back in the office on Tuesday. Why?"

"Why don't we all go back to the tip of the world and spend a few days there? I'll ask Sage if she wants to go too," Will said with a bright smile, as if he was already looking at the glittering sand and sparkling water.

"You mean Montauk? So get out of this surreal world and go to the tip of the world for a few days? Sounds like a great idea." Lu was surprised Will remembered how she once had referred to Montauk as the tip of the world.

The closer they got to the elevator, the slower they walked, as if that way their journey downstairs could last forever. "Which floor are you on?" Will asked quietly as he pushed the button.

"Thirty-seven, only two floors down. I could have walked down."

"Yes, you could have."

The elevator came up quickly, and they got in. By coincidence or by design, the soft background music was Dionne Warwick's "I'll Never Love This Way Again."

They stood steps away from each other in the elevator, forgetting to push the button for the thirty-seventh floor.

"Have you noticed that the music they play here is at least twenty years old?" Lu said.

"Yes, I noticed that in my hotel too," Will mumbled before he realized they had not pushed the button yet. So he did.

The elevator door opened seconds later. "Good night. Have a safe trip back, and I'll see you soon," Lu said, looking up at him.

"Yeah, I'll see you soon." He leaned over and kissed her softly on the cheek and then watched her walk away. The door automatically closed, but the elevator did not move. He did not want to push the lobby button. *Oh, to hell with it,* a voice in his head said, and he pushed the door-open button and stepped out into the hallway. A few feet away, Lu stood silently, staring at him with feverish eyes.

"I just want to be with you tonight," he said. He did not care that he was in a surreal world; if he was not with her tonight, things would not be right once he returned to the real world.

She remained still until he was right next to her. Then they proceeded down the hallway until they came to the door of her room. With her card key in hand, she shot him a glance as if asking, "Are you sure this is what we want?"

She opened the door. The room was opaquely dark, the interior of the room and the cloudy midnight sky outside blurring into one. Then they were swept into a passionate storm—the thud of his watch dropping on the floor, the thump of shoes being kicked off and bumping into the furniture, the popping sound of a button coming off his shirt or Lu's dress, a flash when she let her satin dress slide off her body and pool on the floor.

Then their body touched. Their feverish movement gave way to tenderness as she slowly pulled him into her and held him, tighter and tighter, until they melted into one and drifted away with utter abandon.

CHAPTER 18

· · · · ·

"WE'LL SOON BE ARRIVING at the nation's capital. The local time is approximately 2:00 p.m., Saturday afternoon, and the temperature is …"

Will awoke to the captain's announcement for arriving at the Dulles International Airport outside of Washington, DC. He looked at his watch; the digital display read 2:00 a.m., Sunday. He realized he hadn't set his watch back; it was still on Shanghai time, exactly twelve hours ahead. He had slept for almost ten hours. He pushed his seat back to sitting position and stowed the footrest as memories of the previous day whirled back into his mind.

He remembered Lu's warm body, intertwined with his, floating away into the tenderness of the night. He remembered the first dreamy rays of dawn stirring them awake and her embrace, so feverish, as if she wanted to crush herself into him. And then he'd had to hurry away, back to his hotel. He'd thrown everything back in his luggage and dashed to the airport.

He remembered how she had watched him, smiling as he'd picked up his clothing lying on the floor like debris after a storm. "I guess it's time to get back to the real world," she'd said.

"But we have the tip of the world to look forward to, and you can save a soul," he'd said while putting on his shirt.

"What do you mean?"

"Remember the Flying Dutchman, who was cursed by the devil to wander the sea forever unless the right woman came along to save his soul? I'll let you save my wandering soul if you're willing."

"I'll think about it," she'd said coyly.

A silly grin had risen in his own face, and all had been good in his life.

Out of habit, he reached out for his cell phone sitting in the armrest console. He had turned it off before boarding the plane. While still in the airport he had received a text from Kevin, asking when he would be back in town so they could meet at the pub for a drink. Apparently Kevin had to brief him on something important. He wondered what had put Kevin in the mood to reach out. He had texted Kevin back about when he would be touching down and had said he would meet him at the pub for a drink or a light dinner if he was not too tired. Well, he felt pretty good having slept for ten hours, and he was in a very good mood.

He decided he would let Kevin know their drink/dinner was on right after the plane touched down, but first he would text Lu that he had arrived, and maybe he would call her after dinner with Kevin, when it would be morning in Shanghai. But before doing that he would go home and alleviate Sage from her dog-sitting duty. Maybe he and Louis could go out for a long walk. He wondered how Sage and Joe were doing. Maybe he would convince Sage to come along to the pub with him. It was Saturday night, the busiest night for Joe, so he would have to be at the pub. He thought about what he should tell Sage about Lu and himself, or maybe he should let Lu tell her first …

• • •

When Will arrived at the pub in Alexandria at six o'clock, Kevin Jagger was already sitting at their usual table at the window, a tall glass of dark beer in his hand. "Hey, boss, welcome home!" he called out to Will jovially, a grin stretched across his face.

Will seldom saw Kevin this relaxed. He waved at him from the bar, where Joe pulled the lever for his favorite Hefeweizen.

"Sage said she'll be stopping by for dinner later," Will said, taking the beer.

"Yeah, she just called and said she would be by," Joe said, his eyes twinkling.

The two of them must be getting along splendidly, Will thought as he walked over to Kevin.

"How was the flight? Sorry to drag you out here on such short notice, but I think you need to know the latest development on this joint-venture thing with the damn Chinese," Kevin said, as if he was the person who had propelled the latest development.

"What new development?" Will was perplexed.

"Be honest with me, boss; you and I go back a long time. If you had your way, or if both of us had our way, would you seriously consider involving our business with the Chinese?" he asked, his shoulders suddenly stiffening under his black T-shirt.

"I think we've covered this before. Personally I think it would be much simpler for us to remain a stand-alone company. But the Chinese were pursuing Matrixtech before we became a part of the company, and now the Chinese have come back and sweetened the pot. It's not for me to decide whether we get involved with them or not. I understand you would have preferred to stay where we were; it was familiar and comfortable. But technology keeps changing, and the industry is becoming more competitive. If we don't come up with new products and services, we could disappear in a few years' time."

"Okay, okay, you don't have to preach to me about long-term strategic thinking. We are part of Matrixtech now, and as you said, you have enough money to play with your innovative ideas. But I have a lot invested in the company too, so I am doing my best to help. From what you've said, I gather you would have told the Chinese to get the fuck away if you were the boss of the company," Kevin said, his tone acid and cutting.

Will did not respond. He admitted to himself that, when it came to the Chinese part, there was some truth in what Kevin had said.

"Well, I take it that you agree with me. The good news is the deal is off," Kevin said, putting on a conceited smile.

"You mean the joint-venture deal with Great China Telecom?"

"Joint venture, partnership, whatever, it's off, or at least it's not going anywhere for a long time," Kevin said smugly.

"You mean the board dismissed it? Nobody has told me that."

"Not the board; I made it happen. I happen to believe letting the Chinese take any interest in our company has serious national-security implications. I voiced my concern to Congressman Kessler, and he said Congress had been looking into similar risks, like allowing Chinese telecom-equipment makers to bid on US network-system contracts, especially if those contracts are related to defense or national security. I told him how the Chinese are offering us large R&D funding in exchange for majority control of our company, all in the name of marketing our cybersecurity products and services to their customers all over the world."

"So what did the congressman say?" Will was curious.

"He was alarmed but told me there is no law for the government to tell us we can or cannot form a partnership with the Chinese."

"So what did you do?"

"Well, you told me that the Chinese woman from Wall Street is the sister-in-law of the head of Great China Telecom's parent company. He's got to be a high-ranking government official or must have close ties to the Communist government, don't you think?" Kevin said.

"What does Lu have to do with this?" Will asked. Suddenly he felt there was something sinister in what Kevin had said.

"Don't you think that relationship could be interpreted as colluding for personal gain? At least perception wise."

"But Lu has nothing to do with the joint-venture deal; she's there because of Great China Telecom's IPO," Will said, his voice raised. His heartbeat quickened, and all his blood seemed to surge up to his head. It felt as if it was about to explode.

"It doesn't matter in reality. In situations like this, perception matters, boss." Kevin went on, "And the congressman did some digging. He found out that this Lu woman used to work for his uncle Earl Kessler, who was a senior official at the State Department at one time and later led a very well-known technology company. The world is small, isn't it? According to the congressman, his uncle fired Lu because, as the chief financial officer, she couldn't even keep the company's books straight. She was the reason the company his uncle spent so many years building went down."

"Sage and I know exactly how his uncle's company went down, and Lu was actually trying to stop his uncle's extravagant spending habits. How could you do this? How could you drag her into this?"

"Hey, boss, I'm just trying to protect you." Kevin put up one of his hands, gesturing for Will to calm down. "Don't let this woman fool you; all these Wall Street people are selfish and greedy. The congressman agreed with me on this. He said he wouldn't be surprised if Lu was helping her brother-in-law behind the scenes so her firm could get more of those lucrative IPO deals down the road. Because of the congressman and because of me, she'll have to look for something else now, Matrixtech is off limits."

"What did you do?" Will seethed, glaring at Kevin.

"I didn't have to do anything," Kevin said casually. "Thanks to the congressman's uncle, who still has good contacts at the State Department. The Chinese have been notified through diplomatic channels that the deal is off due to national-security concerns."

"How could you do this? How could you do this to her?" Will muttered. His face was sheer anger, desperation, and horror.

"Good God, don't tell me you fucked her." Kevin let out a cry and then yelled, "You fucked her, you son of a bitch." He slammed his beer glass down on the table and stood up, his face turning red and spidery veins bulging through his forehead. Will stood too, placing his hands flat on the table and leaning in close, his face inches from Kevin's.

The whole pub turned quiet, all eyes on the two men standing across the table from each other, face-to-face, engaged in a standoff.

A moment later, Will was the first to sit down. "You're lucky. If this weren't a public place, I would have punched your eyes out," he said through clenched teeth.

"Go ahead, if it makes you feel better," Kevin sneered. "But you are a coward, Will Donavan, a coward and an ingrate. You couldn't have gotten where you are today without me spending years of my life pounding the street to get your business started. You've made millions, but it's not enough for you. You want to be the visionary genius of the tech world, and I was dumb enough to let you sell our company to those sharks at Matrixtech, telling myself that Will Donovan has to be happy now since he has enough money to play around, having fun inventing his next great program or system. But no, you want more; you're willing to sell your soul to red China and be snowed by that fucking Chinese bitch. You think I'm going to let you do this while I and many of your long-time, loyal employees are supposed to be happy just sitting around, worrying if we'll still get to keep our jobs next week or next month?"

Will stared at Kevin's contorted face and listened to his ranting. But all he could think was he needed to let Lu know what had happened. He was supposed to call her. He had texted her a couple of hours ago telling her he would call her after his dinner, when she woke up. He stood up and grabbed his cell on the table.

"What do you think you're doing?" Kevin asked, his eyes icy blue. "One last bit of advice from me: you'd better cool it with that bitch. Stop all communications with her, not for yourself, but for the company. You don't want to drag the entire company into a scandal and let the world know that Matrixtech's senior executive Will Donovan is involved with a Wall Street woman who colluded with the Chinese Communist government to gain access to US technology secrets and garner huge profits in the process."

"How do you know that perception is already out there?"

"It may not be as bad as you think—*yet*. It's up to you to prevent that perception from getting worse," Kevin said shrewdly. "The Chinese have only been notified that Matrixtech could not finalize its joint-venture agreement with Great China Telecom due to the US government's concerns about the deal's potential cybersecurity risks. I only used your girlfriend's personal relationship with her brother-in-law to raise enough urgency with the congressman so he would take immediate action to stop the deal from going forward. Now the Chinese may feel they have lost face, since their courting Matrixtech has been highly publicized, but so what? They may be mad, but not a single person on either side has been implicated or blamed. But if you are going to continue your relationship with that bitch, I will make things difficult for you, and in the end, we'll all go down. Remember—perception is reality these days." He gave Will a scornful smile, stood up, and walked out.

Will sank back into his chair, the anger inside him slowly turning into numbness. For a long moment, he was completely at a loss about what to do next, a feeling that had last been familiar to him in his pre-navy days, when he hadn't known what he wanted to do with his life, though at least he'd known going surfing would make him feel better temporarily. What now? He glanced out the window and saw Sage's car maneuvering into a just-vacated metered parking spot in the front of the pub. Soon Sage stepped out and went around to slip coins into the meter slot. She turned around and saw him through the window. She waved at him.

He watched her stop at the bar and lean over to kiss Joe across the counter, and then she was in front of him.

"Hi, big brother, glad you're home," she said, her voice as cheerful as the lemony-colored T-shirt she was wearing. She bent down to drop a kiss on the top of his head before sitting down.

"Hey, Lu and I have been texting each other just now. She said you guys had fun together in Shanghai and that you've invited her to spend Labor Day weekend with you in Montauk next week. She said she has so much to tell me but stopped texting because she was waiting for you to call her. Have you called? I think somebody is in love," she chirped, and Will could not help but smile. It was a faint smile tinted with sadness. And Sage noticed it immediately. "What's wrong? You look pale. Are you tired? Sick?"

"I'm fine. I just have a lot of things I need to figure out," Will said. He thought he sounded pathetic.

"What happened?" Sage studied his face, her smile and chirpiness fading quickly. "Now I've seen that look before. Don't tell me your insecurity is taking over again."

"What are you talking about?" Will feigned ignorance, but he knew exactly what Sage was talking about.

"I think you like Lu, and she likes you. Something happened between the two of you when you were in Shanghai, but now you're back to your old self, wondering if she is good enough for you or if you can commit yourself to the relationship."

"It's not like that," Will said, avoiding Sage's glare.

"I am your sister; I know you. When it comes to relationships with women, you have been playing the same game with yourself all your life. You find ways to self-destruct, and you don't let anybody get too close to you, acting like the women you date are either trying to trap you or are too headstrong for you. You can have all the money you want and can build up your business like an empire, but you'll grow old a lonely man."

"But it's different with Lu," Will said, his voice shuddering, as if uttering those words caused him unbearable pain.

"You bet it's different! She is my best friend, and I'll kill you if you think you can just have some fun and walk away like nothing happened. Now, have you called her yet?"

"I can't."

"What do you mean you can't?"

"I'll tell you when I have things figured out. Can you tell her that I can't go to Montauk next week? Perhaps you two could go there and catch up?" Will said feebly. Suddenly he felt the need to get out, leave this place and get away. He stood up and began to walk away from the table.

"Where are you going? Are you okay?" Sage shouted.

He paused and turned around. "I have to go away. I'll call when I have things figured out."

· · ·

On the short cab ride to her mother's apartment, Lu held her cell phone and checked for messages constantly for fear that the hustle and bustle of the traffic somehow could drown the chiming of incoming messages. Will had texted her early in the morning to tell her he had arrived safely and would call her later. But that was eight hours ago. Since then nothing had come through, no calls, no voice messages, no text messages.

Maybe he was too tired and fell asleep, she thought and let herself drift back to the euphoric state she had been in since Will had left her hotel about thirty hours ago. After he'd left, she'd gone for a run in the gym, listening to "Romance" of *The Gadfly Suite* on her new iPod God knows how many times. For the first time, the achingly beautiful melody had also been tender and uplifting. After her run, she had gone shopping. She had found herself looking at lacy underwear in the window of a lingerie store and had actually gone in and bought something contrary to the athletic style she usually favored, something delicate and feminine. Since then the haze in the air had been gradually thickening, but to her it did not dull the deep green of the plane trees and the soft green of the weeping willows. Her mind was not sure if it was love, but her heart sure feel like a teenage girl suddenly in love, and there were moments she would pause and laugh at herself.

Standing in front of the door to her mother's apartment on the eighth floor, she checked her cell one more time before raising her hand to knock. To her surprise, the door came ajar under her first touch. She pushed it open and stepped inside. "Mother, are you here? The door is open," she called from the hallway.

Nobody answered. She had decided not to arrive early to seek information regarding Juin's father. What Will had said about some secrets being left alone had made her think. Regardless of her feelings toward her mother and Juin, she had a sister she cared for. So what if Juin was indeed the son of the man who had persecuted her father? Was she going to force Mei to divorce him? Mei may not be content with her life, but it would be up to her to determine whether she wanted to change her life. Lu did not know Mei well yet, and she should focus on building a relationship with her before doing something that could tear her life apart. So she arrived exactly as told, at noon, and she would do everything to enjoy the dim sum brunch.

It was actually a few minutes past noon, and nobody seemed to be around. "Mother, Mei?" she called again.

After another few moments of quietness, her mother said, "I am in the living room." Her voice was muffled, as if she were speaking from a floor below.

Lu wound her way into the expansive living room but did not see anybody. There was a soft stir from across the room, and a white helmet-shaped head rose from a high-back chair by the window facing the tower of the Garden Hotel across the street.

"Where is Mei? Are we ready to go?" Lu asked curiously.

"Mei is not coming, and Juin is not coming either." Still dressed in her nightgown, her mother went to stand by the window. "You have ruined everything for them."

"What do you mean?"

"Oh, don't pretend you don't know what you did. I knew we should never have let you back into our lives. From the minute you were conceived, you have brought nothing but bad luck," she said, casting a bone-chilling look of disgust and contempt at her daughter.

"I don't know what you are talking about." Confused, Lu began to step toward her mother.

"Don't come closer. You should leave and never come back to bother us again. You are just like your father, so pigheaded about everything for your so-called principles, but you don't care about anybody else."

"Mother, can you at least tell me what happened?"

"I don't understand business, but you told the American government that Juin was a Communist spy. How could you do that? Juin is a successful businessman. He just wanted to buy your boyfriend's company," her mother screeched. Without heavy makeup and thick foundation, her face was a sallow crisscross of pleats and furrows.

"But I never said that to anybody," Lu said. She thought about how she had mentioned the national-security risk to Juin in that meeting a couple of days ago, but she decided not to say anything to her mother about that. She would only be complicating things; her mother would never understand. "I'll call Juin later to find out exactly what happened. There must be some misunderstanding."

"He doesn't want to see you. He'll never want to see you. Do you know how humiliating it is for him? Inviting your boyfriend over, entertaining him, and throwing banquets and parties for him, and what did he get? Nothing but humiliation and shame. Now please leave. I don't want to see you ever again," her mother shrieked, pointing her bony, clawlike hand at the hallway.

Suddenly, anger surged inside Lu. She wanted the answers to so many questions she'd had for so many years. "Why do you hate me, Mother?" she heard herself ask.

Her question seemed to calm her mother down, as the heaving of her chest slowed. "I don't hate you; I just don't want to see you. You remind me of my miserable marriage to your father and the shame and disgrace I have endured because of him." She snuffled a breath and turned away to look outside the window.

"So you never loved my father. Why did you marry him then?"

"You think life is about love? Does love buy you food, clothes, or a roof over your head? Back in my time, women were laughed at and considered worthless or defective if they didn't get married by a certain age. I didn't want to be the laughingstock." Her mother grimaced, as if still feeling the sting of being laughed at as an old spinster.

"So you deigned to marry my father?"

Her mother shrugged. "I could have put up with him if only he had shut his mouth and just been a surgeon. But no, he was so principled and moral, always telling everybody the government was not doing the right thing, talking about how the Communist Party should adopt more-progressive ideas like in the West, simply because he had spent years in America studying medicine. I told him he was asking for trouble, but he wouldn't listen. So when the Cultural Revolution started, he became a prime target."

What her mother said was harsh but not unexpected. It pushed Lu to find out more. "You mean he became the target of the party secretary at the hospital?"

"How do you know that?" her mother asked, still staring out the window.

"Father told me one day when I visited him on the duck farm. He told me the party secretary of the hospital was the one who came to our apartment and dragged him away. I saw the man too and remember what he looked like." Lu paused to steady her nerves. "I want you to be honest with me, Mother. I believe Juin is related to that party secretary. They look exactly the same."

For a moment, her mother was silent, still like a statute. When she finally turned to face Lu, her thin lips were trembling, and tears had seeped into the crevices of her face. "How dare you to come here to judge me like this? You have no idea what I had to do to keep us from being thrown out of our apartment and into the horrible slum area," her mother hissed. Her face was so contorted her features had all lost their symmetry.

Lu found her mother's reaction strange. Why would her mother say she was judging her? She merely had asked if Juin and the party secretary were related.

Voice trembling, her mother continued, "I simply made a deal with him. I had to be with him whenever he wanted; otherwise, we would have been forced out of the apartment and would have had to move into a dirt-floored little hut in the slum area, and I would have either been put in a labor camp like your father or been subjected to what your grandma suffered. You, at five years old, could have been all alone."

"So you did this for you and me, not for my father."

"It wouldn't have made any difference. Nobody could have saved your father. He was too pigheaded to be saved."

Lu looked at her mother, her erect, elegant form hunched and shriveled up. That was why she had never been home, always on so-called business trips. She felt sorry for her, pitied her. But it was hard for Lu to accept the fact that her mother had been willing to sell her body and soul to that snake party secretary. She said she'd done it for Lu, but for years, Lu had hardly seen her mother. From what Mei had told her, her mother might have spent more time with Juin, taking care of him when his father had been hunting down antigovernment capitalists around the country.

"You know, Mother, I never asked you what relationship you had with Juin's father, but now it's safe for me to say that Juin is that party secretary's son. I simply asked you if Juin and the party secretary are related. But you took my question as a chance to alleviate your conscience. You said you didn't do that for my father, but you didn't do it for me either. When Grandma died, I was only five. You were never there for me. And even when you were home, you never paid me any attention. I think you bargained yourself for comfort, money, and power, just like you bargained Mei for this luxury you are living in—"

Lu did not get to finish what she wanted to say, as her mother jolted up and grunted like a wounded beast, "Get out of here, and get out of my sight! Don't you dare drag Mei into this and poison her with your high morals and principles."

"You mean you don't want her to leave Juin so you lose all this," Lu said calmly.

Her mother was blundering across the living room toward her, as if she wanted to get hold of her daughter and drag her out of the apartment. But halfway across the room, her mother stopped. She simply stood in the middle of the large Persian rug covering almost the entire living room area. When she spoke again, her voice was cool and contemptuous. "Just get out. Leave me in peace, and never ever come back here again."

"I won't bother you again, Mother, but I will not cut all communication with my sister."

Her mother began to laugh, a creepy, eerie, bone-chilling laugh.

"Your half sister. Your father was not Mei's father."

"You mean Juin's father …" Lu was tongue tied for the first time since she'd stepped inside the apartment.

"Oh, please, don't be so perverted; even I was not that evil. Juin's father had nothing to do with Mei. He died before Mei was born."

"So who was Mei's father?"

"He used to be one of the generals in the People's Liberation Army. The first time I met him was right after your father was arrested and sent to toil in a labor camp. The general had stomach cancer, and nobody in the hospital was qualified to operate on him. So they dragged your father out of the labor camp and ordered him to operate on the general, and your father saved the general's life. After the general recovered from the surgery, he was the one who suggested that your father be sent to the duck farm so he could be called upon to operate on senior government or military officials when they got sick. You may hate the general, but in a way he saved your father's life. Your father either would have rotted in the labor camp or had his hands broken as punishment, to make sure he would never be able to hold a scalpel again. Back then Red Guards were breaking dancers' legs so they could not dance again and shoving shoes down singers' throat so they could never sing. You were too young to understand what was going on. Everybody did what they had to do to survive."

"But how did you get involved with the general?"

"He went back to Beijing after he recovered from the surgery. We never really kept in touch. When Juin's father got sick, a new party secretary was assigned to the hospital. He told me to be prepared to move because as the wife of an antigovernment spy and counterrevolutionary, I should have been thrown out of our so-called luxury apartment long time ago. Then Juin's father died, and fortunately the general came back to attend his funeral. They were good friends, you know; they used to be foot soldiers together in Mao's army. I asked for the general's help."

"So you became his mistress."

"I did what I had to do to protect you and myself."

"So you just pretended that Mei was my father's daughter even if he was seldom home and the two of you hardly talked. Did my father know Mei was not his daughter?"

"I think he did. He never even touched me after he was sent to the labor camp. But he acted as if Mei was his daughter. I guess even your father wanted to save face; he didn't want anybody to know that his wife was unfaithful to him."

"Is this the same general who adopted Juin after his father died?"

"I see you have been fishing for information from Mei. Yes, but Mei doesn't know what happened between me and the general or Juin's father, and I intend to keep it that way. So you better keep your mouth shut for once. If you don't, I guarantee that you will never see or speak to her again."

Remembering again what Will had said about some secrets being left buried, Lu decided that this was one of those secrets. It would only hurt Mei. She gave her mother a crisp nod of agreement and then asked, "Does Juin know about the relationship between you and his adoptive father?"

"Yes, and he knows the history between me and his real father too, but he accepted it because he understands we sometimes have to make hard choices in life that don't necessarily make us proud. Why do you think he married Mei? Somebody with Juin's background would never have married Mei if—" Her mother stopped short.

"If what? If Mei were truly the daughter of my father?"

Her mother ignored the sarcasm. "Now you know everything. I slept with your father's enemies, your sister's father was one of your father's enemies, and your sister married the son of another of your father's enemies. So you can do nothing but hate me. Good-bye, Lu."

Lu took a last look at her mother. There was nothing left for her to say. All her questions had been answered, all her doubts removed, and all her suspicions cleared. She had been prepared for the truth to be devastating and upsetting, but she felt none of that, only finality.

"Good-bye, Mother," she said and turned to walk out of the apartment for the last time.

C H A P T E R 1 9

· · · · ·

TWENTY-FOUR HOURS AFTER LU left her mother's apartment, she boarded a United Airlines Boeing 747 at Shanghai Pudong International Airport. She slid her carry-on, with her laptop inside, into the overhead compartment and placed her compact handbag on top of the storage console next to her seat. She would not be doing any business-related work on this long flight back to New York, a very rare occurrence during her ten-year career at Lehrer & Schuler.

The past two weeks had been surreal and bizarre, and the past twenty-four hours had been tumultuous and draining. She pulled out her cell phone from the handbag and sank into her designated seat, hoping for an expeditious takeoff so she could stretch her tired body and just go to sleep. By the time she woke up, she would realize everything that had happened during the past two weeks had merely been an extended dream.

Automatically she tapped her cell to check once again if any new text messages or e-mails had come in. She had texted Mei after she'd left her mother's apartment the previous day, telling her she would be leaving Shanghai soon. She'd let Mei know that things might appeared to be all messed up now but that she had not and would not do anything to hurt her and her husband's business. She'd said she would explain everything if Mei wanted to know the whole story. But above all, she'd told Mei she hoped they would remain sisters.

But Mei had not replied to her message.

She'll need time to figure things out, and she will, Lu thought. And for now, Lu was content to know that she had a sister in China, and she would always care about her.

She hadn't received any new work-related e-mail since early that morning. It was Sunday night in New York, the last weekend in August, and not too many people were working the week before Labor Day weekend. And she had forwarded her boss, Jack, everything she had gathered or written up so far regarding the Great China Telecom IPO project. Hopefully nobody would bother or want to bother her for a while.

When she had gotten back to her hotel from her mother's apartment a day ago, Jack had left her e-mail and voice messages urgently asking her to call him. She had, even though it had been in the middle of the night in New York City.

"What the hell is going on?" Jack had asked as soon as she'd called.

"I was going to ask you the same question," Lu had said, remembering what her mother had told her about the deal between Great China Telecom and Matrixtech.

"You tell me. Fred called me this morning, furious, and wanted me to take you off the IPO project right away. He said the Chinese told him that you are very unprofessional."

"Did he give you any specifics?" Lu had asked.

"No, but he said you must have something to do with the feds' intention of investigating the joint venture still in discussion between Matrixtech and Great China Telecom. I told him we don't have anything to do with that deal. Did you hear anything or do anything to trigger the feds' attention?"

"No, all I did was make one comment at a meeting with Great China Telecom's parent company. I said I was concerned about Matrixtech's federal-government contracts for national-security reasons and would have to disclose that in our due diligence study for Great China Telecom's IPO."

"But Dick Witherspoon told me the head of Great China Telecom's parent company is your brother-in-law. Is that true? How come you didn't tell me earlier?"

An uneasy feeling had nauseated her. "That's because I only found out after I arrived here, toward the end of my visit. Are you saying the US government suspects me of some kind of unethical or conflict-of-interest behavior? But I don't have anything to do with the joint-venture deal. Where is Will Donovan? He's the one at Matrixtech working with the Chinese on the joint-venture deal. Has anybody talked to him?" Lu suddenly had remembered Will would be a better person to shed some light on what was going on.

"Dick tried to reach him, but both his e-mail and voice mail said he was going to be away for a while. You should have known that perception is reality these days. Technically you may not have anything to do with the joint venture, but you are on Great China Telecom's IPO project, and they happen to be the company that wants Matrixtech as a partner. Outsiders will view these two projects as closely related," Jack had said with slight annoyance in his voice. He had never talked to Lu that way before.

"It sounds like I'm considered the bad person by both sides. The US government thinks I'm colluding with the Chinese, and the Chinese think I'm unprofessional because I expressed concerns about the joint venture's potential risks to our homeland security."

Jack had been quiet for a moment. Obviously he had not thought it that way. He'd softened his tone a little and said, "Well, it may look that way, but nobody really has accused you of anything. Just do me a favor: Can you forward me everything you have so far on the Great China Telecom IPO? You need to come off the project immediately. Hopefully the Chinese aren't going to take the IPO away from Fred; he will be pissed if that happens."

"Okay, I'll do that. I'll see you next Tuesday in the office, then," Lu had said.

"Don't worry about coming into the office right away. Stay away for a few days; wait for the storm to pass," Jack had said before hanging up.

And she had not heard from anybody else since then—nothing from Dick, Jack, or Fred, or anybody on the Great China Telecom side or her brother-in-law, Juin.

And she did not really care. She only wanted to hear from one person, be it a phone call, an e-mail, or just a text message—Will. But it was as if he had dropped off the face of the earth. She had heard nothing from him since he'd arrived in DC two days ago. She was deeply hurt but had not had time to dwell on it yet considering the chaotic events of the past twenty-four hours. What Jack had said about nobody being able to reach Will made that hurt less cutting. Will was not just ignoring her.

Something had happened, and it had put her in the position of being a suspect to both governments. Will must somehow be aware that he might be the cause for that, directly or indirectly. He was facing some kind of dilemma, and he might have a tough choice to make.

She suddenly realized there was a chance she would never see him again. Before he'd left her hotel room two days ago, he had compared himself to Wagner's Flying Dutchman and asked her if she wanted to save his soul that had been wandering the sea all his life. She had told him she would think about it. But since then he seemed to have drifted back to the dark sea. That thought saddened her.

"Excuse me, may I put my briefcase in your overhead bin?" an Asian male passenger about her age asked as he stood next to her seat. "Mine is really full already."

She looked up and said, "Sure, I only have one carry-on in there, still plenty of space."

"Thanks." The man placed his briefcase in the overhead bin right above her and settled into the seat next to hers across the aisle. He smiled at her and asked, "Where are you going?"

"Home," she said

"Me too."

The captain announced the plane would be pushing back shortly. Lu was about to turn off her cell phone when it began to ring. She didn't bother to look at the caller ID before pressing the answer button.

"Hi, Lu."

She immediately recognized Will's voice. "Will, where are you? Are you okay?"

"I'm fine. Are you all right?" Will's voice came through background static.

"I'm on the plane, ready to take off."

"Lu, I want you to listen to me. I'm sorry to have dragged you into this mess, and I've been a coward for the last two days …"

"What's the mess all about?" Lu interrupted.

"I made the mistake of mentioning your relationship with Juin to Kevin, and Kevin used it to stop the joint-venture deal. Kevin has always been against any merger or partnership for fear of losing his own job." The background static had become more pronounced.

"What did Kevin do?" Lu unconsciously raised her voice.

"He told Rob Kessler about you and Juin, and then through a State Department contact of Earl Kessler, they blocked the deal."

Lu processed what Will had said quickly in her mind, and instinct told her what had happened. "So they created the perception that you and I are colluding with the Chinese. You could have called me earlier about this. It's not your fault."

"This is where my cowardice came in. Kevin somehow figured out what happened between you and me. He threatened to go public with our relationship and make things difficult for me and Matrixtech if I continued to have anything to do with you. I was afraid I'd lose the business I've spent so many years building."

"So why are you calling me now?" Lu asked.

There was a long pause on Will's side.

"Will, are you there?" Lu thought they'd lost connection.

When Will spoke again, his voice was softer. "Yeah, I'm here. Remember the first time we met and Sage said if I'd lost control over my business, I could end up in the sad position of being too young to retire and too old to surf?"

"Yes, I remember."

"Well, Sage is right on a lot of things, but I think she is wrong on this one. I think I am old enough to retire and still young enough to go surfing."

Lu smiled, but her eyes welled up. She opened her mouth, wanting to say something, but had to fight back a lump in her throat first.

"Lu, still there?"

The plane's engines grew louder as it prepared to push back and taxi. "Yes, I am still here, and I know where you are, the tip of the world ..." she almost shouted into the phone over the roar of the engines. The man sitting on the other side of the aisle looked at her funny, but she didn't care.

• • •

Once the plane was in the air, Lu eventually fell asleep. She dreamed she was back in her old apartment in Shanghai, alone. A perfectly round moon, like a big silver plate, hung in the midnight-blue sky.

"Xiao Lu, glad you could come and visit," a familiar voice said from outside the window.

She looked up. The moon had gotten so close. It seemed to have placed itself right on the windowsill. "Grandma? Oh, Grandma, you're coming back," she called out to the moon.

"No, Grandma is not coming back. I am just here to see you." Slowly, her grandma's smiling face faded in to the forefront of the moon.

"But don't you feel sad you're all alone?" she asked, her arms reaching out to touch her grandma's face.

"I was sad when I had no choice but to leave you many years ago, when you needed somebody around to take care of you. I am so happy that you are okay now, so Grandma is not sad anymore. Besides, the moon is quite a beautiful place, quiet and peaceful. It's been my home, and I can always see from here where you are and how you are doing. And I know where you are is quite beautiful too; just look down there."

Lu climbed on her stool by the window and looked down.

She saw herself and Louis, the Doberman, sitting on a white sandy beach, looking out to a deep-blue sea. The waves were rolling in, splashing on the rocky shoreline, bursting into millions of white diamonds.

She looked up again. Her grandma was no longer there, but she could hear her voice: "Go and live your life."

She looked down again. More waves were rolling in, rising, cresting into dazzling white walls dappled by rainbow-colored surfboards.

CPSIA information can be obtained at www.ICGtesting.com
Printed in the USA
BVOW11s1815141015

422513BV00007B/65/P